I0618974

Moral Order

Book One
The Rise of Luca C. Mariner

Phil Pauley

Clink Street
London | New York

Published by Clink Street Publishing 2014

Copyright © Phil Pauley 2014

First edition.

The author asserts the moral right under the Copyright, Designs and Patents Act 1988 to be identified as the author of this work.

All rights reserved. No part of this publication may be reproduced, stored in a retrieval system or transmitted, in any form or by any means without the prior consent of the author, nor be otherwise circulated in any form of binding or cover other than that which it is published and without a similar condition being imposed on the subsequent purchaser.

ISBN: 978-1-909477-22-3
Ebook: 978-1-909477-23-0

Part One: Acacia Burj

Chapter One

Luca did not intend to die today. But sometimes, life didn't co-operate with his intentions.

He was falling headfirst towards Earth. His headset protected his face from the freezing temperatures in the atmosphere, but he could still hear the rush of the icy air as his body shot through it. Once he hit the clouds, he would activate his bodysuit, but it would be a waste of battery power to turn it on while he could still see the curve of the Earth, but his headset was always charged, as were those of his team mates.

Luca had been the first to jump from the aircraft. Looking behind him, he saw two other bodysuits, straight as arrows, hurtling after him. The Heads-Up Display, or HUD, on his visor identified the bodysuits. Asia Mae was right behind Luca, and shortly behind her Ceibastian was steadying himself.

Asia Mae's voice resonated through Luca's headset. "Luca, can you hear me?"

"Yeah, I hear you. Ceiba, what about you?"

"I can hear you, but my communicator is picking up some static."

"Don't worry, it'll clear up as we get closer to Earth."

1

"Okay. I'll let you know if it doesn't."

"Great," said Luca. "Now, guys, prepare for suit activation."

They were approaching the clouds and Luca kept his body straight as his HUD calculated the distance between him and the wall of clouds: two hundred metres... one hundred metres...

"Activate bodysuits in three... two... one... Bodysuit on." As Luca finished the countdown, he could hear Asia Mae and Ceiba echoing his orders through his communicator.

Luca surged forward as his bodysuit powered up, increasing the speed of his descent. His HUD display glowed with the digital information that his suit was now at full power and his body's vital signs were normal. Once he had flown below the cloud barrier Luca braked, turning his body parallel to the Earth's surface so that he could fly straight towards the lights of Acacia Burj in the distance. The city was visible from hundreds of kilometres away; its lights shone even brighter than the stars overhead.

"Keep close to the land," Luca said to his teammates. "We don't want the A'Rmillari to see us coming."

"Should we try stealth mode?" Asia Mae asked.

"Nah, save as much power as possible," said Luca.

"How do we approach the city, then?" asked Ceiba. "We can't just waltz in!"

"We're going through the waterfall tunnel."

Asia Mae and Ceiba both made sounds of protest. "Don't you think that's a dangerous risk for such a small mission?" Asia Mae asked.

"Not if it gets us closer to neutralising some aliens," said Luca. "C'mon, follow me."

Turning his body to the right, Luca headed towards a small mountain range that formed a natural wall along the right side of Acacia Burj. The lights stopped a few kilometres before the base of the mountains, and Luca knew that the ruins of a 21st century city lay there, sprawled out along the dark earth. The ruins were just a piece of history now, crumbling away in the wind and the rain in the shadow of the mountains.

Asia Mae and Ceiba followed Luca as they flew towards the base of the first mountain. They held back as Luca flew up along its ridge until he reached the waterfall he was looking for. He slowed momentarily, observing the water flowing down a cliff

Phil Pauley

face, then angled his body and flew at full speed towards it. He momentarily imagined flying straight into the craggy side of the cliff, but refused to let his fear hold him back. Even as he closed his eyes water sprayed his headset.

After a heartbeat, Luca opened his eyes. He was flying through a dark, narrow tunnel, straight through the mountain, and Asia Mae and Ceiba were calling to him through his communicator.

"Luca? Luca, are you all right?" Asia Mae's voice was heavy with worry.

"Did you make it?" Ceiba asked.

"I made it!" Luca said. "The tunnel is clear. Come on through."

Luca was approaching the end of the tunnel. As the mouth widened into the light, he slowed and pulled to a stop, landing on his feet just before the exit. Moments later, Ceiba and Asia Mae landed behind him.

"So what's this tunnel doing here?" Ceiba asked.

"It's a cave system," said Luca. "But luckily for us, the A'Rmillari doesn't know that it goes all the way through the mountain."

"What's the plan?" asked Asia Mae.

Luca paused for a moment, surveying the city beneath them. The neon lights stretched on for kilometres, ending where the ruins of the ancient city began beneath their feet. Luca's HUD scanned the decaying buildings and overgrown streets. An alert showed one A'Rmillari hiding in the cement corpse of a building.

"Asia Mae, there's an A'Rmillari hiding in that building. I want you to scout ahead. Use stealth mode, and don't attack unless you're spotted."

Asia Mae nodded and changed her bodysuit to its stealth setting, making her body almost invisible except for a blurry outline. She dived straight down the mountain and into the ruins. Luca and Ceiba watched as she disappeared into the darkness below.

"Ceiba, I want you with me. My HUD caught readings of an A'Rmillari in that building, there. He may be a scout sent ahead to prepare for an invasion. We need to neutralise him and find out if an attack squadron is on the way."

"All right," said Ceiba, looking nervous.

But before Luca could give any more orders, a flash of blinding white light bathed the entire mountain. He dropped to his knees as the sound of bombs assaulted their eardrums and the earth trembled in the wake of a barrage of explosions. Luca could hear Asia Mae's voice through his communicator, but could not make out what she was saying.

Gaining his bearings again, Luca scrambled to his feet and looked around for Ceiba. As the smoke and dust cleared, Luca saw he was now all alone in the tunnel.

"Ceiba?"

Luca peered over the mouth of the cave and looked down at the ruins and the city in the distance. All he could see was A'Rmillari. They were sweeping through the streets, checking in every ruined building and behind every crumbling stone wall. They were in the air, jumping out of drop ships, which were shining white light down to illuminate the ruins.

Their glasslike battle armour glistened in the light from their ships and their heads were covered by helmets. Beneath the clear armour, the aliens shimmered and vibrated with colour as they moved in and out of the light. Luca knew that the A'Rmillari had cuttlefish-like skin, able to adapt colour, texture and pattern at will to adjust to their environment and state of mind. If you weren't careful, their stunning, dancing body displays could mesmerise you into submission.

Luca knew they were dangerous. He knew firsthand about their mind control capabilities; he had even heard they could crush your brain from the inside just by using their invasive thoughts. However, they had to be in close range to take control of your mind. Luca was not sure how close, but he was determined to make sure they never got near enough for him to find out. His headset came equipped with protection from mind control, but it was very power hungry and caused his bodysuit's battery to drain twice as fast. It could only be used once, so he would need to save it for an emergency. Through his communicator, Luca heard Ceiba shout out.

"Ceiba? Ceiba, where are you?" Luca surveyed the battleground below with his HUD for any sign of his friend.

"Luca!" Ceiba sounded hysterical. "Help me!"

Luca honed in on Ceiba's signal, and he shot off down the mountainside.

"Stay calm, Ceiba. I'm on my way."

Asia Mae's voice filled Luca's headset. "Luca, are you all right?"

"I'm fine, but I think Ceiba's in trouble. I'm going to help him. What about you?"

"I'm all right, but I think it's safe to say this is bigger than we thought. I'm still in stealth mode. They haven't noticed me yet. What do you think I should do?"

Luca hesitated for only a moment. "Be careful! We can't let them get into Acacia Burj."

"Understood."

Luca stopped about ten metres from Ceiba's location. His breathing grew heavier and his heart thudded in his chest, but if there was one thing Luca was getting better at, it was controlling his emotions. Taking cover behind a crumbling wall, he peered around the side to see a street strewn with rubble. Someone in a bodysuit was kneeling in the middle of the street, surrounded by four A'Rmillari. The headset completely covered the face beneath, but Luca's HUD told him this was Ceiba. Luca could tell that Ceiba was trying to form electro-energy orbs for protection, but he was too distracted to do it properly.

Luca moved back behind the wall and held his hands together. He felt the energy from the sensors building up in his hands and, as it peaked, he pulled them apart. Suspended between his bodysuit gauntlets was a red ball of pure energy.

Peering around the wall once more, Luca yelled, "Ceiba, get down!"

He threw the energy orb, and it hit one of the A'Rmillari in the chest. The alien was thrown onto the ground, and as it lay writhing in agony, its body imploded into nothing more than a pile of smoking armour.

The other three A'Rmillari turned to Luca and hissed. Luca whipped back around the side of the wall and prepared another orb.

"Ceiba, you have to distract them," Luca said into his communicator.

"Luca! I can't concentrate. I feel like my brain's being fried..."

"Ceiba, focus. They can attack your mind, remember? I need you to distract them, so I can take out the other three. Can you do that?"

Ceiba whimpered. "It hurts, Luca."

Ceiba was in shock. There was no way he could fight.

"Okay, Ceiba, I want you to activate your brain block, all right? Sit tight. I'm coming to get you."

"But it'll drain my battery," Ceiba said.

"Just do it," Luca said, frustrated.

"Brain block on," Ceiba said, and Luca heard Ceiba's communicator switch off. The brain block stopped all incoming communications.

Luca stepped out from behind the wall and threw an orb at the group of A'Rmillari that was moving towards him. The three aliens scattered, and the orb missed them completely, but Luca was ready with another, and this time he did not miss. A second A'Rmillari fell to the ground and this time seemed to shatter into superheated component parts.

While the remaining A'Rmillari were distracted, Luca glanced at Ceiba, who was lying on his side amidst the smoke and rubble. He wasn't moving, but Luca's HUD showed that he was still alive.

The last two A'Rmillari had pulled back, and one of them let out a guttural scream, flooding Luca's ears with pain. Luca instinctively clamped his hands to the sides of his headset, but could not muffle the sound assault.

Too late, Luca realised that the screech was not a form of attack, but rather, a call. Behind the A'Rmillari, crystalline figures began to take shape, and as the fractured forms grew more solid, Luca grew more afraid. He moved back behind the wall.

"Asia Mae," Luca said into his communicator. "I need backup. Ceiba is down."

Asia Mae sounded as though she were in the headset with him. "How many are there, Luca?"

"They have Nanobes."

"Nanobes?" Asia Mae paused and Luca could hear her taking a deep breath. "I'm on my way."

Luca spoke to his HUD. "Search info on Nanobes."

"Nanobes," said a robotic voice in Luca's headset. "A sub-microscopic alien race conquered by the A'Rmillari and used as slave soldiers. They often swarm together to feed on neural energy. By touching a bodysuit, they can drain it of power, and by touching bare skin, they can drain a human's life force in minutes. Because they absorb energy, electro-energy orbs do not harm them but will distract them and hold them off for a few minutes. The only way to destroy a Nanobe swarm is by destroying the A'Rmillari that summoned it."

"Damn," Luca said under his breath.

Forming an orb in his hands, Luca rounded the corner and looked for the last two A'Rmillari. They stood either side of Ceiba and behind three Nanobe swarms. Luca's orb vibrated in tune with his emotional energy pattern. He remembered: the stronger his thoughts, the stronger the orbs. He instinctively switched his mindset to one of winner; conqueror. Luca shot at one of the A'Rmillari with his orb but it hit a Nanobe swarm, which was knocked back, unaffected. Luca fired a second, bigger orb, temporarily paralysing both swarms in waves of electric current. The first Nanobe swarm gathered itself and darted towards Luca again. *Damn!*

Luca's HUD told him that he was at 32 percent power. He could use his remaining power to try to fight off the A'Rmillari and the Nanobes, or he could use it to transport Ceiba and himself to safety, where they could recharge their bodysuits and rejoin the fight. The only problem would be getting to Ceiba without either the A'Rmillari or the Nanobes attacking his mind.

Suddenly, as if from thin air, Asia Mae appeared behind the A'Rmillari and blasted one of them with an energy orb, killing it stone dead. One of the swarms disappeared along with their summoner in howling screams. Before the other Nanobes or the last A'Rmillari could react, Asia Mae threw an energy orb straight at the A'Rmillari's head: the swarm and the A'Rmillari collapsed into the dust.

"C'mon!" Asia Mae called to Luca as she put one arm under Ceiba's shoulder. Luca ran forward and took the other shoulder, lifting Ceiba off the ground and onto his feet.

"How much power do you have left?" Luca asked.

"I'm at 24 percent. Stealth mode really drained me."

"I've got 30 percent. Ceiba turned on his brain block, so if he isn't already at zero, he will be soon."

"What should we do?" Asia Mae asked, as they ducked behind a building while an A'Rmillari squadron ran by.

"We need to find a place to recharge. We don't have much time left."

Luca and Asia Mae got out from behind the building and continued moving, dragging Ceiba along. They rounded a corner and found themselves face to face with an A'Rmillari unit.

Before they could attempt to defend themselves, a high-pitched bell sounded. The A'Rmillari troops fell away, as did the smoking ruins and even the night sky. There was nothing; darkness. And then...

Luca opened his eyes and gasped, blinking at the bright light emanating from the wind tunnel beneath his feet. He lifted the sensory helmet off his head and looked around at Asia Mae and Ceiba, who were doing the same.

A woman's automated voice resonated throughout the room. "Your allotted game time is now up. Please remove your head sensors, unplug your gaming vests, and exit the game room. Thank you for playing at the Arcade."

"I have to admit, I'm glad that's over! A bit scary this time, but otherwise, great job you guys," Asia Mae said as she unplugged her vest from her sensor. The sensors coiled into the ceiling above the sleek glass walls of the circular game room. Their voices echoed off the glass as they relived the game.

"Sorry I lost it, Luca," Ceiba said.

"It was only your third time in there. You'll get better with practice," Luca said with a smile.

"I think you did well, Ceiba," Asia Mae said, running her fingers through her long black hair to smooth it down.

"Thanks, Asia Mae," Ceiba said, but he still lowered his angelic sky blue eyes as they walked out of the game room.

In the hallway outside, the next group of gamers was preparing for their mission. Most of them looked about sixteen, the same age as Luca, Ceiba, and Asia Mae. As the three friends walked down the hallway back towards the lobby, many of the waiting boys glanced at Asia Mae. She had a way of attracting male attention. She had wide, almond-shaped brown eyes sitting either side of perfectly straight nose, covered with dark freckles. Her silky black hair almost reached her waist. *Move it guys, nothing to see here,* thought Luca, feeling a little uneasy at the stares, but not really knowing quite why he should be bothered by them.

Asia Mae was the friend Luca and Ceiba were most protective of. Not because she was female, but because she was *special.* The three of them had known each other since they were very young, and had remained friends ever since. Luca thought all of his friends were a little bit in love with Asia Mae, though none of them would ever admit it.

"Luca, you all right?" Asia Mae asked as they stepped into the lobby.

Luca turned to her, jolted from his thoughts. "Fine. Fancy grabbing a bite to eat on the way home?"

"Sure," Ceiba said.

"I have something to tell you two, actually," said Asia Mae. "I wanted to wait until we were clear of the Arcade."

The three of them walked out through the exit.

"What?" Luca asked.

"Well, I think the game might have been glitching up. Did you notice it?"

The boys shook their heads.

"Well, when I was in stealth mode, I heard a couple of A'Rmillari talking," Asia Mae continued in a whisper.

"Talking?" Luca was surprised.

"But they don't talk, do they? They just screech and growl," said Ceiba.

"That's what *I* thought," said Asia Mae. "But these two were speaking, clear as day. Their voices sounded mechanical, but they spoke in English."

"Maybe it's a new feature to the game," Ceiba suggested.

"Nah, we would've heard about it," said Luca. "Wouldn't we? Our virtual contacts keep us informed on the latest updates." Luca gave an exaggerated blink of his electric green eyes, where the digital lenses that kept him – and everyone else – constantly connected to iT, the World Internet were housed.

"I know," said Asia Mae. "But that's not the most interesting part. The A'Rmillari sounded as if they were planning something."

"So?" said Luca. "Whatever it was would have ended as soon as the game shut off."

"I don't think so," said Asia Mae. "They were talking about an attack outside the game. Something much bigger – something *out here* – and they talked like it was happening soon. Luca, what if there's a *real* alien invasion coming?"

Chapter Two

Ceiba smiled. He always thought Asia Mae exaggerated everything and this talk about an invasion must be one of her fantasies. She could be quite a drama queen.

Luca didn't want to think about an intergalactic war, full stop. And he agreed with Ceiba – generally – that Asia Mae had a vivid imagination, always dreaming up things that weren't necessarily real. But he didn't want to tell her that.

Arms linked, Luca, Asia Mae and Ceiba headed to their favourite hangout near the Arcade called the *Game Stop Café*. Most people gathered there on Saturday nights after they left the Arcade. It was one of the few places in Acacia that served old-fashioned burgers and shakes, reminiscent of 21st century junk food.

As the friends made their way down the sidewalk, Luca couldn't help but admire the beauty of Mega City 21, Acacia Burj. It was an iridescent multilayered city of lights, a utopia that never failed to amaze him, especially at night when the lights shimmered and bounced off the sides of the buildings. Luca knew he was very fortunate to be living here. He had heard that the other mega cities on the planet weren't nearly as advanced.

Metallic, chrome and glass buildings were fashioned into spirals and complex geometric shapes that soared into the sky. Brilliant lights pulsated from the facades of the buildings as if they were living, breathing entities. Glass monorails blitzed by on the multi-storey freeways in a blur. The very rich travelled freely around the multi-storey buildings in their private pods as if floating on air. People used to call them the Opulent Society, then out of that was spawned the nickname: Opuls. "What are you looking at?" Asia Mae said, punching Luca in the arm.

"The lights. They're so bright. Don't you think?"

"Luca, you are a dreamer." Asia Mae laughed; her tone and inflection carrying like music on the light breeze. "What other sixteen year-old boy would notice the lights?"

"Don't you take music lessons in one of those buildings?" asked Luca.

"Yes, and I love it," she said. "From the top, you can see the entire city."

"Even the docks?" asked Luca.

"Even the docks." She nodded. "And while a portion of the docks are old warehouses, there are loads of interconnecting buildings to rival the architecture in Acacia Burj, especially the ones that are partially undersea."

"Guys, looks like the *Game Stop* is just as crowded as ever," said Ceiba as they stepped up to the popular nightspot.

People mingled and greeted each other outside the front door. Some of the guys had luminous spiked hair and interactive skin on their arms and necks. They wore trousers that were called jeans, which had been popular more than a hundred years ago and today were very costly – if you could even find them. Of course, most were reproductions. Girls wore thigh high leather boots and short skirts, and had all kinds of hairstyles, including digital hair extensions and head pieces. Some of the guys even had luminous facial markings. Luca knew they were trying to look tribal, but he thought they looked a bit ridiculous. He and his friends much preferred the comfortable white and black sensory bodysuits that most people wore, and kept their hair and faces fuss free.

Ceiba punched Asia Mae and Luca in the arm, grinning. "Look at them." He nodded towards a couple of local celebrities who were sitting at the counter. The young starlets glowed in

11

the ambient tones of reds and blues that emanated from their bodies. Watching their lives on camera 24/7 was nothing short of mind numbing. Luca knew Asia Mae found them pretentious. But when you were famous, it seemed that nothing was too weird or fanciful.

The friends giggled. Luca and Asia Mae rubbed their arms where Ceiba had playfully punched them. Sometimes, he forgot how strong he was. Ceiba quickly secured a booth in the corner by a window where they could view the city lights. It was also a convenient spot if any breaking news was displayed onto the ten storey high opti-video walls.

They sat down and swiped their hands over the table. An optigram displaying the menu appeared and the digital form of a female hostess, a Persona, materialised beside them. She had short white hair and the bluest of blue eyes rimmed in thick black liner. She wore Retro clothes consisting of a short black skirt, knee-high boots and tights.

The streets of Acacia Burj were full of humans, Bions, and Artificial Intelligence (AI) machines. The boundaries became very unclear, especially when you threw the new consumer bionics into the equation. Luca knew that Ceiba was always wishing he was completely human and felt inferior to him and Asia Mae because he was a Bion.

Nearly all citizens were Wired – possessing permanent controls that were connected to the i5D eye lenses they all used to access iT, the World Internet, and other virtual interactivity for their daily use. They could choose to turn off all the comms at the end of the day, though they were required by law not to tamper with the devices, especially when they were students or employed by the military, or if they belonged to one of the Civil organisations. When they turned twenty one, citizens were implanted with a permanent sensory board, and only those with special permission were exempt. It was just one of the ways the leaders monitored them, studying their location, brain waves, body chemistry and DNA. They said it was to keep everyone safe, in the same way that the sensory shield which controlled the air and modulated the temperature kept them safe.

Luca wasn't sure he liked the idea of being permanently Wired, but most people didn't seem to mind. And at least it also allowed people to connect themselves to consumer bionics – electronic add-ons which connected to the nervous system. More and more Civils were using the new mimicry suits, including ones with insect-like wings which allowed them to fly for short distances around Acacia Burj.

"Good evening, young Civils," the Persona said, smiling. "My name is Hopi. What would you like to eat this evening?"

"I want the burger and chips," said Ceiba right away. "And a vanilla shake."

"House pizza for me," said Asia Mae. "That sounds good."

"The same as him, please," Luca added. He had to admit, this was better than going home and having the computer embedded in his bedroom wall print him a meal. Bland. His mum was working away tonight along with his older sister, Gaia, and Gaia's boyfriend, Tanner, was off on some kind of military training expedition, so there would be no one at home.

"It will only take a moment," said Hopi. "I'll be right back."

After she left, Luca said, "Okay, Asia, spill it. What exactly did you hear back at the Arcade?"

"I may have misunderstood," she said, smoothing her long black hair back from her face. "But I overheard a transmission from someone who didn't look like anything I have ever seen before. When he talked to the A'Rmillari soldier, the soldier addressed him as Overlord and outlined their mission. I could only hear parts of it because the transmission went in and out."

"That's awesome," said Ceiba. "But why would that be in the game?"

"Do you suppose the game picked up some interference from a spaceship as it entered our solar system?" joked Luca. "Let's face it; we all think there are alien spaceships out there, even if everyone denies it."

"It is possible," said Asia Mae, her eyes widening. "This is one of the newer games at the Arcade, and they might be getting some interference."

"Come on, Luca! The glitch could have come from satellites instead of spaceships," said Ceiba. "We have no proof that aliens exist in our solar system. Maybe in other galaxies but not here."

"I believe they interact with our leaders," said Luca. "Of course, that's just *my* theory. But as convincing as they seem in the game, A'Rmillari and Overlords are all supposed to be just myths."

"What's fascinating is that they were all talking about an invasion here on Planet Earth," said Asia Mae. "And I don't think they were referring to the game. Honestly, guys, something *big* is about to happen and it involves intergalactic beings – targeting Earth. I can just feel it!"

"You're just fantasising again, Asia Mae," said Ceiba, laughing. "I don't think there's a war coming. And it's only conspiracy theorists who believe that Earth communicates with aliens." He looked pointedly at Luca. "The crews on our mining ships on the Moon and Mars have never reported running into aliens. If they did exist, I think they'd mind their own business in their own galaxies. Plus, this was just a video game – it wasn't real, guys."

"Think about it. The game we played tonight was *Markarian Attack*," said Asia, leaning in and speaking in hushed tones. She looked around to check that no one was paying attention to them before continuing. "And the myths say that the A'Rmillari came from the Markarian Galaxy, that they were hybrids, as a result of interbreeding with humans. And there was a mention of Overlords, I remember that."

"So?" said Ceiba. "How do you even remember that stuff? It's just fantasy. A myth. Most of the virtual environments at the Arcade are based on some kind of mythology or ancient lore. They even have games that feature prehistoric dinosaurs and dragons. We're talking *really ancient*! And let's just suppose for one second that the A'Rmillari are a real race. We were *playing a game*, Asia Mae. How could the A'Rmillari be communicating for real in a game? Do you really think that's possible?"

"I don't know. I guess my imagination is running away with me as usual," said Asia Mae. "But, what if the stories *aren't* myths?"

"I suppose it *is* possible," said Luca. "I, for one, believe there are aliens and that they may have communicated with Earth, and I like your idea that the game could have intercepted an actual transmission from the A'Rmillari." As he watched her across the table from him, he realised he found it difficult to ever disagree with her.

"Okay, fine, I'll play along," said Ceiba. "So, what if this race has learned to merge its consciousness with the sensory circuits of the games?"

"I'm not sure," said Luca. "If there's an alien race in contact with us, why would they want to merge their consciousness into a game? It would be too risky for them."

"Very mysterious," said Asia Mae. "All I know is that it sounded ominously real. It gave me the creeps. I almost lost my focus in the game."

"You always kick ass in those games," said Ceiba. It was no secret that he admired Asia Mae just as much as Luca did, even if he did think she exaggerated far too much.

"What do *you* think, Luca?" asked Asia Mae. She pulled a hand-kerchief from her pocket and twirled it in her long, slender fingers. When she was deep in thought, she always twirled things.

"It's weird. I never thought about the virtual games being a source of realtime communication," said Luca. "But anything is possible. That's what Grampa Sol and Dad always told me. Mum is more of a disbeliever, the scientist who has to have proof before she believes anything."

"I got the feeling this was real," said Asia Mae, pursing her lips together in a little pout, as she looked out over their city. "I think I heard a transmission I wasn't supposed to hear. This means we could be in trouble. It's not something I want to think about, but it could affect all of us in a big way."

"Did the A'Rmillari see you when they were talking inside the game?" asked Luca. Asia Mae looked at him intently with those big chocolate eyes and he suddenly felt very self-conscious. *Could she read his thoughts?* He tucked his hair behind his ears. He only hoped it wasn't sticking out too much after being inside the wind tunnel's virtual environment. His hair had a mind of its own and seldom looked tame. And it was far from the perfect blonde curls that Ceiba had.

"No, I'm positive they didn't know I was there," said Asia Mae. "I hid from them underneath a stairwell, and I closed my electro-orb in my palms so they couldn't detect the energy signal."

"What *exactly* did they say?" asked Luca, swallowing hard. "Do you remember?"

"I remember every word. The first one said, 'Xsar Tiandi, they won't stand a chance against us. They don't know anything about our capabilities and because of the treaties, they think they're safe.'" Asia Mae spoke in a deep, sinister tone, trying to imitate the voice she had heard.

"That doesn't sound too scary," said Ceiba, grinning. Luca guessed he was hungry and was ready for this A'Rmillari talk to be over.

"I'm not finished," she said. "He kept talking and said, 'That's why it will be so easy to take over Earth.' The one named Xsar Tiandi just snarled, and I swear, his teeth looked like blood-stained fangs."

They all shivered.

"I have to agree with you, Asia," said Luca. "It does sound really scary."

"I know, right?" said Asia Mae.

"If they *are* real and they really can communicate through the virtual games, then what can we do?" said Ceiba. He didn't want to think about the possibility of communicating with aliens and intergalactic wars. He had enough trouble balancing his half AI systems and half human biology. He kept thinking he should have some advanced skills because of his wiring, but so far, he hadn't detected anything.

"I don't know," said Asia Mae, folding her hands on the table. "The authorities wouldn't believe anything we said – we're just teenagers, and of course, we have no real proof – just a game."

"Hey, did they say anything about activity in the ocean?" asked Luca. He was always curious about activity underneath the sea. In fact, he was obsessed with it. The teachers didn't talk much about the undersea mines in iT school and his mum barely mentioned it, even though she worked in the Intergalactic Research & Science Organisation.

"No, I didn't hear anything about the sea," said Asia. "And I was listening for any information I could get."

The food appeared from the centre of the table. It smelled delicious. Without waiting, Ceiba took a bite.

"Oh, guys! This is the best tasting burger I've had in ages!"

Luca picked up his burger. With just the right blend of spices and herbs, it tasted perfect. He always wondered what original burgers had tasted like, but his teachers had told them that they weren't as good for you as their manufactured food was. Through his eye i5D, he could identify the information in his visionary field and read the calorific and nutritional content of everything he ate.

"I don't know if I believe aliens have ever visited our planet, but I do know that something weird has been going on for a while," said Ceiba, wiping his mouth with a handkerchief.

"What have you heard?" asked Asia Mae, as she picked up a slice of her pizza.

"You know my dad heads up the security services at the docks, right?" said Ceiba. "Well, he's been saying there's been unusual activity lately. But every time Mum and I question him further, he just says it's top secret."

"What about your mum, Luca?" asked Asia Mae. "She's a scientist and researcher... maybe she knows something."

"Honestly, if Mum did know anything about aliens having ever been on Earth, I doubt if she would ever in a million years tell me," said Luca as he sipped his milkshake. The thick, creamy drink felt good in his throat, and he tried to avoid looking at the nutritional information appearing on his i5D. Sometimes, that took all the fun away from eating.

"Mum is always trying to protect me," he continued. "But my sister Gaia is an apprentice with Mum, and she's been working extra late and on weekends, too, as if there's some big project going on."

Gaia was three years older than Luca and was considered something of a genius. Unlike him. Luca was more of a *good* kid – with potential. He admired Gaia and her boyfriend, Tanner, who was in a training programme in the military. They both lived at home with him and their mum, but they were very independent. Luca's father had died a few years ago. It was something he didn't like to think or talk about.

"I told you," said Ceiba. "There is something big going on! And if what Asia Mae has told us is true, then this proves it! But, honestly, Asia, I think it might have been a trick of the mind. The A'Rmillari game is designed to incorporate mind tricks."

"I know all that," said Asia Mae. "But it felt so real, Ceibastian." Asia Mae was the only one who called him Ceibastian. To Luca, it sounded too old and he always called him Ceiba.

"I have an idea," Luca said. "Why don't we finish our food, then go down to the docks and see if we can find out anything."

"You mean spy?" asked Ceiba. He loved the idea of an adventure, even though he didn't like the idea of aliens one little bit.

"Yeah, sort of," Luca said, laughing lightly. "This gives me a good excuse. I love going to the docks."

"I know," said Asia Mae. "Your favourite place, right?" She

placed her hand on Luca's forearm and smiled sweetly. Ceiba noticed the smile and kicked Luca underneath the table. When Luca looked up at him, Ceiba winked. *Ceiba, knock it off!* Luca said silently, hoping Asia Mae didn't notice his cheeks were burning.

"I'd love to go to the docks," said Asia Mae.

"I'm in," said Ceiba. "And Pop's not working tonight, so I won't have to hear a lecture about how dangerous they are."

"Great!" said Luca. "Let's finish and get outta here."

Luca couldn't help wondering about what went on inside the walls of the Arcade. The real and the virtual. The fun and the sinister. It was a place where people played, but it was also a place where people died. Where the virtual blurred with dreams and masked the edges of reality until people weren't sure where the boundaries lay. And, it was rumoured, the Arcade was a place where mercenaries, liars and killers were born.

Chapter Three

"What a beautiful night!" exclaimed Asia Mae as she slipped her arms through Ceiba's and Luca's. Silvery moonlight slanted between the crystal and chrome, glistening like diamonds off the buildings in the Acacia Burj realm. A few Civils flew between the skyscrapers, and even from this distance, the friends could hear the buzz of their wings. The air around them had a periwinkle tone and smelled of honeysuckle – tonight's mood-enhancing scent. Asia's eyes glittered like jewels in the twilight.

"A perfect night for an adventure," said Luca.

"A perfect night for *spies*," added Ceiba, laughing. "All we need are hoods to cover our faces."

"You laugh now," scolded Asia Mae. "You might not find it quite so funny if it turns out everything I heard was real."

"Okay," he said, "I surrender. Let's go find us some aliens."

Everyone laughed a little bit too hard.

They walked the short distance to the monorail that would take them to the docks. A tourist or visitor to Acacia would be able to select the city's information on their i5D and read:

<u>City</u>: Acacia Burj 21 of 112 Mega Cities on Planet Earth

19

Safety Enclosure: Sensory shields over city provide year-round
protection from outer unstable Planet Earth environments.
Area: 20 square miles
Elevation: 901 metres
Weather: 17°C, Wind NW at 6 km/h, 63% humidity. Temps
vary, but remain mild, within 4 simulated seasons of spring,
summer, autumn, and winter
Local time: Saturday, 8:00 p.m.
Population: 819,702 comprising Humans, Bions, AIs
Life Expectancy: 150+ years

As they had learned in their geography classes, Acacia was not
the largest of the mega cities on the planet, but it was still one
of the grandest, with sky-high buildings filled with apartments,
shops and offices stacked upward into the heavens. From the
sides of many of the buildings emerged huge 3D figures present-
ing daily news updates, as well as promotions that touted tour-
ism on the Moon and the latest inventions. The city's citizens
could interact with immersive experiences everywhere and anywhere if they wanted to. Luca felt it was all a bit confusing at
times and he saw how easily reality could blur with the virtual,
but he loved his city. It was all he had ever known, and to him,
it was mostly perfect. He did wonder about what was 'out there',
beyond the safety of Acacia, in the Wilds – or, as some called
it, The Garbage Pit – but he doubted if he'd ever find out. He
was more interested in deep sea and space exploration. That was
where he hoped his future lay.

A few stars blinked overhead and a crisp breeze filtered
through the air. The air was calm and clean, thanks to the sensory shield that protected the residents of Acacia from Earth's
violent weather patterns, the outcome of a runaway greenhouse
effect. Long ago, its atmosphere damaged, much of Earth had
been almost obliterated by increasingly extreme weather, the
Climate Wars, and occasional meteor strikes. Those cataclysms
had changed the surface of the planet and had prompted those
countries that could afford it to build enclosed mega cities like
Acacia Burj, where the environment could be controlled and the
citizens protected. Outside, in The Garbage Pit, where disease
and savagery were rife, nothing could live for very long.

As Luca and his friends climbed aboard the monorail, they

passed a few passengers, mostly people who were out for the evening and probably going to the theatre, sports arena or cinema. A toddler, wearing a child's version of a gaming body-suit, sat on his own, swiping away at his sensorpad quite happily. Luca thought he looked sad and wondered how old this Bion actually might have been.

A couple of random teenagers sat together, dressed in sleek black and white gaming suits, like Luca and his friends. Nobody paid them much attention as they looked like most of the teenagers in Acacia. However, there was one guy with dark brown hair pulled back in a ponytail and wearing a glowing hoop through his earlobe, who looked a little suspicious. Generally, only the Retros wore earrings. The man's eyes followed Luca and his friends, and he even turned in his seat to watch them walk down the aisle. *Was he a spy?* There had been rumours that spies from other mega cities were lurking around Acacia Burj and reporting any unusual behaviour. *He looked so familiar.* Luca felt positive he had seen him at the Arcade and the *Game Stop*. But he wasn't sure. He shook the feeling away. It was more than likely just his overactive imagination and nothing more.

They sat down in their seats, which instantly moulded around them. Asia Mae sat in the middle, which suited Luca and Ceiba just fine. The monorail glided gently, and then zoomed past the city buildings topping 400 miles per hour. From the panoramic windows, everything was a blur of light.

"Hey – let's prep our bodysuits for surfing," said Asia Mae, swiping at the optographic sensors on her wrist. In this mode, the suits were designed to mimic wetsuits and protect their bodies from any toxins in the sea.

"I thought we were spies looking for aliens," protested Ceiba. "Not surfers."

"Just in case the water looks good and we can go in," said Asia Mae, grinning. "We can go in the water first, and then do a bit of investigating," she said, smiling reassuringly at Luca. "Unless they have warning sirens blaring everywhere..."

Asia's knee bumped up against Luca's and he felt a tingle course through his body. *Did she feel it?* Outwardly, he remained composed, but he sincerely hoped she wasn't reading his vitals, as his pulse rate would certainly give the game away.

"Just last week, a sub-sea earthquake stirred up tidal waves that almost hit the docks," said Ceiba. "If it hadn't been for the shields, the docks would have been damaged. Pops said they were almost too late."

"That's a bit too close for comfort," said Asia, shivering. She placed her hand on Luca's knee as the monorail rocked gently and he was sure she would hear his heart thudding like a million jackhammers. But no one seemed to notice. He didn't move. He didn't breathe.

"Yeah," said Ceiba. "A tidal wave could do some serious damage, but we should be safe tonight. Pops would have mentioned if there were any unusual weather patterns."

They all knew that a huge tidal wave could destroy most of the protective shield that was anchored around Acacia through digital and biotechnological interfaces. They had heard stories of other cities across the planet being severely damaged by tidal waves.

The docks that linked the outer world to inner Acacia sat right at the edges of the shield, and led down into to the sea where corporations and manufacturing facilities had established subterranean offices underwater. Because there was always talk of Earth becoming increasingly inhospitable – which it already was in the Wilds – some of the elite Opul families had built homes beneath the sea, and from what Luca had heard they were magnificent.

The docks were Luca's favourite place to go. Civils were only allowed there at certain times of the day when the weather was calm. Sometimes, they were allowed outside Acacia's sensory realm, but if violent weather threatened, they were required to follow emergency protocols. Luca and his friends hated dealing with the constant threat of unpredictable weather and the tireless alarm sirens.

When the monorail stopped, Luca and his friends got off. They went through the first massive wall gate easily enough, but then there were security personnel at the gates of the final airlock chamber, as usual. The security guard scanned their wrists. He nodded, and then unlocked the massive door to the chamber. Luca waited patiently for it to open while the chamber hissed and groaned as it depressurised.

They stepped through, and into, the raw, open world. The sight before them took Luca's breath away. In fact, the heat and humidity was overpowering – he always forgot how cool it was within the city compared with outside. The second thing he always noticed was the smell. It was muggy and musty with seaweed and a scent of oil – unlike the crisp, clean air of Acacia. Luca breathed in deeply, inhaling the raw salty air hungrily, relishing every nuanced scent and imperfection. In front of them was the tumultuous open sea and away to their left, barely accessible from here, The Garbage Pit. To their right, were Luca's favourite places – the sub-sea and terrestrial docks.

This doorway wasn't the only way out of Acacia. The outside could be accessed through runways, which led down into the ocean and connected the outer world of Earth to Acacia. The docks consisted of a monstrous infrastructure built half below the waves and half on the surface, almost as big as a city itself. Submarine pathways were illuminated by white lights to help guide deep sea cruisers, and ramps circled in loops down into the sea in one direction and to portals into Acacia in the other.

There were screeching and clanking sounds coming from the docks, and engines purred in the distance. Luca felt oddly at home here, and often slipped out of Acacia to wander through the massive infrastructure. Submersible cargo, giant amphibious vehicles, underwater trains, and cruise liners with detracting wheels travelled through the water and docked inside massive maintenance hangars above and below the waterline. Impressive by anyone's standards. And they made him curious. He wondered where everyone was going and what they were doing.

Luca stopped for a moment and turned off the comms on his sensorpad and i5D. They wouldn't really work anyway out here on the docks as they didn't have any security clearance.

"I always forget how huge the docks are," said Asia Mae. "They're as big as the skyscrapers in Acacia Burj!"

"You could definitely get lost here," agreed Ceiba. "It's a maze."

"Look at that!" Asia Mae said, pointing to a very large Pathfinder: a long, sleek cruiser ship rising nose first from the undersea world. It broke the surface and rose out of the water like a shining glacier. Streams of water cascaded down its wings.

"It's magnificent!" said Luca. "See, once the ship nears the harbour it releases its wheels for travel on land."

They watched as the security wall opened so it could slide

through into Acacia. It looked like a private vessel. *Probably just a group of wealthy people who enjoy a Saturday afternoon cruise under-sea,* thought Luca.

"It would be wonderful to take one of those cruises someday," said Ceiba. "Can you imagine?"

"Only the very wealthy can afford it," said Luca.

"I know, but it's fun to dream," said Ceiba.

"I *would* like to," said Asia Mae. "Think of all the awesome things we could do, the places we could go."

"Yep, maybe someday..." said Luca. His eyes wandered to the horizon. The last glow of the sun had almost completely disappeared and a misty grey fog now shrouded the heights of Acacia, as if trying to penetrate its invisible shields. A few mangy birds squawked overhead, a sound he rarely heard inside the city. It reminded Luca that it was nearly impossible to recreate all the natural sounds perfectly in a pseudo-world.

"Where should we go first?" asked Asia Mae, remembering their mission.

"Come on!" said Ceiba. "Let's go and dip our feet into the sea first."

"What about our mission?" asked Luca. "Don't you want to find out if there's anything suspicious going on in the docks? We're spies, remember?"

"Absolutely!" said Ceiba. "I just thought we could take a moment on the beach while we're here."

"I would love to," said Asia Mae, once again wrapping her arm through his. "Let's go."

They heard laughter amidst the roar of the ocean waves. There were other groups of teens on the beach, enjoying a Saturday evening of freedom outside Acacia's sensory walls. Luca looked in the direction of the laughter and recognised three guys and two girls from his iT school. They were wearing dark wet suits and were effortlessly paddling and gliding on the water's surface. Sometimes Luca wished he was more athletic.

Luca and his friends stood transfixed, watching them surf and roll with the waves. And then the magic happened and for a moment, none of them could utter a sound. As the waves broke and started frothing forward, a bioluminescent light shone through in a symphony of deep neon blue... almost like blue fire chasing along the coastline.

It was the most beautiful thing Luca had ever seen – next to Asia Mae, of course. He and Ceiba had surfed in virtual environments before, but it was nothing as spectacular as this.

"Come on!" Luca laughed, kicking off his shoes.

"Are you sure?" said Ceiba. "What if there is a strong undercurrent in the sea? I'm a strong swimmer but I've heard stories–"

"Look," said Asia Mae. "Those guys and girls are out there surfing and they're all right."

"Right!" said Luca. "Come on, let's go!"

They kicked off their shoes and headed to the water. Luca noticed that each step sent a little shockwave through the water, making it glow momentarily around his feet. Asia Mae and Ceiba saw it, too.

"*Whoa!* This is so cool!" said Ceiba. "What is this?"

"It's magic," said Asia Mae, walking in the edges of the sea. "Bliss."

Luca scooped up a handful of sand and threw it out into the sea. As the grains hit, there was a burst of light. He found some little pebbles and threw them into the sea, watching as the water created blue glowing splashes.

"It feels like we're on an alien world. Don't you just love it?" Luca was in his element.

"It's breathtaking," said Asia Mae. She lay down at the water's edge and swished her arms back and forth. Luminous blue water bubbled around her body. With her long hair flowing, and bathed in neon blue, Asia Mae looked like a mermaid from another world.

Ceiba and Luca started kicking and splashing each other but eventually lay down on the edge of the shore with Asia Mae. The water was cool to the touch, but their bodysuits kept them warm. They kicked their legs and swished their arms back and forth, watching the blue light ripple through the waves.

After a few minutes, Asia Mae stood up, wiped her hand on her bodysuit and watched the water sparkle at her touch. "Come on, maybe those guys will let us borrow their surfboards. I want to ride the waves!"

"I don't think we should bother them," said Ceiba as he stood up, shaking the water from his hair. "I can't surf very well."

"Um, I haven't surfed that much either," said Luca.

"Actually, I haven't surfed at all," said Ceiba.

"I'll teach you!" said Asia Mae, watching the water sparkle with blue lights on her fingertips.

"Look, it's just enough to be here and see this amazing sight," said Luca. "And we still have our investigating to do…"

"Yeah, that's right," said Ceiba. "And we shouldn't stay out too late."

"Okay, okay," said Asia Mae. "But next time I'll bring my surfboard and I'll teach you how to surf."

"Cool," said Luca.

"What causes the blue light?" asked Ceiba.

"It's red tide algae, which turns the sea a blood-red colour at certain times of the year. When it's agitated, the algae glows this blue colour," said Luca.

"I've never seen it before," said Asia Mae. "And I've surfed a few times out here, back when I dated…" She stopped when she caught Luca's eye. "Oh, never mind. It really does feel like magic."

"I've never seen this before either," said Ceiba.

Luca had studied bioluminescence for a couple of years. It was one of the beautiful things about science that he loved, and the sight was always mesmerising. Jaw dropping. He had been told that was why so many of the buildings in Acacia Burj were trimmed in similar blue light – as a way of mimicking nature.

It was completely dark by now and the laughter of the surfers had faded into the distance as they surfed further and further away, blue lights rippling and splashing outward from their boards.

"Hey, Asia Mae, what're you doing out with these losers tonight?" A voice shouted out behind them.

Luca recognised his neighbourhood's local troublemaker, Prince, and wished he'd go away. A hulking guy with tight, bulging biceps, Prince swaggered towards them as if he was the toughest, meanest dude on the planet. *And he probably is,* thought Luca. He was flanked either side by his two thuggish friends, Thitis and Tatio. All three were top athletes in iT school, but they had a reputation for picking fights. Most the top athletes were honourable students and positioned for sporting excellence or great careers in the military. But some of them had become insecure bully boys. And rumour was that Prince and his friends were Bions because of their superhuman abilities. Luca thought perhaps they had trouble with their circuitry systems and it caused them to have aggressive personalities, but he didn't know for sure. Prince and his friends were eighteen years old, and had just graduated. Luca had heard from his sister's boyfriend that they had signed up for next month's intake at the Military Centre. Although dangerous, military service was a guarantee of a stable income once they completed training.

Although Luca couldn't access much information through his comms on the docks since he was out of range, he could still scan body reads. He switched his comms back on and quickly swiped his sensorpad.

STATS:
Approaching: 2 Male Bions, 1 Human Male
Blood pressure: 190/80, 230/90, 220/75
Moods: Volatile, Erratic, Hostile
Assessment: Do not approach; do not trust

Oh, just great! Not everyone had access to this application. His mum had copied the app from the military training programme for Luca a couple of years ago to help him identify potentially dangerous people. She always worried when he went out to the docks. And since his father's death, there had been many adversaries. She was overly protective that way.

Luca didn't really need an app to tell him that these troublemakers were bad news. Nothing like a bunch of bully boys to bring down what had so far been a perfect evening. *What did they want?*

"I said, what brings you out here tonight with these losers?" Prince shouted again.

"I'm enjoying a peaceful evening with my friends tonight," said Asia Mae, standing tall, folding her arms, and trying to look tough. "We're not bothering you or anyone else."

"Aha, traitor-son?" said Prince, looking straight at Luca. "What're you doing out here, isn't it past your bedtime?"

Luca clenched his jaw. *Steady,* he told himself.

"Not much," Luca replied. He tried hard to ignore all traitor insults. "I'm just out enjoying the sea like everyone else."

"Ya gonna try your hand at surfing, baby boy?" Prince asked, sneering.

"Nah, he can't do it," jeered Tatio. "He's a coward like his old man was. Don't know why a pretty girl like this one would be hanging out with two losers like the traitor and sissy no-pulse over there."

Luca looked over at Ceiba, silently pleading with him to not say anything. Jerks sometimes called Ceiba a no-pulse because he was a Bion. And sometimes they called him a sissy because of his long, gangly body that he hadn't quite grown into it yet, and those damn blonde curls, and because he was… well, he was *pretty.* People were often surprised by how strong Ceiba was, despite appearances. His bionic parts made him far superior to his friends. And he was no sissy. Just the mention of it got Ceiba riled up. Luca understood. It was the same way anger rose in him when anyone mentioned that his father was a traitor. And as for calling him a no-pulse, well two of these bullies were Bions, as well. *But maybe they don't know it themselves,* thought Luca. Some parents hid it from their children, even though there were always rumours.

Luca briefly recalled an incident with Ceiba when they were only seven years old, after the accident, when his circuitry malfunctioned. His parents had not been able to afford the annual upgrades like other families, and once, Ceiba had tripped and fallen on the ground. Bleeding, he started twitching in spasms. Luca hadn't known what to do. He screamed for someone to help. At that time, the older students, Tatio and Thitis, in particular, had made fun of Ceiba. A teacher had called for an ambu-rail and they quickly took Ceiba for emergency care. Ever since then, Ceiba had been especially self-conscious of his AI condition, and Asia Mae and Luca had been especially protective of him.

"Maybe this one – this traitor-son – needs to be taught a few lessons," piped in Thitis, clenching and smacking his fists together – hard. He had a scar across his cheek under his eye, and if it weren't for his upscale bodysuit and slicked back hair, he would look like someone the Civils or Military would cast out into the Wilds for being a troublemaker.

"Ya know something? I'm in a mood for a good fight tonight," said Prince. "And wouldn't you know it, there's not a single person around to stop me."

"Not a single soul to bother us," said Tatio. He heaved his shoulders, spat on the ground and dug his heels into the sand like some tribal hunter who was about to fight one of the mutant animals that apparently ran rampant in the Wilds.

"Look," said Asia Mae, squaring her shoulders. "Just leave us alone. Go back to the city and we won't tell anyone that you threatened us. You'll get in lots of trouble for this. We're not bothering anyone."

Luca didn't like to fight. He believed it was smarter to reason with people and use logic to come to an amicable conclusion. But these kinds of guys didn't understand logic and had no control over their emotions. And Prince, Tatio and Thitis had clearly already worked each other up into a frenzy.

Compared with Prince and his gang, Luca was short. And though he had some muscles, he just didn't have the bulging, overblown kind.

These idiots were acting like infants and the way Luca saw it, he, Ceiba and Asia Mae only had two options: stay there and fight and get badly hurt and humiliated… or run. Luca looked at Asia Mae and Ceiba and nodded. They decided to run.

Before spinning around on her heels, Asia Mae dug her foot into the sand and deftly flicked it up into the gang's faces. They all bent over, spluttering and trying to clear it from their eyes.

"Run!" yelled Asia Mae.

Chapter Four

"You can run but you can't hide!" yelled Thitis, fast on their heels.

Luca ran with every ounce of strength he could muster. He could barely think. But he knew his friends had three things going for them: one, it was dark, with only a sliver of moonlight marking the walkways; two, both he and Ceiba were very familiar with the docks, and, hopefully, Asia Mae was, too – Luca wasn't sure; three, they were all healthy, extremely lithe on their feet and could run like the wind.

Luca dared to look back and saw that Prince, Tatio and Thitis had decided to turn back and were heading for their dune choppers: one-person motorbikes running on deep tread wheels which were perfect for tearing up the beach. *Oh, no!* How in the world were they supposed to outrun them?

"Guys, we need to split up," he called. "It'll be easier to lose them!"

The friends ran as fast as their legs would carry them and separated inside the passageways of the docks. The older guys wouldn't easily be able to ride their dune choppers through these narrow alleys. This was the only thing that could save Luca and his friends. They had to disappear amongst the buildings. It was

Strategy 101 from their defensive training in iT school.

The cargo hold area of the docks comprised of hundreds of huge, bulky containers and rose fifteen storeys high. There were a dozen automated loaders positioned in front of them.

Luca knew that Ceiba would be okay because of his familiarity with the docks. And while he didn't like to fight, he would be able to look after himself if he had to. As for Asia Mae, she was proficient in all kinds of martial arts, and besides, Luca doubted if the gang would harm her, unless... unless they wanted to take advantage of her. There had been stories. Luca's vision waxed into white-hot fury and he was near-blinded with anger.

He heard Asia Mae scream and then Tatio laughing. The sound bounced off the sides of the walls and could have come from anywhere. *Where was Asia Mae?* He had to find her. He had to rescue her from these brutes. His heart beat wildly in his eardrums – *so loud, so fierce* – it sounded like someone was pounding with a hammer on his back. *He had to protect Asia Mae!* This was no virtual game. This was real.

The three thugs had separated, too, and Luca chanced a brief look over his shoulders and saw Prince jump off his chopper and start after him. "You can't escape me, you traitor!" screamed Prince.

Although Prince was big and fast, he was also bulky and his size kept him from squeezing through some of the narrower nooks and crannies on the docks. Luca darted left onto some conveyor tracks, which were almost completely hidden in the dark. They were used to courier small cargo supplies to and from the docks, but because it was Saturday evening, there were no illuminations, no optigrams, and no one was operating the tracks. The tall warehouse storage buildings and containers on either side buffered the noise of the roiling, choppy sea and Luca ran effortlessly down the tracks. His lungs were about to burst; he stopped briefly to look back to see if Prince had followed him. He couldn't see much in the dark, but he was quite sure Prince wasn't there. If nothing else, he would have been able to hear him panting. Now, he had to zigzag through the maze of equipment and machinery to see if he could find Asia Mae and Ceiba. What he'd give to have real electro-orbs in his hands right now!

There was a security fence in front of a large building that looked like it might be used for the storage or manufacture of boat parts. Luca ran his hand along the perimeter of the fence and found a small gap at the bottom. He was thin enough, and he could crawl under it. Asia Mae would have done the same thing and it looked as though someone had prised it open, so maybe she was in there.

Just then, through the fence, he saw Asia Mae's long black hair whip around the corner and into a door in the large building. He was relieved to see that she was all right, but he would go and find her to make sure all was well.

Once inside the boundary, he headed towards the door where Asia Mae had disappeared. It was quite far away. *Was someone behind him?* He charged through the corridors where tall containers were stacked all the way up to the ceiling. His only thought was to protect Asia Mae first, and then find Ceiba. Faint lights illuminated the walkway. There wasn't a sound anywhere except for his thudding heartbeat and the soft padding of his feet. *Where had she gone?*

He finally spotted an open door in a vast hanger and made a beeline towards it, hoping that it was the same door Asia Mae had entered.

Inside, Luca stopped. *He could not believe it.* Instead of finding manufacturing parts for boats or more storage containers, what he saw was unbelievable.

Chapter Five

Asia Mae lay on the bed in her room, flipping through the optigraphic magazine pages that glowed from her sensorpad, trying to decide if she should get her long hair cut into one of the new short choppy styles that everyone was wearing. She seldom did what everyone else did though. She liked being her own person and not a follower of fashion.

Asia Mae entered her body size and style preference into the opti-mag and a short party dress and high heels appeared next to her. Asia Mae stepped into the clothes and looked at herself in the mirror, twirling to see how the sides and back looked. With a blink of her eyes, she was able to tailor the dress into a more pleasing style, then record and save the image to her comms. She'd ask her mum to order that dress for her birthday next month. She had plans to ask Luca to go out to dinner with her that evening to celebrate turning seventeen.

She turned off the opti-mag and stretched out on her back on her bed. She loved her bedroom, from which she currently had a 180 degree panoramic view of stars and galactic landscapes that served as a substitute for a window. Most often, her window – just like Luca's and Ceiba's – featured rotating planets, dazzling stars and mesmerising nebulae projected seamlessly on interactive surfaces combined with optographic imagery. She and her friends were all a little obsessed with space. She heard music in the stars and wanted to travel to them, to determine what sounds vibrated from them. Luca wanted to explore the seas, as well, and Ceiba would go with them wherever they went.

Her comms buzzed and she raised her sensorpad.

"Hello?"

"Asia," said Luca. "Turn on your screen."

She glanced at the right icon and suddenly, there was Luca, standing before her on the wall of her bedroom. "What is it?" she asked him.

"I need help. Ceiba needs help. Can you come?" he asked. Surrounded by storage containers and high walls, her best friend, Luca, wearing his sleek gaming bodysuit, looked shaken and scared. His brown hair flopped carelessly over his forehead, covering his green eyes. She liked it when he combed his hair back so she could see his eyes... really see them. They were the colour of the sea early in the morning at sunrise.

"Where are you?" Asia Mae asked. She got up and walked over to the wall. The image on the screen seemed so real, she felt she could reach out and touch Luca.

Within seconds, the screen turned dark on her bedroom wall and Luca was gone.

"I'm coming, Luca," she cried out to him. She turned and tried to get out her door, to run to Luca, but her arms and legs felt heavy and weak and she couldn't move.

Asia Mae woke up in a cold sweat. Talking to Luca had been a dream. It had all been a dream. Prince and his thugs, Thitis and Tatio... and the chasing... *No, wait.* That *hadn't* been a dream. *Where was she?* Her ears throbbed with pain. She was lying in a puddle of mud. Rain was beginning to drip on her, cold and icy. Oh, that's right. She was in the docks. It was never like this in Acacia – the rain always felt refreshing and mild, but this rain reeked of rot and chilled her to the bone. She pushed herself up, every muscle screaming. Now, she remembered.

When Tatio cornered her, she had screamed. He had just laughed and, pushing her against the wall, had tried to kiss her. "Oh, come on now, pretty," he had said, his teeth like sharpened fangs, waiting to cut deep into someone's throat. "You know you want it."

She twisted her head from him as he leaned in closer and pinned her arms back against the wall. Just remembering his breath, the staleness and foulness of it, disgusted her.

Instinctively remembering her martial arts training, Asia Mae had kneed him in the groin and he had bent over groaning. Quickly, she had slipped out from under him and, light on her feet, had run deeper into the maze of buildings. She had looked for Luca and Ceiba, but couldn't see anything or hear anything except for footsteps running in the distance. She couldn't have been sure if it was security personnel, or the thugs, or her friends. And then something had hit her on the head. She wasn't sure what.

By now, the rain was slanting down in hard sheets and Asia Mae was getting drenched. She shook with cold. A pale glow in front of her indicated that there was a room open in one of the buildings that might offer some warmth. And at this point, she would welcome the sight of a security guard.

Surely, Tatio and his friends had moved on by now. She hurried into a hangar where there were numerous sea ships that seemed to be in various stages of disrepair.

Something caught her eye in one corner of the hanger. *Oh, no!* She ran toward the body and saw Ceiba, lying in a heap of bruises and twisted arms and legs. He had been beaten badly. "Oh, no!" she cried quietly, for fear someone might hear her. She knelt down and pressed her fingers to his throat to feel his pulse. *Thank God.* He was alive. Even though he was part AI, he didn't have enough advanced programming systems to withstand beatings like this. Asia Mae had always known he was more human than AI. His emotions were proof of this.

"Oh, Ceibastian," she murmured softly, her eyes swimming with tears. "What did they do to you?"

Chapter Six

Luca tried to wrap his mind around what he was seeing. He had never even known this existed. Over his head hung an old, dilapidated metal sign that read: *Acacia Pathfinder Museum*. The hangar was full of huge sub-seafaring vehicles stretching as far as the eye could see. They all had huge retractable wheels to allow them to drive onto land from the sea. They were the original generation of Pathfinder, incapable of flight. A couple of red security lights illuminated the walkways, but the building was mostly shrouded in long, dark shadows. Perfect for hiding.

A series of marine ships from the past century were lined up like proud soldiers in front of him. Iron staircases stood at the side of each, leading up to platforms, with hatches opened wide on the decks, beckoning anyone to enter.

Disappearing amidst the row of ships, Luca quickly hid from anyone's line of sight. He heard the sound of footsteps running outside. He wasn't safe yet. He had no idea if any security personnel were around or if Prince and his friends were still searching for him. *And what had happened to Asia Mae and Ceiba?* He hoped they had escaped to their homes by now back through the security chamber, as they had agreed. It felt like he had been running for hours. Luca desperately wished he was safe at home, as well. If his mum were home by now, she'd already be worried. He never stayed out this late.

His heart pounding rapidly, he sat down on the stairs by one of the ships and breathed in big gulps of air, resting for just a moment. Outside, the wind was beginning to howl like a deranged wolf through the pathways and the waves were crashing wildly against the docks. It sounded like a storm was beginning to gather strength. The surfers would be gone by now and the bioluminescence would have shifted into gales of seaweed and waves, thrashing the shore.

Suddenly, he felt very alone. He looked at the ships beside him. They were things of beauty. Long and sleek with oval bodies of dark grey glass. With slender and graceful lines, they resembled submarines, some with wheels and some with tracks. The Pathfinders had evolved from the old-style armoured vehicles that prowled the Wilds looking for escaped criminals or Outcasts who were forming guerrilla armies. There was always the threat of attacks from some of the Outcasts beyond Acacia Burj.

Luca couldn't help but think about his father and Grampa Sol. He felt small and alone in this cavernous hangar, and he missed them terribly when he thought back.

Born into a naval family, Luca rarely saw his dad – a born leader and legendary Pathfinder racer in the Navy – while he was alive, because he was constantly away on naval military service and secret missions. Grampa Sol had been in the Navy as well and naturally Luca had wanted to follow in their footsteps.

There had been a few rare occasions spent alone with his father, Commander Delmar C. Mariner, a champion Transatlantic Pathfinder Race Winner and Naval Officer. He was one of the original men to cross the Atlantic underwater in a Pathfinder, which had been built by Grampa Sol, in the first ever global race.

Broadcasts of Commander Delmar and the ship's crew had been splashed across the video walls on the sides of buildings and across all personal communications, announcing the great naval hero who had achieved the impossible. Optigrams of Commander Delmar and Grampa Sol had even been featured on the moving sidewalks throughout Acacia and a new line of sea and land bodysuits similar to their outfits had been created and marketed to the richest fashionistas. Supposedly, these broadcasts had been featured on news announcements worldwide. All of that should have made Luca swell with pride, but it didn't.

Apparently, during a later sea mission, his dad's abandoned vessel had been attacked by a mysterious, unknown force – no one knew who, what or why according to all the news reports. The Pathfinder was found badly damaged, floating out at sea with the crew dead inside. None of the crew members were recognisable – their bodies has been crushed, seemingly by great pressure. The military alleged that one of the bodies belonged to Luca's father. There had been many inquiries and meetings, attended by his mum, behind closed doors. Even his sister Gaia had been interrogated. Luca never saw the body and, being only nine years old at the time, was too young to have been questioned by the authorities.

Rumours started to spread in Acacia, whisperings that his dad was a traitor who provided information to sea pirates and even to some of the Wild's savages, about planetary security systems. At first, Luca had cried himself to sleep every night because of the accusations.

"Luca, don't believe what you hear," his mum had told him, hugging him close to her. "Your father was an ethical, moral man. He would never do anything to jeopardise our planet and its people... or his family. He loved all of us very much."

"But everyone calls Dad a coward," Luca had protested.

"Those people don't know what they're talking about," his mum had said. She fiercely tried to protect his father's name.

Grampa Sol told Luca that they were all lies, too. That his father was absolutely not a traitor. Luca took comfort in his Grampa Sol. It was only a couple of years later, though, that Grampa left Acacia to go to another city to work with scientists on a top secret military sea project. *To search for the truth,* he told everyone. Luca hadn't seen him for a long, long time and they only communicated on the comms at appointed times. Luca missed his Grampa Sol.

Because of the rumours, though, Luca had mostly been ashamed of his dad. He hated feeling that way, but Prince and his thugs hadn't been the first ones to call him a coward and traitor-son.

All of a sudden, amidst the rain and wind, Luca heard voices not far outside the hangar. Luca hurriedly climbed the stairs and stepped through the hatch into the ship nearest to him, at the end of the row - a Racer Class Pathfinder. He tried to close the hatch as quietly as possible, but the sound made a squeaking, grinding noise that echoed throughout the hangar. *Damn!* So, he stopped, leaving it ajar a few centimetres.

He scrambled down a narrow corridor where, in the shadows, he noticed there were two sleeping quarters on either side, a small mess hall, a medical room, and a storage unit amongst the glass cables and wires. It felt like a relic of time gone by; like the images of old-fashioned submarines his father had showed him. When he came to the cockpit, he sat down in one of the two seats in front of the control board. He couldn't see much because only a small amount of light came in through the hatch, which he had left slightly open.

Terrified, he sat and waited, straining to hear movement or even a footstep out in the hangar. Had Prince or one of the other gang members followed him? Were Ceiba and Asia Mae close by? Was it the military? His breathing was loud and he tried to be quieter. He dared not make a sound. He shivered and his teeth chattered... too loudly.

After what seemed like hours in the cold and damp environment, Luca decided it must be safe to leave. His legs ached as the cold made its way through his body and his feet were almost numb. He wasn't used to being out in the elements like this. However, just as he made a move to stand up, he heard the loud, screeching sound of his hatch door as it slammed shut.

Stunned by the sudden darkness, he slowly stood up, deciding that he would feel his way back through the hallways of the Pathfinder to the exit. As he stepped forward, he leant on the control board to balance himself and accidentally triggered a switch. To his horror, the Pathfinder began to kick into life. *Oh, no way!* Lights flashed on the control board and the humming sound of a computer system start-up vibrated in soft tones through the ship. A series of graphs emerged on the panoramic screen, outlining the ship's diagnostics. In the foreground, Luca could now see the hangar before him.

"*Standby to launch engines in thirty seconds,*" a voice blared from the intercom system. "*Prepare all crew for departure.*"

No! Stop! Luca had no idea what to do. He had to think fast. He tried to flick switches to shut it down but had no idea which ones to press. He could get severely disciplined for being on board this ship. He could be suspended from iT school. This could keep him from getting into one of the sea and military training programmes. His mum would be so disappointed. Overwhelmingly, he just wanted to be safe at home.

As the countdown ended, the engines fired up into a deafening roar. Out in the hangar, Luca saw that the entire area was flooded with blinding white light. Luca saw Prince running and hiding behind another sea ship in the long line of vessels.

Desperately looking around for the off switch, Luca saw some names embossed on the dashboard of the cockpit:

S. C. Mariner
D. C. Mariner

Sol C. Mariner and his son, Delmar C. Mariner. This Pathfinder was the original transatlantic race-winning model that had been built by his grandfather, Grampa Sol, and which had made the Mariner name famous.

Chapter Seven

Curiosity overcame Luca's fear. The lights outside the old Path-finder were glaring and the noise of the engines could probably be heard for miles around. Even though the ship was revving up, and he knew he was risking *everything*, he had to investigate the cockpit a bit further. A strange feeling of connectedness swept over him like a tidal wave – that familial and emotional connection to his father and his Grampa. A strange feeling tore at his gut and tears formed in his eyes, but he brushed them away. Somewhere deep inside, he just knew that his father wanted Luca's initials, L. C. Mariner, to be the next ones carved beside his and Grampa Sol's.

Then, something unexpected happened. As Luca rested his hand on one of the panels, he felt a piece of metal scrape along his fingertip.

"Ow!" Luca pulled back his hand and rubbed his finger, not spotting any blood.

A voice announced, "Scanning DNA for identification."

What?

"DNA identification complete. Luca C. Mariner authorised."

And from out of nowhere, a lifesize opti-image of his father appeared right in front of him on the control screen. Luca was shocked. It was so lifelike he was transfixed. Every cell in his body vibrated as he watched his father stand before him. He wanted to reach out and touch him.

"Dad!"

"My son, Luca, thank the stars you have found me. Son, I love you. I love your mother and sister with all my heart. I promise you, we will see each other again. You must listen very carefully to what I have to say. This is of the utmost importance. Our planet is in great danger. You must maintain order in the universe or humanity will become extinct —"

Before Luca's father could continue, an alert was triggered and a loud automated voice boomed: *"Unauthorised file access."*

The opti-image disappeared and the Pathfinder's engine began powering down.

What? Wait a minute! What was Dad going to tell me to do? Tears spilled onto his cheeks. *Dad was not a traitor or a coward! He was a hero!* He quickly searched the controls, scrabbling around for the opti-file, so could take it with him. Remembering that his DNA was connected to the power source, he pressed his hand on the glass screen again and a slim piece of metal appeared from a slot in the control panel. It looked tarnished and weathered, and it curled slightly at the ends. Luca grabbed it. As he looked at it in the palm of his hand, rolling it around in the dim light, it seemed to slip towards his index finger as if a magnetic field was drawing it there. As Luca watched, astonished, the strand of metal wrapped itself around his finger. He yanked at it, trying to take it off again but it held fast. Perhaps it was his father's? Perhaps it had been meant to reach him?

Luca scurried back to the hatch, heaved it open and ran down the stairs, glancing back just once at the Racer Class Pathfinder. He ran out of the hangar door and onto the walkway between the buildings on the docks. The rain was furious, beating down hard on his shoulders. He looked in all directions, searching for another opening, desperate for a way out. He was sure Prince and his friends were long gone, or captured by security. He prayed that Asia Mae and Ceiba were safely at home.

The wind whipped and howled around the sides of the buildings like a giant sea monster. A few red emergency lights blinked at random corners of the buildings.

He thought he saw a door ajar and hurried towards it. By now, he had only one thought: *nothing is as it seems.*

□□□

"There's a signal from Earth," said Pihaa. "You're going to want to see this."

"It is what we have been waiting for, for a long time," said Xsar Tiandi. "With this signal, we will be able to get into Murias."

The A'Rmillari Overlord, the first of the Thirteen Overlords who ruled numerous galaxies, turned to a few members of his council. With human features, he stood tall and regal with a bald, shiny silver skull. White lines swirled all over his body, as if they were white veins pumping oxygen across his skin. He wore a black full body armour suit and around his neck was the red amulet he used to control any environment or atmosphere to his liking.

"We haven't been allowed there for many years," said Pihaa. "The boy's DNA is the same as Delmar C. Mariner's," said Xsar Tiandi. "Yes, I am sure this is what we've been waiting for. He has the Key."

With that, he turned and went to the wall panel that pulsated with the lights from galaxies throughout the universe.

Chapter Eight

Luca was freezing. The kind of freezing that made your bones ache and your skin burn. The rain was hurling down so fiercely, he could barely see in front of him. He had completely lost his bearings. He felt miserable and lonely. He ran towards the closest cargo container, and triggered its door to open. As he ran inside, it closed automatically behind him. The cargo hold was filled with boxes and equipment. Luca decided it would be his sanctuary. He'd stay there until it stopped raining, and then he'd make his way back through the security wall and into the warmth and safety of Acacia.

Just as he started to get sensation back, he felt the container jerk forward. He span his head back toward the door. *What was that?* He ran back over to the door and tried to open it. Only then did he realise that the container had locked itself shut. *He wanted to be safe, not locked up!* Terrified, he banged on the door and shouted: "Help! Help me! Is anyone out there?"

But all he could hear was the faint sound of the rain and wind. The storm was so violent; Luca feared it would rage all night long and trash anything in its path. Maybe he had no option but to stay there and wait out the storm.

"Please! Is anyone out there?" cried Luca. He banged on the door and then went around the walls, pounding them as hard as he could until his fists hurt.

But no one came.

What would his Grampa Sol tell him to do? *Just stay calm, relax and wait out the storm.* Someone would eventually come. So, Luca went behind some boxes in the corner of the cargo container and slumped down against the wall and tried to sleep. He had a lot to think about.

Luca sank like a boulder to the bottom of the sea. No matter how hard he tried to swim, he kept getting pulled down deeper and deeper. Some-where, far away, he thought he heard Asia Mae's voice. And then there were male voices – Ceiba and his father, telling him to swim harder. He never thought he'd die in the ocean. Luca fought off the panic and swam harder. But the waves rocked him back and forth, keeping him from moving forward. And the roaring sound assaulted his ears...

Then, standing before him was a glittering sea creature... The light was so bright he could barely see. No, wait... It wasn't a sea creature. It was a...

Luca came to with a jerk. He had slept more soundly than he thought he would and now, the cargo container seemed to be moving! *What on Earth was happening?*

Sweat rolled off his forehead and his clothes were damp. It was hot and muggy inside the cargo container, and the air smelt stale. There was a faint hum that he couldn't quite make out. He heard men's voices outside and someone flung open the cargo container door with a loud screech. Peeking around the boxes, Luca could see three men in Navy uniforms walk inside and start to pick up crates with their exo-shifters.

This couldn't be happening! Luca realised he could possibly be in the cargo hold of a military Pathfinder – they had special ships designed for deep sea and space exploration.

Oh shit! What was he going to do?

He heard the men moving heavy machinery around the cargo unit, unloading boxes. A minute dragged on like an hour. Luca held his breath.

"See you back at Central," said one of the men.

Luca heard him shut down his exo-shifter. Were they gone?

"Well, well, well. What have we here? Some kind of stow-away?" one of the Navy submariners asked as he peeked around the corner of a box.

"He's just a teenager!" said another. "Hey, kid, what are you doing here?"

"I... I... I got lost," stammered Luca.

"Well, you're not supposed to be here," the Navy submariner said. He was a tall man with short brown hair and a beard. Heavy lines burrowed deep in his forehead, as if he got angry often. "It's strictly forbidden for non-authorised personnel to be on board the *Sibylline*." He grabbed Luca by the arm and dragged him up off the floor. "Come with me, kid."

"Ah, go easy on him," the other one said. "He's just a boy."

"This could get us in all kinds of trouble," wrinkled forehead man said. He held onto Luca's arm firmly and guided him out of the cargo container and down a hallway.

"Please, could you just take me home?" pleaded Luca, but the men didn't seem to hear him.

The kinder, rounder man addressed his sensorpad and a true-to-life optigram of two Navy officers popped up, hovering in front of them as they walked.

"We have a breach, Commander," he said.

"What do you mean?"

"A stowaway, but I think he just got lost."

"Oh, for goodness' sake. Where did you find him?"

"He was in one of the cargo unit containers."

"Bring him here immediately."

"We're already on our way."

They walked through numerous brightly lit hallways. Luca noticed a few other Navy men and women carrying boxes through the halls to cargo containers. They finally came to a room that had *Security* printed in bold letters on the front. The guy with deep ridges in his forehead pushed Luca into a room with a long table and chairs – much like the conference rooms at his mum's offices.

"Have a seat," Luca's escort said.

Two Navy officers sat around the table.

"This is Lieutenant Commander Dillon and First Officer Marco," said one of the officers, motioning to those at the table. It was immediately apparent to Luca that Lieutenant Commander

Dillon was a Clone. She looked to be about fifteen years old, which meant that she must still have her memories and experiences from her days as a Lieutenant in a previous body; a previous lifetime. The military honoured this, after they performed numerous tests to ensure the original officer's consciousness had 'rooted' in the Clone, and gave them tenure after so many years of service. It felt strange being hauled before such a young-looking commander, though. Luca was reminded of people's obsession with immortality and his Grampa Sol had always said that it could be the undoing of humanity in the future. Luca wondered if the future was now.

"Thank you, Petty Officer Hunter and Sergeant Santiago," said Lieutenant Commander Dillon, nodding to each in turn. "You may get back to your stations."

The two Navy men saluted the officers and then left the room. Luca could have sworn that the nice guy, who was apparently Sergeant Santiago, winked at him as he exited the room.

"Hello," said Luca.

"Well, welcome to the *Sibylline*. We're in charge of security on board this ship. Who are you and what are you doing aboard our Stealth Class Lazer Pathfinder?"

So it *was* a Stealth Lazer ship!

"My name is Luca C. Mariner and I wasn't doing anything wrong, honestly. I'm a student and was with some friends last night and just got lost during the storm and accidentally got locked in, that's all," insisted Luca. "I swear." But he knew he was in big trouble. "There was this gang threatening me and my friends on the beach and we ran to hide, and–"

"Mr. Mariner," said First Officer Marco, interrupting him. "How old are you?"

"I'm sixteen, sir," said Luca.

"You must understand this is a grave offence," said Lieutenant Commander Dillon. "You've put us in an awkward position. I'm responsible for all personnel on board this ship and you have placed the entire operation in jeopardy. Just you being here is a major breach of security."

"But it was purely by accident, Commander," said Luca. "I meant no harm. I didn't know I was on the ship at all. I just want to go home, please."

"Was anyone else with you?" asked First Officer Marco.

"Yes, like I said… my friends, Ceibastian and Asia Mae," said Luca. "We were out last night watching the bioluminescent surfing and, as I said, these guys came up and threatened us so we ran and hid in the docks."

"So no one else was with you in those containers?"

"No, sir," said Luca. "It was just me. As far as I know. I'm not sure what happened to the others… and really, I'm so sorry about all of this."

"Well, it's too late now," said Dillon. "We've already started our voyage."

"You… you mean we're on an expedition at sea right now?" Luca's eyes widened and his heart sank.

"Oh, yes," said Marco, dryly. "We've already started our voyage. We can't turn back now."

"To an undersea location?" asked Luca. He felt as though if he didn't hold his breath his whole body would start trembling in fear.

"Well, first we have to deliver some supplies to our mining base on the Moon," said Dillon with tight, thin lips. She barely moved her mouth at all when she talked, as if her jaws were wired together. "But that isn't your concern. You're a stowaway and as such, you will be taken to our security lockup. It's not a punishment, but for your own safety. We can't have teenagers running amok around our ship."

"What about my mum?" asked Luca nervously, remembering suddenly that he hadn't been home all night and now, it was very early morning. "Can you contact her and let her know I'm all right? She'll be worried sick."

"Who is your mother?" asked Marco.

"Her name is Skye Mariner," said Luca. "She works for the Intergalactic Research & Science Organisation. You might have heard of her?"

The two lieutenants exchanged looks and Marco raised his eyebrows. Luca suspected that they knew who she was, but they were trying not to let on. That made him very curious.

"Don't worry," said Marco. "We'll contact your mother and notify her of your dilemma."

"Thank you, sir," said Luca. "Could you let me know if you find my friends?"

"If we uncover any information about them, we'll let you

know," said Dillon. She had a slender build and looked much shorter than Luca. There was something about her eyes that belied her age. They darted around the room constantly as if on high alert.

"Thank you, Commander."

"By the way," Marco asked. "Do you know a young man named Phaeton?"

"No, never heard of him. Why?"

"Are you sure?"

"Positive."

"Very well, then. Your escort will be waiting outside the door to take you to your room. You'll have a screen from which you can watch our voyage in safety."

"Thank you, sir."

Luca had no choice but to be agreeable. After all, he was more or less a prisoner. His pulse raced with apprehension as he reminded himself that he was on a military spaceship and heading to the Moon.

Chapter Nine

Asia Mae had blood on her hands. And now it was smeared on her clothes. Its characteristic smell of rusty iron punctured her nostrils. She was going to be sick.

"Help! Help!" she screamed over and over as Ceiba lay crumpled in her arms. He had cuts on his arms and gashes and nicks across his face. His blonde curly hair was tangled with red. One arm hung limply and lifeless across his lap as if it were broken. She tried to be very still as she held Ceiba in her lap in case his spine or circuitry were damaged but she was filled with panic and fear. Ceiba was really strong and he could fight. More than one person must have done this to him.

"Somebody, help me!" she screamed again.

Boots echoed on the rain-sodden pathway outside. A door clanked open and next thing she knew, two security guards stood in front of her.

"Asia Mae? Is that you?"

She looked up and saw the Chief Security Guard Red Ammos, Ceiba's father.

"What the hell's happened? Is that Ceiba?" He dropped to his knees.

"He was beaten up by some guys from iT school." Asia Mae sniffled, trying to hold back the tears.

Red checked his son's neck for a pulse. He then activated his sensorpad and called for help. "We have a boy down at Dock 51. Looks like he's been attacked by a gang. Send help and hurry. He's my son."

Immediately, sirens filled the air and within minutes, medics came in with a pod stretcher that floated beside them in the air, propelled by energy from their sensorpads.

After they had carefully placed Ceiba on the stretcher, Red turned to Asia Mae. "Are you hurt?"

"No, I'm fine. I got away before they could hurt me."

"Still, I want you to come to the hospital with us on the ambu-rail. You need to be examined just to be safe."

"Okay, I want to stay with Ceiba anyway."

"On the way, you can explain exactly what happened," he said, more sternly.

Asia Mae nodded. "Mr. Ammon, Luca was with us and I don't know what happened to him. If they attacked him, or–"

"I'll put out a distress call and have my men search for him. Hopefully, he got away and is safe at home."

Asia Mae nodded. Maybe Luca was home by now. But in her heart of hearts, she knew he'd never leave the docks without her and Ceiba. She simply had no idea what had happened to Luca and the mystery of the night's events deepened further.

The ambu-rail was waiting outside, hovering in a glow of light. Asia Mae was grateful for the warmth inside its cabin and hoped that Ceiba would be all right. Within seconds, they would be at the hospital.

Outside the ambu-rail, the storm raged on with fury. Somewhere below them, the archaic Pathfinder Museum exploded into a fiery maelstrom.

Chapter Ten

Unfortunately, Luca's escort wasn't Santiago or Hunter. He would have felt more comfortable with those familiar faces. Luca didn't know who this military man was and no one had introduced him. Sergeant Santiago had been rather friendly.

This security officer, a hardened military man type with a shiny bald head and small, beady black eyes, had suddenly appeared when Marco and Dillon had finished questioning him. Luca quickly realised he was a very unwelcome guest in the highest tech military vehicle on the planet. However, there was a part of him that couldn't help but feel like the luckiest space-travelling captive alive.

Luca had seen six or so military crew as they had walked through the hallways. They were tall and lean, with ropy muscles, and the men had hair that was cut short on the sides with a zigzagged fringe falling over their foreheads. They were all wearing tightly fitting black military bodysuits comprised of mesh and leathery chest, leg, knee, and arm coverings. A thin line of silver coursed around the knee and arm pads – the colour of the Acacia Military. Each of the uniforms had a stiff, high collar around their necks that could transform into a headset complete with a covering over their eyes. Around their hips were metal belts laden with weapons, sensory tabs and controls. Luca suspected the weapons were the real version of the energy orb that was simulated in the virtual games at the Arcade. He couldn't wait until he was old enough to be accepted into the Navy and intergalactic military training programme and wear one of those uniforms.

"How long will we be gone, sir?" asked Luca. "When will we return? Will my comms work in here?"

The security officer grunted and ignored his questions. Luca realised he was probably a basic model AI. The military often used AIs for missions.

The officer gently pushed him into the small room. "When you hear the countdown for takeoff, sit yourself in your sleep pod. It can be a bumpy exit from the sea."

"Can I watch?" asked Luca.

"You'll be able to see from your viewing screen," said the officer. "Even from your sleep pod."

The officer then turned around and left, locking the sliding wall door with a wave of his sensorpad. Despite his homesickness, Luca was starting to feel a little bit excited. He was going to be able to watch the *Sibylline* take off from the sea!

Looking around, Luca saw the built-in sleep pod, a small sensory desk, exercise equipment to one side, and an enclosed toilet, shower and wash basin in the corner. The whole room was softly lit with a glowing, luminous light that seemed to ooze out of the walls and ceiling. Luca felt suddenly relaxed, exhausted, and wondered if the pale light was having a calming effect.

Luca thought back to his history lessons and recalled that a long time ago, space explorers had to float around in cramped capsules and be hooked up to all kinds of biological machines and wires in order to survive entering alien atmospheres. He was grateful that the ships were now organically designed to accommodate different planetary biosystems and the insides were built to look like ordinary ship environments.

There was a large panoramic viewing screen filling one side of the room. Luca ran over and studied the scene before him. All he could see was darkness as they plunged deeper into the sea. He knew from what Grampa Sol had told him that launching into space required the *Sibylline* to plunge deeper into the sea and reach 3,000 metres below sea level before it could build up enough speed to escape the Earth's atmosphere. Launch sites were scattered all over the world's oceans.

He stared at his sensorpad, trying to connect with his family. But there was no signal. Then, he tried to contact Ceiba and Asia Mae. No signal. He gave commands to activate his i5D to connect with the World Internet, but there were no responses.

"Hello!" said Luca to the four walls. "Is anyone out there?" He didn't know why he was yelling. He was alone in this adventure. Oddly enough though, he was too excited to be afraid. Surely, the Navy crew wouldn't harm him? His mum was important to the government and military as a researcher. Lieutenant Commander Dillon had said she would try to contact her, so hopefully she wouldn't be worried. Luca just didn't know what they were going to do with him or how long he would be gone. Luca reasoned that Acacia's military were the 'good guys', and as such, he shouldn't have a thing to worry about. And yet, things seemed *odd*. That was the only way to describe it.

It was eerily quiet with only the constant hum of the engine somewhere in the belly of the ship. Luca thought he heard a bump next door, but couldn't be sure. He thought about the things he had learned in the Pathfinder Museum, and wondered about the significance of his father's message. The past few hours had been surreal.

Luca's father had been very familiar with this world. He used to drill Luca on the importance of Acacia, which was a major hub for global trade and a strategic military base where naval tankers docked after months or even years below the sea. When Luca was a child, he and his father had spent many days playing optographic puzzles featuring tankers and military bases. The vast tankers were like floating cities themselves and were used to control strategically important regions of the underwater landscape that were rich in minerals and crucial in space exploration and heavy industries.

On many days, when Luca could steal away from the city, he would go to the docks and watch the most advanced vehicles break through the waves and rise to the skies while other vessels plummeted from the skies at high speed to make subaquatic landings on the horizon. He had just never dreamed that he would be on one of these ships at the age of sixteen. Especially not as a stowaway!

For the Navy, travellers, and even expert nautical racers like Luca's father, the sea had become a perilous place where huge waves and unpredictable currents destroyed ships. But to Luca, the sea was still a hauntingly beautiful place.

Luca sat down on his sleep-pod, which automatically secured his bodysuit against its surface, and waited. For what, he didn't know. He ran his thumb over the metal of the opti-file wrapped around his index finger. The Lieutenants might have confiscated his father's file if they had thought it was more than just a normal ring.

It must be still very early in the morning, Luca reasoned. He was so tired from last night and wondered what had happened to his friends. He felt a pang of loneliness as he thought of them and wished they were with him. If all went well, though, he'd be back home soon and could share this incredible story. *They'd never believe it!*

Luca wondered what Asia Mae was doing. He remembered a year or so ago when he and Asia Mae had gone out to the roof-top of her apartment building where there was a terrace garden filled with rose bushes and trees. They had sat near the edge of the glass fence, looking out over Acacia Burj. Civils in winged bodysuits had whizzed by them, some close enough to almost reach out and touch, and the crystal and glass buildings had almost been blinding.

"What do you want to do when you get out of iT school?" Asia Mae had asked.

"Hopefully, I'll get into a pilot trainee programme," Luca had said. "Maybe in the military with Tanner. What about you?"

"I want it to be something that helps people," she had said. "I mean, I applaud you for wanting to pilot Pathfinders and all, but I'd love to do something that uplifts humankind in some way. Maybe something with my music. I really believe that there are musical vibrations in our galaxy and I'd love to study that. I don't know, really. Perhaps Mum and Dad would both like for me to be a palaeontologist like they are."

Luca had watched the sunlight on her eyes and marvelled at how prisms of golden light reflected in the brown. He remembered how he had wanted to hold her hand and kiss her, but had grown shy at the thought. She was best friends with him and Ceiba. She'd think he was silly for wanting to kiss her. And he had let the moment pass like he had so many times before.

He remembered a music recital where Asia Mae had performed. He and Ceiba had perched themselves in the front row of the symphony hall to give her all their support. That particular night, she had played a version of an old instrument, the cello. She sat in the centre of the stage, her body folded over the instrument, caressing it. Her strokes were fluid and harmonious, filling the auditorium with a sound that vibrated through the rafters. The music was always reflected in her smile, her eyes, and through her hands, whether it was gaming or playing a cello. *How could her parents not appreciate the gift of such a thing?*

After several announcements, it felt like the ship was shifting to move upwards and Luca realised that it must be on its way to breach the sea and soar into space. *Space!* Amazement finally overcame his desire to go home and be with his family. Thrilling was the only word he could use to describe the feeling.

Luca turned his attention to the viewing screen and watched as the ship breached the sea. Like a giant whale, the *Sibylline* exploded upwards, breaking through the surface. Rivulets of water streamed across the screen, illuminated by the lights lining its exterior. Luca was pushed back into his pod. For a moment, he couldn't tell if they were in the sea or outside. It was incredible. For a second or two, there was nothing but sheets of water that sparkled with a kind of fusion of white and blue. He wished he could take an opti-video of the sight. *Dammit!* If only his comms worked.

Then, the viewing screen cleared and the ship tilted to the side. Luca could see the city lights of Acacia grow smaller and smaller as the ship lifted faster than he could have ever imagined travelling. The city looked tiny compared with the sea and land surrounding it.

They lifted higher, and for the first time in his life, Luca started to see the curvature of the Earth with his own eyes. A mass of infinite beauty. Swirls of filmy white clouds hovered over parts of the Earth. In a few spots, he saw orange film, and in the distance he saw dark, roiling clouds of a supercell thunderstorm that looked menacing. The sea looked like one immense pool of the deepest blue with dots of land interspersed here and there. It was breathtaking. To think, he had been on land just hours before. And now, somehow, Acacia Burj seemed like just a speck on a massive planet. It overwhelmed him. That speck was his home. His stomach churned. Gradually, Luca could feel the ship levelling out. They were in space!

Luca felt his bodysuit release from the pod and as he leant forward to look at the viewing screen properly, his thoughts turned to home. He wished Asia Mae and Ceiba were there to share this with him. How could he ever explain how magical it was? Would they even believe him? It would just seem to them like a fantastical tale.

Suddenly, and without warning, the wall opened up, and there stood a young military trainee with a tray of food.

"Luca?"

"Tanner!"

"What are you doing here?"

"What are *you* doing here?" Luca asked. He was shocked. Never in a million years did he suspect that Tanner, his sister's boyfriend, was on the *Sibylline*.

Tanner looked just as shocked as Luca.

"I'm training on this ship," said Tanner. "It's part of my military training programme." His dark blonde hair was cut short around the sides with a fringe that fell straight over his forehead, looking dishevelled, as though he had rubbed his hand through it repeatedly. He was dressed in the same uniform as the other military crew members, except he had a red seam coursing through his to differentiate between being a trainee and a full-fledged military member. "So what's your excuse?"

"I was with Asia Mae and Ceiba last night at the docks. We got separated and it started to rain. I took cover in one of the containers," said Luca. "I honestly didn't know I was on board a ship."

"Does your mum know?" Tanner asked as he set the tray of food down on the desk. "She'll be worried!"

"They said they'd contact her and let her know," said Luca. "But could you get a message to her somehow? Make sure she knows?"

"Maybe," said Tanner. "I'll try."

"Tan, am I in trouble here?" asked Luca.

"You could be," said Tanner. "I've never known what they do with prisoners…"

"They said I wasn't a *prisoner* – that I was put in here for my safety, that's all."

"Well, fact is, they've locked you in here for a reason," said Tanner. "And you're not the only one. We have another prisoner, too. Luca, how in the world did you get yourself in this mess? Why didn't they send you home instead of bringing you along?"

"When they found me, the ship was already moving and it was too late to turn back," said Luca. He suddenly wished he could disappear. He felt ashamed and embarrassed in front of Gaia's boyfriend. They would forever tease him about it. It might even ruin his dreams of being accepted into a military sea voyager training programme someday.

"What happened to Asia Mae and Ceiba?" asked Tanner.

"I don't know," said Luca. "I never saw them again after we separated. I'm assuming – hoping – they went home after it started raining."

"Was anyone else with you?"

"No, but we were being chased by Prince, Tatio and Thitis – you know, those idiots from iT school who graduated last year?"

"Aren't they getting ready to enter into the military training programme?" asked Tanner.

"Yes," said Luca.

"Well, this might affect their applications," said Tanner.

"It should," said Luca.

"Luca, did you see anything else suspicious on the docks last night?"

"What do you mean?"

"Oh, I don't know… just anything out of the ordinary?"

"There seemed to be loads of people running around, and at times, I couldn't tell who was chasing who," Luca said, remembering when he saw Prince running to hide in the hangar. Tanner didn't say anything, though he looked as if he wanted to. He turned to leave.

"Wait," said Luca. "You said there's another prisoner? Who is it?"

"Don't know yet," said Tanner. "I just gave him his food. All

I know is he was found in one of the ship's containers on the docks last night, like you. Maybe he was running from Prince and those guys, too."

"So, it's not Prince or one of his friends?"

"No," said Tanner. "I know them from all the sports games. They just have big egos. Always have. I don't know who our other prisoner is and he isn't talking."

"Tanner," Luca began, "I found something when I was on the docks. I think you–"

"Look, that can wait," said Tanner, interrupting him. "We need to figure out what the military is planning to do with you."

"I heard them say that they have to go to the Moon to deliver some supplies and then back to Earth to a deep-sea mining base. I guess you already know that," said Luca.

"Yeah, yeah," he responded. "I know what we're doing on the ship – what our mission is – I'm just not sure what they have in store for you and that other prisoner."

"They wouldn't hurt me, would they?" asked Luca. "After all, Mum's job is important. That should help my case, shouldn't it?"

"Maybe," said Tanner.

"*Maybe?*" said Luca. "Why *wouldn't* it help?"

"Look," said Tanner, "I'll see what I can find out. Go on and eat your food and I'll come back as soon as I can."

"Thanks, Tan," Luca said. "It helps knowing you're on board."

"Try to get some rest," said Tanner. "You'll enjoy our landing on the Moon."

"When will that be?"

"Not for several hours," said Tanner. "Get some rest and see you later, Luca."

Luca noticed that Tanner was frowning. He was worried. That had to mean Luca was in some kind of trouble.

The wall closed softly behind Tanner. Luca sat at the desk and ate his manufactured food – a plant-based meat loaf of some kind and orange vegetables. He drank the bottle of water and thought about his predicament. He wondered if he was being monitored or opti-recorded. Probably. He also wondered if there was a way out. But why would he leave his room and what did he hope to find? It wasn't like he could run home. And who was the other prisoner? Although Luca didn't consider *himself* a prisoner, exactly. Something didn't seem quite right. Tanner had seemed too fidgety and nervous.

He couldn't help but wonder if the *Sibylline* really was on a mission to deliver supplies, or whether it was something else. He remembered his father's words of warning and his plea for Luca to restore order in the universe. *But what in the world did it mean?*

Chapter Eleven

An odd silence hung over the hospital waiting room. Asia Mae sat slumped in one of the chairs, her body aching and sore. She couldn't stop shaking even though they were safe inside the sensory walls of Acacia Burj and the storm couldn't hurt her. And nor could Prince and his thugs.

As she and Ceiba were being whisked away in the ambu-rail, she had looked back at the docks and heard a massive explosion. Through the rain and wind, she had seen a blaze of fire shoot into the sky. What had blown up? Why? And why did she feel like something had happened that went further than just being chased by Prince and his thugs? Something sinister seemed to be bubbling just beneath the surface, but Asia Mae couldn't figure it out. Things didn't add up. It was just supposed to be a fun Saturday evening, but it had almost turned deadly. She couldn't help but wonder about what she heard in the A'Rmillari game and if that had anything to do with all the secrecy at the docks. It had been fun thinking about it – thinking that maybe the game was intercepting a real live message from aliens somewhere in the galaxy! It was fun pretending they were spies.

Where was Luca? If he were with her, it wouldn't be so bad.

Luca was the one person who could calm her and make her feel better. Just the touch of his hand or the way he looked at her with those clear emerald eyes, and his dark hair sticking up all over his head, seemed to make all her worries disappear. Luca had no idea how handsome he was – gorgeous, really – and that was one of the most endearing things about him. He had the biggest heart in the world and some girls thought he was a bit too soppy and sentimental, but not Asia Mae. She loved how he wasn't afraid to show his softer side, but when he had to be tough, he could be. Make no mistake about it, Luca was stronger and more mature than most guys his age.

She had tried to contact him on her comms when she arrived in the hospital, but there was no response. She left a message for him to contact her immediately. Maybe he'd come over and stay with her tonight since she was alone. He had never done that before, but she had wanted him to several times when her parents were gone. He had always declined. He was just shy, she told herself. Or, maybe he didn't find her attractive *in that way.*

Several people – men and women, old and young – sat on the deep-padded benches in the waiting room near Asia Mae. They all looked worried, their brows furrowed, charcoal circles under their eyes, hair tousled, clothes wrinkled.

Asia Mae had been so relieved when the security guards and Mr. Ammos had found her and Ceiba. He wouldn't let the other security guards arrest her. Technically, she could have been held in the Detention Centre and questioned about why she was on the docks during a storm in the first place.

They weren't sure about Ceiba's condition, but he was young and strong. He had that going for him. So they said. The fact that he was a Bion could be either an asset or a liability. She didn't know which.

After tonight's beating, there were lots of things wrong with Ceiba. He had a collapsed lung and a ruptured spleen and a nasty gash on his leg. The AI circuitry in part of his brain was misfiring as well. One of Prince's thugs must have kicked the hell out of him. And there was internal bleeding, broken ribs and probably more. All Asia Mae could remember was the blood. It had been everywhere.

The doctors had immediately transported Ceiba to an advanced healing pod for hybrids inside the hospital, and Asia

Mae had been allowed to see him for only a moment. The healing pods were very good and utilised a mixture of sound waves, physio-biomeds, circuitry repair nodules, light wave emissions and the latest in medical laser inventions to treat and heal bodies.

Still, Red was beside himself with worry. As was Asia Mae. Ceiba's mum had become hysterical after seeing him and the doctors had to administer a sedative to calm her down. She was now asleep in a recuperative room in the visitor's Serenity Lounge, which was imbued with calming sensors in hazy, mellow light, and it had helped her relax and drift off into a dreamless sleep. They had tried to get Asia Mae to go in there and rest as well, but she had refused. She wanted to stay awake in case Ceiba woke up or she heard from Luca.

Asia Mae had a few cuts and bruises from fighting with Tatio, which the hospital staff tended to with ointments and a couple of bandages, but luckily there was nothing too serious. Red had offered to contact Asia's parents, but they were travelling into The Wilds for a subsea dig and weren't home at the time. She had tried to message them on her comms, but again there was no answer. Being an only child, she had no one else at home. She considered Ceiba and Luca her real family.

On the ambu-rail, Red had looked at her closely and said, "Asia, did you and your friends see or hear anything suspicious around the docks?"

"What do you mean?" she asked, guardedly. "Like I told you, Prince and his friends chased us, and–"

"I know, I know," said Red. "Just wondered if you saw or heard anything else that didn't seem quite right while you were on the docks. We're always on the lookout for suspicious behaviour, and with the storm and all last night, it was hard for the visuals to pick up any unusual activity."

"No, honestly," said Asia Mae. "We just got lost. We were being chased by Prince and those guys from iT school and the storm started and it got dark fast and we all got separated." She felt like she had explained this a million times.

"Okay," he said. "It's not safe out there on the docks at night – especially in storms. None of you should have been out there at all. Look what happened to Ceiba."

"But that was because of those guys from iT school," said Asia Mae.

"I know," said Red. "But you never know what you'll run into out there."

"Mr. Ammos," asked Asia Mae. "Did you find Luca?"

"No, not yet," said Red. "We contacted his mum, but she hasn't heard from him. Everyone's looking for him though. We should find him soon."

"And what about Prince, Tatio and Thitis?"

"Those older guys from iT school with the dune choppers?" asked Red.

"Yeah, those guys."

"No word," said Red. "But if I have anything to do with it, not one of them will get into the military training programme this year." He clenched his jaw. Asia Mae knew he was very upset about Ceiba. So was she.

"That's good," said Asia Mae. "They're just mean guys who had way too many privileges because they were worshipped in sports. And, they shouldn't get away with this. I'm so sorry about Ceiba, Mr. Ammos."

"He's a strong boy," interrupted Red. "He'll make it. He has good DNA and his circuitry is repairable. It's a good thing I found you when I did though. Now you go on home and get some rest."

"I will in a while," said Asia Mae. "I just want to look in on Ceiba one more time, and then I'll go home. I promise."

"I'll be around if you need me," said Red. He put his hand on Asia Mae's shoulder and gave it a little squeeze. "I know your parents are out of town, so remember, I'm here if you need anything."

"Thanks, Mr. Ammos."

Even though Asia Mae knew she was all right, that Ceiba would more than likely heal fast, and that Luca was probably safe at home, she had an uncomfortable feeling in her gut. About everything.

Chapter Twelve

"I don't think the Mariner boy knows anything," said an older male's voice.

What? Luca couldn't believe that he could hear a nearby conversation from just the other side of the wall. He quietly climbed from his sleep-pod and moved closer. The voices were faint, but he could still hear.

"Well, Earth Central will decide when we get back, after we've done further investigations," a second voice said. "We can't take any chances after the explosions last night on the docks at the museum. After all, he was there. You *do* know who his father and grandfather are, right?"

The museum? Did they know that Luca had been in the museum? *What explosion?* His heart started racing.

"I know," said the first voice. "But his mum and sister work for us and the young man can't be blamed for what his father and grandfather did. Although, you never can tell. We've been fooled before."

"If he clears Security Investigations, and proves he's not a threat and that he has nothing to do with the museum blowing up, then maybe we should leave him on the Moon at the resort when we arrive," argued the second voice. "That way he can travel back to Earth on a Space Cruise Liner. It would be more comfortable for him and we wouldn't have to worry about what to do with him when we reach Mariana."

"Right, seems like a good idea. What about our other prisoner?"

So, they did consider Luca a prisoner!

"He's a different story entirely. He's some kind of outcast, who was exiled from Acacia a couple years back, and he's now wanted by the military. Could be a spy, we're not sure. He might have had something to do with the explosion at the museum also."

Luca heard some shuffling, a few footsteps, and then the voices faded into the distance. His head was whirling. What did they mean? He didn't want to be left on the Moon to come back in a tourist Space Cruise Liner. He wanted to stay on the ship and continue on with the deep sea mission. He wanted to talk to Tanner. Surely, Tanner wouldn't let any harm come to him? *Maybe he could pull in some favours.* According to Gaia, Tanner was doing exceptionally well in his military training programme and was well liked by his superiors.

Luca walked over to the wall that had opened for Tanner before and tried to make it open for him. He focussed on several different commands in turn on his sensorpad, hoping he could reactivate it, but nothing happened. Obviously, the frequencies had been adjusted to work only with the ship's personnel.

He didn't know how long he was standing there, but he soon heard a knocking on the other side of his room. He went over to the wall and knocked back. "Is anyone in there?" Luca yelled.

"Yes! Can you hear me?" a muffled voice called.

"I can hear you, but it's faint. My name's Luca. Who are you?"

"I'm Phaeton. Can you get us out of here?"

"I've tried to get out, but I haven't been able to breach the door. My comms don't work in here. Have you tried?"

"Yeah, but no go," Phaeton said. "Hey—"

Footsteps, banging and a clanking sound. Scuffling. Someone entered Phaeton's room and now there was silence. Luca felt a sense of foreboding, but reminded himself that his sister's boyfriend was on board and his mum worked for the same people as the military. He'd be all right.

Luca went back to the panoramic screen. He couldn't believe

they were already approaching the Galileo Resort's runway and he didn't want to miss it. He wondered if he should sit down again, but this landing shouldn't be as tumultuous as the breaching of the sea, and since no one told him otherwise, he stayed put before the screen.

What he saw before him was extraordinary. A metallic grey horizon with rounded mounds, craters and hills spread before him. Like a grey-white desert, barren of the blue sea Luca was so familiar with on Earth. Galileo was a space resort station that had been built by remotely operated robots from Earth many years ago, and it showed signs of ageing. Nowadays, people wanted to go to the newer resorts on Mars.

As for the docking station and its neighbouring runway, it was quite different from the docks at Acacia Burj. The station was built inside a crater, and various worm-like canvas shoots formed covered walkways out into the resort.

All living areas on the Moon were enclosed in an invisible sensory shield like the one on Acacia Burj. That way, lunar tourists didn't have to wear spacesuits or headsets like they used to long ago. The sensory shield adjusted for gravity, oxygen and essential Earthly conditions and protected people from the vacuum of space, the extreme variances of the temperatures from the brilliant heat of the sun and the deep cold of the night, and from the impact of micro-meteors.

The resort, with the distant blue sphere of Earth as a backdrop, looked gorgeous. Luca sighed. Earth was a brilliant jewel against the black velvet sky.

The *Sibylline* was landing in a deep valley with mountains in the distance that looked like they were covered with a layer of bright new snow. Luca knew it wasn't snow, but a layer of rock dust with sparkling beads of glass caused by meteor impacts. It was stunning.

When the ship slid into the docking station, it was surprisingly steady and calm. Outside the viewing window, the ground looked like grey, talcum-powdery dust with rocks scattered about.

Luca couldn't take his eyes off the screen. He had no idea where his mysterious fellow prisoner was, and at the moment, he wasn't too concerned. All he could think was how incredible this moment was. He was on the Moon! *Wait until Ceiba and Asia Mae hear about this!*

Luca didn't know how long he stood there but, finally, some land transporters rolled off the *Sibylline*, loaded with supplies. Military personnel, who were stationed on the Moon, darted around the transporters on foot, or in their lunar vehicles, and guided the ship's crew onto a service road leading into the resort.

Luca had no idea that there was so much housing and tourist development on the Moon, or that the Galileo Resort was so large. Of course, most Opuls vacationed on Mars nowadays and ignored the Moon. But both the Moon and Mars were real getaways from Earth and its problems. Luca wondered if Earth looked as beautiful from Mars as it did from the Moon. *Someday,* he promised himself, *I'll travel there and find out.*

He wished Tanner would come back. Maybe he could persuade him to let him visit a little bit of the Galileo Moon Resort. He remembered what he heard those crew say out in the hall – that they might leave him to return on a tourist ship. He didn't want that, so maybe he should just stay quiet.

No doubt the *Sibylline* would be in a hurry to go back to Earth and wherever else it was going. It was all so exciting; Luca couldn't believe he was part of it. Even through the excitement, he worried about Asia Mae and Ceiba. What had happened to them?

As Luca stood transfixed, watching the land transporters, something changed. So fast, so sudden, that Luca wasn't sure what he was witnessing. A black cloud made up of masses of random shapes descended from the air and swarmed through the docking station area and then, out of nowhere, a three pronged dark pearlescent grey spaceship landed in front of the *Sibylline*. Immediately, twenty or so bulky, armour-clad figures rolled out of the ship and started blasting large fiery red energy orbs at the Pathfinder's crew.

¤¤¤

"So the attack is underway," said Pentu, one of the Dark Alliance observers currently on Ramessu, the A'Rmillari's mother ship.

Xsar Tiandi, Overlord One of the A'Rmillaris, nodded. This mission was of the utmost importance to the Dark Alliance. He couldn't believe their luck when the Key was activated from Earth.

"The tracking signal from the Mariner's Key is loud and strong on the Earth's Pathfinder," continued Xsar Tiandi. "We should be able to seize the ship and the young man, if needed, and with that Key, we can get back into Murias and activate the anti-gravity weapon that will allow us to collect Earth's water resources to sell across the Universe."

"I've sent the best of your soldiers to capture the ship," said Pentu. "I think we should take the young man alive. The Key might only work with his DNA."

"We must take every precaution," said Xsar Tiandi. "Ever since the tracking system was severed on his father's whereabouts, it has been impossible to penetrate the new portal at Murias. This Key is crucial."

"Yes," said Pentu. "We will recover the key. And Xsar Tiandi?"

"Yes, Pentu?"

"Your life depends on it."

"As you wish," said Xsar Tiandi.

Chapter Thirteen

Asia Mae watched closely as a medical attendant escorted the floating trauma pod through the hallway. Inside it, a young man was encased in an orange light. He appeared to be sleeping.

In the waiting room with her was a young woman with a little brown haired girl on her lap.

"How long will Poppa be in surgery?" the girl asked, pointing to the medical pod as it floated by, twisting in her mother's lap. The woman, who didn't seem much older than Asia Mae, had been crying and her eyes were red and swollen. "Honey, it shouldn't be long," she said. "They have a very good medical crew here. Your Poppa is going to be okay." The mother hugged her little girl tightly in her arms, rocking her back and forth.

Sitting on the sofa by the wall, a grandfatherly type with a small protruding belly, white hair, and bushy eyebrows, sipped on a hot drink. He wore a grey overall bodysuit like many of the elderly men. Asia Mae wondered if he was drinking coffee or one of the calming brews that the hospital gave out freely. As she looked at him, she also wondered why he was there. She didn't like the thought of getting old and it made her understand why many of the Opuls went to the Translation Institute to have their consciousness transferred into a Clone when their physical body grew too old.

Asia Mae hated hospitals. Even though they were supposed to heal the sick, hospitals seemed like very negative environments, not conducive to healing at all. They made her feel depressed. After Ceiba's father had left her in the waiting room, Asia Mae had felt more alone than ever. She tried to get comfortable in the chair, which was impossible. It was more like a padded bench that ran all along the wall instead of a chair. All the plush chairs in the centre of the room were taken. She decided to wait a few minutes, then, when none of the medical staff was looking, she'd sneak into the trauma ward to look in on Ceiba.

A nurse with short yellow hair, alabaster skin and wide eyes, wearing a computerised dress and sleek, skinny white trousers, appeared in the waiting room. Asia Mae knew that the medical staff could monitor chemical reactions and vital signs of the patients very efficiently from wherever they were.

A girl who was sitting beside her in the waiting room, and who appeared to be a little older than Asia Mae, looked over and rolled her eyes. In a loud voice, she said, "I don't know which is more disgusting – a Persona doing medical work or the fact that everyone is wearing those stupid-looking computer tops."

Since the girl was talking directly to her, Asia Mae said, "Well, supposedly, it's very efficient for the medical personnel to wear those LED dresses, and–"

"Complete crap," announced the girl. Her short brown hair stuck up in spikes on the top of her head. She had a wild-looking, animalistic look about her, with heavy dark eyeliner and black eyeshadow around her enormous brown eyes. She was a Retro, no doubt, dressed in ripped, holey vintage blue jeans, a low cut t-shirt, and an expensive leather jacket like some of the people wore at the *Game Stop Café*. An ornate necklace spiralled across her chest. Asia couldn't see exactly what it was, but it looked like some kind of snake.

"It's rubbish. We're getting further and further away from things that are *real*, if you ask me. We're living in a Persona world! People hooked up to sensors and machines and letting their Personas do their work? How do we know they can even be accurate? And wearing computers as their clothes to help them with patients? It's all nonsense."

"I guess..." said Asia Mae hesitantly. She had never heard anyone be so outspoken against modern technology. She always thought it was *good* for progress. She couldn't imagine living without her sensorpad, her i5D, or any of the multiple apps that were part of her everyday life. Of course, there were the elders in Acacia Burj who said that everyone was addicted to technology, but she disagreed. Technology was necessary and she loved it.

"Of course, it's just the Opuls or the medics who can even afford the fancy-schmancy digital clothes or those goddamned materials that encircle you in ambi-lights. Ugh, it's just awful and *so* pretentious."

"Uh-huh," said Asia Mae, suddenly feeling self-conscious about wearing the newest fashion in gaming bodysuits and her embedded wrist sensorpad.

The nurse glanced over in their direction, raised her perfectly arched eyebrows slightly, and then went back to entering information on her optigram charts.

"If they're so obsessed with creating happy moods for everyone," said Retro girl, lowering her voice a little, "then why don't they make them affordable for *everyone* – not just the Opuls?"

"I think it would be great if we could all afford those clothes," said Asia Mae. "It would be nice to control my mood by clicking my fingers."

"Mine would probably be on 'angry' all the time," Retro girl smirked. Her dark brown eyes flashed. "Everything about this place makes me angry and I *like* feeling that way. I don't want to feel like roses and sunshine. That's all fake. I want to feel in control of my erratic emotions."

"Yeah, I understand," said Asia Mae. She didn't know what else to say and generally, when someone was angry, she felt it was good to not antagonise them further. "So why are you here?"

"My brother was found beaten up on the docks tonight and he's in critical condition," said Retro girl. "He barely survived. He was with me and my boyfriend. And they arrested my boyfriend." She wiped away tears that were forming in the corner of her eyes with the back of her sleeve. She was obviously far too tough to let anyone see her crying.

A mild shock zipped through Asia Mae and she sat up straighter in her chair. Who was her brother?

"That's strange," said Asia Mae, inquisitive. "Is he okay?"

"I think so. Yes." She nodded to herself. "He *will* be."

"Who's your brother, if you don't mind me asking?"

"Elton," she said. "Elton Madden."

"Oh, I thought I might know him."

"Do you?"

"No, I just thought–" Asia Mae said.

"They said he would pull through, but they talk crap all the time, so who knows?"

"I'm sure he'll be okay," offered Asia Mae. "That's one thing that's good about this place. They have a great medical staff." She shifted on the bench. Could it be a coincidence that Retro girl's brother and Ceiba had both been beaten up? *Who knew the docks were so dangerous?*

"Do they know who beat him up?"

"No one's talking," said Retro girl. "I have my theories, but that's all they are. And I don't know where they've taken my boyfriend."

"Well, I'm sorry," said Asia Mae. "What were you doing on the docks?"

"My boyfriend was supposed to meet someone about some business and my brother just went along. What about you?" Retro girl asked. "You have someone in here?"

"Yes, a friend," said Asia Mae. "He was found beaten up on the docks, too."

Retro girl's eyes grew big as saucers. "Well, ain't that something?"

"What?"

"Oh, nothing," said Retro girl. "Just adds to my theory, that's all."

"What's your theory?" Asia Mae was curious.

"If I started on that, we'd be here for hours," Retro girl said, laughing and picking at one of the shredded holes in her jeans.

Asia Mae decided to change the subject. This girl looked familiar. *And the name Madden...*

"Do you use iT school at Acacia Central? I'm not sure if I've ever seen you before..."

"Name's Sumer. I'm named after a season, apparently. I used to log in to classes at Acacia Central," she said. "I graduated a couple of years ago. Now, I'm trying to *find myself*, as my parents say."

"Oh, that's a pretty name. It's unusual." She just couldn't figure out where she had heard it before.

"I guess..." Sumer said, shrugging her shoulders. "My parents were into unusual names."

"Are your parents here?"

"Nah, they're always travelling. Elton and I are left on our own a lot. Enough about me. What's your name? You a foreign princess or something? You have an exotic look about you."

"Asia Mae." She blushed. "I'm no princess, that's for sure. Just a regular Civil in Acacia Burj."

"Humph. Could have sworn you were a princess. Are you in Level Two at iT school?"

"Yeah, I still have another year before I graduate, then, hopefully, I'll get into a Third-Level programme. Doing what, I'm not sure yet. Maybe music or palaeontology."

"Well, good luck to you," Sumer said. "And look, forgive my manners. I'm just fed up."

"It's okay," said Asia Mae. "It's not easy when our loved ones are in here."

Asia Mae looked over at the Persona nurse behind the reception desk. When people's bodies became older and more decrepit, they sometimes chose to go to Hibernation Clinics where they lay inert in a pod for hours at a time, while their consciousness was hooked up to sensors and computers temporarily to wear his or her perfect duplicate-body called a Persona. These bodies looked just like the originals – only much better. They were the perfect versions of their human selves.

At that moment, the Persona Nurse gestured towards Sumer and Asia Mae. Sumer rolled her eyes again and under her breath, said: "Oh no, she probably heard me carrying on. If this gets back to my parents..."

Perfect Nurse smiled politely, showcasing polished white teeth. "Don't you two young ladies want to go home and get some rest? It's early morning and you must be tired."

"I'll go home when I'm ready," said Sumer, puffing up her chest. "And I'm not ready yet."

"I'll go in a little bit," said Asia Mae. "Can you tell me if you've had anyone come in from the docks by the name of Luca Mariner?"

The nurse accessed some files on her clipboard, looking for new patients.

"Besides Ceibastian Ammos, your friend, and Ms. Madden's brother, we have a couple of unknown males in from the docks," the nurse said in a pleasant, almost musical voice. "Unfortunately at this stage we don't have any information about their identities. Which is unusual. One of them is in critical condition and the other, I'm afraid, is dead. Do you think you might know them?"

"Yes," said Asia Mae, her stomach clenching. Could one of them be Luca? Tears filled her eyes. "Can I see them?"

"I'll have to check to see if that's permissible," said the Persona. Her name tag said that her name was Nurse Lorelai.

"Thank you, Nurse Lorelai," said Asia Mae, sweetly. "I'd really appreciate it if you'd check."

"Come on," Sumer whispered, as she grabbed an old-fashioned backpack from beside her feet and stood up. "Let's go to the morgue."

"But, Nurse Lorelai said..." began Asia Mae.

"Screw Nurse Fancy-Top," said Sumer. "We don't have to wait for her. I've seen where the morgue is. Come on!"

"You sure it's safe?"

"Of course. There aren't any laws that say we can't go look at bodies in the morgue."

"Um... right." Asia Mae was doubtful.

The other people in the waiting room looked up at them questioningly as Sumer took Asia Mae's hand and pushed her out into the hallway.

Just as they were scurrying across the gleaming polished floors, it all clicked into place. Asia Mae almost stopped in her tracks. Then it dawned on her. She remembered where she had heard Sumer Madden's name before. She had watched the news feeds all over Acacia of Sumer with her family.

Wow! Sumer's father was President Madden, Acacia Burj's leader.

Chapter Fourteen

Chaos ensued. Shouting and screaming raged outside and inside the hallways of the *Sibylline*. Huge orange orbs shot through the air and exploded on the ground, wounding everyone in their paths. A dozen or so military crew and a few of Galileo's residents lay bloodied and lifeless over their land transporters under the blazing sun. It had all happened in an instant.

An attack on the Sibylline? Luca couldn't comprehend what he was seeing. He stood there at his viewing screen and watched as the black shapes moved and disappeared like the wind into the interior of the landing station where the Pathfinder was docked. Were they on board? Was this some kind of illusion? A game?

Luca's heart drummed so loud he thought his insides would burst. This couldn't be happening! Luca didn't understand. They were there to unload supplies for the settlements on the Moon. Who were these intruders?

And then, a second group of unknown armoured soldiers – nearing three metres tall, bodies flashing in different shapes and colours beneath glasslike armour, descended from the spaceship. They quickly scattered among the lunar vehicles, wielding long weaponry and firing red and orange energy orbs that shattered anything they hit.

Even inside the *Sibylline*, Luca could hear the explosions and ripping of fire outside the ship. Footsteps pounded down the hallway outside Luca's room. He was afraid, but the wall door opened and there stood Tanner.

"Come on, Luca! We're under attack!"

"What's going on, Tanner?"

"There's no time for explanations. Hurry, come with me!"

Luca ran out the door and followed Tanner. Emergency lights blinked on and off through the smoke. The smell stung his senses. Men were running through the halls, shouting orders to one another. Luca saw Sergeant Santiago running with a couple of weapons. Sweat streamed from his brow and he looked scared.

Lieutenant Commander Dillon rounded the corner. "Get to the bridge," she yelled as she ran.

An emergency strobe lighting system flashed into action.

Tanner handed Luca an Electro Turbo Neutraliser and asked: "Do you know how to use this?"

"Sure!" said Luca. Truth was, he had only used a Neutraliser in his virtual games, but he wasn't going to let Tanner know that. Grampa Sol had told Luca that all those games had been designed to simulate reality, so, hopefully, he could manage. He had no choice, really, if he wanted to survive.

The halls were dark, with only the pulsating emergency lights in the far corners to see by; the random explosion of fiery orbs hitting their eardrums. Tanner and Luca were running blind, looking for stairs that would take them to the bridge. Military crews were running all over the ship.

Brilliant flashes of white, red and orange blazed through the hallways at intervals. Trails of smoke followed, creating a thick, hazy film that reminded Luca of deep fog on the docks in Acacia.

An armour-clad enemy burst around the corner. They were on the ship! Tanner blasted him with his Neutraliser, but the giant soldier was too fast and Tanner missed. The attacker grunted and lurched forward again. He lunged at Luca, but this time, Luca aimed and shot at him, hitting him squarely in the head. Arcs of bright red light exploded from his Neutraliser and the attacker crumpled.

Without stopping to think, Tanner and Luca fled down another hallway, leaping over a tangled pile of dead soldiers and fallen crew. Luca wanted to stop and take off the headsets of the dead soldiers to identify them, but Tanner told him they didn't have time.

"Someone should be remotely fighting these soldiers," said Tanner.

"What do you mean?" asked Luca.

"We've got the ability to fight remotely from the Command Centre," said Tanner. "The corners of the hallway ceilings are equipped with blasters – all you have to do is aim and fire. If we can get there, we'll be in a better position. I don't know why the Captain hasn't been taking out these guys from there. We'll lock ourselves in there and should be able to seal off all entrances to the ship. Come on!"

As they climbed stairs to get to the higher level, three more of the giant soldiers lurked at the top, blocking their way. They were impenetrable hulks – only red shiny beads peering out from their headsets where their eyes should have been. They were the scariest things Luca had ever seen. Luca and Tanner both fired their Neutralisers, defending their position. The soldiers jumped high into the air and practically flew back into the outer hallway. *What the—?* Luca and Tanner looked at each other with big eyes.

Luca whirled around and saw that the soldiers were now behind them at the bottom of the stairs, aiming their blasters at him and Tanner. In a flash, he remembered something. In the A'Rmillari game, Luca's electro-energy orbs vibrated to his emotional energy pattern: the stronger his thoughts, the stronger the orbs. He instinctively switched his mindset – he wasn't about to let these attackers kill him or Tanner! With all his might, Luca blasted his weapon at the soldiers and out shot huge, round blood-red orbs. The soldiers crumpled to the ground in a pile of hiss, ash and smoke.

"How'd you do that?" Tanner exclaimed.

"I'll explain later," said Luca, grinning. He wasn't sure he could explain to Tanner, because he really didn't understand how he had done it either; it was all part of something he had learned in the A'Rmillari game.

They hurried through passageways and rounded another

corner. Two of the *Sibylline's* men lay bleeding. Sergeant Santiago was tending to them.

"Are you guys all right?" asked Tanner.

"Yeah, we're good," Santiago said. He shook his head sadly. "I can't believe this is happening."

"Look, we'll be back!" yelled Tanner. "We're going to see if the Captain is all right."

The men nodded and Santiago said, "Hurry! I think some of those goddamn monsters are still on board."

"Try to get the wounded to the medic bay and lock yourselves in!" shouted Tanner.

When they finally reached the Command Centre, Tanner scanned his sensorpad on the door panel and a voice announced: "Verification confirmed."

The door slid open and he and Luca stepped inside. Tanner quickly closed and sealed the door behind them.

"Hello? Captain?" called Tanner. "Is anyone here?"

"Where's the Captain?" asked Luca.

"I don't know," said Tanner.

From behind a row of controls emerged a tall, young man, as white as a sheet of paper. He was non-military, dressed in Retro clothes, with long brown hair tied back in a ponytail, holding a Neutraliser. He was trembling.

"Stop right there! Put your weapons on the floor!" he shouted at Luca and Tanner.

Luca looked at Tanner. *What now?* The ponytail guy was definitely older than Luca – probably closer to Tanner's age – maybe early twenties.

"Wait! Wait a minute!" said Tanner, putting his weapon down at his side. "Aren't you supposed to be in lockup?"

"No," he said. "That was a mistake. Do as I said – put down your weapons or I'll shoot!"

"How'd you get in here?" asked Tanner.

"I said put down your weapons or I'll shoot!"

"Do it, Luca," said Tanner, nodding at him. "All right. You don't have to shoot. We're putting down our weapons."

Luca and Tanner slowly put down their Neutralisers.

"Good. Are you alone?"

"Yeah," said Tanner. "It's just us."

"There were... there were..." began Retro guy. His shoulders slumped as he loosened his grip on the Neutraliser.

"What?" asked Tanner. "There were *what*?"

"I don't know how to explain it," Retro guy said. "Just moments ago, there were these *things* in here, and now they're gone. Disappeared into thin air..."

"*What?*" both Tanner and Luca said, looking at each other with disbelief in their eyes.

"I'm not lying! They disappeared into thin air! Just like that!" Retro guy said.

"Probably an optigram," said Tanner.

"Yeah, possibly," Retro guy said. "Both of you, move over to the control screens. Either one of you know how to fly a ship?"

"Look, we're not pilots either," said Tanner. "I'm in training and while I've observed the Captain, I can't fly a Lazer Stealth Pathfinder. We've got to find the Captain."

"He's dead," said Retro guy, blank-faced.

"How do you know?" asked Tanner.

Luca's heart dropped.

"Where's the Captain?" shouted Tanner. "And what about First Officer Marco? Where the hell are they?"

"They're dead," said Retro guy. "But I didn't kill them. It was those enemy soldiers."

"But how—?" persisted Tanner.

Retro guy cut off Tanner's question and aimed his weapon at Luca and Tanner. "Look, I don't know. Both of you – get over to those controls and figure out how to fly this bloody thing and get us back to Earth."

"Okay, okay," said Tanner. "Put the gun down. We'll try to figure this out."

Luca and Tanner approached the control screens that covered one entire room from the floor to the ceiling, wrapping around them in a semicircle. Data streamed on the glass-walled panels, reading out planetary stats, oxygen and gas levels. Opti-visuals surrounded them in the concurrent helixes that diagrammed the ship's inner and outer walls. On one panel all around them, Retro guy, Tanner and Luca were able to see the outside of the *Sibylline*; the full scale attack happening on the moon base, and the tranquil stars above. On another panel, when they walked to it, they were standing in the hallways in the ship, able to walk through the halls and rooms, using their hands to flip to their destinations.

Luca's head was spinning. He didn't know what the hell was going on, but he knew one thing for sure. Since there was only one other prisoner, this had to be the guy who had been next to him in his cell; the one who had called himself Phaeton. Was he going to kill them next?

Chapter Fifteen

"Look, we're all on the same side here," said Tanner. "You can put down your weapon, too."

"How do I know you won't put me back in the lockup?" Retro guy asked.

"Because I suspect you should have never been put in the lockup in the first place," said Tanner. "Besides, we don't know if any of those soldiers are still on board, and we don't know who is dead and who is still alive. We're all we've got. We need each other."

"Are you Phaeton?" Luca questioned.

"You're the kid that was next to me?" Retro guy snorted under his breath.

"Yeah, I was in the room next door."

"Yeah, I'm Phaeton," he said, finally lowering his weapon. "So, when did the military start arresting kids?"

"He wasn't technically a prisoner," said Tanner. "He was just in there for his own safety."

"I'm not really a kid," protested Luca. "I'll be seventeen next month."

"Well, we're all screwed," said Phaeton, relaxing for the first time since they came in. Phaeton was dressed similarly to most Retros. Worn, holey jeans, torn white t-shirt under a black trench coat. Even old cowboy boots. He looked like he had stepped right out of the history books. He had a glowing hoop in one ear. Even though he looked rather unapproachable, Luca could see Phaeton had a look that some people might find intriguing.

"If we can't figure out how to pilot this ship, then we might just be forever stuck on the Moon with those nasty soldiers." Phaeton slouched into the Captain's chair.

"Who are they?" asked Luca.

"Maybe our military trainee friend can tell us," said Phaeton, nodding toward Tanner.

"I honestly don't know. It could be a faction of the military that has decided to rebel or a group from the mines. Or, another group on Earth I don't know about. I don't recognise their armour."

"But they're too tall to be human. And we couldn't see their faces," said Luca. "They have armour like the soldiers in the A'Rmillari game at the Arcade. Surely that's our clue."

"Aliens? Ugly sonofabitches, if you ask me," said Phaeton, nodding.

"Right now, we've got to get control of the ship's piloting system," said Tanner. "We need to get off the Moon, or you might be right – we'll get stuck here, stuck in a fight that we can't win. I've never seen orb blasters like the ones they were using."

"Okay, truce it is."

"But shouldn't we see if the people at the resort need help?" asked Luca. He didn't like the idea of abandoning them.

They glanced at the viewing screen and saw that much of the Moon colony seemed to be evacuating in personal spaceships.

"We won't be any good to them." Tanner frowned. "We don't have that many crew members on board. And I have no idea how many were killed on the Moon. We need to get in touch with Command Central in Acacia Burj. Phaeton, have you seen the Captain's body?"

"No, but I saw two of those big soldiers dragging him and that First Officer out of here and when they turned their backs, I had only a sliver of a moment, but was able to slip through the doorway before it closed shut. I'm just assuming they were both already dead."

"Or they were alive and being kept hostage," Luca said.

"Don't know. We can deal with that later. Come on; let's get this ship in the air." Phaeton was impatient.

The three of them walked closer to the control screens which spread before them like wet glass. The panoramic view ran from floor to ceiling. Underneath the glass control panels, lights blinked off and on and all controls were set on automatic.

Tanner stroked his chin. "Here's what I know. We have very few crew members on board. The ship has been pre-programmed to return on a security mission to the Mariana Deep Sea Mining Base on Earth. It's a fair distance from Acacia Burj. This trip to the Moon was just a minor detour to deliver some supplies."

"Then who the hell is attacking us and why?" asked Phaeton.

"I don't know." Tanner rubbed his forehead. "Could be that someone on the resort planned the attack. Could be that the soldiers were trying to confiscate our supplies. With all the mining going on these days on the Moon, it's big money and mercenaries have been known to launch attacks."

"But what about that armour? Where did they get that? I've never seen anything like it," said Phaeton.

Luca had been wondering the same thing.

"Maybe they created the armour at the mines," said Tanner. "That ship could have come from the same place."

"I have other ideas," said Phaeton, folding his arms.

"What do you mean?" asked Tanner, before changing his mind. "Look, that can wait. Right now, we need to figure out how to get out of here."

"We're on autopilot," said Luca. "Are the controls voice-activated?"

"We might not need to worry about that. From what I've been studying, these Lazer Stealth Pathfinders and all the life-support systems are assisted by electronic impulses and intelligence from the chief engineer who built the ship. In this case, that's Dr Brett Tycho." Tanner acted as if he was giving a lecture to an iT school class.

"You mean a Persona?" asked Luca.

"Yes," said Tanner. "Except in this case, Dr Tycho has been working with our Captain and First Officer to pilot the *Sibylline*. He's a valuable resource."

"Damn!" Phaeton shook his head. "Those things can't be trusted."

"Well, how do we access the Persona of Dr Tycho?" asked Phaeton. "If we can't get in touch with him, our asses could be toast."

"I've only been in here a couple of times," said Tanner, looking around him. "I'm not sure."

"Comforting." Phaeton smirked.

Luca looked around at the rows and rows of lights and commands on the control screens. Again, he was surprised by how similar they were to some of the virtual games he and his friends had played.

Luca understood roughly how Personas worked. He knew that any biological material left behind measurable energetic traces that contained significant information. Those energetic traces could be amplified to appear as optigrams, and actually interact in real-time. Luca instinctively swiped at the control panel just like he had done numerous times in his games. For once, he was very proud of his gaming skills and the fact that he, Asia Mae and Ceiba had played at the Arcade every weekend.

There was a swish and a humming sound near the control screen. Phaeton and Tanner watched as an optographic glow formed near Luca's body. Instantly, Dr Tycho appeared before them.

"What's this?" asked Phaeton.

"I think Luca somehow just accessed Dr Tycho's Persona." Tanner sounded nervous. Perhaps he would get into a lot of trouble by letting a sixteen year old man the controls, but Luca knew their only hope was Dr Tycho. Optographic Persona or not.

"Welcome," said Dr Tycho, looking around at all of them in the room. "Young man, are you training as a Pathfinder pilot?"

"Hello doctor," said Luca. "I'm—"

"I'm military Trainee Tanner Elliott, Sir," Tanner said, interrupting Luca and stepping in front of him. "And this is my intern, Luca. We've been attacked on the Galileo Moon Resort, and we need to return to Earth. We're pre-programmed to land at the Mariana Deep Sea Mining Base and we don't know where the Captain or first officer are. Sir, we need help getting home."

"I wondered what happened. I've been working with the Captain on this journey," said Dr Tycho. "My last communication with him was when you first came under attack. All systems went down for a while and I couldn't access your ship. Who's the attacker?"

"We don't know," said Tanner. "They were dressed in strange mesh with some kind of headsets – not sure what they were made of – and they didn't speak. We suspect they projected optigrams to distract us."

"Strange, indeed. A new military tactic, perhaps." The Captain frowned. "How many are dead?"

"We don't know that either," said Tanner. "But we didn't have many crew members on board in the first place and many of them are hurt or dead. We need to get out of here and find those soldiers, rescue the Captain before they come back and break into the Command Centre."

"Dr Tycho, with your help, I think I can pilot the ship," offered Luca. "It's very much like many of the virtual games I've played."

"Ah, yes. Those new games have been designed to pre-train the youth. I'll guide you," said the engineer. "What is your name?"

"I'm Luca. Luca C. Mariner."

"Any relation to Commander Delmar C. Mariner?"

"He was my father."

"Well, then, it's in your blood, son," Dr Tycho said, smiling faintly. "You should do fine and you may be the ship's only hope."

"Thank you for your confidence, sir." Luca felt overwhelmed at the enormity of this responsibility, but he was also excited about the challenge.

"As long as the internal systems have not been compromised – and I wouldn't be able to communicate with you if they had been – I should be able to steer you home."

A nervous excitement filled Luca in the centre of his chest. Could he do this? He remembered his father's message to him in the Pathfinder Museum. Was this part of his mission? Something his father knew would happen someday?

"All right, young man," said Dr Tycho. "Sit down and interface with the ship's controls. Not everyone can do it, so let's see if you can."

Luca sat down in the chair before the control screens. Sweat beaded up on his forehead and he smoothed his hair back. *I can do this! Just think of it like a game*, he thought. He tried desperately to ignore the shaking inside his body.

"First thing is to seal all doors on the *Sibylline*," ordered Dr Tycho. "And check the hull has not been breached."

Luca made the directive and on the monitors they could see all the internal and external doors being closed and sealed.

"Now, let's do a sensory scan to determine how many non-authorised bodies are on board," said Dr Tycho. "How many are dead or alive?"

As Luca followed orders under the Captain's tutelage, they all watched as silvery rays beamed and penetrated every room and hallway on the ship, including the Command Centre. The rays identified four shapes on the fourth floor – just below them. They were like a dark cloud, wavy and fluid. They disappeared into thin air while they watched. As the sensors scanned each room, the final tally of crew outside the control room was: two humans dead, four humans wounded, but alive. Lieutenant Commander Dillon and First Officer Marco, plus Sergeant Santiago were among them. The rest of the crew was no longer on board. Finally, in the galley on the second level, two enemy soldiers were identified and one human military crew member. A non-living form was heaped in a pile in the corner.

"That has to be the Captain with the aliens," said Tanner. "The soldiers must have locked both officers and themselves in the galley."

"What do the scanners mean by unidentified *alien* soldiers?" asked Luca. He already knew the answer.

"It simply means that the attackers are not human and not known by the *Sibylline's* database and therefore, are referred to as alien," said Dr Tycho. "They could be from the mining bases on the Moon. You all must figure out a way to rescue the Captain as soon as we launch and go onto autopilot."

"At least he's still alive," said Tanner. "But we have one dead."

"It could have been worse," said Dr Tycho. "It's time to get out of here. Come now, Luca."

Everyone nodded. They were all fidgety and nervous. They just might very well perish on this voyage. The odds seemed greatly stacked against them ever reaching Earth.

Tanner and Phaeton stood by wordlessly as they watched Luca and the Captain. With his directions and guidance, Luca was able to interface with the ship. Using the engineer's thoughts to assist him, Luca relaxed and instinctively knew which hand movements to make; what commands to voice.

Luca showed great skill at piloting the *Sibylline*. It felt natural to him and it was as if he had been born to do this. His Grampa Sol and father would be so proud. *And Asia Mae and Ceiba!* Luca could just imagine them hugging him and telling him how proud they were of him. He couldn't wait to see them again. He hoped he would.

While interfacing with the Persona of Dr Tycho, Luca lapsed into a trance-like state and was startled when he saw the Captain's memories flash into his mind like pages in an opti-photo album. Luca had complete access to his intelligence, memories, and instincts. It was surreal. He saw memories of Earth, of earlier voyages, glimpses of the Captain's wife and children. Luca felt like he was eavesdropping on someone's life and it made him feel uncomfortable. Then, the fog of memories cleared and he saw a clear blueprint of exactly what he was to do with the controls.

Before Luca knew it, the ship was disengaging from the landing dock, counting down to takeoff and hyper-speed warping into space, heading for Earth. Luca felt a wave of homesickness and didn't know if it was the Captain's emotions or his own. Probably both. On the screen, Luca could see the small blue globe of Earth far in the distance. *Home.* His heart squeezed.

As they lifted, Luca could also view the Galileo Moon Resort where bodies lay and smoke still spiralled upwards from the attacks. It was sickening. Buildings were burning and people were panicking. Personal spaceships were evacuating the Moon base. *Were they headed home or to Mars?* It looked like a war-ridden village in one of Luca's virtual games. Luca felt awful about abandoning them.

As Luca watched, the strange ship reappeared, shooting high in the air like a bullet, and leaving a particle stream trailing behind it.

"Look at that!" Luca pointed.

"Bloody hell!" exclaimed Phaeton. "So, that's who attacked us!"

"Do I need to contact the ground crew on Earth?" asked Luca. "Maybe that ship is headed to Earth. Maybe it will follow us!"

"Yes, now that we're on the correct trajectory, I'll patch you into Earth Acacia Central," said Dr Tycho.

Within seconds, the screen was filled with a panel of executive military crew, seemingly surrounding Tanner, Phaeton and Luca.

"I'm Admiral Maasaw. We lost communication with you about an hour ago. What's happening on board the Sibylline?" A colonel in full military dress with a cluster of shiny medals stood before them; his cohorts were in the background. "We heard there was an attack on Galileo. Where's the Captain?"

"Sir," said Tanner. "My name is Military Trainee Seaman Recruit Tanner Elliott, No. 5487, and the attack is official. We're working with Dr Tycho to pilot the ship back home. We were attacked by an unknown aggressor. The Captain and the first officer are on board but we're not sure at the moment who is dead and who is alive." Tanner's voice broke.

"Go on, Seaman Elliot," said Admiral Maasaw.

"We don't know how many are dead at the resort, but it was badly damaged." Tanner rubbed his eyes. He went on to explain the condition of the *Sibylline* and the crew.

"Who were these attackers?" Admiral Maasaw asked. "Did you do a body scan?"

"Our body scans couldn't penetrate their armour, so we simply don't know. We have no intelligence about them. They wore full mesh body armour and were covered from head to toe. They used weapons similar to our own, but more advanced and more powerful."

"How many were there?"

"At least forty or fifty at the Moon base."

"Any reports on the damage to the resort?"

"We're not sure what happened or what damage was done. Our sensors weren't able to get any readouts on the resort. Not sure why, sir."

"How soon did they attack after you landed?" asked Admiral Maasaw.

"A few minutes in, after we started unloading the supplies. I was getting ready to help some of the crew and saw them when they swarmed our ship. I held them off as much as I could, and ran back on board to strategize and take a defensive position on the ship. But, well... you know the rest of the story, sir."

"Who else is with you in the Command Centre?" the colonel asked, looking around at the small crew.

Phaeton raised his eyebrows and held his breath. He hunched down behind one of the big monitors and acted like he was working on something behind the screen. Luca slumped low in the chair so he couldn't be seen. Neither one was dressed like a military trainee. Neither of them was exactly invited to be on this ship.

"Oh, uh... they're part of my team," said Tanner slowly. "Interns, you know... in training and all."

Dr Tycho interjected: "Admiral, these young trainees are proving to be astute and skilful working alongside Seaman Elliott. We should have no trouble getting the *Sibylline* back home. I have every confidence in them."

"We're assessing the situation from here and we'll get back to you," said the admiral nervously. "Keep me updated."

Admiral Maasaw and Earth Acacia Central disappeared from view. Luca relaxed. He had been worried that the crew on Earth would learn about him being a stowaway.

Now Luca had bigger worries. He had to land the *Sibylline* back on Earth. He had never trained to do this. What if he killed everyone? Plus, he might just be bringing the attacking ship and a crew of giant enemy soldiers with him!

Chapter Sixteen

"We'll be on autopilot for a few hours, Luca," announced Dr Tycho. "Just stay alert at the screens for any unusual activity. And do periodic scans to see where bodies are on the ship. When it's time for re-entry, I'll help you again. Of course, if there are any problems, you can voice-activate me. I'm on standby."

"Thanks, Doctor."

The engineer's Persona disappeared and Luca no longer had access to his thoughts and memories. He looked up at Tanner and smiled.

"Wow! That was the coolest thing I've ever experienced! Scary though – I was totally worried that he'd learn I was a stow-away... a prisoner."

"Me, too, brother," agreed Phaeton. "All I needed was for him to see my clothes properly. They'd be waiting to arrest me again!"

"I don't think he suspected anything unusual, given the circumstances," said Tanner. "We can thank Dr Tycho for helping us out."

"Yeah, who knew a Persona would save our ass?" Phaeton smirked. Then, he looked over at Luca. "Who knew a kid could pilot a Stealth Lazer Pathfinder? Way to go, dude!" He high-fived Luca and grinned broadly. Luca decided he liked him.

"We're on course for Earth," said Tanner, looking over the controls. "I would never in a million years have thought you could pull this off, Luca. I'm impressed!"

"Thanks, Tan. Think this will help me get into a military training programme like you?" Luca leaned back in his chair.

"Yeah, absolutely. It should do, anyway." Tanner rubbed the back of his neck nervously.

Luca settled in, gazing about the command centre of the *Sibylline*. It was sleek and otherworldly with polished chrome beams arcing over the ceiling and plush pod-like chairs scattered around the controls. The viewing screen in front of Luca's seat swept across the whole room, so that it felt as if he was one step from falling into the void of the galaxy. It was dizzying. What was even more impressive was that after they lifted from the Moon, swirling blue bioluminescent lights curved into multiple helixes of the galaxy – part of a optographic map in real-time – and spun from an axis through the entire room concurrently, as if Luca and his friends were part of the galaxy itself. Muted blue and white lights tracked in patterns on the floor and in the ceiling. Before Luca, the multilayered glass control display panel – along with the rotating helixes in the entire Command Centre – lit up with information on the star networks of the galaxy.

"Well, that's all good and sweet, but we have bigger problems to worry about in case you two have forgotten," said Tanner, bringing Luca and Phaeton back to the issue at hand. "Why were we being attacked in the first place? And what are those soldiers going to do with the Captain? They're on our ship right now, remember?"

"You're right," said Phaeton. "We're really not safe with those attackers on board and there's still a lot of danger in piloting this ship back to Earth. It's possible it won't make re-entry."

Luca didn't want to think about that.

Tanner went over to a wall and waved his sensorpad. The wall slid open. He pulled out a fresh military trainee uniform and handed it to Phaeton. "Here, I think you need to change out of your Retro clothes and put on one of our military trainee uniforms. It's designed with sensory armour and will give you a little bit of protection if we're attacked. Plus, if the Captain contacts us again, I don't want him to see you dressed like that and we don't know who we'll bump into at Mariana."

"Eurgh! Do I have to really put this on?" Phaeton asked.

"Yes, I think it would help," said Tanner.

"Can I have one?" pleaded Luca.

"There's only one here, and besides, I don't think you need it. Your gaming bodysuit isn't out of the ordinary, and Dr Tycho has already seen you. He didn't really get a good look at Phaeton."

"Fine." Phaeton stripped and slipped on the form-fitting military trainee suit. He opened the panel closet door and looked at himself in the mirror. "Don't look bad if I say so myself, but my girlfriend would freak out if she saw this on me!"

"Man, it looks good on you," said Tanner, winking. "She might like it."

"You don't know her," said Phaeton. "She's anti-establishment and trust me, she would hate it."

Luca was a little envious. He would have loved to wear one of those. But, it didn't matter. Not really. He was piloting the ship!

"I need to get out there and see if anyone needs help and if I can get some backup to rescue the Captain," said Tanner.

"But you can't go out there, Tan!" said Luca. "What if some of those soldiers are waiting for you? They seemed to have some supernatural skills. Not to mention their weapons."

"I'll be okay. We know from our scans where they are and I can access the scans at any time. Do your comms work in here, Luca?"

"No, I tried them when I was in lockup. My sensors aren't synced up with the ship."

"I can take care of that," said Tanner, swiping at his sensorpad, arranging the coordinates to match the sensors on board the *Sibylline*. "There! That should do it. Now we can communicate."

"What about you, Phaeton?" asked Tanner. "Do your comms work in here?"

"Don't have any comms," said Phaeton, proudly.

"Haven't you been permanently Wired?" asked Tanner. "I mean, you're at least 21, right?"

"Right," said Phaeton. "But I wouldn't let them Wire me."

"How did you get out of that?"

"I was expelled from Acacia," said Phaeton. "That's how."

Tanner was impressed. "Has it been beneficial?"

"Yeah, for now," said Phaeton. "Of course, it has got me into trouble more than once and partly why I was arrested..."

"What do you mean?" asked Tanner.

"There's time for that later," said Phaeton. "We have to get the Captain, remember?"

"Yeah, right."

Luca couldn't wait until he had a chance to talk to Phaeton about being able to forgo the permanent sensory wiring. It was one thing he definitely didn't want.

"Do these comms work with the ones on Earth?" asked Luca.

"It's tricky," said Tanner. "Sometimes, we're able to use these to communicate with people on Earth and sometimes we can't. I don't know why. If they don't work, you'll just have to wait until we get to the Mariana base. You should be able to use your comms there."

"I didn't think they worked outside Acacia Burj at all," said Luca.

"Mariana is wired for universal contact," said Tanner. "However, we've been told we aren't allowed to get off the ship once we're there. Only the Captains and the docking crew have permission to go on the base."

"Why is that?" asked Phaeton, still admiring himself in the mirror.

"I don't know," said Tanner. "Probably security issues. Probably to keep the trainees safe. The military keeps many things secret from the public."

"That's an understatement," said Phaeton under his breath.

"What?" asked Tanner.

"Oh, nothing!" said Phaeton, rolling his eyes.

"We need to focus on our problem of having bloody aliens on board," said Tanner.

"At least we know *where* they are," said Phaeton. "Any ideas about *what* they are?"

"If you've ever played some of the virtual games that tie in mythology and wars, then these soldiers – and those creepy tall guys – are A'Rmillari aliens," said Luca. "And the weird black clouds are Nanobe swarms which can steal your thoughts and confuse you."

"I haven't *played* virtual games for years," said Tanner. "They're called military training programmes these days! Phaeton, you still play those games?"

"I *study* those games," Phaeton said. "They're revealing."

"Well, this isn't a game, and we still haven't decided what we're going to do with those enemy soldiers on board," said Tanner, feeling a little out of his depth.

"Awesome!" said Phaeton. "This imaging system is amazing."

Luca and Phaeton walked to the panel that took them outside the ship. As they stood looking at the planets and stars surrounding them, Luca could see Earth in the distance. A round blue sphere; it made him feel homesick again.

"Well, we need to rescue the Captain," said Tanner. "Phaeton, you want to come with me? We know that Luca can interface with the former Captain's Persona; he'll be all right here alone, and safe."

"Not if I have a choice!"

"No choice. The last thing we need is for them to attack us once we land," said Tanner. "We know where they are. Let's go get 'em."

"Tanner..." Luca said. "I think I should come with you. I don't think you all should go out there alone – you need all the manpower and backup you can get – and the *Sibylline* is on autopilot at the moment."

"No, you need to stay here. You're the only one who can get the ship home," said Tanner.

"Well, be careful, okay?"

"Sure, Luca. I'll be fine. I'll continually do scans to see any movement and report anything unusual to you."

"I can do scans from here if you need my help," said Luca.

Tanner nodded, and then he and Phaeton headed for the door.

Luca took a calming breath and kept his eyes glued to the monitors before him. He was flying the *Sibylline*! Was this really possible?

Any moment, he expected to wake up and find it was all a dream.

Chapter Seventeen

"Come on, princess! We have to hurry before they find us!" Sumer said, holding Asia Mae's hand and tugging her along. They sped along the scrubbed and polished hallways of the hospital. A couple of Persona Nurses quietly walked by with optographic charts in hand. They barely glanced at the two girls.

Asia Mae and Sumer sped up, racing through a labyrinth of hallways, and passed numerous doors with headings such as: *Trauma Intensive Care Unit Pod* – which was where Ceiba was; *Serenity Pod* – which was where his mum, Elsa, was; *Infectious Disease Pod*; *Operating Room Pod*; and *Warning! Biological Biohazards: Do Not Enter Pod*. They next passed a multitude of unmarked doors. The hospital was even more massive than Asia Mae realised.

"Sumer, can we stop and check in on Ceiba before going to the morgue?"

"We'll do that afterwards," said Sumer. "I want to look in on my brother, Elton, too. And make sure he's all right."

"Sumer, who beat up your brother?"

"I don't know for sure, but I have my suspicions. I'll tell you later."

Asia Mae nodded and the girls hurried to find the lift.

"Should we take the stairs instead?" asked Asia Mae. "What if they catch us?"

"This will be faster," said Sumer. "And there aren't many people on duty this early. It's weirdly deserted around here. We should be fine. We just need to get in there before they tell us we can't."

They stepped inside the lift. It felt weird to Asia Mae to be in cahoots with this strange girl. She seemed pleasant, but what was the president's daughter doing wearing Retro clothes and rebelling against everything in sight? Sure, there were some Opuls who detested their wealth; perhaps Sumer was one of those. The most interesting thing was that Asia Mae found that she liked her. Sumer was feisty. With the exception of Luca and Ceiba, Asia Mae had never met anyone who was so outspoken, honest. It was refreshing.

Exiting the lift, they were almost knocked out by the strong smell of antiseptic. The morgue was cold as ice, like when the storms hit the docks, and as sterile as what Asia Mae assumed a Translation or Hibernation Clinic would be like. She shivered. Underneath all the smells was an underlying, unsettling odour of death and decomposition.

"I don't like it in here," said Asia Mae, her teeth chattering.

"Nor do I, princess," said Sumer. "But if we want to find out who the dead guy is and make sure it's neither one of our friends, then this is necessary."

There were two sections in the morgue. In the regular unit were multiple rows of glass-covered pods where bodies lay, ready to be taken to crematoriums. In the other section were rows of pods filled with AI body parts, artificial heads, wiring sticking out everywhere, microchips, and tools. There were whole walls filled with tanks containing bodily fluids and body parts such as brains, stomachs, and even eyeballs. That part of the morgue was disgusting. There was another room at the end of the hallway called 'The Organ & AI Donation Room'.

"Let's skip the Morgue Factory and just look in the regular morgue," said Sumer, shivering.

"I agree. That place looks awful."

Sumer nodded. She and Asia Mae walked by the glass-covered pods, carefully peering in each one.

"I don't see anyone I know," said Sumer, breathing a sigh of relief. "At least I know my boyfriend didn't get killed."

"I thought you said he was arrested?"

"Yeah, he was," said Sumer. "It would be just like him to fight the authorities and that could get him killed."

"I'm glad he's not in here, too," said Asia Mae, placing her hand on Sumer's arm. "Did you try to message him?"

"No, we don't wear our comms most of the time," said Sumer. "So, there's no way I can find out how he is."

"Aren't you Wired?" asked Asia Mae.

"Um, no," she said. "I was exempt."

"Why?"

"Oh, you know... personal stuff."

"Oh." Asia Mae didn't really know what she was talking about. She thought it weird that the president's daughter wasn't permanently wired, but said nothing. Of course, he was only president of Acacia Burj – not the world. Each mega city had its own president and military.

"So, you finished looking?" asked Sumer with her hands on her hips, her backpack flung back over her shoulder.

"Just give me a second." Asia Mae walked down the last row of pod-enclosed bodies. Her pulse was racing. The odour of death permeated her being through and through, and she thought she just might be sick. It had been a long night. If she discovered Luca in one of these pods, she didn't know what she'd do. She had almost lost Ceiba and now, if she lost Luca... well, she couldn't let herself think about that.

When she came to the very last one, she stopped and bent over to look closer.

"Oh my God!" Asia Mae gasped.

"What?"

"I recognise this one," she said, trembling. *This didn't make any sense!*

"Is it your friend?" asked Sumer. "Luca?"

"No. It's one of the guys who chased us on the docks last night. His name is... *was*... Prince."

"Well, Bions can be killed just like anyone else," said Sumer.

"I know that," said Asia Mae. "But why would anyone want to kill Prince when everyone said he was getting ready to go into the military trainee programme? It doesn't make sense!"

Luca or Ceiba couldn't have done this. As the girls stared at Prince's face, Prince's eyelids fluttered and both girls screamed.

Chapter Eighteen

Tanner shouldered his Neutraliser and said, "You ready, Phaeton?"

"Ready as I'll ever be," he said, picking up his weapon. If Phaeton didn't have his long hair, he would look exactly like a military trainee in his new uniform.

"How'd you get out of your cell?" Tanner asked before pressing his sensorpad to open the door. "And where'd you get your Neutraliser?" It had just dawned on him that Phaeton had somehow escaped the impenetrable cellblock.

"It was easy," said Phaeton. "When the sensors went out initially, my cell door automatically opened and I slipped out. One of the crew was dead and his weapon was just lying there, so I picked it up and ran."

Tanner nodded. That made sense to him. He desperately wanted to be able to trust Phaeton, but he wasn't sure. *Did he have anything to do with the Captain being captured?* Tanner couldn't help but wonder. Phaeton was a Retro – that was clear. And those Retros often got into trouble with the law with their freedom rallies and anti-Persona marches. Tanner and his girlfriend, Gaia, had had many discussions about Retros, Civils, AIs,

Bions, Personas, Opuls, and the entire world of Acacia Burj. He had never had much interaction with a Retro. Gaia had sympathy for them, but Tanner was neutral. He thought mostly they were just rebellious punks.

"So can I ask why you were arrested?" asked Tanner.

"It's a long story," said Phaeton. "In a nutshell, I was on the docks in the wrong place at the wrong time. I can tell you more after we've taken out these militants. No big deal, really."

"Okay," said Tanner, tentatively. "I figured it was something like that." Tanner needed to trust him. At this point, he didn't really have any other choice. "Let's go!"

Being alone was the perfect opportunity for Luca to listen to the rest of his father's message while Tanner and Phaeton were gone. He waved his hand against the control panel so that the ring might activate its message. He held it there for a few seconds, hopeful that it would work. Once again, his father's image appeared before him, so lifelike. Luca could barely believe it was just a message. There he stood in front of him, smiling, dressed in his Naval Commander's uniform, looking as trim and fit as he had been on the last day of his life. Luca looked at him – *really looked at him* as if he were seeing him for the first time – and tried to record the image in his mind. His father had thick dark brown hair that never moved, unlike Luca's unruly hair. His green eyes were the same colour as Luca's and he peered into him as if he were trying to imprint his thoughts onto his son.

"Luca, you will notice that each time you access this file, you receive different information. This is my biological blueprint. It accesses my thoughts and memories from an ancient entanglement that connects our quantum particles and family's DNA. Each time you access it, the message will change and evolve as a growing, living entity. So, it is imperative that you keep this Key with you at all times.

"The Moral Order was established years ago to keep peace and develop life on Earth and in the Universe with a coalition of like-minded intergalactic beings. However, there has been a disruption to this universal peace by a merciless alliance of Thirteen Overlords who have come from the most ancient, deepest, darkest corners of the universe. These Overlords are masters at taking everything, destroying one Galaxy at a time without reason. They are predominantly inorganic machines; alive, but not life as you or I know it.

"You will come to know that all beings have evolved in some way from alien species, particles omnipresent in space and time. We are all connected."

"We, on Earth, trade our thoughts with many aliens from other galaxies. Our common purpose is to further our knowledge and understanding for the greater good. Every galaxy has one special planet with abundant liquid water, capable of supporting an intergalactic portal. In our galaxy, that planet is Earth. Each custodian of that planet has their own Key to enter the intergalactic portal. The Dark Alliance would have these portals destroyed in a bid to take control of the entire galaxy. We must keep your Key from these Overlords. Your Key is a passport to the universe."

His father's image was disrupted and disappeared when Tanner buzzed Luca from somewhere out in the hallways of the *Sibylline*. It appeared that the opti-file was set to shut off any time there was interference from another message. Luca would have to find another time to listen to more of his father's message. It all seemed like a virtual video game.

"What?" Luca responded to Tanner.

"We need you!" said Tanner. "Hurry! We're down one level and we're trapped!"

"I'm on my way!"

Luca grabbed a Neutraliser and headed for the door. He waved his sensorpad and it automatically opened. He looked down each direction of the hall and saw that this floor was empty. Smoke was still floating like billowy white clouds along the floors and everything smelled of phosphorus.

Luca crept along the deserted hallway, his breathing quiet, his heart pounding loudly. It felt like a ghost ship. He knew they should all have just stayed locked in the Command Centre. There would be a whole military crew on standby when they landed. But they had to rescue the rest of the crew. They needed them. The mystery soldiers could attempt another attack on them and the Command Centre before they ever reached Earth. He knew they'd be lucky to make it there in one piece as it was.

Luca inched his way down the stairs as quietly as he could. Two dark shadows whirled in front of him and Luca's heart stopped. He raised his Neutraliser to shoot, but they disappeared again like hollow wind. *Where did they go? Were they being con-*

trolled by the enemy soldiers? They were too fast for Luca to detect any real features – if there were any.

When he got to the floor beneath the Command Centre, he saw Tanner and Phaeton huddled in the corner at the far end of the hallway. There was a cloud of black smoke in front of them, but other than that, Luca couldn't see any sign of trouble. His friends looked scared, trapped. Luca waved, but they didn't respond.

Luca cautiously walked down the hallway towards Tanner and Phaeton. *Couldn't they see him? Had they been temporarily blinded by the enemy soldier? What was going on?*

"Shh, I think I hear something," said Tanner, sinking back into the wall with his Neutraliser poised to shoot.

"Sounds like footsteps." Phaeton wasn't going to take any chances. He'd blast his way out of there and leave the enemy soldiers in a pile of ash. "Where's Luca? Shouldn't he be here by now?"

"I don't know," said Tanner. "Maybe he had trouble after he left the Command Centre."

A haze of darkness clustered again in front of them. Phaeton fired an orb and the Nanobe swarm disappeared again.

"What the hell was that?" said Phaeton.

"They're optigrams, I think, to throw us off." Tanner wasn't sure.

"An optigram, my ass," said Phaeton. "More like creepy real time Nanobes."

"Optigrams or not, they're definitely creepy – I agree."

"Prepare to fire. I think the enemy soldiers are with them in stealth mode and getting ready to attack!" shouted Phaeton. He raised his Neutraliser and started to press the lever.

"Guys!" cried Luca as he ducked, just missing the blast as it veered off to the right of him. "Don't shoot! What's going on?"

"Luca? Is that you?" asked Tanner. He lowered his Neutraliser.

"Oh my God!" said Phaeton. "We almost shot you."

Luca stood just in front of Phaeton and Tanner. "Couldn't you see me?"

"No," said Tanner. "All we saw were those *things,* and then they disappeared and left nothing but black smoke. That's why I messaged you. I thought they had us trapped. We heard your footsteps and thought you were one of the enemy soldiers."

"I saw the Nanobe swarm on the stairs," said Luca.

"Those Nanobes, if that's what they are, were playing with our minds. C'mon," said Tanner. "Stick together and get to the galley."

As they cautiously slipped through the hallways and down the stairs to the first level, they stayed on the lookout. Instead of more Nanobes, they were greeted with the quietest of quiet. They could only hear their own breathing and hearts thudding. They had just one more floor to go.

"Should we round up some of the crew to help us?" asked Phaeton.

"There aren't many crew to round up," said Tanner. "Let's just blast in and surprise them," said Tanner.

"I don't know," said Phaeton. "Might be a good idea to have some backup."

"Let me see if I can patch into any of the crew's comms," said Tanner. He shook his sensorpad, but no one responded.

"It's like they're all offline," said Luca, his voice low. "I did a quick scan before I left Command Centre. The two alien attackers and one human were still in the recreation room. From the scan, it looked like the Captain was sitting at the table with his hands tied behind him and the two alien attackers were standing with their weapons aimed at the door. I don't think we should blast our Neutralisers before going in. We could hit the Captain."

"Agreed," said Tanner. "Okay, boys, get on either side of me and let's go in now. As soon as we take out the soldiers, we'll take the Captain back to the Command Centre."

Luca and Phaeton nodded. They quickly moved to the door of the lounge. Standing in front of Phaeton and Luca, Tanner waved his sensorpad and a voice announced: "Verification confirmed." The door slid open. Luca, Phaeton and Tanner poised their Neutralisers to shoot and moved inside. They stopped dead in their tracks. The room was empty.

Chapter Nineteen

"That was so scary!" said Sumer. "I do not like Bions when they're dead and misfiring!"

"It doesn't make sense that Prince would be killed. Who would have done that?" Asia Mae folded her arms, trembling.

"Oh, princess," said Sumer. "You have so much to learn, sweetie." She took Asia Mae's hand and squeezed it.

"I know he was mean, sure. He thought he could do anything and get away with it. But for someone to kill him?" Asia Mae couldn't comprehend it. She just stood there in the hallway outside the morgue, feeling the chill of death.

"Come on, princess," said Sumer. "Let's get out of here before Nurse Fancy-Top finds us."

Sumer led her away. Asia Mae still couldn't grasp what she had just discovered. She had to see Ceiba and make sure he was all right.

"Sumer, let's go to the trauma pods. I need to see Ceibastian."

"Sure," said Sumer. "My brother will still be there, too. We need to make sure they're safe and where they're supposed to be."

They jogged to the lift and rode up to the floor where the

trauma pods were. Asia Mae was nervous. She desperately needed to see Ceiba and touch him, to feel his pulse and know he was getting better. She didn't think she could take much more of this hospital – of the fake Persona Nurses, of the sterile, polished floors. Of optographic charts and quiet hallways. Of morgues, Morgue Factories and AIs with fluttering eyelids.

The room was easy to find and when they walked in, the young man was sleeping peacefully in his medical pod, hooked up to a variety of tubes and wires.

Elton was in the room next to Ceiba's, so Asia Mae told Sumer she'd meet her in the hallway after her visit.

"Okay. See you in a few." Sumer nodded and left the room.

Asia Mae walked over to Ceiba's pod. The lights were low and their glow cast soft, comforting shadows across the room. She felt the tension in her own body release as she stepped forward, and suddenly she felt so very tired; she just wanted to sleep.

She looked at Ceiba and took his hand in hers. "Ceibastian, I'm here. Everything is okay. You're going to be just fine." Tears spilled down her cheeks.

He had several wires and sensor nodes attached to his head and a chest tube going into his lungs, with bandages around one arm and leg. His other arm was in a sling. His cheeks were shadowed with pale bruises, but Asia Mae could tell he was healing. She wasn't sure which parts of him were AI and which were human, and she didn't care. To her, he was all human.

And then, just a flicker... *Could it be?* Another flicker. Her heart dropped. She didn't think she could bear it if Ceiba expired. And then his hand squeezed hers ever so slightly.

"A... Asia..."

"Ceibastian?"

"Where am I?" He opened his eyes.

"You're still in the hospital, but you're okay," said Asia Mae, wrapping both her hands around his good one. "The doctors are taking good care of you. I'm here, Ceibastian."

"Luc... Luca..."

"He... he's at home," she lied. "Please don't worry. We're both all right." She was not going to tell Ceiba that Luca was missing. Hopefully, Luca really was at home and all was well.

"You... you okay too?"

"I'm fine, Ceibastian. And your mum is in the Serenity Pod...

I can get her for you. Your dad's gone back to work but he was here most of the night."

"I know. Asia..."

"Yes, Ceibastian? Don't worry, those guys won't hurt you anymore."

"No..." Ceiba said faintly. His breathing was laboured and Asia Mae leaned closer to hear him.

"What is it?"

"Prince... his friends..."

"Yes, I know," Asia Mae said.

"It... it wasn't them."

"What?"

"They didn't hurt me."

"Then who did?" she asked.

"Soldiers."

"Soldiers? Ceibastian, are you sure?" she asked. Her head was reeling. What in the world was going on? He nodded.

Nurse Lorelai appeared in the room behind her and said, "I'm afraid your time is up. Mr. Ammos needs his rest now. You can come back tomorrow."

"Ceibastian, I'll be back as soon as I can," whispered Asia Mae. She leaned over and kissed him lightly on the forehead and tried to let go of his hand.

He clutched her hand tighter and whispered back, "Be careful."

"I will," she promised. "And I will find out why this happened."

Ceiba let go of her hand and closed his eyes. Asia Mae stood up and headed for the door, where Nurse Lorelai stood stoically.

"Thank you for letting me visit him," Asia Mae said.

The nurse smiled her fake smile again. "You can't pay any attention to what they say," Nurse Lorelai said.

"What do you mean?" asked Asia Mae.

"When they're on the pharmaceuticals, they have fanciful imaginations," she said. "That's all. I hope you get a good rest now, Ms. Morningstar."

The nurse disappeared and Sumer came out of her brother's room.

"Everything all right with your friend?" she asked.

"No," Asia Mae said, shaking her head. She still couldn't comprehend anything that was happening. "Something's very, very wrong."

"What do you mean?"

"Ceibastian told me he wasn't beaten up by Prince or any of his friends. The attackers were soldiers!"

"I'm not surprised," said Sumer. "Come on, let's get outta here. We need to talk."

Chapter Twenty

"Where are they?" asked Phaeton, whipping his head around the room.

"This is strange," said Luca. "Something about this room just isn't right."

"They've moved," said Phaeton. "Probably knew we were coming."

"We would have seen them or heard them," said Tanner. "When we called Luca, we were just down the hall."

"Maybe there's a back door we don't know about," said Phaeton.

"Maybe the floor plans have been altered," said Luca. "Although it did seem like the scans identified actual bodies in the room."

"Well, they must have left because they're not here. Maybe they detected our scans," said Tanner. He relaxed his position and lowered his Neutraliser.

Phaeton spoke up. "I think we need to get back to the Command Centre. I don't like this and we're putting ourselves in danger by being out in the ship like this."

"Agreed," said Tanner.

Before they could turn and leave, a stealth-mode wall in front of them dissolved and two enemy soldiers appeared, clad in bronze mesh with massive shoulders, massive legs… and aiming weapons straight at them. Beneath the mesh, their skin rippled with changing colours. As their skin dulled to a soft metallic sheen, Luca realised that they were adapting their bodies to blend in with the ship.

The Captain sat slumped over the table with his hands tied behind his back and his mouth gagged. Blood trickled from his head down onto the front of his clothes. Either he was knocked out or dead. It was impossible to tell. On the floor beside him lay First Officer Marco.

"What the…?" exclaimed Phaeton.

"Fire!" ordered Tanner.

They fired, but the enemy soldiers went into stealth-mode individually. One of Tanner's orbs came dangerously close to hitting the Captain.

Tanner looked questioningly at Phaeton. "They're using invisibility shields!"

Luca, Tanner and Phaeton dropped to the floor and slid behind a counter. They poised their Neutralisers again and fired. The enemy soldiers appeared again, standing in front of the door, and began firing at them. One of the orbs grazed Tanner's shoulder and the smell of burning flesh permeated the air.

"That bastard shot you!" shouted Phaeton.

"It's nothing," said Tanner. "We've got to get the Captain! We can leave Officer Merrimac and get him later."

"We can't. If we move towards the Captain, they'll take us out."

"We're going to have to blast our way out," said Luca. "There's no other way."

"Okay. Let's go!" said Phaeton.

"I'll move towards the Captain while you cover me," said Luca.

"Hurry!" said Tanner.

Luca edged towards the Captain.

Phaeton blasted his orbs like an electric bolt of lightning into one of the soldiers, hitting him in the leg. He and the other soldier turned and made for the hallway.

"Let's grab the Captain!" said Luca.

Phaeton and Tanner hurried over to Luca and helped him untie the Captain. They took the gag out of his mouth, and then tried to stand him up.

"Captain? Can you talk? It's Tanner, we're going to take you back to the Command Centre."

"Check his pulse," said Luca.

"Tanner – he's dead!" cried Phaeton. "Come on, let's go."

"No! No!" screamed Tanner angrily. "It was all a trap! They used him as a decoy to lure us here. Don't you see? They knew we'd be able to find him with our scans and..."

"Come on, we're not doing him any good right now," said Luca. "Let's get back to the Command Centre. We'll come back later and get him."

"I agree with Luca," said Phaeton.

"Well, we're not leaving him here," said Tanner. "We'll take him back to the Control Room. Or, we'll drop him off at the Medic Centre. Leave his body there." He sniffed. Tears formed in his eyes, but he didn't want to cry. Soldiers didn't cry.

"Come on," said Phaeton. "Let's get him out of here."

Phaeton and Tanner stood him up, threw his arms around their shoulders and began carrying him through the hallway. The Captain's legs and feet dragged behind him as Luca led the way.

Luca sensed the Nanobes before he saw them. They bore a specific odour of death and decay that was strong and penetrating. And then there they were. A cluster of them, coming at them head-on around a hallway corner. Luca started blasting them right away with his orbs.

"Oh, damn!" shouted Phaeton. "They're using Nanobes to stop us catching them!" With his free arm, he started blasting his Neutraliser, too. They simply swarmed and disappeared, missing his orbs altogether. *What in hell were those things?*

The wound on Tanner's shoulder seared. Looking at it briefly, he could see that some of his wiring was exposed. Sparks fizzed underneath his human flesh. He tried to use his good arm to fire his Neutraliser at the Nanobes, but in doing so, dropped the Captain's slack body to the ground.

When all the Nanobes had retreated, Tanner leaned on the wall for just a second. "Let's pick him up and keep moving."

"Tanner, you're bleeding," said Phaeton. "Let's leave the Captain's body here for now and just get the hell back to the Command Centre."

"No... we can't leave him," said Tanner.

"Tanner, don't worry," said Luca. "We'll come back for him."

Footsteps that sounded like boulders slamming into the floors echoed through the hallways.

"They're coming again!" shouted Phaeton. He ran down the hall and up the stairs. Tanner and Luca stood their ground and fired their orbs at the enemy soldiers. It appeared that the one soldier who had been wounded was already healed. He bounded up the stairs and ran after Phaeton. The other aimed at Tanner and blasted him in the leg. Tanner crumpled.

Before Luca could move, the remaining soldier turned towards Luca and blasted him in the arm. The pain seared through him and blood gushed out of the wound and ran down his side. The soldier turned his attention back to Tanner, holding an orb of blue-fire energy in his hands. Luca slammed his fist hard into the soldier's gut. The soldier was caught by surprise and doubled over. Luca scrambled and tried to run. The soldier was too fast for him and brought his hand of blue-fire down towards Luca. Dodging, Luca rolled out of the way in a split second and reached for his Neutraliser. The soldier moved toward Luca, hovered over him and laughed. A low, growling laugh that sounded like it came from the bowels of hell.

"I'm not going to kill you," bellowed the soldier in a thick, strange accent. "You're coming with me."

The wound on Luca's arm was bleeding profusely. The energy had been sucked out of him. Was he going to be kidnapped? Why would they want a teenager? All Luca could see was a torpedo of blue-fire orbs coming his way. In a brief instant, he thought about Asia Mae and Ceiba, about his parents, his Grampa Sol – and then, everything went black.

Chapter Twenty-One

The early morning air was refreshingly clean beneath the protective covering of Acacia Burj: another perfect day inside the city. Crystal blue sky, diamond studded sunlight falling on the leafy trees, even the subtle smell of cinnamon wafting in the air. No one would suspect that a storm had ravaged the docks last night. Nor would anyone suspect that such savagery had taken place at the edges of Acacia Burj the previous night.

Asia Mae and Sumer walked towards a moving sidewalk, hopped on, and watched as optigrams appeared before them and advertised the latest fashions and sensorpads. There were even optigrams touting the newest versions of Personas:

> The All New Upgraded Persona 2240!
> You need one, too!
> Easy, affordable payments!
> Get your Persona now and save your real body!

They stood quietly, listening to the pleasant voices while the sidewalk transported them beyond the hospital grounds. Now and then, Sumer would start to say something, but when Asia

Mae looked at her questioningly, Sumer would shrug her shoulders and say, "Never mind."

Asia Mae was still trembling over what Ceiba had told her. Her gut told her something was terribly wrong. Was it only last night that she and her friends had gone to the Arcade and enjoyed gaming, then to the Game Stop Café, and then, of course, to the docks where everything happened? She couldn't grasp that it was only last night that everything had changed. Yet, to the world, this was a normal day in Acacia Burj.

At the end of the moving sidewalk, Asia Mae and Sumer got off, and headed towards the monorails that would take them to their respective homes. They had been quiet, both of them exhausted from lack of sleep and deep in thought.

"I've been thinking," said Sumer. "If soldiers beat up your friend, Ceiba, last night on the docks, then it's possible they were the ones who beat up Elton, too."

"What makes you think that?" asked Asia Mae.

"Because Phaeton and I found my brother beaten up on the docks just like you found Ceiba. We had been together in our secret meeting place and heard all this commotion on the docks. It was so noisy with the rain and wind, that at first we thought it was the storm, but then we heard voices and footsteps. I heard my brother scream out and that's how I knew it was Elton. Phaeton and I waited until it was quiet, then we slipped out and found Elton. In just minutes, security guards were there and they arrested Phaeton and called for an ambu-rail to take Elton to the hospital."

"If they beat up your brother, why would they call for an ambu-rail?"

"I'm not sure," said Sumer. "I wonder what my brother saw that made them beat him up so badly. He almost died, and still could. He was still unconscious at the hospital, so I didn't get the opportunity to ask him anything."

"I wonder if Ceiba saw the same thing?" said Asia Mae.

"We've got to talk to them later after we've all rested," said Sumer. "I need a shower and a nap before I can even think straight."

"I agree. Look, Sumer, thanks for everything," said Asia Mae, smoothing her long hair back off her face. She felt self-conscious about her dirty, bloody bodysuit. "Just having you to talk to last night helped."

"Look, why don't you come over to my house?" said Sumer, heaving her backpack farther back on her lap. "We'll shower, change, maybe take a nap, and have some lunch. Then, we can talk more about this."

"What about your parents?"

"They're travelling."

"So are mine," said Asia. "But I need to check on Luca first."

"You can do that at my house," said Sumer. "Trust me, we have the latest technology and if you can access him anywhere, it will be from there."

Asia Mae felt bone-tired and, really, all she wanted to do was go home, contact Luca, and go to sleep. In that order. But the fact that Sumer was President Madden's daughter made her very curious.

"Are you sure?" Asia Mae said.

"Honestly, you'll be doing me a favour," said Sumer. "With my brother in the hospital and my boyfriend arrested, I could use the company."

"Okay," said Asia Mae. "Maybe for just a little while."

After a few minutes, they left the monorail and stepped onto a private one that Asia Mae had never been on before. It was designed for the families who lived in the elite suburb of Amaryllis, just on the edge of Acacia Burj. Asia Mae also knew that this was where most of the Opuls lived. There were only a handful of people on the monorail this morning. Asia Mae hunched over even more so that her long dark hair would partially cover the stains on her chest from Ceiba's blood.

Sumer said very little. Her petite, willowy-thin body looked overwhelmed. As they were nearing their destination, she looked at Asia Mae with her wild panther eyes.

"Don't be too impressed by what you see when we get to my house."

Asia Mae nodded. "Sure, I understand."

The monorail stopped at each private residence in turn and people dressed in the latest fashionable bodysuits stepped off. Finally, they came to a wooded area and Asia Mae and Sumer stepped out. Sumer waved her hand at the entrance of a tree-lined path and said: "Come on, follow me."

"I thought there'd be a privacy fence," said Asia Mae.

"There is, it's just concealed. My mother didn't want a fence to mar the view."

For a moment, Asia Mae felt transported back in time. The Madden property was such a contradiction to the sleek glass of Acacia Burj. The rural scenery before them looked like it came out of a book from the 18th century. They walked along a dirt path that was lined with every kind of tree and flower one could imagine. There were pink, blue and white asters, as well as red rhododendrons and pink chrysanthemums. Asia Mae only knew what they were because of her botany classes. Never had Asia Mae seen so many different types of flower and tree in one place.

"This whole area is a hobby of mine," said Sumer. "Mum let me design the gardens in front of our home. Naturally, I went Retro." She smiled and looked at the trees, pleased and proud.

"It's gorgeous," said Asia Mae. "I didn't know there were any places like this in Acacia Burj."

"Most people don't realise," said Sumer. "Of course, our house is a different story. You'll see."

At the end of the path, they stopped and a door opened up. Asia Mae couldn't believe it. The front and side of the house had perfectly mirrored sides so the trees were reflected against it, and as such, the house was totally camouflaged from the outer world.

Asia Mae gasped as they stepped into the massive hallway. The foyer was several storeys high, with a tiered glass stairway that led up to multiple floors that were stacked like a lopsided jigsaw puzzle.

Sumer took Asia Mae by the hand and led her up the glass stairs. "Come on," she said. "We'll go to my room first."

"Don't you have AIs?" asked Asia Mae, looking around. When she entered her own family's apartment, the maid greeted her and asked if she could get her anything.

"When my parents leave, I turn off all the artificial intelligence," said Sumer. She rolled her eyes at Asia Mae. "It's just too much sometimes, you know?"

It wasn't too much for Asia Mae. She loved the technology and would be in heaven if she lived in a home as beautiful as this. As they climbed the stairs, the floor-to-ceiling glass windows showcased the surrounding forest and Acacia Burj. The higher they got, the more of the city they could see. The sky-high crystal and glass buildings of Acacia Burj glistened in the distance and monorails and personal space pods glided evenly through the air, one on top of the other as if they were stacked towards heaven.

When they finally reached the highest level of the house, Asia Mae had to stop and take it all in. She could even see far outside the city where the docks spread out before the sea. It was beautiful. The sun shimmered across the water and white-tipped azure waves rolled lazily to the shore, belying the fact that there had been a storm last night. There was just a solitary rising trail of smoke in one area of the docks, perhaps where the explosion had been last night. Off to the far right of them were the Wilds, a rustic, barren world of desert with sparse shrubs and trees. Such a contrast to the beauty of the sea.

"Sumer, this is just breathtaking."

"Um, I don't know."

"How can you not be proud of this?"

"Because of the price my father pays to live here. Because of the people who can't afford anything but a tiny room to live in. It's too much, really."

"I don't understand," said Asia Mae. "Isn't your father President Madden?"

"You knew?"

"Well, yes," said Asia Mae hesitantly. "Your face is all over the newscasts at times with your parents and even though you're always dressed in bodysuits on the news and not retro clothes, I still recognised you, sure."

"Please don't hold that against me," said Sumer. "I try my best to stay under the radar and blend in with the Retros. I find them to be the most real people I know. People judge me if they think I'm an Opul. Especially when they find out who my father is."

"No, I wouldn't," said Asia Mae. "I mean, I understand. What do you mean about your father paying a price? Isn't this house furnished by the people – the government – of Acacia Burj?"

"Yes, but I'm not talking literally. What I mean is that it's all politics," said Sumer. "Too often, he has to compromise his principles. That's all. My father is a good man, deep down, but he has done some things he's not proud of – things I hate – because of politics."

"Oh." Asia Mae didn't really understand.

117

"Enough about that right now. Let's get cleaned up, maybe take a nap, and have something to eat. Then we can talk."

"That would be good. I feel so disgusting after last night."

"Yeah, you look a mess," said Sumer. When she saw Asia Mae's face drop, she quickly added, "I'm just teasing. You could never look a mess." Then she laughed. It was a small laugh, light and lyrical. And surprising.

When Sumer opened the door to her bedroom, Asia Mae gasped again. The room was practically as large as Asia Mae's entire apartment. Sleek silver and glass tables punctuated the area with a long white sofa, tons of grey and black pillows, a fireplace at one end, white marble floors, and a digital wall where all comms and videos were utilised. Rounding the wall was a floor-to-ceiling window, displaying the centre of Acacia Burj in all its glory. There was a deck outside that looked like it was dangling in the clouds, leading to a clear infinity pool. Swimming in that would feel like you were swimming in the sky.

"Oh, my goodness! That pool! And, this looks more like a lounge area than a bedroom," said Asia Mae. "It should be showcased in some architectural opti-magazine."

"Well, actually it has been, but it only embarrassed the hell out of me. But this is just *part* of my bedroom." Sumer motioned for Asia Mae to follow her and went into another large room off the lounge. A monstrous bed that could easily sleep several people floated on a platform at one end of the room, piled high with pale blue silk comforters and pillows. The floor in here was marble, as well. On one side of the bedroom was a door that led to what Sumer called her 'Retro Room'. Inside were an old-fashioned overstuffed sofa, a wrought iron bed, lamps, and bookshelves full of real old-fashioned hardback books. The floor was made of real hardwoods.

"Real books?"

"Yes," said Sumer. "There's nothing like the feel of paper."

"I thought they only existed in the museums and libraries," said Asia Mae.

"Well, if you know where to find them, you can still get them," said Sumer. "I try to collect as many as I can, even though they're quite expensive."

"I love it!" said Asia Mae. She walked over to a bookshelf and started perusing the titles.

"This is where I sleep and it's my favourite part of the house," said Sumer. "I designed it, and fortunately, Mum and Dad don't mind it. They think I'm going through a phase. Here, let me get you a robe so you can take a shower. I have two, so you can use the one in here and I'll take the other. Don't worry, it's not Retro. It has lots of hot water, jet sprays – the works! And then, let's take a nap. I'm really tired."

"That sounds wonderful," said Asia Mae.

"You take my bed in the outer room and I'll take the antique bed. Meet you down in the kitchen in a couple of hours? Then, we'll see if we can contact your friend Luca and my boyfriend. I need to talk to him."

"Great," said Asia Mae.

When she stepped into the ultra-modern shower, she activated the water by speaking to it as Sumer had instructed. Immediately, it rained down thousands of drops of soft, hot water, rushing over her body like a waterfall on a mountain hillside. Not that Asia Mae had ever been on a real mountain in a real waterfall, but it was similar to what she, Ceiba and Luca had experienced when they first entered the A'Rmillari game last night and went through the waterfall. *Was that really just last night?* Asia Mae shivered, remembering what had happened afterwards. It was all so surreal.

Drawing her mind back to the present, the water trailed down Asia Mae's body, kneading the sore muscles and calming her. She could have stayed there forever, but sleep was beckoning. When she finally stepped out, she stood below a sensor which drenched her with warm air, drying her hair and body in seconds. Then, a soft dew-like scent sprayed all over her, perfuming her with a touch of jasmine. She could barely keep her eyes open.

She wrapped a robe around herself, and then sank into layers and layers of silk comforters and pillows on Sumer's enormous bed. She was asleep almost before her head touched the pillows.

Asia Mae didn't know how long she slept. It was a deep, dreamless sleep, but she woke up refreshed. She saw that Sumer had left Retro clothes for her to put on. *Her idea of a joke.* Clean, faded, ripped blue jeans, a huge sweatshirt and trainers. Asia Mae laughed, but put them on anyway. Her mum would kill her if she saw her dressed like this, but she had no choice and besides, her parents were travelling. Her bodysuit was bloody and dirty, and was missing anyway. Even if it were there, she wouldn't want to put it back on. It reminded her too much of Ceiba and what had happened to him last night.

Asia Mae slipped into the clothes and found them surprisingly comfortable. She brushed her long hair until it glistened and went out to find Sumer.

"You look lovely," Sumer said, as Asia Mae walked into the kitchen. "Those clothes look great on you."

"Thanks so much for the shower... and the nap... and the clothes," said Asia Mae. "I feel so refreshed after that."

"Me, too," said Sumer, who was now wearing another pair of blue jeans with a shirt. "I've already put your bodysuit in to be cleaned, so it will be ready after we've eaten if you want to change back into it."

"Thanks so much," said Asia Mae.

"Right now, I'm famished. C'mon, let's go to the kitchen." Sumer motioned for her to follow and they went out into the hallway and down the glass stairs. Passing one lavish room after another, they landed on the second floor where the kitchen was situated. Asia Mae gasped again. It was as large as two apartments, lined with shiny white and glass cabinets from wall to wall, which curved in semicircles at both ends. Glistening glass countertops, chrome sinks, glass tables and cabinets punctuated the room.

"I'm going to treat you to a real Retro meal," said Sumer. "Straight out of the machine!"

"You mean you aren't going to cook them yourself?" asked Asia Mae, laughing.

"No, but I would if we had the real ingredients."

"I like Retro food," said Asia Mae. "A cheeseburger and coffee sounds wonderful."

Within a few minutes, their meals were nearly completed. The smell of the food made Asia Mae's stomach gurgle, and she realised she was starving. The two girls sat down at a glass table that overlooked the forest around the house. Asia Mae was starting to feel comfortable with Sumer, as if she had known her all her life.

"I really need to message Luca," said Asia Mae. She gazed directly at her sensorpad, then listened. But no message came through on her i5D. She rubbed her eyes, as if that would some-how make a message come through. Finally, she left another mes-sage, "Luca, please contact me as soon as you get this message."

"No news?" asked Sumer, as she sipped her coffee.

"No, which is strange," said Asia Mae. "Something's wrong. He would have contacted me by now."

"He wasn't in the hospital, so perhaps he and his family have gone to a spiritual service or something."

"No, I don't think so," said Asia Mae. "I can't remember the last time they went to any kind of religious service."

"Could you try to send a message to his mum?" asked Sumer.

"That's a good idea, I'll try." Asia Mae sent a message to both Gaia and Skye, Luca's mum, but there was no answer.

"Maybe if I go to his home, I can find something out," said Asia Mae. "We live very close to one another."

"Tell me what happened last night," said Sumer, taking a big bite of the burger.

Asia Mae proceeded to tell Sumer everything – beginning with the game at the Arcade, what she overheard in the game, then their dinner at the Game Stop and finally, their venture out to the docks. Sumer listened carefully, stopping occasionally to get another food item out of the refrigerator. First, olives. Then, a plate of cheese. She could not stop grazing.

"Would Ceiba's father perhaps know something about Luca – about what happened on the docks?" asked Sumer.

"Maybe," said Asia Mae. "I'll go back to the hospital this after-noon and talk to Ceiba again, and see if I can get in touch with Mr. Ammos. What do you think about all this, Sumer?"

"I think something's going on," said Sumer. "It's bigger than you realise. I think what you heard in the A'Rmillari game is a bit too real to be just a game and I think it all ties in with what my boyfriend and I have learned."

"What have you learned?" asked Asia Mae, wide-eyed, as she took a final bite of her burger.

"That Acacia Burj is on the brink of war."

Chapter Twenty-Two

Dammit! Dammit! Dammit! Phaeton couldn't leave Tanner and Luca behind no matter how much he wanted to just get back to the Command Centre and be safe. He just couldn't leave them.

After he had climbed the stairs, he ran down the hallway to his left and tucked himself into an alcove. The enemy soldier paused at the top of the stairs, trying to decide which way to go. Thankfully, he headed in the opposite direction to where Phaeton was hidden.

Phaeton tentatively stepped out, knowing he had to go back for Tanner and Luca. As quietly as possible, he ran back to the stairs and down to the level where he, Luca and Tanner had just been. The Captain's body was on the floor, and beside him, Tanner was slumped against the wall and out cold. The giant enemy soldier had his foot on Luca's stomach and Luca seemed to be unconscious, too. Blood trailed from a wound on his arm. It didn't look good.

The assailant had some kind of blue-fire orb flashing out of his hand. It popped like firecrackers and looked even more lethal than his weapon. He had raised his arm to slash down at Luca and the blue-fire spun like atoms.

No! Phaeton hoisted his Neutraliser and fired a massive orange electro-orb just as the attacker's arm started coming down with the blue-fire. Phaeton hit the enemy attacker in the chest, but instead of falling to the ground, the enemy soldier – with his face covered in head armour – just stood there, defiant as ever.

The enemy's head snapped around to where Phaeton stood and he took his foot off Luca's chest and squared his shoulders directly at him. Terror swept through Phaeton. The soldier was coming after him!

The attacker roared: a sinister, animal-like sound that made his blood run cold. The assailant threw his blue-fire at Phaeton, knocking the Neutraliser out of his hands. He fell backwards onto the floor and the noise of the weaponry screamed in his ears.

Luca opened his eyes and for a moment and registered the blurry outline of a massive figure standing over him. He felt the foot on his chest, and then it was gone. Was that Phaeton across from him on the floor? Pain blazed white-hot in his arm. He looked to the side and saw his Neutraliser centimetres away. He reached with his good arm, stretching as long as he could, and then edged his body towards the weapon. Finally, he grasped it and just as the enemy raised his arm to throw another blue-fire at Phaeton, Luca shot the Neutraliser, blasting him in the back of the head.

The soldier slumped to the floor next to Luca.

Phaeton got up and moved over to where Luca lay. "Thanks, man. You saved me," said Phaeton. "You hurt?"

"It's just my arm. And I think you saved *me*," said Luca, propping himself up with his good arm. "Thanks for coming back. What about Tanner? Is he all right?"

Phaeton walked over to Tanner and checked his pulse. "He'll be fine, I think." Phaeton was surprised at the wires fizzing beneath the skin. He hadn't realised Tanner was a Bion. "But we need to get him back to the Command Centre. I think we'll all be safer in there than anywhere else, and you need to be back at the controls for re-entry."

They looked at the enemy soldier lying on the floor. Luca's orb had hit him directly in the back of the head in the neck area at the base of his headset. A black, blood-like substance pooled around his head.

"Tanner, you awake?" asked Phaeton. He didn't move.

"We can carry him," said Luca.

With their Neutralisers slung over his shoulder, and the enemy attacker's weapon cradled under his arm, Phaeton heaved Tanner up and slung one of his arms around his shoulders. Luca took the other side, and then they both dragged him to the stairs. It was awkward and difficult and took several minutes to get him up the stairs because Tanner was out cold. It was like dragging a dead body.

Finally, after what seemed like an eternity, Phaeton and Luca reached the Command Centre. Leaning Tanner's body against the wall, Phaeton waved his wrist and the wall door opened up. They took Tanner over to one of the pods and stretched him out.

"He really should be taken to the medical room," said Luca. "If only we had an engineer to check him over - I hadn't realised he was a Bion. Will his wiring repair itself?"

"It should do, yes," said Phaeton. "For now, it's too risky to go back out in the hallways," said Phaeton. "Remember, there's still another alien out there on the loose somewhere."

"They were using some kind of invisibility shield in the kitchen galley – something that absorbed their atoms," said Phaeton. "I'm surprised they didn't use it in the hallway just now," said Phaeton.

"Well let's concentrate on getting Tanner healed and getting this ship back in one piece. Maybe our comms will come back on in a while," said Luca. "Everything seems to be offline right now. Even the scans on the rooms are blank. We have no choice but to do the best we can right here."

"Let me take a look at your arm," said Phaeton. "They got you good."

"It just burns," said Luca.

Phaeton proceeded to tear a larger hole out of the sleeve on Luca's bodysuit. He found an arm band amongst the emergency supplies and wrapped it around Luca's scabbing wound. The blue-fire had just grazed it, but the open wound and surrounding burn looked painful.

"Thanks, Phaeton," said Luca. "That feels better already. We need to tend to Tanner."

"Tanner should be fine. I think he hit his head when he fell back and that's what knocked him out. Or maybe some of his wiring has short-circuited. Hopefully it will repair itself. He can rest here. We'll get Tanner to Earth and the medics can take care of him there," said Phaeton. "And, once we land, we'll have the resources we need to take care of that other alien, too. I've had enough of those things for one day."

"Phaeton."

"Yeah?"

"That enemy soldier spoke to me," said Luca.

"What? What did he say?"

"He said, *I'm not going to kill you. You're coming with me.*"

"Why would he want you?" asked Phaeton.

"I have no idea," said Luca.

"Well, we know they can speak English," said Phaeton. "Maybe Tanner can provide some insight when he wakes up."

As they took care of Tanner, bandaging his wounds and applying solder to the exposed wires in his shoulder and leg, and making him comfortable, neither one of them saw the alien ships on the video screens.

They were being pursued.

Chapter Twenty-Three

"Warning! Warning!" the voice on the *Sibylline's* Command Centre announced.

"Command Centre?" said Luca, turning his head towards the main sensory screen. "What is it? What's going on?"

"Enemy ship approaching."

"What on Earth?" screamed Luca.

"Identity unknown. All sensory probes are blocked."

"Let me try!" said Phaeton.

"You're not Wired, remember?" said Luca. "You need your comms in order to connect."

"I don't think so," said Phaeton. "I can interface with the command centre. No problem."

He swiped at the controls, looking for the coordinates and incoming data on the screen in front of him. But the *Sibylline* could not identify the ship. The aliens they had just encountered in the hallway had to be the same ones as on the ship. Luca and Phaeton were quite sure they were the A'Rmillari. An alien race that wasn't supposed to exist.

"They're blocking us!" said Luca, pressing on the glass control screen, trying to bring up the Captain's Persona. "Dr Tycho, are you there? I need you – *now!*"

There was static and a sizzling sound but the Captain didn't respond.

"This is so weird," said Luca. "Security protocols are intact, but the Captain's Persona has been severed. Phaeton, what do I do?"

"Crap," said Phaeton, running over to Luca's side. "There must be some kind of major interference. Maybe there's a problem with one of the communication satellites. Can you land this thing?"

"I don't know much about the *Sibylline's* operating systems," said Luca. "It's pre-programmed to land at the Mariana Mining Base, though."

"That's what the Dr told you," said Phaeton.

"Well, we're on automatic piloting right now, and if there are no disturbances, our re-entry into the sea *should* go smoothly."

"Well, let's hope we can get this baby to destroy those ships," said Phaeton. "Or we're in for a world of trouble."

"Yeah, they could destroy us before we get to Earth!" said Luca.

Luca looked up at the display and saw an alien ship approaching. It was like the one from the Moon. It could even have been the same one. "You think it's planning to attack us?" asked Luca.

"Hell, yes! We can't take chances," said Phaeton. "Let's figure out how to engage the firing systems."

"Warning! Warning! Incoming fire! Prepare defence shields!" the command centre blared.

"Phaeton, how do we prepare the defence shields?"

"Can you give the command centre a verbal command?"

"I don't know," said Luca. He turned toward the controls and ordered, "*Sibylline*, activate and engage all defence systems now!"

Nothing happened.

"I think you have to be connected to Dr Tycho's Persona," said Phaeton. Sweat had beaded on his forehead. Luca watched him wipe it off and curse under his breath. He looked scared.

Just at that moment, Luca and Phaeton saw an explosion of fire on one of the opti-panels, indicating that the *Sibylline* had been hit. Both Luca and Phaeton could feel a tremor run through the ship.

"Dammit!" shouted Phaeton. "This is all we need!"

"Warning! Security breach! Fire in left quadrant in hull of

ship!"

"Dr Tycho, please activate," said Luca. *We're going to die! We're going to die!*

The Captain's Persona flickered slightly next to Luca.

"I'm here," said Dr Tycho. "Is everything all right?"

"No!" cried Luca. His heart scratched its way up into his throat. "We're being attacked by an alien ship. Can you help me engage our weaponry to counter the attacks?"

"I'll try my best. Just take a seat at the controls."

Luca sat down and leaned back into the sensory chair as the Captain's consciousness melded and intersected with his. The Captain's thoughts were calm and reassuring. Luca was amazed again at the technical information that flowed through his consciousness.

Luca then followed Dr Tycho's commands. Within seconds, Luca was blasting a stream of fiery laser bursts at the enemy ship. But it was firing at them in return.

Phaeton stepped into the opti-panels on the floor that mimicked the outside of the ship. He was able to report back to Luca all the damage to the other ships.

"You hit it!" he said. "Great job, Luca! Take this goddamn ship out!"

Luca fired again, but missed. The alien spaceship could careen left and right too quickly to lock a shot.

"You're getting close to the Earth's atmosphere," said Dr Tycho. "Let's accelerate to make your descent faster."

"Won't this ship just follow us?"

"Not if we can fire the lasers in all directions to distract it, then accelerate and lose them," said Tycho.

Luca followed the engineer's commands, letting his thoughts and the Captain's intersect as one. But, just as the engineer's Persona had faded in and out during the whole journey, it disappeared all of a sudden, and Luca knew he was on his own. He immediately felt the disconnect. His stomach churned. Luca had to rely on the abilities and the skills he had developed in gaming. He was having trouble accelerating the ship in the comparatively short distance between the upper atmosphere and the ocean floor.

"Come on!" said Phaeton. "You can do it, Luca!"

It happened very quickly. Luca saw on the screens that they

had entered Earth's atmosphere and were approaching the ocean... fast! It was bumpy and forceful and he and Phaeton had to hold on to keep from being thrown into the floor. One small error could kill all of them.

Luca couldn't take his eyes off the screens as the ocean sped closer and closer. Lightning flashed outside, painfully intense and close. The radar display on the control screens flickered.

He knew he shouldn't worry. He was a Mariner, after all, and came from a long line of expert pilots and champions. It was in his DNA. Surely, the protective shields of the *Sibylline* would save them. *Wouldn't it?* Of course, no one had counted on an enemy ship attacking them.

"The enemy ship is still with us," said Phaeton, standing in the middle of the wall panel optigram. "We didn't lose it."

"We have no choice but to land," shouted Luca. "Dr Tycho has gone again and I can't get his Persona back. I'm flying blind, Phaeton." He tried to breathe and stay calm. He had piloted replicas of similar ships in games a few times in the Arcade. They were rapidly approaching the ocean, and Luca had no control over the speed or angle to smash through the ocean waves and land safely into the depths of the sea.

"Warning! Warning! Brace for impact," alerted the Command Centre.

Phaeton checked again to make sure that Tanner was fastened in his pod. They were 10,000 metres from impact.

"Here we go!" shouted Phaeton.

The *Sibylline* ploughed into a raging wall of rain and hail. It began to buck and Luca used every ounce of power he had to keep the ship level manually. His breathing was ragged and his pulse hammered in his ears like a million drums.

"Easy going there," said Phaeton. "Come on, Luca, you can do it!"

On the monitors, Luca read they were now at 3,000 metres and dropping like a meteor. There was a burst of static and thunderous crashing as the ship hit the ocean hard. It felt like the *Sibylline* had slammed into a boulder and Luca and Phaeton lurched forward, then back in their seats. Dr Tycho's Persona faded in and out in a prolonged sizzle. Then, it was gone altogether.

All Luca could see were blinding sheets of water on the screens in front of him – infinite rolls and foamy waves as they plunged to the sea floor. Deeper and deeper, the *Sibylline* sank, rocking and jerking from side to side, until it finally stabilised.

According to the Command Centre, the impact had ripped away some of the external armour plating. *But they were alive!*

"Earth Acacia Central, Admiral Maasaw, come in, please," Luca shouted into the comms. His voice was urgent. "Does anyone read? This is the *Sibylline* Stealth Lazer Pathfinder, on a return trip from the Moon. We've just landed in the sea and are headed to the Mariana Deep Sea Mining Base. Does anyone read, please?"

Silence. Luca pounded his fist against the control screen and shards of fire fizzed beneath the glass panels.

"Do you see the enemy ship?" he asked Phaeton.

"No! I can't see anything!"

Chapter Twenty-Four

The words shocked Asia Mae. She felt like a knife had pierced her heart. Her world was turning upside down.

"*What?* Are you being serious?"

"I don't mean to upset you, but I don't think it was just a game that you were playing last night at the Arcade, and I don't think our instincts are wrong about an intergalactic war coming," said Sumer. "It will start with an invasion of Acacia Burj, I imagine. Then, the war will follow." She walked over to the kitchen counter and asked for refills on their coffee. Within seconds, she returned to the table and handed a steaming mug to Asia Mae.

"Thanks," she said, wrapping her hands around it to get warm. All of a sudden, her body had gone cold. "So, you believe the characters in those games at the Arcade are real?"

"Some of them. What I'm about to tell you is strictly confidential," said Sumer. "I believe I can trust you. I hope so, anyway. Truth is, you feel like a sister to me. I've never had a sister, but... can you keep a secret?"

Sumer reached out and touched Asia Mae's hand.

"Yes," said Asia Mae. Shyly, she added, "I've never had a sister either. And yes, you can trust me. I promise. I've been wondering about everything since I heard those A'Rmillari characters talking in the video game. I thought it was just my silly imagination and after *everything* else that happened last night, I kind of forgot about it. But, wait a minute – are you sure it's safe to talk in here?"

Asia Mae looked around the room. This modern home – the president's home – must be wired for automatic recording. *How could anything be secret in here?*

"As I said this morning, I've turned off almost all the comms in the house, and we *won't* be recorded. I can promise you that. Phaeton – that's my boyfriend – he taught me how to do it. My parents don't have a clue what I know. They think I'm just some Retro-chick who hasn't found her place in life yet and who loves gardening and antique clothes and books. We're safe, I promise. Of course, when my father gets back in town, that's a different story."

"I hope you're right," said Asia Mae. She took a sip of coffee. The hot liquid felt good trickling down her throat. "What do you know?"

"My boyfriend studies the games at the Arcade," said Sumer. "They're not all just *games*. Phaeton is a genius, by the way." Sumer smiled. Her face lit up whenever she mentioned her boyfriend.

"He was kicked out of Acacia Burj a couple of years ago and sent into the Wilds because of his activities with the games and the underground news alliance. He was getting ready to expose the truth about the future of Acacia Burj."

"What truth?" Asia Mae's eyes widened. "The war?"

"Yes." Sumer took a big gulp of coffee and lowered her voice. "And about aliens!"

"But aliens don't exist, right?" said Asia Mae.

"That's what we've been told all our lives," said Sumer. "But, I think that was a lie. I know, some people would think we're crazy to hear us talk like this. Last night, I believe you had some real-life interference on your video game. You picked up some communications between a real alien race called the A'Rmillari. Of course, I'm not one hundred per cent sure of this. My boyfriend has told me all of this and he doesn't have any proof. Not yet. He thinks these aliens have been planning a take-over for decades now.

"I wonder if my father knows about it," continued Sumer. "I've never felt like I could ask him. And now he and Mum are at the Galileo Moon Resort."

"What would the aliens want with us?" asked Asia Mae. She glanced around the room, as if the walls could hear. "Why would they attack us, Sumer?"

"Phaeton has been trying to find that out," said Sumer. "We're honestly not sure yet. It could have something to do with our mineral resources, or our water, or our planet. Who knows? But that's another reason Acacia Burj threw Phaeton out into the Wilds. Maybe they wanted to stop his research before he learned too much."

"How has he survived out there?" asked Asia Mae. "It's so dangerous."

"I've been helping him and he has found others out there, as well." Sumer nibbled on a biscuit, and then added: "The Wilds aren't exactly what we've been told either."

"But if your boyfriend is living in The Garbage Pit, then how was he arrested at the docks last night?"

"I've been helping him – meeting him on the docks and even getting him fake IDs and passes into Acacia Burj. He went to the Arcade yesterday and played the A'Rmillari game, too, to conduct research. We met on the docks later and he was about to tell me what he had learned when a couple of men from the military found us when we went to the aid of Elton. So, see, princess, what you told me about overhearing those soldiers in the A'Rmillari game could have definitely been a real conversation."

"Honestly," said Asia Mae. "It sounded real to me, but Ceiba and Luca thought it was just a game."

"Well, I trust Phaeton," said Sumer. "We've been meeting at the docks in our secret place for a long time and when Mum and Dad aren't here, I can sneak him into our house. Those are the best times." For a moment, she stared out of the wall window and got a far-off dreamy look in her eyes as if she was remembering something very special.

Sumer looked back at Asia Mae and said: "Anyway, somebody reported seeing him on the docks, apparently. Those security guards work closely with the military, you know. Even though Phaeton had a fake ID that I had bought him, they knew who he was and took him away in handcuffs." Her eyes glistened with tears. "Now I don't know if I'll ever see him again."

"Did they know who you were?" asked Asia Mae. "That you're the president's daughter?"

"No, they didn't. At least I don't think so. Generally, no one knows who I am when I dress in Retro clothes, which is one reason I love doing it."

"What about the sensors?"

"Neither Phaeton or I am permanently Wired, remember?" said Sumer. "Plus, they can't access my personal information on the docks when we're outside Acacia Burj. That's another reason we like to meet there."

"What does all of this have to do with Ceibastian?" asked Asia Mae.

"You said that Ceiba told you some soldiers had beaten him up, right?"

"That's what he said," said Asia Mae.

"Maybe, just maybe Ceiba *found* something on the docks last night that he wasn't supposed to find."

Chapter Twenty-Five

Rocking from side to side, the *Sibylline* began to dive to the bottom of the ocean and glide bumpily through the sea towards the mining base.

"What's happening?" asked Phaeton. "Is this baby actually taking us to our destination?"

"Hope so," said Luca, feeling a sense of heightened anticipation. "But I'm a bit worried that the ship could fall apart before we get to Mariana."

"What do you mean?"

"The assessment panel indicated that our external shields are damaged and our weapons systems are gone."

"So, we have no fire power if those aliens are coming after us," said Phaeton.

"Exactly," confirmed Luca.

"I don't see the enemy ship right now," said Phaeton. "Looks like our panels are still down, but the last time I looked, that ship was right on our tail – just as we entered the ocean. You'd damaged it and there was fire everywhere, but it was still flying."

"Then it's probably not far behind us." Luca felt like panicking.

He had no control of the ship, Dr Tycho's Persona was gone, and the *Sibylline* had been damaged. He had to stay calm.

"Maybe we lost them," said Phaeton.

"Maybe."

"But we've still got one of those soldiers somewhere on our ship. And he's got that goddamned invisibility shield. We have a live one and a dead one – remember?" said Phaeton.

"With his invisibility capabilities, it's going to be hard to find him. We'll have reinforcements when we reach the mining base, surely?"

"See if you can connect with anyone at the base," said Phaeton.

Luca nodded, and then said, "Mariana Deep Sea Mining Base, this is *Sibylline* Command Centre. Is anyone there? Do you copy?"

There was no response. Luca then tried to reconnect with Admiral Maasaw from Earth Acacia Central, but again, there was no response. He and Phaeton were still alone.

"The comms might be severed for good this time," sighed Phaeton.

"When we reach the mining base, we'll go and find any remaining crew members from where they're holed up, then find some personnel at the base to help us," said Luca. "And if that alien ship has followed us, then we should have enough resources to fight them."

"If we can get around that sonofabitch alien," said Phaeton.

"I can't imagine where he is," said Luca. "Our last scan didn't reveal his location."

"We should be able to handle one measly soldier," said Phaeton. "With or without his invisibility capabilities."

Luca watched as the *Sibylline* sailed through the icy waters close to the bottom of the ocean to reach its destination. There was turbulence and, now and then, the ship moaned and creaked as if it might come apart any moment. Hydrothermal vents funnelled up from the ocean floor every so often. The steam temporarily obliterated the view, and Luca could almost feel the searing heat they brought up from deep inside the Earth.

Even though Luca was worried – after all, he had almost crashed the ship he wasn't even supposed to even be on; and he had been pursued by enemy soldiers; and they still might die – he was also so excited about being in the depths of the ocean he could barely contain himself. Even Phaeton stopped talking as the Pathfinder's exterior lights highlighted the surrounding water and they watched the mysterious deep sea unfold before them

At first, there was only murky darkness. Luca felt as though he and Phaeton were completely isolated from the rest of the world. Before them was a barren, desolate lunar-like plain. Luca knew there was much more to see. After all, many luxury homes had been built deep in the sea – closer to Acacia Burj, of course – and there were the mining bases scattered all over. He had no idea how many. Luca and Phaeton watched as rugged mountains and a vast plateau stretched out before them. People had always claimed that a great abyss lay behind the ocean ridges and rift valleys. All of a sudden, a flurry of white snow began floating around the ship, giving the sea an ethereal, otherworldly feel.

"What is that?" asked Phaeton.

"It's dying plankton and sand," said Luca. "I know it sounds weird, but they form marine snowflakes after a while."

"It's bizarre if you ask me," said Phaeton. "I've never heard of snow in the ocean!"

"From what I saw in iT school, this marine snow is the foundation of certain ecosystems." Luca thought it was beautiful, but he didn't want to say that. Phaeton would think he was being overly sentimental.

"Wow! What's *that?*" exclaimed Phaeton, pointing.

Before them, a huge school of glowing neon-blue fish with extremely large, bulging eyes sailed by them. Luca remembered his night at the docks with his friends, and how Asia Mae had been surrounded by the bioluminescent waves. A pain seared through his heart. He wanted to see her. Even though they had only been apart a day, it felt like an eternity. He suddenly felt tired – he hadn't slept since accidentally climbing aboard the ship. He'd try to contact Asia Mae the first opportunity he got at the mining base. She'd never believe the adventure he'd had. It worried him that he hadn't been able to contact her since he was discovered as a stowaway.

"What are they?" asked Phaeton.

"Those are bioluminescent fish," said Luca.

"I have to admit, they're cool," Phaeton said. "And strange."

"They're remarkable," said Luca.

"All systems, prepare for the approach to the Mariana Deep Sea Mining Base," the Command Centre announced. "Destination: ten kilometres. Time: three minutes and counting."

All of a sudden, the *Sibylline* entered an underwater cave.

"What the—?" said Phaeton.

Luca wasn't sure what he had expected, but it wasn't this. As the ship sailed into the cave, a world opened up. They were headed upwards into a huge dry cavern within a rock, which was accessed through this cave tunnel. All around them were high, rocky walls that completely encompassed an underground world with land, buildings and bright lights that was free from water. As they emerged from the sea, the wheels descended from the *Sibylline* and they drove onto land. Rolling up the ramp, the ship slid into the dock.

"Destination complete. Welcome to the Mariana Deep Sea Mining Base. Doors will unlock in 30 seconds. Decompression activating. Unfasten security holds and prepare to disembark."

"Where are we?" Tanner said groggily from his makeshift bed at the far end of the room.

"Tanner, you're awake!" said Luca. "How're you feeling?"

"Er, not too bad. Where are we? Why am I in this pod?"

"We're at the Mariana Base," said Phaeton. "Thanks to Captain Luca, here. We had to secure you in the pod for landing."

"You mean we're back on Earth?" asked Tanner. "Already?"

"Yep," said Phaeton. "We're at the mining base. You've missed most of the excitement, I'm afraid!"

"Glad you're finally awake," said Luca. "We were worried about you for a while."

"Well, somebody, come and help me out of this," said Tanner. "And tell me what I've missed. Last thing I remember was an enemy soldier standing over me."

"Uh-huh," said Phaeton. "That's when I found you, and saved your ass, I might add."

"You took him out?" asked Tanner, looking up at Phaeton – the wayward Retro who looked too thin to fight anything, much less one of those giant enemy soldiers.

"Uh-huh," said Phaeton. "If it weren't for me, you would be dead as a dodo."

"What about the other one?" asked Tanner. "There were two of them, if I remember."

"One got away, I'm afraid," said Phaeton. "We don't know where he is."

"We think he's in hiding," said Luca.

"Makes sense," said Tanner. "He could be hiding until his people come for him."

"I thought of that, too," said Phaeton. "An enemy ship may have followed us into the ocean, but we haven't seen it since then. You sure you're okay?"

"Yeah, I'm a little sore and stiff," said Tanner, "but I'm fine I think. Thanks, Phaeton. Really... thanks."

"Sure," said Phaeton, nonchalantly. "You would've done the same for me."

"Come on, Phaeton," said Luca. "Let's help him up."

They went over and unfastened the security holdings on Tanner in the pod. His hair was dishevelled and he looked a mess. His face was swollen on one side with black and purple bruises. His wounds still looked bad, but they could get medical help at the base.

Luca ran back to the command centre screens. Something didn't seem right. Outside the Sibylline, Mariana looked abandoned. The site was littered with giant caterpillar track-based mining machines, but no one was operating them. It seemed as though all the men, women and mining vehicle control pods that operated the machines were gone.

Where was everyone?

Chapter Twenty-Six

BREAKING NEWS!
Terrorist attack on the Galileo Moon Resort

President Madden & the First Lady
Kidnapped on the Moon

Details on the hour!

Sumer and Asia Mae stood and watched the newscast on the private Amaryllis monorail in horror.

"This can't be happening!" Sumer said as quietly as she could to Asia Mae, presumably so other people on the monorail wouldn't hear her. Everyone's eyes were glued to the newscast on the optigram by the monorail.

Asia Mae put her hand on Sumer's arm. She was trembling. Asia Mae said as gently as she could, "Sumer, it's going to be fine. They didn't give any details, which means they aren't sure of anything. It could even be a false alarm. They've given plenty of false alarms on the news before."

"No, you don't understand," said Sumer, shaking her head.

She was trembling. "This all makes perfect sense in light of what Phaeton has been telling me. They really did it this time!"

"I don't know where my parents are either," said Asia Mae. "They might be at the Galileo Moon Resort, too. All I know is they were travelling. They could be anywhere."

"Well, if they're not into politics, they have a chance of surviving this," said Sumer.

"They're both palaeontologists. I'll have to check their schedules when I get home," said Asia Mae. Her stomach knotted. Surely her parents weren't on the Moon. They would have told her, wouldn't they?

"I think they'll be okay, then," said Sumer. "They've only kidnapped my father because of who he is."

"Look," said Asia Mae. "We'll visit Ceiba and your brother at the hospital, then I'll contact Ceiba's father, and see what he knows. And maybe Luca will have his comms on and I can contact him. He might know something. His sister's boyfriend, Tanner, is a military trainee and both his sister and Luca's mum work at the Intergalactic Research & Science Organisation. They might know something."

"Oh, no!" said Sumer, covering her eyes with her hands and trying to hold back the tears. "Don't you understand, Asia Mae? This is part of a big plan that's been going on for a long time. It's part of something much bigger and Phaeton was just about to tell me about it when he got arrested. I swear if anything happens to my parents, those damn aliens are going to have hell to pay."

"We don't have any *proof* that it was aliens," said Asia Mae, immediately realising how naïve she sounded.

"It's all a load of garbage," said Sumer. "Everything we've been told has all been lies."

"Come on, let's go find out what we can," said Asia Mae. "Don't worry. I'm sure your father is alive and well. Anyway, even if it is true, whoever's got him wouldn't hurt him. They'll need him for leverage – to get something they want. You know how the media blows up everything to sound more exciting and dangerous."

"I don't know," said Sumer, shaking her head.

The two girls had decided to go back to the hospital to see Ceiba and Elton. Asia Mae had repeatedly tried to contact Luca, but he had not responded. She was worried that something had happened to him, and after all the weirdness with Ceiba and Sumer's brother being beaten up, Sumer's boyfriend being arrested, and Prince being killed, nothing would surprise her. Or so she had thought. She had not been prepared for this news at all.

BREAKING NEWS!
Warning! Huge solar flare expected to hit Earth sometime in the next 24 hours.
Massive flares can trigger strong geomagnetic storms that knock out satellites,
cause comms blackouts and disrupt power grids.
Details on the hour!
Stayed tuned to more information and ALL Breaking News First in Acacia Burj!

"What now?" said Sumer.

They had just switched monorails when the breaking news about the solar flare blared at them from all sides. It alternated with the news about President Madden.

"Our world is falling apart," said Asia Mae. "This just can't be happening."

A live video feed showed a 3-dimensional image of the Sun, a flashing circle pointing out to viewers the huge loop of electro-magnetic energy bursting out from its side. Suddenly, the image crackled and went dead. The first communications satellite must have already been taken out.

Asia Mae reached over and took Sumer's hand. They were both scared beyond belief. When the monorail reached the hospital, they hurried through the hospital doors. It was eerily quiet, the way it had been last night. They rode the lift to the trauma ward where Ceiba and Elton were. First, Asia Mae went into Ceiba's room. But the room was empty.

"They've moved him!" shouted Asia Mae, running over to the medical pod that had been freshly cleaned. "He's not here."

"Maybe they've moved him into a regular medical ward – one that's not trauma," said Sumer, holding tight to her backpack slung across her shoulders.

"Let's look in on your brother," said Asia Mae. She didn't like this feeling – as though something even more weird was about to happen.

They ran to Elton's room and just as Asia Mae expected, he was gone as well. The girls looked at each other, panic rising in both of them.

"C'mon, Asia Mae," said Sumer. "We've got to find out what's happened."

They ran to the information counter at the end of the hallway. Asia Mae asked the Persona Nurse at the desk, "Excuse me, ma'am, can you tell me where Ceibastian Ammos is?"

"And I need to know where Elton Madden is," said Sumer, edging in close to Asia Mae at the counter. "They were in rooms next to each other, in the trauma ward."

"Let me see," said the perfectly groomed Persona Nurse. This was a different nurse from Nurse Lorelai from last night. With short blazing red hair and brown-topaz eyes that sparkled, she had the same perfect, fake look of plastic and makeup like all the other Personas. She pulled up the opti-chart and a page of names appeared. "It appears that someone checked Mr. Ammos out earlier today."

"What about Elton?" asked Sumer. "Elton Madden?"

"Someone checked him out, as well. Now, can I be of further assistance?"

"Was it his father?" asked Asia Mae. "Did Mr. Ammos take Ceibastian home?" Her heart was beating so fast, she felt like she was having a panic attack. What was going on?

"I'm sorry, but I'm not supposed to say, really." She smiled at them and after a couple of moments, motioned for them to come closer. "But I guess it would be all right to tell you. It's nothing major. They were simply transferred to the military hospital."

"Why?" asked Sumer. "Why in the world would they be transferred to a military hospital? They're not in the military."

"Well, it says that they were removed as a precaution, for protection."

"Who are they being protected *from*?" asked Sumer. "They're not criminals."

"I don't know," said the Persona Nurse.

"Come on, Asia Mae, let's get out of here. I can hardly breathe."

"I'm sorry to have upset you," said the Persona Nurse. "I'm sure they're all right."

Sumer took Asia Mae's arm and pushed her out the front doors of the hospital. Sumer let go of her arm and stood outside

143

on the entryway for a moment, too overwhelmed to move. She leant her head against the wall of the building. Tears streamed down her cheeks.

"Sumer, are you all right?" asked Asia Mae, putting her arm around her. A cool breeze brushed through her hair and Asia Mae shivered slightly. She was still wearing the sweatshirt and jeans that Sumer had given her earlier that morning. To the rest of the world, she and Sumer were just two Retros trying to be different from the rest of the trendy bodysuit-wearing people of Acacia Burj.

"No," said Sumer. "I just know too much about what's going on, and I can't breathe. Asia Mae, my parents have been kidnapped by alien terrorists on the Moon, my boyfriend has been arrested by a corrupt military faction, and now, my brother has been taken to the military hospital, which could be a prison for all I know... And our planet is about to be hit by a huge solar flare."

"Well, the solar flare could miss us – we've had warnings like this before and nothing happened. Maybe Ceiba and your brother really were moved for their protection," said Asia Mae. "There has to be a way to find out what's going on." She wanted to crumble too, because she was very, very afraid. She realised that if her new *tough* friend, Sumer, was this upset, then something was very wrong with the world. Asia Mae still didn't have any idea where Luca was. He might have been arrested for all she knew, or worse. He might have been beaten up on the docks and left for dead. She shivered again. She couldn't think about that. He had to be alive, somewhere.

Luca, where are you? I need you!

"C'mon," said Asia Mae.

"Where?" said Sumer. For once, Sumer seemed speechless and didn't know what to do.

"First, let's go to Luca's house and talk to his mother. We'll get to the bottom of this."

"Okay," said Sumer, "and then I'll tell you more about what I know."

"There's more?" asked Asia Mae.

"Oh yes," Sumer said. "Much more."

Chapter Twenty-Seven

Sumer and Asia Mae had decided to cut back to Sumer's estate in Amaryllis and pick up her ultra modern *Bullet,* a sleek super-bike designed for flight racing, although she never used it for that. It had come in handy a few times when she met Phaeton at the docks.

"That's amazing," said Asia Mae when Sumer opened their garage and rolled out the Bullet. "Is it safe?"

"It's fast and we need speed right now," said Sumer. "Plus, if power is turned off to the city, we can still get around."

She handed Asia Mae a full-face headset and then they climbed on top of the *Bullet.* Asia Mae held onto Sumer's waist as they raced through the streets, which wound up in concentric circles several levels to Luca's apartment building. As the bike picked up speed, it lifted off from the ground and soon they were flying high over the road. Asia Mae's stomach lurched and she squeezed even tighter onto Sumer, feeling her new friend's body shake with laughter. Monorails glided beneath them on invisible tracks and private space pods cluttered the air as people began to find their way home to see loved ones. Sumer expertly wove between them, soaring over Acacia Burj.

The news blasted from the giant opti-screens across the buildings:

UPDATE! BREAKING NEWS!
Citizens of Acacia Burj are urged to stay CALM!
Take precautions and seek undersea and underground shelter!
Solar flare to hit Acacia Burj in 10 hours! Details on the hour!
This is not a drill... This is not a drill!
Stay tuned to Breaking News First in Acacia Burj!

Asia Mae needed to know Luca was safe and they were hoping his mum and sister could tell her something about his whereabouts. Sumer was scared stiff, and furious at the world. She hated to admit it, but for the first time in a long time, she was confused. It was one thing fighting people and stupid ideologies, but it was another to try to fight a natural disaster like a major solar flare. Earth was vulnerable.

Sumer and Asia Mae stopped on the landing pad on the rooftop of Luca's apartment building. It was all glass and very artistic, but a little too cold in its sleekness for Sumer. *Goddamn aliens*, she thought to herself. She had done some snooping of her own in her father's private office at home and gathered as much information as possible for Phaeton. It was nothing concrete, but information was power and as long as Phaeton had information out in the Wilds, he had a better chance of survival. However, now that he had been arrested, that information wasn't doing him much good. Sumer didn't know what the aliens planned to do with her parents and that upset her. And now, she had to deal with a ball of solar energy hurling through space towards Earth.

She and Asia Mae went to Luca's apartment and knocked on the door. There was no answer. "Keep trying to contact him," said Sumer. "He has to be around somewhere."

Asia Mae nodded, but her lower lip wavered. Sumer knew she was afraid that something had happened to Luca. Sumer didn't want to say it, much less think it, but she knew Luca could be dead. She watched as Asia Mae continued pressing her sensorpad, trying to contact Luca. Her new friend had to be one of the coolest girls Sumer had ever met, courageous, too, and although she was still only a second level student, she showed remarkable maturity and finesse in the way she handled herself. Wearing Sumer's antique clothes, Asia Mae almost looked Retro herself.

"Come on," said Sumer. "We can't hang around forever. We need to find a place of shelter before the solar flare hits."

"Where can we go?" asked Asia Mae. "From what the news said, we should all get underground or undersea and I don't know anyone who has an undersea home, do you?"

"Yes," said Sumer. "My family has one and I can take us there. We just need to get to the docks, where I can get our private shuttle."

"You have a house undersea *and* a shuttle?" asked Asia Mae.

"My father's the president, remember?"

Chapter Twenty-Eight

"Can you walk?" asked Luca as Tanner struggled to get up from his makeshift bed.

"Uh-huh, I think so. Where's everybody else?" asked Tanner. "The rest of the crew?"

"They were in the lounge part of the ship a couple of floors down the last time we scanned," said Phaeton.

"We need to gather the rest of the crew and assess the damage to the ship. It wasn't a smooth landing," said Luca. He was worried that his inept attempt at landing and the firing from the alien ships had caused irreparable harm to the ship. A Stealth Lazer Pathfinder was very valuable – very expensive – and the authorities might put him in jail for trying to pilot such an elite military machine.

"I'm just impressed that you managed to get us home," said Tanner. He smiled at Luca.

"Hey, it was on automatic pilot, remember?"

"Still..." said Tanner.

"Don't let him mislead you," said Phaeton, ruffling Luca's hair. "The kid has talent."

"At least you weren't hurt," said Tanner. He started walking around the room, trying to flex his wounded leg. It was stiff and painful.

"I think we need to get off this ship and see what's going on at the base," said Phaeton. "I haven't seen a sign of life on the monitors. We need to do some investigating and find some medics if anyone's here to tend to the injured."

"We aren't allowed to go into the base," said Tanner. "We were told that only the officers would disembark and pick up some mining materials. The rest of us are supposed to stay on board."

"I think it's safe to say those orders are void," said Phaeton. "We've got dead crew members, we can't get in touch with anyone at Earth Acacia Central, and there doesn't seem to be anyone here at the mining base."

"You have a point," said Tanner, rubbing the back of his neck. The wound on his shoulder looked like it was healing nicely, but his leg was still in bad shape. Blood oozed through the pack that Luca and Phaeton had wrapped around the leg.

Luca looked at the control screens. He felt uneasy about switching off the engines and getting off the ship, but what an opportunity. He had to agree with Phaeton. Security cameras were positioned in all the hallways on the *Sibylline*, and suddenly, Luca saw movement.

"Look!" Luca said. "The rest of the crew are coming out of hiding!"

Luca and his friends watched as Lieutenant Commander Dillon and Sergeant Santiago carefully made their way down the hall, and then proceeded up the stairs with their fellow crew.

"I imagine they'll head here," said Tanner. "Like we did."

"If they're smart, they'll get their asses in here fast," said Phaeton.

In a matter of minutes, the door slid open and Dillon looked around, surprised to see Phaeton, Tanner and Luca standing there. From her viewpoint, she saw a very unqualified group piloting the *Sibylline*. There was one military trainee who was beaten up quite badly, a Retro guy with a ponytail wearing a non-authorised military trainee uniform, and a young stowaway lad in a body gaming suit. Out of the three of them, two were supposed to be in lockup. She'd have to deal with that infraction later, but right now, she needed to take control of the ship.

"What's going on here?" she asked. "Where's the Captain? And what about First Officer Marco?"

"They're dead, ma'am," said Tanner, leaning against the control screen.

Tanner quickly briefed Dillon on all that had transpired – the death of the Captain and Merrimac – and how Luca had saved all of them by piloting the ship by intersecting his consciousness with Dr Tycho's Persona.

"Impressive," said Dillon, glancing at Luca. Dillon's military uniform was ripped at the shoulder. Her headset-hood lay in shreds around her neck thanks to several skirmishes with the enemy herself.

Luca, Phaeton and Tanner described the two enemy soldiers on board, their invisibility capabilities, and the fighting in the hallway.

"I'm sorry about the Captain. He was a good man," said Dillon, with a stoic, emotionless look on her childish face. She pursed her lips tightly before continuing to speak. "What about you, Elliott? I see you've been wounded."

"Yes, Lieutenant," said Tanner. "One of those enemy soldiers almost took me out, but Phaeton... um... Trainee Wilding here, saved me."

"*Trainee Wilding?*" asked Dillon, looking quizzically at Phaeton. "He's supposed to be in lockup. Last I remember he was a Retro, an outcast, and a prisoner."

"I shouldn't have been locked up and–" said Phaeton, puffing up his chest in defiance.

"Ma'am, he saved my life," said Tanner, interrupting Phaeton. "He's been a great asset through this ordeal and he's been helping us."

"Two more crew died in the lounge, including First Officer Marco," said Santiago, who was standing next to Dillon. He shook his head. "Their wounds were too severe." He had been rather quiet until now. Despite all his years of being in the military, Dillon imagined he had probably never encountered anything like this.

"First Officer Marco is dead?" asked Tanner shakily.

"Yeah, so it's only us left," said Santiago, wiping his brow. "I'm sorry." Dillon noted that his blue eyes, which had looked so warm and cheerful before, were now dulled with battle fatigue. "First Officer Marco was a good man and a good friend, and the Captain and First Officer Merrimac behaved commendably. Where are the bodies? We will need to arrange a memorial service for them and the others when we get back to Acacia."

"Merrimac's body is in the kitchen and the Captain's was in the hallway on the level below us, ma'am," said Phaeton. Both he and Tanner lowered their eyes. Perhaps they were ashamed to leave his body, thinking it disrespectful. "We had to leave it there to escape the other soldier."

"Have you been able to contact anyone here at Mariana?" asked Dillon.

"Our comms were taken out, Commander," said Luca. "And there's some damage to the ship. We haven't seen anyone here at Mariana on the monitors. Looks like they've cleared out."

"Even though our crew is small, we should be able to get the comms repaired," said Dillon.

"We were followed into the ocean by a ship like the one on the Moon," said Tanner, cautiously.

Dillon nodded sternly and strode straight to the control screens to view their surroundings. She paused and looked around the room at the rest of her crew. She felt slightly dizzy. Perhaps it was shock.

With her hands on her hips, she said: "We don't have time to discuss the enemy soldiers and their ships right now. Let's just hope they don't find us. Santiago and I will go and get the supplies and documents we were scheduled to get at Mariana and the rest of you can wait here where you'll be safer. Shouldn't take us long. Then, we'll head back to Earth Acacia Central and report to Admiral Maasaw."

"Yes, ma'am," everyone chorused.

"You think you can pilot the ship back to Acacia Central?" asked Dillon, looking at Luca.

"Yes, Commander," he answered. Dillon thought he looked queasy and she wondered whether he was really capable of what she was asking him to do.

"Good. Right now, we need to get the comms repaired. Plus,

we need to find that other enemy soldier," said Dillon. "He might be waiting for his comrades to show up before he comes out of hiding." She turned and gestured to Santiago. "Come with me."

When they left the Command Centre, Luca and his friends gathered around to watch the monitors.

"I still don't like this," Phaeton said. "We need to go out there and do some investigating on the base ourselves. I want to find out what's going on."

"Let's just hang tight," said Tanner. "We're lucky Dillon didn't throw all of us in lockup."

"That would have been idiotic," said Phaeton. "She needs us to get her back to Acacia."

"She only needs Luca," said Tanner. "We're dispensable."

"Like hell we are," said Phaeton. "If it hadn't been for us, those enemy soldiers might have killed the rest of the crew. She needs to be thanking us."

"Well, maybe the commander will remember this when we get back to Acacia," said Tanner.

"I agree," said Luca. "She can't put Phaeton back in jail after all this."

"Hopefully," said Tanner. "But look, we'll probably be in big trouble when we get back to Acacia. That's just the way it is. After all, Phaeton, you were a prisoner and Luca, you were a stowaway. Even though you managed to pilot the ship back to Earth, that doesn't mean there won't be repercussions for what you did. And the ship is damaged – that's very expensive for our military. Phaeton, well, they'll probably arrest you as soon as we get back to Acacia. Sorry, dude."

"I'd like to see them try," said Phaeton. "I'll make my getaway before that happens. Now, let's go and see what we can learn at the mining base. Luca, you stay here in case someone tries to get in contact with us."

"I'd like to investigate the base, too," said Luca. "Besides, you're hurt and not getting around so well. Why don't you stay here?"

"No, if we're gonna go, let us go first," said Tanner. "We'll check out the damage to the ship. You have a Neutraliser here in case the aliens breach the door, and you're our only real hope to pilot the ship. We need you in good shape."

Luca reluctantly agreed to stay behind. After Phaeton and

Tanner were gone, he'd wait a few minutes, then go exploring on his own. He'd come back in plenty of time before any of them returned. He didn't want to lose this opportunity to explore an actual undersea mining base no matter how dangerous it might be. This was the kind of thing he had dreamed of doing.

Luca waited and waited. Finally, he had to go exploring. Just as he prepared to leave the ship with his Neutraliser, his i5D comms signalled he had a message from Asia Mae. *Asia Mae!* Luca had been so absorbed in the *Sibylline* and everything that was happening, he had forgotten he could contact Asia Mae. He looked at his sensorpad and it connected the message to his i5D. He could see Asia Mae standing in front of him.

"Hey," said Luca, excitedly. "Asia Mae, are you there?"

The image was blurry and Luca wasn't sure, but he could swear she was wearing Retro clothes. What was that all about?

"Luca?" she said. "Is that you? Is it really you?" She had tears in her eyes.

"Yes, Asia Mae," he said. "I'm so happy to hear from you. Are you all right?"

"Yes, I'm fine," she said. "Ceiba and I are both fine. I've been worried sick about you. Where are you?"

"You'll never believe it," said Luca. "I'm on a Stealth Lazer Pathfinder."

"What?! she said. "Are you at sea? Or in space?"

"I'm at the Mariana undersea mining base," said Luca. "I have so much to tell you!"

"Luca, have you heard the news?"

"No, our comms are severed. I'm surprised my sensorpad is working!"

"President Madden and the First Lady have been kidnapped from the Galileo Moon Resort. It's all over the news here in Acacia," said Asia Mae. "It's so awful. I've got so much to tell you, too. And there's going to be a–"

The connection went dead.

"Asia Mae?" said Luca. "Are you there?"

There was no answer. No visual on his i5D, no buzzing from his sensorpad. Evidently, whatever was going on at Acacia Burj was interfering with communications. He shook and swiped at his sensorpad over and over again, trying to reconnect. *Damn it!*

Chapter Twenty-Nine

All over Acacia Burj, news optigrams were blaring on the sidewalks that they only had minutes left.

NEWS UPDATE!
WARNING! WARNING! WARNING!
Take cover NOW! Get undersea! Get underground!
Solar storm to hit in 10 minutes and counting...

Asia Mae was hanging on tightly as Sumer careered above the multi-tiered streets of Acacia Burj on the *Bullet*. They had little time to waste and had to get to the docks quickly, where the president's shuttle was hidden.

Asia Mae couldn't believe the turmoil in the city as they passed over swarms of people who were running and screaming. Parents were dragging their children along the streets, and there were outbreaks of violence between ordinary people. Personal space buggies were zooming through the air around them and the monorails were crowded with hoards of Civils trying to get as far away from the city centre as possible.

Finally, Asia Mae and Sumer reached the docks.

"Maybe we should just head out to the Wilds," said Asia Mae.

"We'll be safer undersea," said Sumer. "The solar flare might take out part of the Wilds, too."

People were beginning to crowd the outer docks, looking for old boats and canoes – anything to escape in. Security guards were trying to keep everyone away, shooting rounds of ammunition into the air as a warning but Civils were knocking them down and ploughing over them.

Landing near the docks, the girls slipped through narrow passageways to the president's private docking area. Wind and ice-cold rain whipped around the corners and the docks croaked and groaned under the pressure of the oncoming storms. The sky was illuminated with a green and red aurora.

"We don't have long before all hell breaks loose," said Sumer. "We have to get to the shuttle and get out of here. Undersea will be the safest place we can be."

Sirens were blaring across Acacia Burj. There was still no word about Sumer's parents and they still didn't know if they were alive or dead. The whole city was focused on the impending solar flare and had forgotten about President Madden.

Chapter Thirty

All alone in the *Sibylline's* Command Centre, Luca was worried. So, the President of Acacia and the First Lady had been on the Moon and had been kidnapped in that attack, he presumed. What did it mean for Acacia Burj's future and their world? *Obviously, it had to be those strange soldiers who kidnapped them, but why?* He recalled his father's message and realised that the pieces were beginning to fit into a giant puzzle. He just wasn't sure how he fitted into this puzzle, and all he could hope was that he could figure out what he was supposed to do.

Many things were worrying him, but the news that Asia Mae and Ceiba were safe had lifted his spirits, and he clung to the hope that things would be back to normal in Acacia when he got home. Although he was having the ride of a lifetime on the *Sibylline,* he had so much to share with his friends and he couldn't wait to hear about their experiences on the docks. He hadn't been gone from them that long in reality, but in many ways, it felt like years. So much had happened. Luca couldn't wait to see them. Especially Asia Mae.

After a few moments of watching blank monitors and not

being able to see anything happening outside the ship, Luca decided to disembark and investigate the Mariana base. He heaved the straps of his Neutraliser over his shoulders just in case he was confronted by that lone alien. For all Luca knew, he might have died from his injuries by now.

As he stepped out of the ship, it felt weird to be in a cave that was half undersea and half on land with a sensory shield that protected it from the ocean itself. *A marvel,* thought Luca. It was almost like being on a rocky planet somewhere in the galaxy. The high walls of the mining base were a mixture of quartz and andesite rock, which could have been left over from old volcanic sites. The most interesting part was that the walls were punctuated with rare crystals, along with marble and bright white lights that sparkled on the sides. It was truly beautiful, and Luca understood why a mining base had been set up here.

The wound on Luca's arm was healing nicely, and although it was still stiff and sore, it didn't slow him down as he hurriedly ran across the base to the main building. When he got inside, he realised the crew must have left in a hurry – the place had been abandoned. Half-filled cups and plates sat on tables in the kitchen. He heard Phaeton and Tanner in a room at the end of the hallway.

"Hey, you were supposed to stay on the *Sibylline*," called Tanner. He and Phaeton were leaning over a filing system that comprised both rare vintage manila folders and opti-files on a digital desk and viewing screen.

"And miss all the fun?" said Luca, smiling. "By the way, I was able to talk to Asia Mae for a couple of seconds."

"What a relief," said Tanner.

"Yeah, she and Ceiba are fine," said Luca. "I didn't get to talk to her for long before the comms died, but she said they were good and she seemed fine."

"I'm glad you got to talk to your friend," said Phaeton. "Any news from Acacia?"

"Well, the president and the First Lady were on the Moon when the aliens attacked. The news is reporting that they've been taken hostage."

"I knew this would happen someday," said Phaeton. He and Tanner exchanged a worried glance.

"Where's the lieutenant and everyone else?" asked Luca.

"They're in another building *allegedly* getting supplies or documents or something," said Phaeton. "Who the hell knows?"

"What's this?" asked Luca. Inside an open safe was an old fashioned manila file folder labelled *Classified.* He picked it up, flicking through the worn pages. It seemed to be a top-secret series of files, most pages referring to an underwater station called Sub-Biosphere 2.

"Whoa!" said Phaeton, looking over Luca's shoulder and grabbing a few pages. "Here's everything I've been hearing about in the Wilds. Don't you see, dude? This is proof of some top secret stuff."

"Maybe it's all legitimate," said Luca. "We have mining bases everywhere in the sea. This could just be another one."

"Look carefully, Luca," said Phaeton, pointing at the page in his hand. "Here – this Sub-Biosphere 2 is an elite research facility designed to observe different alien species from across the galaxy! It says it right there."

Luca started flipping through different opti-pages on the viewing screen, but he couldn't get the classified files to open. Suddenly, a thought came to him. *Perhaps my father's Key with its digital file could unlock this?* After all, his father seemed to know secrets and was trying to share them.

"No," said Phaeton. "We're not going to be able to access this file. But these old papers contain a lot of information. I wonder how old they are."

"Wait," said Luca. "Let me try something."

He held the ring, still wrapped around his finger, against the viewing screen.

"Verification for Delmar C. Mariner identified," a voice announced.

It worked! There was a click and secret files related to the Sub-Biosphere 2 filled the entire room.

"Most of this info is too technical for me to understand," said Tanner. "By the way, Luca, where did you get that thing?"

"I'll explain that later," Luca said. "We need to figure out what they're planning to do with this and how it affects us."

"Well, after those major asteroids hit Earth years and years ago, that's when they created the few mega cities that exist today," said Phaeton. "I think it scared global leaders enough to start developing and creating safe seed banks, to protect all life, past and present, from future disasters."

"So this could save our lives someday," said Luca. Had his father been trying to explain this facility to him? *Is that why his Key had opened these old secret files?*

"The question is, why are these files top secret?" said Phaeton.

"If they fell into the wrong hands, perhaps it would cause problems," said Luca. "The Opuls would try to buy it. I don't know. I'm just guessing here."

"Maybe this Sub-Biosphere 2 is being built for military purposes. Honestly, this is what I've been researching with my contacts in the Wilds."

"I think you're wrong," said Tanner. "I think, like you said, it's for the good of the planet, not just a select few."

Luca walked over to the paper file folder that lay on the desk. "Look, here's a map that tells us how to get there. It's quite a distance from here – deep in the middle of the ocean. I'm going to take it."

"You could get in trouble for that," said Tanner. "We shouldn't take anything from this place."

"We might need it," said Luca.

"Well, since our military tells us that we don't have any contact with alien groups, then I agree, Luca should take it. Thing is," said Phaeton, "our military has been communicating with alien groups for a long time, and I'm not just talking about one alien group – I'm talking about loads of them!"

"How do you know?" asked Luca.

"You don't know what you're talking about," said Tanner.

"I've learned a lot from gaming," said Phaeton. "I've intercepted quite a bit of their communication in those games. I'm not sure if they're aware that we can do that, but it happens. Besides, I've been working with people in the Wilds and we've been gathering information for a long time."

"What information?" asked Tanner.

"We can discuss it later," said Phaeton. "I agree with Luca that we need to take these secret plans and map so we can find it later. I have a feeling that the Sub-Biosphere 2 will answer a few of our questions."

"Hey," said Luca, in a moment of clarity. "I've just remembered something. I think I saw you the other night when my friends and I were at the Arcade. Did you leave on the monorail and go to the docks afterwards?"

"Yeah," said Phaeton, "A-ha, I remember seeing you, too! When I saw you get on the monorail, I wanted to approach you and ask if you had heard anything suspicious at the Arcade – if you had intercepted any communications – but was afraid I might alarm you. You had been playing in the A'Rmillari game, right?"

"Right," said Luca, nodding as he remembered. "Asia Mae said she overheard the A'Rmillari characters talking about a plot to take over the Earth, but we all thought it was just part of the game."

"Oh, they're clever," said Phaeton. "I'm not sure why or how we can intercept the frequencies, but we can sometimes. Everyone thinks they're just games, but some of what we hear in those games is real. These alien comms interfere with the programs and manifest in real time."

"Guys!" said Tanner. "Can you hear yourselves? You are both letting your imagination run away with you. This Sub-Biosphere 2 is probably a legitimate structure for our future. Nothing mysterious about that."

"The file says *Classified*," said Luca. "That means we're not supposed to know about it."

"I say we take all the documents we can and get the hell out of here," said Phaeton. "Maybe it's what the A'Rmillari are after."

Suddenly, the base shuddered and they heard the sound of explosions around the mine.

"Oh no!" said Phaeton. "C'mon, guys!"

"They've found us!" said Luca. "Those alien ships have found us!"

"If we don't get back to the *Sibylline*, we could all die here," said Phaeton as he darted out into the hallway of the administration building.

"I do *not* want to drown in this place," said Phaeton.

"Neither do I," said Luca. He saved the secret Sub-Biosphere 2 opti-files onto his Key and safely zipped the old paper folders of documents inside his bodysuit. There was another explosion and they could all feel a trembling under their feet. Luca ran with his friends out of the building and towards the *Sibylline* as fast as they could.

A blinding orange orb the size of a football torpedoed through the air, heading straight for the administration building.

Chapter Thirty-One

Phaeton shoved Luca out of the way as a giant steel girder crashed behind them, trapping his foot.

"Dammit, Luca, run! Get inside the ship now!" yelled Phaeton. "And prepare for takeoff! I'm right behind you!"

A swarm of ghostly Nanobes swirled around Mariana. Phaeton had noticed that when he was near them, his thought processes became muddled and he couldn't think straight. He vaguely recalled the A'Rmillari game. The Nanobes' purpose was to disorient, and perhaps even steal their thoughts. And they were controlled by their alien masters.

"Block your thoughts from those Nanobes!" shouted Phaeton to Luca and Tanner. "I think they can read our minds!"

Tanner and Luca nodded.

The two alien ships were tens of metres high. They had completely blocked the entrance to the mine. In rapid succession, the ships fired missiles and torpedo blasts from their prongs at the Mariana base. Round, fiery orbs hurtled through the air. A massive volley exited from the front prongs of the ships and smashed into a couple of the mining vehicles, exploding into deadly pieces on impact. Tanner, Luca and Phaeton shot desperately back with their orb-blasters, dodging the enemy's fire.

A siren rang out on the base and within minutes Dillon and Santiago were scrambling out of the administration buildings at the other side of the base.

Multiple projectiles hit the ground a couple of metres from Phaeton. He could feel the blazing heat from the fireballs as they whizzed past him. He finally managed to free his foot as Nanobe swarms floated in and out of sight around the ship.

A'Rmillari piled out of the two alien ships. Slashes of red and blue streaked across the mining base. The rock walls shuddered with the explosions and Phaeton worried that the sensory protection would be breached and they would all drown in the ocean. He had to get to the *Sibylline* as quickly as he could, but that wasn't going to be easy now.

"Phaeton?" a voice yelled at him through the din of explosions and screams.

Phaeton whipped his head around and was alarmed to see Scar – a renegade pirate he had met while in the Wilds. He was carrying one of the massive alien orb thrusters and running straight towards him. Scar had been born and raised in the Wilds and often acted like a feral wolf. Scar and his pirate friends believed that all of the Earth should be free and people should be able to live wherever they wanted – even in the protected mega cities. Scar and Phaeton had been friends until the moment he joined the renegade pirates. After that, Phaeton distanced himself from him, wanting no part in their thuggery and criminality.

"Bloody hell! What are you doing coming out of that alien ship?" asked Phaeton.

"Bloody hell, my ass!" said Scar, scowling through the scars that criss-crossed his face in deep jagged lines. His teeth were broken and crooked, and added to the deranged look of the wild man. "What are you doing fighting *with* the military? Thought you were against those bloodsuckers."

Phaeton ducked behind a boulder as an enemy soldier blasted an orb towards him. "Look, it's a long story. I'm just trying to save my butt here. I'm not *with* the military. What's *your* story?"

More pirates spilled out of the alien ships along with the aliens. Smoke and fire tumbled over the mining base. Phaeton could see it was going to be a massacre.

"We pirates figured we'd be more effective if we fought *with* the aliens *against* the military instead of trying to take them on by ourselves."

"What are you talking about?"

"Phaeton, we're working with the aliens, the A'Rmillari. Far superior beings to these scum military. You're either with us or you're not. I figured I'd give you the chance to join us. We used to be friends, and we used to look out for each other. But it looks like you might have turned traitor."

Phaeton realised in a flash that this was why the aliens had been delayed in reaching Mariana - they'd been waiting for the pirates to join them. The pirates were dressed in a mishmash of old military clothing and antique camouflage that could blend in with the green and brown foliage in the Wilds. Some had even pieced together bits of old glass and metal over their tattered clothes, tied with leather straps in an attempt to create make-shift armour.

"I have not turned traitor. Scar, you're out of your league here. Do you know what you're doing?"

Just as a blast hit the ground near him, Scar scurried behind the boulder next to Phaeton. "Yep, for the first time in my life, I know what I'm doing. The A'Rmillari are going to give us the money and supplies we need and we'll help them take down the military. Then, everyone will be free."

Phaeton studied the expression on Scar's face and realised that for him, this was a logical solution. Scar had never had anything. He could barely read or write, but he was good at hunting wild game and foraging. He knew how to survive. Now, he and the pirates were being promised everything. And in Scar's mind, this was the best way to survive in a world that was teetering on chaos.

"So, you gonna fight with us?" asked Scar, pointing his alien weapon at Phaeton. "I'm gonna give you one last chance."

Chapter Thirty-Two

A roaring blast shook the ground for the second time and black smoke coiled into ominous clouds within the mining base. Flames spiralled upwards through the smoke and licked across the rocky walls of the mine, creating a ring of fire around the *Sibylline*. There was no doubt. Mariana's rock walls were going to cave in, the ocean would flood the base, and the Pathfinder would explode.

Luca's ears ached from the noise and a sharp burning sliced through his nose and lungs from the fire, as he leapt across the ground towards the *Sibylline*. Enemy soldiers – and what looked like a ragtag army of humans – were pouring out of the alien ships behind him. *Humans fighting with the aliens? What next,* wondered Luca? He had learned from this short voyage that there was much about his world that he didn't know.

As he ran through the entrance of the *Sibylline*, the enemy hybrid soldier who had been hiding on the ship burst around the corner a few metres away. He ran towards Luca in his glass armour with a deep belly roar.

So, now you come out of hiding, you coward, thought Luca. He aimed at the head, focused, pulled the lever back and fired his

Neutraliser. Red orbs blitzed through the hallway and blasted the enemy. Immediately, the enemy soldier went down, lying in a hissing heap of fire and ash. Luca jumped over the pile and ran towards the Command Centre.

The alien ships had found them and weren't planning on Luca and the *Sibylline* escaping. Or, did they still want to kidnap Luca? He remembered what that soldier had said when they were fighting. And why were the personnel at the mining base gone? Had they been forewarned?

Luca didn't stop running until he reached the Command Centre. He had only a few moments to make it, and he knew the Sibylline could go up in flames. All through the ship, the alarm system was buzzing, announcing: *"Danger! Danger! Enemy ships attacking!"*

Luca approached the control screens. "Dr Tycho, come in! *Please!"*

The comms linking Luca to the outside world were dead. There was no Dr Tycho. Not even a sizzle of a sound. Not a glimmer of a Persona. Luca was going to have to pilot the ship by himself to Acacia. He didn't have time to panic and doubt himself. He had handled the descent into the ocean by himself, hadn't he? He could do this.

"Warning! Warning! Prepare for takeoff."

On the screens, Luca watched as Tanner helped Dillon board the *Sibylline.*

"Luca, you all right in here?" asked Tanner.

"Yes, I think so," Luca said. "I'm going to have to pilot this blind. We still don't have comms with the outer world."

"You can do it," said Tanner. "Remember, Phaeton and even Dr Tycho said the games were all designed to simulate the real thing."

"Phaeton isn't on board yet!" said Luca. "We can't leave him here."

"We don't have a choice," said Tanner, limping over to the weaponry screens.

Where was Phaeton? Come on, hurry, thought Luca! He didn't want to leave without him. Luca powered up the controls and commanded: "Charge Interceptors, attack enemy ships. *Now!"*

Their orb-crushers torpedoed the air and hit the enemy ships in front of the *Sibylline,* crippling them but by no means destroying them. Instead, the blasts only fed the circle of fire around the *Sibylline* and made it grow even larger.

Luca shouted, "Command Centre, can we extinguish the fires?"

"Fires cannot be contained. All systems prepare for lift off in 3 minutes and counting."

Two more crew members boarded the *Sibylline*, but Luca didn't see Phaeton anywhere.

From the mining base, there were openings that led to numerous other caves throughout the area. Luca wasn't sure, but he knew that those caves could fill with water at any point. Hesitant and scared, Luca froze for a moment. With the mining base compromised, he had to get the *Sibylline* out of the cave. Where was Phaeton? How could he leave anyone behind?

"If you're going to pilot this ship, then act like it and get us the hell out of here!" screamed Dillon as she fired into the foot soldiers. "That's an order!"

"Yes, Lieutenant," said Luca. He had been shocked back into action, but he trembled as he sat before the control screens and gave the instructions for takeoff. He positioned his hands on the manual controls. This was different from leaving the Moon because their destination had been pre-programmed. Luca had done this many times in a simulated environment at the Arcade, but never in real life. He wished Dr Tycho's Persona was with him. The *Sibylline* was a large ship and it wasn't going to be easy to manoeuvre with alien ships blocking its path and a ring of fire surrounding it.

While Sergeant Santiago and Lieutenant Commander Dillon monitored the instrumentation on the control screens, Luca went through every basic manoeuvre he could remember from gaming.

The craft shook and rocked. Wrenching on the manual controls, and swerving and careening to avoid the aliens and the fire, Luca had to find another way out of Mariana. The two alien ships blocked the main cave entrance and there was no way he could go out the same way he came in.

The aliens fired at the *Sibylline* as it ascended. Try as he might, he couldn't seem to shake their fire. Luca took several hits, but managed to dodge multiple attacks while navigating upwards and away from the opening at high speed.

"Remember, when piloting a ship, the first thing you do is focus," his

father had told him when he was a boy. "*Block out all other sounds. Listen to your own voice and no one else's. Follow your instincts.*"

Luca saw an opening at the back of the cave where water was pouring in. He wasn't sure it was big enough, but it was his only hope of escape before the ship would be obliterated.

"Hold on! This is going to be tight," he called out.

Luca had to hurry. Sparks and smoke flew everywhere. All the explosions were causing the cave walls to collapse. Rocks and debris pummelled the Pathfinder. They had to get out of there, and fast! Luca fought the controls to maintain the *Sibylline's* trajectory.

"*Calm your mind. Focus,*" said his father's voice from far away.

"It's not going to fit!" screamed Dillon. "We're going to crash!"

"We'll fit," said Luca as calmly as possible. He maintained full power as he aimed for the narrow cave opening. It was several metres wide, and jetting water straight at them.

As if intersecting his father's consciousness, and connecting to the memory of all that his father had taught him, Luca suddenly remembered a network of caves that his father had drawn for him and made into opti-puzzle pieces. They had played this game many nights when he was a small child. Luca suddenly thought the cave opening might lead to an expansive cave network that would take them to freedom. He wasn't sure how he knew, but he felt confident he was right.

"Come on," said Tanner. "You can do this, Luca."

They held their breaths. If Luca had miscalculated the ship's size in proportion to the opening, then the *Sibylline* would crash. No one would survive.

While tilting the *Sibylline* to match the narrow opening of the cave, Luca flew the ship through the gap, barely fitting. It was so close, it made the hair on Luca's neck stand up and his heart went into overdrive. Luca honestly had no idea where this skill had come from. But he didn't have time to think about it now.

Everyone shouted and Tanner slapped him on the back. "Way to go, Luca!"

Lieutenant Commander Dillon said, "Thank God! Now, take us back home, young man!" Even though she was being stern, she had a grin on her face.

"I'm trying, Lieutenant," said Luca. "I'm doing my best."

"I think he's doing a great job," said Santiago, as he winked reassuringly. "Those were some gutsy moves."

"Thank you," Luca said. He was inwardly pleased, but he knew they were still in danger. If the cavern walls caved in on those alien ships, then it could cause massive explosions throughout the ocean. And he was still flying through unknown cave systems.

Luca stilled his mind and focused all the ship's power to the engine thrusters to get them away from the Mariana Mining Base and those aliens. He thought he could hear his father's voice from long ago when he used to tell him about piloting a Path-finder. *Just follow the blue lights on the cave walls. They will take you to freedom.*

Chapter Thirty-Three

For a few heartbeats, Phaeton stared at Scar, his old friend from the Wilds, his muscles numb, his mind fervently scattering through various scenarios about how this could play out. He had no doubt that Scar would kill him if he didn't go along and pretend to be on his side. Besides, the *Sibylline* was gone.

"Look, I don't like the military either," said Phaeton. "I was arrested and they forced me to fight with them. I'm with you, Scar."

"Glad to hear that, old friend! Let's get out of here and I'll take you back to the ship," said Scar. "Our leader will want to meet you."

"Are you sure they won't kill me?" asked Phaeton. After all, he was wearing a military trainee uniform.

"Nope, I'll vouch for you," said Scar, taking his arm. "Besides, they have these procedures they do on all their allies."

"Procedures?" asked Phaeton, alarm bells ringing in his brain.

"Nothing major," said Scar. "It doesn't hurt. Just helps all of us fight together."

Phaeton wanted to get out of there.

"Come on, don't be a girl," said Scar. "I came out of it okay and you will, too. Now, come on, if you're serious, or else I'll hafta shoot you, Phaeton. That's all there is to it. It's our law now."

"Okay, let's go." *No! No! No!* Phaeton was hoping there would be a way to escape from Scar and get back to the *Sibylline*, but it was impossible now. As they ran towards the alien ships, the air was shattered with screams, water jets, rocks crashing into the sea, smoke and fire all around them. There were swarms of Nanobes interweaving through the mine. Broken bodies lay bloodied and in piles of ashes on the ground of the Mariana base.

Phaeton looked around frantically for someone to help him, but he was alone. Scar kept Phaeton close to his side so that he had no choice but to go along.

Inside the alien ship, a soldier stopped Scar at the entrance, but Scar told him that Phaeton was there to fight with them. The soldier made him leave his weapon with him, growled and waved them past.

Phaeton's heart raced. His legs wobbled as they walked. *This is it.* He felt naked without his Neutraliser now. He was sure the aliens were planning to kill all the pirates when the fighting was over and would kill him along with the rest of them. He had never been so scared in his life. The mayhem from outside was muted and all Phaeton could hear was his breathing and footsteps. And the pounding of his heart.

"Are you sure we can trust them?" Phaeton asked Scar, still curious about why his friend would side with aliens.

"Absolutely. They want us to be free. This is summin' all of us have been dreamin' about in the Wilds. You'll see."

It was clear Scar had drunk whatever magic potion they were feeding him.

The interior of the alien ship was constructed out of an organic substance. The walls looked as if they were moving. And they were. Tiny, living, breathing nanobots that were an integral part of the ship. They could adapt any environment into the A'Rmillari's native atmosphere. With its cold interior and its living, breathing environment, there was nothing warm about this ship.

Scar led him into an inner control centre where there were three A'Rmillari, standing and looking at monitors. Maps of the galaxy swirled on panels in the chamber, revealing a network of stars Phaeton had never seen – not even on a game in the Arcade. And there were maps of Earth's undersea environment.

Most of the A'Rmillari soldiers were dressed in black mesh bodysuits with silver cords of organic, stretchy fibres coursing across the arms and legs. These three weren't wearing any kind of headset, exposing shiny grey heads. They had human-like features, but their skin shone a lustrous white-silver with raised white lines that swirled over their faces, hands and bare heads like a network of arteries. One was obviously female because she had breasts underneath her black armour suit and wide yellow catlike eyes. The men looked similar, but their features were more masculine and hard-edged, like they had been drawn with a thick black pencil.

"Did you bring us a prisoner?" the female A'Rmillari said in perfect English, but with an odd, robotic accent.

"Not really, Pihaa," said Scar. He turned to Phaeton and out of the corner of his mouth, said: "She's the Captain."

Then, Scar turned back to Pihaa and said, "He has joined us to fight against Earth's military. I was friends with him in the Wilds. He's on our side now."

Pihaa walked over to Phaeton and took her long silver finger and traced her razor-sharp nail along his face and down his throat. Phaeton held his breath. He knew if he moved one muscle, she would slice his throat. The two male A'Rmillari watched with apparent amusement. Phaeton knew that they probably thought of Earthlings as scum.

"We do not think of you as scum," said Pihaa, withdrawing her hand from his face.

They could read his mind!

"I... I..." Phaeton stammered. *He reminded himself to block his thoughts.*

"We think of you as children," said Pihaa. "A helpless race. But not scum. Some of you are useful, as your pirates are proving to us."

She nodded towards Scar, who beamed with pride. *Clearly, he has been fed a lot of crap,* thought Phaeton.

"You want to help us?" said Pihaa.

"Yes," said Phaeton.

"Scar, take your fellow comrade to the programming chamber to be scanned and refitted for combat."

"What does that mean?" asked Phaeton.

"We must scan your body – your mind – to make sure you have not been programmed by Earth's military to infiltrate our systems. It is difficult to differentiate between Earth's AIs, the Personas, the Bions, the Clones, so we scan your bodies to make sure you're clean. Then, we can imprint our agenda onto your mind and use you in our fighting the way we have with the pirates."

"What about my memories?" asked Phaeton. He didn't want to forget his feelings for Sumer. Or his friends. His parents had died a long time ago, and he didn't want to forget them either. Really, all he had were his memories.

"You will keep your memories," said Pihaa. "But if there are any implants or warfare in you that could harm us, we will know and they will be erased."

Scar took Phaeton by the arm and said, "Come on, follow me. It doesn't hurt."

"Wait," said Phaeton, trying to stall for time. "Who are you people?"

"Well, our Overlord would say that we're specialist soldiers – models, if you will, from him. A particle – a cell – from the Overlord. Though we've been created to carry out his mission in life, we still have individual thought and can enact our free will as long as it's for the good of The One, our Overlord. If not, we're in danger of being eliminated. It's as simple as that."

"I don't really understand..." said Phaeton.

"You don't need to," said Pihaa. "And I wouldn't be telling you this if you weren't joining us, but since you are, you too will now receive direct orders from our Overlord, and will be privy to some of his thinking and commands."

"And those Nanobes?" asked Phaeton.

"Ah, nothing more than energy nanobots enslaved to help us achieve our mission. We can crush a human's brain if we can intersect with the human's mind. That's all." Pihaa licked her lips as though she was enjoying the thought. "You'll understand more when your mind is merged. Now, Scar, please escort our new recruit to the programming laboratory."

Phaeton couldn't breathe. He wanted to run. To scream. To

hide. Anything to prevent this scanning and imprinting which sounded more like a mind control procedure than anything else.

"What do they mean, that they serve The One?" asked Phaeton when they went out to the hallway. He was really trying to stall for time, trying to think of a way to escape.

"It's not that bad," said Scar. "You'll just receive orders from time to time from their master. The A'Rmillari used to be a big race of beings, but something happened on their planet, and now there's no one left and no way to sustain life. Everyone died. The Overlord and a few others escaped. So, this Overlord dude created printed clones of him as his army – some female, some male, as far as I know. His goal is to recreate life on his planet again using a small amount of Earth's water resources."

"You seem to know a lot about them," said Phaeton.

Scar tapped his head. "It's all info downloaded from the Overlord." He then smiled his goofy grin. Phaeton just shook his head. He was in an impossible situation.

There was a great explosion outside and Phaeton knew the aliens' ships had been hit. *Or were the rock walls at Mariana caving in?*

Attaboy, Luca, he thought. Then, he remembered he was being shot at, too, and no matter which side he was on, or what ship he was on, he wanted to live.

Pihaa turned towards her pilots and said: "Get us out of here and try to track the Earthling's ship. If they get away you will both be eliminated, understand?"

"We can't track them through rock," said one of the male pilots.

"We will try to find them once they emerge from the under-water cave system," said Pihaa. "His Key should be all we need to access that map and breach the barrier to Murias."

Chapter Thirty-Four

Safely beyond the Mariana base and sailing through the cave network, Luca followed the luminous blue lights that appeared like beacons from time to time in the caves. He felt as though he had connected with his father's consciousness in the same way he had with Dr Tycho's – he was hearing him speak to him from inside his mind – and it both delighted him and alarmed him because he wasn't sure how he was able to do it.

Luca directed the coordinates on the ship to take them back to Acacia. In the monitors, they could see explosions in the background, so it was a safe bet that the alien ships were being destroyed in the collapse of the Mariana Mining Base. Luca hated to admit it, but he was sure that Phaeton was dead. This was something he wasn't going to forget easily. In the short time he had known him, Luca had grown to like him very much. He admired him for his independent thinking and tenacity.

"I know what you're thinking," said Tanner.

"About Phaeton?" asked Luca. He felt so guilty.

"Yeah. But you can't think like that. You did the best you could and Phaeton knew the risks."

"I know. I just can't stand the thought of leaving anyone behind, the thought of them being killed."

Tanner put his hand on Luca's shoulder and said, "Phaeton would be proud of you."

"Tan... did you see Phaeton's body out there before you got to the *Sibylline?*"

"Honestly, Luca, the last time I saw him, one of those pirates who was fighting with the aliens had him cornered. Before I could get to him, there was a blast and the path was blocked. I'm sorry, but I don't know what happened to Phaeton after that."

"Who were those pirates?" asked Luca.

"I don't know," said Tanner. "Probably some of the savages from the Wilds. Not much more than animals themselves."

Luca nodded, but that didn't ease the guilt he felt about leaving his friend behind.

The *Sibylline* shot through the underwater cave system. It was dark and murky, but with the natural light emanating from phosphorous rocks, Luca definitely recognised some of the caverns from the opti-games and puzzles his father had given him as a child. Remembering the intricate digital games, Luca steered the ship safely through the dangerous caverns. In the background, he could hear explosions continuing from the collapse of the Mariana Mining Base.

The command centre announced, "*Warning: The Sibylline is losing energy. Set coordinates to recharge.*"

Luca looked up from the controls and, not wanting Dillon to hear, he quietly said to Tanner, "I have to recharge the energy cells. Our last thrust out of the cave depleted normal reserves and we're going to lose power fast."

"Can you do it?" asked Tanner.

"I think so," said Luca. "It just requires powering down and voice-activating the controls. I *think...*"

"Men, I'll be back in a moment," said Dillon. "I think we're out of danger for now and I need to rest."

"Sure," said Tanner. "We can message you if needed."

Luca didn't want to alarm her, but he wasn't so sure they were out of danger. The ship was still damaged and unstable.

Tanner sat down by Luca and smiled reassuringly. "Really, Luca, you've been very impressive. This is going to get you into a Military Training Academy, I can promise you that."

"We're not exactly safe yet," said Luca. "But thanks for your vote of confidence."

"I trust you," said Tanner. "You're a good man." He leaned back in the chair and watched the scenery on the control screens. Luca noted that Tanner said 'man'. That was the first time he had ever done that.

As the *Sibylline* powered down to recharge its energy cells, they floated through the caverns. Lights on the ship's exterior shone on columns and curtains of calcites all around them, along with a hanging forest of stalactites, both coloured and translucent.

"Wow!" said Tanner. "Look at that! Have we hit the jackpot or what?" He pointed onscreen to walls in the caverns that teemed with life, including bright red bryozoans, smooth, grey sponges and bushy, stinging hydroids. It was spectacular.

"I know," said Luca. "It looks just like the game *AtlantWorld* at the Arcade." Luca had been deep sea diving in a simulated environment in the Arcade, in which similar images decorated the cave walls. He wondered what it would feel like to be out there in the water in fins and diving gear, but then realised he'd be crushed due to the pressure of the water at this depth. *Maybe someday,* he thought, *I'll be able to dive for real.* Currently, only the Opuls could afford the real thing. The rest of the Civils went to the Arcade to act out their dreams.

As the *Sibylline* ascended higher and higher, they exited the cave systems and finally felt safe. They found themselves in a huge sinkhole hundreds of metres below the seabed with a view to the surface. It seemed they had been undersea for a long, long time, and the relief was overwhelming.

All of a sudden, Luca felt a strange sensation – a pulling of the ship.

"What's that?" asked Tanner.

Luca and Tanner watched in horror on the monitors as the *Sibylline* was pulled into a whirling vortex. Like a giant bathtub drain, the vortex was sucking them into the blue hole and they were falling into a seemingly bottomless pit with nothing to stop them. There was no escape.

Chapter Thirty-Five

They could die. In fact, they surely would die. The little air that was left was stifling and oppressive. The reserves would not last. Luca noticed that Tanner was slumped over and already passed out. A chill ran down Luca's spine. *What was going to happen to them?*

Luca grabbed an oxygen mask and put it over Tanner's face, and then put one over his own. He looked over his shoulder and saw that Dillon and Santiago were wearing oxygen masks, but they had passed out. Dillon must have known what was happening. Luca swiped at the control screens to bring up optigrams of the exterior of the ship, but the link up had been severed.

They were drifting in a perfectly circular pool of inky darkness. As they drifted down, Luca's vision blurred. He saw an eerie, luminous green light from below the ship. The *Sibylline* groaned and creaked as it was pulled deeper and deeper into the notorious abyss. Luca squinted at the data on one of the monitors and noticed that the pressure going off the scale. He feared the ship would implode at any moment.

Then, the strangest thing happened. The luminescent green

hue grew in strength all around them. Luca was transfixed. *Was this a mirage? An illusion?*

On the screens, Luca saw an iridescent sea creature floating nearby. He couldn't believe his eyes. It was a human-like sea nymph, like a mermaid from old maritime legends. He honestly didn't know if what he was seeing was real or not. Was he dying? Her face was angelic and her long green hair flowed around her like silky threads of seaweed. Except for her hair, she glowed a neon bioluminescent blue like the colours he'd seen on the beach a few nights before, and her eyes were large and aquamarine with a luminous, almost transparent quality that appeared to be looking directly into Luca's soul. He could think of nothing else – his head, his heart, his body, his soul was filled with this beautiful creature.

Luca was mesmerised. He felt connected to her. He was light-headed and couldn't get enough air. He would pass out any moment like Tanner and the others.

And then, the sea nymph was standing before him *inside* the *Sibylline*. *How did this happen?* He must be dead, he thought. She was an angel. *Of course!* She touched his face, her fingers cool and soft. Gently, she blew air onto his face and it was fresh and reminded him of the sea... and he could smell something rich – plants, seaweed... the headiest of perfumes. A blinding light shot out from her hands and she swirled the light around him. Suddenly, he could breathe again. He gulped in the delicious air.

Luca heard her say, "My name is Serenissima. Do not be afraid, Luca. Trust in yourself. We are connected and I am here to help you."

From far off, he heard music - harps and flutes, a heavenly sound. *Was this what death felt like?* Maybe he had already died. Maybe this was heaven. For what felt like an eternity, he thought that the ship was floating in zero gravity and his own thoughts were buoyant and light.

The sea nymph disappeared in a blinding light and Luca snapped out of his trance. The ship's pipes gave way under the extreme pressure and finally buckled against the force of the pressure. The frame of the ship started to collapse.

All of a sudden, the *Sibylline* rocketed to the surface. Luca lost consciousness and slumped over like the rest of his fellow crew.

The last thing he remembered was the face of Serenissima and the haunting music coming from somewhere in the depths of the sea.

Chapter Thirty-Six

Shapes and footsteps materialised from the dark alleys. The sky overhead was streaked with fireballs. A blitz of orange lightning burst like fireworks in the air and what looked like three mercenaries, carrying Neutralisers, headed towards her. Gangs of fearless oversized AI like this were roaming the streets, looting what little of the city that was left. Skye Mariner sank back and tried to disappear into the wall of her apartment building. She had been looking for Luca when the unthinkable had happened. A major solar flare had hit just as predicted, and now there were residual storms showering down communications satellites. They had been knocked out of orbit and were plummeting back to Earth. She hoped that her son, Luca, was safe out there somewhere.

"I think I saw something up there," she heard one of the mercenaries tell the other in clipped, inhuman tones. "No one is supposed to be on the streets."

"We have orders to shoot," called the second mercenary.

"Shoot to kill?" a third one asked the rest of the team.

"Orders are orders and with all the comms down and the Civils disconnected, the humans are confused and disoriented. They're starting to attack each other."

"There is still a lot of residual fallout," agreed the first mercenary. "The debris from the satellite has been almost as bad as the initial solar flare. I think most of the Civils have packed up and headed out to the Wilds, anyway," it said. "Or gone undersea."

"Or died."

Images flashed in Skye's head. *Fires. Acacia military patrolling the streets. Children screaming. Adults screaming. People robbing and shooting their own neighbours. Buildings imploding. Burning. Crystal and glass windows shattering into smithereens.* She squeezed her eyes shut, trying to get the images out of her mind. Skye had to get back to where her daughter, Gaia, was waiting for her. They had survived the solar flare, but she wasn't sure they were going to survive the hysteria and aftershock.

Just then, all around her the air was pierced with a screeching siren. A drone passed overhead, sweeping its lights over the ground, alerting everybody to the enforced curfew.

Emergency curfew in force! Stay indoors until further notice!

Skye pressed back even further into the outer wall of her building. Then, there was screaming. A group of Civils ran down the street not far from her and the mercenaries turned and lumbered after them. Skye tried to decide if she should go and help the Civils. There were three robots, though, and only one of her. They'd take her down before she could identify herself. The mercenaries opened fire on the Civils, never even giving them a chance to explain why they were in the streets.

Skye's heart dropped. The world had gone mad. She needed to run three more streets to get back. She wished that she was still connected and could wear one of those flying mimicry suits. She tightened the straps of her backpack around her waist, kept her Neutraliser at the ready, and began to run in long strides. Two steps, three steps. Almost past one block. *I'll make it*, she told herself.

She tripped at the corner of a building and stumbled, falling down on the sidewalk and dropping her Neutraliser. As she grappled for the weapon, a huge foot stomped on her hand. She screamed, not seeing what it was. As she struggled to stand up, a cold metal hand wrapped completely around her neck and she choked.

"Stop," a robotic voice said.

Skye shoved her elbow back into the mercenary's stomach armour, but it didn't even flinch.

"Don't move," it said. "Or I'll hurt you."

"Look, I work for the military," said Skye. "Let me go."

"I don't care who you work for," the voice said. "You're not supposed to be on the street. We have orders to shoot anyone. And that means you."

"Please," said Skye. She couldn't get a look at its face. The mercenary had her pinned in front of it. Then, from her peripheral vision, Skye saw a young woman standing in the shadows of the alleyway. A shot from a Neutraliser rang out and the hand around her neck went slack as the AI crumpled to the ground. Gaia came running towards her mother.

"Mum, are you all right?"

"Oh, Gaia, what are you doing out here?"

"I came to find you. You were taking too long."

Another drone flew overhead. Skye and Gaia darted into the shadows to hide. "Mum!" said Gaia in a loud whisper.

Skye brought her fingers to her lips. Footsteps ran past them on the street. More mercenaries. Skye waited for a few minutes until the drone had moved on. She then grabbed Gaia by the hand.

"C'mon on!"

They ran as fast as their legs would carry them, sticking close to the burned out buildings, where they could duck into alleyways if needed. Skye was filled with fear, but also determination.

Finally, they reached the Interplanetary Scientific Research Organisation building. Skye led Gaia to the back where the security door was. Her hands shook as she took out her key. The sensorpad had stopped working after the storms, but, fortunately, someone had installed an old-fashioned key pad on the door when it was first built – for emergencies such as these. She unlocked it, and she and Gaia hurried inside. Skye locked the door behind her and they ran upstairs to her lab where they barricaded themselves inside.

"We have to be ready to go when they come to help us out of here," said Skye.

"Are you sure they're coming for us?" asked Gaia.

"Vice President Vive assured me an escort would come to take us out of the city," said Skye. "I've known Vive for a long time," said Skye. "I trust him. Let's hurry, Gaia. We have to get the files downloaded to hard copies as fast as possible. There's still a lot to do."

"Help! Somebody, help me!" From somewhere outside the ISRO, the screams came again. "Somebody, please help me!"

Neutralisers blasted in the air. Skye couldn't risk going back out again. The emergency systems had blared sirens through-out the city for hours, warning everyone before the solar flare hit. No one had warned them about the rest of it. The city had erupted in flames after the first direct hit from a communica-tions satellite had pierced the sensory shield and sent flames, earth, and debris high into the air. Fire broke out everywhere and people were killed instantly or trapped in buildings that tee-tered on destruction. Some – mostly the Opuls – had escaped in ships undersea. Others were blockaded in the military hospital and jail, and some of Skye's co-workers barricaded themselves in the ISRO building. Hours before the solar flare hit, a few had escaped the city but people were afraid to go to the Moon.

The fact that Acacia Burj, even though much of it was rubble, was still standing at all was a tribute to the strength of the sen-sory shield that had been built years ago to protect them. But even this couldn't withstand the rage of the fireballs, the angry mobs, and a military trying desperately to maintain order.

The ISRO building, a sturdy reinforced concrete military compound, had mostly survived. Gaia had already found the bodies of two senior officers who had died when the left side of the building came crashing down. A continuous fire roared on one end of the compound, and Skye just hoped it didn't breach the wall that separated the sides of the building.

There was no mass media. No opti-news reports. Global com-munications had stopped. People were behaving like the Outcasts in the Wilds. Like animals. Skye Mariner could understand why.

"Mum, right before I came to find you, I was able to contact one of the commanding officers in the navy," said Gaia tentatively. "They found the *Sibylline* floating in the middle of the ocean."

"Thank heavens," said Skye, wringing her hands. "Was Luca on board?"

"He's in the military hospital," said Gaia. "And yes, he's fine. Do you think he'll be safe there?"

"I hope so; I think so."

Although she didn't tell her daughter, hearing that Luca had been found aboard the floating *Sibylline* brought back memories of when her husband's Pathfinder had been found floating on the sea. No one knew what had happened or why the entire crew had been killed. She had seen the bodies, but couldn't really identify Del. Even Sol, Del's father, had agreed with her. "S*kye, we have no proof that Del was in there. It could be anyone's decayed body after floating in water so long.*"

They had cremated the dead crew and she had tried to put it behind her. But she thought about him every single day. Things would be so much easier right now if he were with them.

It wasn't long after Del's funeral that Sol left Acacia Burj. He only explained that he needed to go in search of the truth. Little Luca had sobbed. It had been too much for him to bear at such a young age. First, he had lost his adored father and then he lost his beloved Grampa. Skye had heard nothing from Sol since.

Another scream came from outside. "Somebody please let me in!"

"Mum?" said Gaia. "Should we open the door and help them?"

"No," said Skye. "We can't trust anyone but ourselves."

Gaia and Skye wore the traditional dark formfitting bodysuits with sensorpads and emergency wiring that all research scientists wore. They were designed to withstand power outages, but only for a limited time. Skye deduced that they had about one or two days' power left at most. They both turned back to their work.

"Gaia, have you heard anything about Tanner?" Skye watched her daughter's face. Luca looked like Skye with his dark, dishevelled hair that never stayed in place and green eyes that shone like glistening blades of grass, but Gaia was the opposite. Her shoulder-length brown hair hardly moved. It was rigid, and matched the way Gaia carried the rest of her body – stiff, prim and statuesque.

"I'm not sure if they found him or not," said Gaia, as she retried the sensorpads on her wrist, smoothed down the front of her bodysuit and pulled up several research optigram sheets. "I was hoping we might find him when we went to the hospital to find Luca." Tears welled up in her eyes.

Time was of the essence. They had to try to save the scientific research and information they had accumulated before the generators died. Skye feared that their world was forever changed and didn't know what the future would look like.

"How Luca got himself on board the *Sibylline* as a stowaway has to be a great story," said Gaia, managing a half-smile, trying to normalise the situation.

"Luca has always been so dependable and trustworthy; I can't imagine how that happened. Knowing that Luca's safe in the military hospital takes one worry off my mind," said Skye.

"Mum, what about President Madden?" Gaia asked. "Without our satellites, we can't contact the terrorists on the Moon and we don't know what's happening. If he were here, maybe he could keep peace out there on the streets."

Skye wasn't sure how much she should tell her daughter. True, Gaia had been working with her for a year in research and was privy to many of the top secret military programmes, but the extent of the intergalactic secrets was expansive... and ancient.

"Times have quickly become precarious," said Skye. "Vice President Vive has been doing the best he can in the absence of President Madden."

Skye had a feeling that she was the only one of the ISRO staff who knew that the solar flare had been manipulated to attack Earth. She also had her suspicions that it was the A'Rmillari who had kidnapped President Madden and the First Lady on the Moon. She had been working with the intergalactic military to try to intercept recent alien communication. But they had been too late. Skye and her team never suspected they would attack so suddenly. She thought they had treaties in place to prevent this. She knew what they wanted, of course. They were coordinated by a dark alliance and they had plans to breach Earth's secret undersea facility. *But, what prompted the attack now?*

The solar flare had hit Acacia Burj just hours before, but it felt like it had been a lot longer ago. Skye had never seen such chaos and uproar. Civil unrest had already turned to anger with the threat of diminishing food and water supplies. Factions had started to form and terrified people had banded together to leave the cities and head out into the Wilds.

It was so sad. Many of the elegant glass buildings were now lying in rubble, the monorail systems had stopped and their world was totally exposed to an angry sky that offered dangerous lightning and fiery ash rain. The massive solar flare from the sun and ensuing satellite shower had ravaged Earth, destroyed their communications, and introduced everyone to an ongoing nightmare. The firing of Neutralisers and shouting continued in the streets.

"I hope Vice President Vive hurries," said Gaia.

"So do I," said Skye. "So do I."

What Skye didn't tell Gaia was that she knew of a place that was protected from all of this: a place that the A'Rmillari were trying to find so that they could take control of the planet. She and her fellow researchers had long ago learned of a dark alliance which was trying to gather Earth's water using an anti-gravity weapon that would allow the water to escape the planet's gravitational pull. They planned to collect it and sell it across the universe to the highest bidder. That was what they did; stripping planets of their resources and destroying them in the process. Nothing survived.

Yes, Skye knew of a secret place that had been built by a coalition of intergalactic governments that contained almost the entire DNA of all flora and fauna – species past and present – that had ever lived on Earth. A secret place that held the key to life, which was teeming with benevolent alien beings from all over the universe working together to stop the dark alliance's Overlords from taking control. A place called Sub-Biosphere 2.

Chapter Thirty-Seven

"*Wake up, Luca,*" *Serenissima's musical voice echoed.* "*You have much to do. Wake up, Luca.*"

Bright rays of light shone like a fusion of stardust. So bright, so blinding. Then, all of a sudden, there was a great clatter nearby and Luca's eyes jolted open. He had been dreaming. What were all those voices? Who were they? Where was he? What had happened?

The days had become a jumbled puzzle and Luca didn't know where he was or when it was. He had a splitting headache. Unsure of his surroundings, he looked around, confused and disoriented. He was lying in a medical pod that seemed to be floating in the air. Pulsating sensors were attached to his forehead and a bright hue emanated a soft hum all around him. After getting his bearings, and seeing personnel running by the doorway wearing uniforms, he realised he was in an extremely busy military hospital. There was a flurry of activity and noises outside in the foreground.

"Hello!" he shouted out. "Can anyone hear me?"

A nurse came running over to his pod.

"Can you tell me where I am?" Luca asked. Memories of falling through the blue hole came flooding back.

"Young man, you're lucky to be alive," she said. "It's about time you woke up. The Navy found your ship floating in the ocean and rescued everyone on board. You're in the military hospital." She checked the readings on the sensor on his forehead.

"Do you know where the others are?" asked Luca. His mouth felt dry and his throat, parched. "Did everyone else survive?"

"There were a couple who didn't make it, but the others are scattered throughout the hospital," she said.

"Is everything all right?" Luca asked. He noticed that the nurse was wearing a bloodstained bodysuit instead of the LED dress that medical personnel usually wore and her hair was straggly and unkempt like a stringy rope mop. Generally, hospital personnel were antiseptic-clean.

"I hate to be the one to tell you this," she said, looking at him with sad eyes.

"While you were on your ship, a massive solar flare hit Earth and knocked out all the satellite systems. The global communications network has crashed to Earth and Acacia Burj has taken a direct hit. There are military drones and soldiers patrolling the streets, trying to keep order but it's chaos."

"*What?*" asked Luca, pushing himself up with his hands. "I thought Acacia Burj was protected..."

"It has been until now," the nurse said, pushing her hair out of her eyes. "Civils and AI mercenaries are rioting out there, but I don't have time to talk about all this right now. I have my hands full. We're taking in some of the injured off the streets. Someone from the military should be along soon to tend to you and answer your questions, and we'll get you out of here as fast as we can. We need the pod."

The military hospital sat on the edge of the city near the docks. More like a military compound than a hospital, it had an emergency generator that provided electricity during extreme storms. The emergency generator would only last for so long.

Luca's head was swimming. The world of Acacia Burj had changed dramatically since he'd been away. Since the night he, Ceiba and Asia Mae went to the docks. He decided he had to get out of this hospital. If the military personnel came looking for him, they might put him in jail or worse. He had knowledge of the attack on the Moon and Mariana, and the military might not want him talking and might imprison him. After all, he had piloted the *Sibylline* when he wasn't qualified or authorised to do so.

He took the sensory attachments from his forehead and rolled out of the pod. He was stiff and sore all over and slightly dizzy. What had happened in the water? He couldn't exactly remember. Luca wore only a healing computerised gown, adorned with a row of lights and sensors across the shoulders. If the main grid of the communications systems were down, then the healing lights would soon stop working as well.

There was a side table with a pitcher of water. Luca quickly drank a glassful and then hurried over to the closet and found his bodysuit. He changed and put on his boots. He quickly checked his pockets to make sure that the paper files about Sub-Biosphere 2 were still there. They were. Luca knew that he had to hurry. If any military commander came in to see him, they would confiscate these files and he'd never know what was in them. Good thing they had been inside his bodysuit. Thank heavens that no one had thought to look there when he was rescued. He was sure the files would shed some light on the attack on the Moon and the mining base.

Glancing down at his hand, he was relieved to see that the ring was still wrapped around his finger. He hoped Asia Mae would be safe. But he was worried and couldn't be sure. If her parents were home, they would know what to do in a situation like this. Luca didn't know if they were still travelling or not. Acacia Burj was in ruins. *Where would everybody be?*

First, he decided, he had to find Tanner in the hospital. Luca also needed to listen to his father's message again. He knew he might not find a working computer in time but somehow, he would find a way to utilise emergency power, somewhere.

With his pockets filled with his most prized treasures, Luca quietly walked out of his room and into a crowd of people who were clamouring for medical attention. Luca was shocked. People wearing shredded clothes, with dirt and grime on their bodies and arms in slings. A few on crutches hobbled past him. They smelled of fire and the ocean. Most had a blank stare in their eyes as if they didn't know where they were.

A couple of metres away, Luca saw Lieutenant Commander Dillon wandering aimlessly through the hallway. She wore a hospital dress and had a glazed look in her eyes.

"Luca!" she said when he saw him come around the corner. "You're okay?"

"Um... hello, Lieutenant Commander. Yes, I'm fine."

"You did a fine job," said Dillon, which sounded so strange coming from this young, disoriented girl.

"I'm glad you're okay," said Luca. He didn't know what else to say.

"The world is off-balance right now," said Dillon. "I tried to warn my peers a long time ago that this would happen, but they didn't seem too concerned."

Luca nodded, trying to look sympathetic. Dillon started mumbling to herself about warning everyone and walked past Luca, wrapped up in her own world. He noticed there were military cops, who were carrying Neutralisers, patrolling the hallway. *Why would they have weapons in a hospital?* Luca avoided their eyes. As Luca hurried down the hall, someone called out to him.

"Luca! Luca! Is that you?"

He turned around and there, at the end of the hallway was a blonde curly-haired guy with his arm in a sling. *Ceiba!*

Chapter Thirty-Eight

Phaeton lay horizontally and nanobots moved underneath him like crawling ants. The room looked like more like a computer programming room than a medical pod. There were massive computer modules and panoramic screens. On one, the image of a human brain rotated in 360 degrees, and on another screen, a strange-looking organ rotated too. *Probably the A'Rmillari brain,* thought Phaeton. Then, on one wall, was a panoramic view of the galaxy. There were pulsating lasers, wiring and circuits that looked like the inside of a massive computer chip. Before the computer walls were long dark grey tables where nanobots writhed in unison.

He felt like a slab of meat ready to be butchered. They wouldn't let Scar stand near him, and now a shiny grey-headed A'Rmillari Programmer was poking long needles into his skull. With a wave of the Programmer's hand, a band of red laser-like lights flashed around Phaeton's head and started spinning. Phaeton watched something white like blood pumping through raised white lines on the A'Rmillari's hands. When the alien turned his head, Phaeton could see the same white blood veins coursing over his skull in a spiral. *He's just a 3D print,* Phaeton told himself. *Nothing more than a copy.*

The Programmer hadn't spoken one word. So far, Phaeton didn't feel anything weird in his mind. His heart thudded all the same. Any minute now, he would be implanted with a direct link to the Overlord and his thoughts would no longer be his. He'd be forced to do things he didn't want to do. Phaeton had practically begged Scar to let him escape from the alien ship, but Scar was loyal to the aliens.

"Scar, don't do this to me! Help me, please!"

"There's nothin' to it," Scar said. "You'll still be you. You'll just have these orders inside your head now. But trust me; you want to be fightin' with the aliens – not against them. And the women – good lord! You should see some of 'em. They're real pretty and they take a fancy to us human men."

"But they're printed copies! They're not real!" said Phaeton.

"Aw, don't look at it that way," said Scar. "A woman is a woman, if you get my drift and each one can think for itself. They're not exactly robots."

"Look, Scar," said Phaeton. "It's not too late for you and me to get out of here. Are you sure you can trust them?"

"They've been good to me and my boys," said Scar. "Gave us food and weapons when no one else would. Helped us build a community in the Wilds, and if you remember, it's not a bad place to live. We took care of your ass more than once. Why wouldn't I help them? And besides, you said you wanted to help us, right? Why are you scared all of a sudden?"

"It just feels a little strange to have my mind imprinted, that's all," said Phaeton.

"Have you seen their Nanobe swarms?" asked Phaeton. He thought maybe he could make Scar realise they weren't so great, after all. Plus, he wanted to learn as much as he could about these aliens. He wasn't sure how this knowledge could help him, but he knew one thing, he had to find a way to escape.

"Yeah, I know about 'em," said Scar. "Like Pihaa told you, they're used as tools. And, as far as I can tell, it's a mind control thing. These aliens are real smart. They can second guess everything before it happens!"

"Have fun! I'll be back when it's done!" Scar grinned a lopsided, jagged-toothy grin.

Idiot, thought Phaeton. And he was an idiot for ever following Scar onto this ship. He should have just taken his chances and made a run for it. Phaeton felt suffocated and more helpless than ever. The Programmer was too large for him to overpower. And he'd never make it past the guards at the entrance of the ship. It looked like his days of free, independent thinking were over.

Everything started shaking. A shockwave tore across the entire alien ship. The sudden force propelled the equipment onto the Programmer, crushing him on the floor. He sprawled out, motionless, white ooze dripping from his head.

Phaeton had to get out of there. The ship was being destroyed, but he felt paralysed on the nanobot table. Even though there were no visible straps, Phaeton couldn't move his arms or legs. How was this possible? There was nothing visible holding him down!

"Help!" he screamed. "Somebody, help!"

All around him, the ship was twisting and distorting, circuitry materials melting. It was as if it had been designed to dissolve if attacked. Bloodcurdling alien screams rang out through the ship. The live alien ship was disintegrating, and hopefully, along with it, the aliens.

Scar ran into the room and over to where Phaeton lay.

"Scar! Help me up! I can't move a muscle," said Phaeton, help-lessly.

"Phaeton, it's a mind trick! They've programmed you to think you can't move or leave. Just clear that from your mind and c'mon! The ship is going down!"

Phaeton tried his best to erase all thoughts of being tied down out of his mind. He concentrated and saw his fingers moving. Then, one by one, he was able to move his arms and legs. He stood upright.

"Thanks, Scar," said Phaeton. "I think the Programmer is dead."

"No problem. They can just print another one. We gotta get out of here," said Scar. "The whole ship is about to explode!"

Scar helped Phaeton off the table and they ran out of the room and down the hallway amidst others – pirates and aliens alike. Phaeton couldn't help but wonder if the programming had been completed. Would he now be controlled by the A'Rmillari Over-lord? Phaeton had no idea of knowing whether his mind would be his own from now on. But, right now, he had to get out of here. Everyone was running wildly in every direction. And then, the walls collapsed, folding in on themselves, trapping them inside. It looked like Phaeton and Scar were going to be obliterated along with the ship. Everything went as black as midnight on a cloudy night in the Wilds.

Chapter Thirty-Nine

"Ceiba! Oh my God! Is that you?"

Luca ran to him, pushing past the throngs of people, and threw his arms around his friend. He noticed Ceiba had bruises on his arms and neck and was wearing a hospital gown.

"Oh Ceiba, am I glad to see you!" said Luca. "Are you hurt? Asia Mae told me you were fine."

"I wasn't great. They had to repair some circuitry in my brain and nervous system," he said. "But this human part of me has to heal like regular folks." He smiled wryly.

"Oh, Ceiba!" said Luca. "You *are* regular folk! You're all human, you know!" He hugged his friend again. "What are you doing here, Ceiba? Did you get hurt in the solar storm?"

"I've been here the whole time," said Ceiba. "Since the docks. I think being here saved my life. This place is a fortress. But, what are *you* doing here, Luca? Where have you been?"

"I was on a Stealth Lazer Pathfinder. I was found in the sea with the rest of the crew."

"You *what?*"

"Long story, believe me! But I'm fine. Asia Mae didn't tell me you had been injured."

"You talked to Asia Mae?"

"Only briefly before the comms went down," said Luca. "Ceiba, do you know where she is?"

"I don't know." Ceiba looked from left to right, then back at Luca. "Can we go somewhere private and talk?"

"Sure," said Luca. "But I wanna get out of here. Do you feel up to going to my house?"

"Luca, I'm sorry to tell you this, but I'm not sure you have a house anymore," said Ceiba. "And I'm not sure if either one of us can leave this place. Let's find a private area in here somewhere."

"Ceiba, what's really happened to Acacia? The nurse said—"

"It's worse than you know," said Ceiba, looking at the people passing them in the hallway.

"What happened?"

Ceiba lowered his voice. "Luca, I was beaten up on the docks that night we all went out there after being at the Arcade. Really badly."

"I'm so sorry. Did Prince and those guys get you?"

Ceiba looked around, his eyes searching for *something* or *someone*, and then said: "I'm fine, and no, Prince didn't beat me up. Look, let's go find a place where no one will hear us. I'll tell you what happened."

They walked along the hallway and went out into the stairwell – the only place where people weren't milling about – and sat down on the steps. Luca couldn't help but notice that Ceiba was worried. His usual sunny blue eyes looked cloudy and hollow, and there were still scars on his face from the beating.

"Luca, something big is going on that we're not supposed to know about."

"I know," said Luca.

"When the gang were chasing us, I ran into an old warehouse when it started raining. Just to get out of the cold, you know?"

"I did the same thing." Luca nodded his head.

"I was looking for a place to hide and as I ran through some hallways, I stumbled upon a couple of AI mercenaries." He picked at the lights on his shirt, his fingers, trembling. "I just stood there. I couldn't move."

Luca put his hand on Ceiba's arm, and could feel the shaking in his body. "What happened next?"

"I don't remember exactly, but they spotted me. And that was it."

"Oh, Ceiba..."

"Next thing I knew, Luca, is that they fired something at me, and I flew across the floor. Every bone in my body ached. My head, my sides... I thought I was a goner. They left me for dead. Everything went black and the next thing I know, Asia Mae and my Dad found me. They took me to the hospital, and soon after that, I was transferred to this military medical centre – right before the solar flare hit."

"Oh, Ceiba!" said Luca. "I'm so sorry. I had no idea."

"Asia Mae probably didn't want to worry you," said Ceiba. His eyes were lined with worry and fear.

"We only had a minute to talk. There wasn't time to explain."

"Luca, were *you* hurt that night?"

"No, not that night... and I'm fine now. I think I almost suffocated in the sea on the *Sibylline*, though, but I'll tell you my story later. Do you think we're safe in here?"

"No, I don't. I was trying to find a way out when you found me in the hallway."

"I agree," said Luca. "We need to get out of this place."

"But most of Acacia has been destroyed."

"I *have* to find my family," said Luca. "And Asia Mae. And then we have to find somewhere safe."

"I'm not sure how much time we have," said Ceiba. "I've heard military personnel talking when they thought I was asleep."

"Well, Mum and Gaia should be all right since they work for the ISRO, but I'm not sure about Asia Mae or Tanner, Gaia's boyfriend. He was with me on the *Sibylline*."

The door to the stairwell opened. There stood Red Ammos, Ceiba's father. "Ceiba? Luca! Oh, my God, I'm so glad I found you! Are you boys okay?"

"Yes, Dad, are you and Mum okay?" asked Ceiba. "Did the storms destroy our home?"

"Everything's a mess," said Red. He walked into the stairwell and quietly closed the door behind him.

Ceiba threw his arms around his father. "Oh, Pops, I'm so glad you're here!"

"Well, our home is gone, Ceibastian, but your mum and I are safe."

Luca felt fear prickle inside his skin. "Mr. Ammos, do you

know about my mum and sister? Or about Asia Mae?" His eyebrows drew together.

Red shook his head and narrowed his eyes. "Not sure. Part of the ISRO building was destroyed and I haven't heard anything about your friend Asia Mae since I saw her in the hospital when I was there with Ceibastian."

"Dad, why did they move me here?"

"Ceibastian, I don't have time to go into that now. You boys have to get out of here." Red set his jaw, rigid. "I brought you a bodysuit, Ceiba. You need to change out of your medical wear and I want to adjust some of your micro-settings."

"But–" started Ceiba.

"No time to explain," said Red. "I want you to remember one thing: I know you're tough, but under no circumstances are you to reveal that you're part AI, okay?"

Ceiba nodded.

"It wouldn't be safe for you out there if anyone knew they could get circuitry and wiring from you. Now look, I've got a couple more guys waiting down at the end of the hallway. One is President Madden's son, Elton – his parents have been taken hostage on the Moon – and Tanner is waiting, too." Red nodded at Luca. "I've given them each a small backpack with a few supplies that will help you, and I smuggled a couple of small Neutralisers in your bags. Trust me; you boys have to get out of here. It's not safe for you."

"What about my family and Asia Mae?" asked Luca.

"I promise you, Luca, I'll find them and take care of them," said Red. "I don't want you to worry about them. Your mum is very resourceful, and so is Asia Mae."

"Please, I have to know they're alive," said Luca.

"You can trust me," said Red.

Red then took a tiny laser-pulsing screwdriver and probed it into Ceiba's ear. There was a soft humming sound that emitted from the probe.

"Ouch!" said Ceiba. "Careful, Dad."

"Don't worry, son," he said, "this will adjust your settings to keep your circuitry stable." It only took a moment, and then Red put the screwdriver back in his pocket.

"Dad, what's going on in Acacia Burj?" Ceiba nervously chewed on his bottom lip as he changed clothes.

"I explained a lot of it to Tanner and Elton and they can fill you in. And, Luca, the military is going to do a debriefing and investigate to find out the cause of the *Sibylline's* near destruction, and the way things are at the moment, you could be put in jail if you don't get out of here. You boys simply have to get out of Acacia Burj."

"I don't want to leave you and Mum," said Ceiba. There were tears in the corners of his eyes.

"And I can't leave without knowing my mum and Gaia are all right," said Luca. "And Asia Mae–"

"Forget about them! You boys have to get out of Acacia Burj now! It's crawling with military drones that are arresting anyone who looks suspicious. But that's not the worst of it. Alien soldiers have landed and they're killing randomly and taking people hostage. There's likely to be a full-scale invasion. It's not safe for you here and I'm risking everything by getting you out of here. Your family, your friends… well, you just have to trust that they're safe right now. You two have to rely on each other and get to safety."

Luca couldn't help but wonder if the A'Rmillari had deliberately caused the solar flare to destroy Acacia Burj.

"Regardless of aliens being here, I don't understand," said Ceiba. "We'll *die* in the Wilds. That place is not fit for life." He had never seen his father so commanding; so unbending.

"No, that's not true. You can survive in the Wilds," said Red. "There are communities out there – even some rather advanced ones. Find the Beyul Atoll and you'll understand. We've been lied to, son. None of it's what we think, exactly. You can make it out there until your mum and I come and find you."

"But–," Ceiba started.

"Listen to me," said Red. "Be strong. C'mon, you two!" Red pushed his copper hair back off his forehead. He was sweating. "There's no time to wait."

Red hugged his son, then Luca. He voice was thick with emotion. "Ceiba, your mum and I are safe. And Asia Mae. And Luca, we'll find your mum and sister. Come on, follow me down the hallway and stay quiet. There are so many people, we should be able to get through the crowds unnoticed. When we get to the end of the hallway, I'll hook you up with Elton and Tanner. I've left a door unlocked for you."

Luca nodded. He could feel the urgency to get out.

"I want you boys to find a way out of Acacia Burj as fast as you can. I've explained this to Tanner and Elton. Luca, I've heard about your piloting skills from Dr Tycho – you might be able to find an old aircraft or two at the docks – there's a good portion that's still standing and in working condition – and get out to the Wilds. Remember to look for Beyul Atoll. Head west. And, this is important. Do not go back home and do not try to find anyone. Your life depends on it."

"But, Mr. Ammos—" Luca began. Surely, he could take just a few moments. How could he leave Asia Mae? His mum? Gaia?

"There's no time for anything else," said Red.

He turned towards Ceiba, hugged him again and said, "Trust me. I love you, Ceiba. Your mum loves you. You are our son. We will find you."

"Love you, too, Pops," said Ceiba. A single tear trailed down his cheek.

Luca and Ceiba sneaked down the hallway, walking towards where Elton and Tanner were waiting. But just as Ceiba looked back once more behind them, he saw the guards following, not far behind.

Chapter Forty

Sumer and Asia Mae sat in the tiny shuttle, frozen, still in shock over everything that had happened. They had barely got out of Acacia Burj in time before the solar flare struck. Low on power, it had taken much longer than it should have done to get here. Deep undersea, they were nearly at their destination, Mariana.

Being as practical and as logical as ever, Asia Mae was trying not to worry. Luca had contacted her while he was at the Mariana Deep Sea Mining Base, and she felt sure he'd still be there. If he was, then he would have been safe from the solar flare and the debris from the destroyed satellites.

Asia Mae thought back to all that had happened and the recent events that had changed the course of their mission. They had originally planned to go to the president's deep sea home to take refuge. But, plans had changed at the docks. The newscasts had been counting down the minutes to the solar storm. There had been very few minutes left. Asia Mae and Sumer talked very little, both of them sickened that they couldn't get to their loved ones.

The skies had blackened with red and white lightning zigzagging from the heavens to the ground. Communications had cut out. They had seen the beginning of chaos in the streets: people running like wild animals, not knowing where to go or where to hide; security guards firing warning shots at Civils who were screaming.

When Sumer and Asia Mae had found the president's *Zipper* shuttle parked in the secret spot at the docks, there was no one guarding it. The president's decoy *Zipper* had been destroyed in another area of the docks. *Good thing there had been a decoy,* thought Sumer.

"I guess everyone is on high alert in the city," Sumer had said. "We're lucky we didn't have to fight a mob to get here."

"I don't think we should waste any time," Asia Mae had responded, listening to the screams and shouts from the city.

Sumer had nodded. "You're right. We have no time to lose."

They had quickly climbed into the shuttle. "You sure you can pilot this thing?"

"Don't worry, my father taught me how to do this when I was young. It's like second nature to me. We used to go on adventures in the ocean, and lucky for us, the shuttle always has basic supplies on it, too. We'll be fine once we get to our undersea home."

Asia Mae had looked around cautiously. Would they be okay? The shuttle was pleasant with a comfortable seating area behind them. Alongside the seating were cabinets with supplies. Not nearly as large as a regular Pathfinder ship, but definitely comfortable.

Asia Mae had wondered if this was easy for Sumer. She doubted if things were quite as straightforward as Sumer let on. After all, her parents had been captured, and no one knew if they were alive or dead. Her brother was trapped in the military hospital and she hadn't seen her boyfriend since they had been at the docks.

Neither Asia Mae nor Sumer knew exactly what would happen to Acacia Burj after the solar flare hit. Asia Mae had felt an authentic stab of pain in her heart as they moved off from the docks. Their lives would never be the same again and she wasn't sure how she would fit into the new world. If there was one.

The Zipper had sliced through the choppy water, diving deeper and deeper. Sumer had adjusted the coordinates, sat back and relaxed.

"This is one time I'm grateful for my father's position. This shuttle just might save our lives."

"Thanks for bringing me," said Asia Mae had said. "I don't know what I would have done without you, with Mum and Dad gone, and..."

"Sure, Asia Mae. We're sisters now."

Asia Mae nodded. She now had the sister she had always wanted and it felt strange, but comforting.

They had sailed undersea quickly, heading to the president's sub-sea home, and thought they were making good time. All had seemed to be going as planned until a massive roar had sounded outside the shuttle. The sonar equipment that was responsible for underwater surveillance on the control screen pinged loudly, indicating underwater threats. The Zipper started vibrating and spiralling through the water.

"Oh, no!" Sumer had screamed, grabbing the control lever. "I think the solar storm has started!"

Not far from Acacia Burj, they had approached the under-sea housing development where the president and some of his administrative officials, along with other affluent Opuls, had vacation homes. As they neared the resort, Asia Mae could see it more clearly. Lights glowed like twinkling fireflies in the distance.

"Is this it?" Asia Mae had asked, her eyes wide. She had no idea this even existed.

"Yes. We'll be there soon."

Sumer had powered down the engines, and headed skilfully towards an opening in one of the buildings. But as they started their approach, Asia Mae and Sumer had watched in horror as a massive ball of fire crashed down through the sea and into the complex, causing the entire settlement to shatter. Sumer's shuttle rocked with the explosion.

Sumer had screamed, but thinking fast, had steered the Zipper away from the explosion. They could hardly speak. Asia Mae had turned back and watched the luxurious development collapse and fold in on itself.

"Where do we go now?" Asia Mae had whispered through chattering teeth.

"You said that Luca is at Mariana. Right?"

"Yes, that's where he was when I talked to him last."

"Then, let's go there. It's deep enough and far enough away from Acacia Burj that it should be protected, I would think."

Sumer had checked her systems and all seemed operable. The blast hadn't hurt the shuttle.

"But we don't know how far-reaching the damage is," Asia Mae had replied. "Chunks of satellite could have fallen all over the planet and all through the ocean."

"We don't have another option."

She hadn't told Asia Mae, but Sumer had a backup plan. In her backpack, she had a map to the Beyul Atoll in the Wilds. Phaeton had given it to her in the event that Acacia Burj was ever overrun by aliens or if the military turned on her and her family. He always told her to head there if there was nowhere else to go. And after Mariana, that might be the case.

Chapter Forty-One

"Luca!" shouted Tanner. "Man, am I glad to see you!"

Luca hugged Tanner and said: "I was worried about you, Tan. No one would tell me anything about who survived from the *Sibylline.*"

"I know," said Tanner. "I had no idea either. Last thing I remembered was seeing that blue hole. Everyone, this is Elton. He's President Madden's son."

Luca's eyes widened. *The President's son?* Ceiba, Tanner and Luca nodded at Elton.

"I'll explain everything later," he said. "We need to get out of here."

The four young men rushed to the exit and stepped outside. The door clanged shut behind them and they could hear the unfamiliar noise of mechanical locks clicking into place.

Outside the military hospital, sitting stoically on the edges of Acacia Burj, it was daylight. The first thing Luca noticed was the air. It was thick, searingly hot and burned his lungs. The next thing he noticed was the murky black haze that shrouded the docks and city. No longer was there a shield protecting the city's tall buildings and homes, and people. No longer was the temperature regulated and no longer were the senses of everyone in the city wired and controlled. The city was open to the sky with its bursts of fiery red streaks against grey clouds.

Fires still burned and flames licked their way up the rubble of tall buildings. Great columns of black smoke rose high into the air, spreading thickly into dark charcoal clouds.

The wind blew soot into their faces and Luca tasted the ashy silt in his mouth. He spat it out. To his right, the ocean was rough and choppy with clumps of debris spewing on the waves. Even the ocean had been damaged by the solar flare and falling satellites. Everything looked angry.

Elton was Luca's height and had a shock of coarse chocolate-coloured hair. His eyes were brooding, as if he didn't trust anyone. Elton wore the typical bodysuit that everyone wore in Acacia Burj, but he was wearing sunglasses, which was unusual. He reminded Luca of Phaeton, but that seemed to be the only thing similar about the two. Luca hadn't decided if he liked Elton or not. It was too soon to tell.

"This is our own doing," said Elton, camply, his hands on his hips.

"Why do you say that?" asked Tanner. He checked a backpack Red had given them to make sure they had water and supplies and the Neutraliser he had promised.

Elton shook his head. "We got ourselves into this mess."

"Do you work in the government with your father or something?" asked Tanner.

"No, I'm studying to be an engineer," said Elton. "I really don't like politics. My father's work has turned me against it. It really isn't glamorous and you can't trust anyone."

"I can understand that," said Tanner. "I would have thought you'd be in the military."

"Oh, no, darling, that's a little too rigid for my style," laughed Elton.

"Look guys, I think we need to take Mr. Ammos' advice and get out of here," said Luca. "We can get to know one another later."

"Yeah," said Tanner. "We need to hurry. There could be aftershocks from the solar flare. They might not be over."

"Where do we go now?" asked Ceiba. He felt like if he left Acacia Burj, he'd never see his parents again, and yet, he had no choice.

"Follow me," said Luca.

The group started walking towards the warehouses on the docks. Their senses were numb to the fact that their beloved city had been transformed, citizens killed, and their world mostly destroyed. Luca knew that none of them could afford to contemplate it right now. All they should think of was survival.

Luca recalled that Red Ammos had been desperate to get them out of the hospital. Somebody didn't want them out here and they needed to disappear as quickly as possible. Luca remembered seeing a couple of old Switchblade jets at the back of the Pathfinder Museum.

"Guys, let's see if we can find a functional aircraft in the museum to get out of here."

"There was an explosion there a few days ago before the solar flare hit," said Elton. "I'm not sure any of it is still standing, especially now."

"Well, let's find out."

Moving down the hill, Luca led them to the older part of the docks where the Pathfinder Museum once lay. A group of children, men and women of all ages were huddled nearby at the end of one of the docks, rummaging through a stack of rubble. Their bodysuits were blackened with soot and torn, and their hair dishevelled as if they had rolled around in a rubbish dump. They looked up, their eyes wild and disoriented, as Luca and his friends walked by. Even from this distance, Luca could see the fear and helplessness in their eyes.

Tanner's voice was low. "Keep your eyes on the docks. Don't look at them."

One of the guys yelled, "Hey! Do any of you have any water to spare? Any food? We don't have anything to eat."

Luca and his friends kept walking.

Ceiba said, "Guys, we should give them some water."

"We can't," said Elton. "They'll take everything we have if we stop. We can't save everybody."

"But there's a little girl," said Ceiba.

"Sorry," Elton said. "They could kill us for a piece of bread."

Luca glared at him, but said nothing. Didn't he have a heart? They were Civils, after all. Not a bunch of wild savages.

"Come on," said Tanner. "He's right. We have to keep moving."

The group started towards them and Luca and his friends

then started running. They easily outran them and hid in the docks. Luca led the guys further into the compound. Fortunately, parts of the docks and sections of the museum itself were still standing. Luca and his friends found several Switchblade jets at the far end, protected by a wall. Ceiba rolled up his sleeves and started pulling the debris away from the nearest one. The others watched in amazement as he pushed and lifted bricks and rubble out of way as if they were screwed up pieces of paper. They all climbed aboard, with plans to prepare for takeoff. What was great was that they could fly out of this place almost silently - like a drone - and no one would hear them.

Outside, the handsome world of Acacia Burj continued to burn.

Chapter Forty-Two

"You gonna be able to fly this thing?" asked Elton, sceptically.

"Yeah, I think so," said Luca. "My Grampa always said that the Pathfinders were just more advanced systems of older aircraft like this. It certainly looks simple enough. And strangely familiar."

After checking the instrument panel, Luca felt confident he could fly it. He located the old-fashioned headsets that still sat on the control panel and handed them to his friends.

"Put these on," said Luca to the group. "We'll be able to hear each other talk with these." Luca took control as if he had been piloting the supersonic jets for years. His recent experience with the *Sibylline* had given him more confidence.

They all put on the aviation headsets, adjusting the visors in line with their eyes and pulling the cushioned headgear around their ears.

The jet was very comfortable inside. There was rubble scattered around, but once the boys removed most of it, they were able to buckle into the cracked, worn leather seats.

"I can't believe they don't use these jets anymore," said Tanner. "They're almost as cool as the *Sibylline*."

"I don't think they can fly into space or go undersea," said

Elton, dryly. His expression was cold, aloof. "These old jets are very inferior to what we have today."

"I was just sayin' that I thought they were cool," said Tanner. He shook his head slightly.

"I like these old jets," offered Ceiba. His voice was cheerful but the look on his face suggested otherwise.

"Let's just pray there's fuel in this one," said Luca.

"I remember Dad talking about the museum keeping them partially fuelled, with their batteries charged, at all times for maintenance," said Ceiba.

"Perfect," said Luca.

Luca and Tanner sat in the cockpit with the others seated behind them. Luca switched on the controls and the engine purred quietly, barely making a sound.

"Are you sure you can fly this?" asked Ceiba again for the fifth time. His body looked rigid from stress.

"You can trust Luca," said Tanner. "If he can manage the *Sibylline,* he can certainly manage a little outdated supersonic jet."

Elton raised his eyebrows, but kept his mouth shut. Ceiba's eyes grew wide, his hands gripping the sides of his chair.

"To utopia?" he joked.

"I've got a lot to tell you," Luca said, laughing. Now, let's hope we can get out of here without drawing too much attention to ourselves."

The roof of the museum had been torn away, so there was just open stormy sky and the exterior of the dock's buildings above them. Luca took control of the lever and lifted the Switchblade jet up vertically, out of the museum warehouse. They climbed higher and higher until they were clear of the docks. There were heavy winds and the jet bounced through the turbulence, but Luca maintained control. Even he realised that his skills were impressive. As if his consciousness were intertwined with Dr Tycho's Persona or *someone else*, he rotated the jet in mid-air, dodging a jagged streak of lightning that shot like daggers from the sky. He knew if he could get the plane higher, he would be able to see the world they had just lost to the solar flare.

"Whoa!" shouted Ceiba. "That was close!"

"You've not seen anything yet," said Tanner, smiling, looking back at Ceiba. "I tell you, Luca's the man when it comes to navigation."

"Guys, stay on the lookout in case we're being followed," said Luca.

"We've got your back," said Tanner. "Don't worry."

The plane started to stall, but Luca let his mind relax and heard his Grampa Sol's voice the way he used to talk to his father. *"Use the throttle to control the ascent."* Luca followed Grampa Sol's instructions and levelled the plane. Luca spiralled up and away from Acacia Burj, towards the Wilds.

"So just where exactly are we going?" asked Elton, his arms folded across his chest, resigned to the fact that they would all die.

"A friend told me about a place in the Wilds," said Luca, speaking into the microphone on his headset. "Mr. Ammos told us the same thing. I hope we can find it."

"What friend?" asked Ceiba.

"He was a prisoner on the *Sibylline* and his name is Phaeton. *Was* Phaeton," Luca corrected himself quietly.

"Wait a minute!" said Elton, leaning forward. "Did you say *Phaeton*? Phaeton Wilding? A tall, skinny guy with long hair?"

"Yeah! How do you know him?"

"He's my sister's boyfriend." Elton slumped back in his seat. "He was cast out of Acacia Burj a couple of years ago and has been living in the Wilds ever since."

"Why was he cast out?" asked Ceiba.

"Political stuff," answered Elton. "He was an activist, but he's a good guy. A good friend."

"I'm sorry to tell you this, Elton, but Phaeton was killed in the attack on Mariana." Luca didn't really want to talk about it. He blamed himself for leaving Phaeton at Mariana.

"What attack?" both Ceiba and Elton asked sharply.

"We'll talk about it when we land somewhere safe," said Luca. "Right now, I have to concentrate on flying."

"Yeah," added Tanner. "Listen to Luca. We don't have time to talk. Keep your eyes peeled for any lightning or unusual clouds or anyone following us. We have to avoid them at all costs. We'll have plenty of time to talk about Mariana and the alien attack... and Phaeton."

As the Switchblade soared away from the city, Luca peered through gaps in the clouds and was shocked to see the destruction below. There were no words to describe the roiling fires, the craters in the roadways, the piles of ashes and collapsed build-

ings, the makeshift campsites set up on the streets near abandoned monorails, soldiers corralling herds of people roaming
the streets like cattle. A few buildings were still partially standing – the ISRO building where his mum and Gaia worked, the
military hospital, some of the buildings on the docks, and a few
apartment houses and offices. Overall, their once beautiful city
looked like ruins from a war. As if a nuclear bomb had exploded.
The Earth, at least this part of it, was on fire.

Mr. Ammos had been right about not going back into the
city. Luca and his friends would have found nothing but rubble
and gangs of angry Civils and it would have been dangerous.
He silently wished that his mum, Gaia and Asia Mae were all
right. He felt guilty about leaving the city without trying to find
them. Maybe he could go back once he got Ceiba and the others
to safety. But he had a sinking feeling that he'd never see them
again. He hoped Mr Ammos had kept his word and gone looking for them.

"What do you think we'll find out in the Wilds?" asked Ceiba.

"There are settlements of people," said Elton. "Phaeton used
to tell me about cities – nothing like Acacia Burj, of course. But,
people have banded together and formed little towns like Beyul
Atoll. If we can find that place, we'll have a chance."

"And to think, we always thought it was uninhabitable out
there," said Ceiba.

"It was the way the government kept its citizens under control," said Elton.

"But your father is... *was* president," said Ceiba. "He was in
control of the government!"

"Not exactly," said Elton. "He had to answer to a board of officials who dictated much of what was done. He didn't always have
a choice. One of his goals was to start educating people about the
truth out there."

"Well, he didn't do it soon enough," said Ceiba.

"It doesn't matter now," said Elton, solemnly.

No one spoke for a while as Luca guided the jet safely out west
towards the Wilds in the hope of locating Beyul Atoll. If such a
place even existed, Luca doubted they had much hope of finding
it and suspected no one else did, either.

After an hour or so had passed, they came to a patch of
land where there was no fire. Just clumps of scrub, followed

by stretches of dry desert as far as the eye could see. Luca lowered the plane down through red clouds so they could see more closely. They saw small bands of people wearing Acacia Burj bodysuits walking together to get away from the city. The people looked up to the sky as if hoping Luca would come down and rescue them.

"Don't even think about it, honey," Elton said when they saw the people. "They will steal everything we have." Luca wondered whether Elton was right not to trust anyone.

Luca sat back and tried to relax. They were all hoping Beyul Atoll was the place Phaeton had described and that they would find a comfortable place to rest there. But for all he knew, it was nothing more than a makeshift campsite for outcasts who had been exiled from Acacia Burj.

They continued flying for a couple of hours more. They flew through patches of bright blue sky, and every now and then through red, black and orange storm clouds. Occasionally, lightning spears shot through the sky and thunder rumbled around the aircraft. When this happened, everyone gripped their seats, worried about a direct strike.

"I think we're getting closer to Beyul Atoll, according to the instrument panel and coordinates Phaeton gave me," said Luca. "I think he was hoping we'd be able to travel in the Sibylline, which would mean we'd get there faster, but the coordinates should be the same for this old jet."

The first goal was to find a place to land, hide the plane if possible, and take shelter. Luca knew the fuel would not last much longer, but maybe there would be more in Beyul Atoll. He wished there was a command centre out there somewhere that he could contact for guidance. He even tried a few times to make contact over the radio. "Hello, anyone out there? Luca C. Mariner here on board a Switchblade from Acacia Burj. Anyone out there?"

No one answered.

The numbers glowed on the instrument panel. The fuel gauge was hovering on empty. But Luca didn't want to alarm his passengers. They were hundreds of miles south-west of their initial takeoff location in Acacia Burj. *This should be close to Beyul Atoll,* thought Luca. He hoped. If it came to it, they would just have to get out of the plane and walk. It now appeared they simply didn't have enough fuel to get there and he didn't want to crash.

A *whomp* rocked the jet as if they had hit a hard updraft, and a crackling flash of amber light shone in spurts in the cockpit.

"Are we going to crash?" exclaimed Ceiba, waking violently, his knuckles white as he gripped the sides of his seat.

"No," said Luca, calmly. "We're not going to die today."

The engine started to cough and splutter. Luca pushed the control wheel away from him to descend and reduce power. As if he had been doing this all his life, Luca brought the Switch-blade down safely, deep into the Wilds. In front of them was an endless, mirror-like salt plain, barren of life and unlike anything remotely familiar to the Civils of Acacia Burj.

"Impressive," said Ceiba.

"You did pretty good," added Elton as the jet rocketed across the ground.

"That's it," Luca said. "We're out of fuel."

Chapter Forty-Three

An icy chill ran down Asia Mae's body, so cold that she could see her breath. Sumer looked concerned as she studied the display monitor before her, comparing it with what she saw from the shuttle's windows.

Time: 07:46 a.m.
Depth: 9,508 metres
Location: Mariana Deep Sea Mining Base
11°22' N, 142° 35' E of Acacia Burj, Earth,
Partially on-land cave system and partially
sub-sea structure
Safety Enclosure: Sensory-shields over mine
have been mostly destroyed; above sea cave
structure intact; proceed with caution
Area: 16.0934 km
Status: Unknown, 2 possible life-forms detected

Sumer was surprised that the status was 'unknown', which could mean many things, but she didn't say anything to Asia Mae about it. There was also a light beeping on her monitor that indicated two life forms could be alive in the wreckage. Of course, that could be anything from sharks to sea urchins.

Asia Mae and Sumer had been in and out of sleep all night and it was now pre-dawn in a pitch-black sea as they neared Mariana. The Zipper had heaved and lurched and ocean swells rolled over them as they dived deeper and deeper, both of them nervous about their journey. After all, Sumer had only piloted the Zipper a few times and never to anything like this depth.

There were phosphorous clouds of black and grey and fine silt that floated in clumps outside the cave entrance, while artificial lights glowed on the outer perimeter.

"This is it," said Sumer, checking the coordinates.

"But look at all the rocks and debris around the entrance," said Asia Mae. "That can't be normal. Do you think it's safe?"

"I don't know. With all that's taken place on Earth, could it have affected the mines, too?"

"Something happened here. Most of this place seems like it's been destroyed. I don't like the look of it," said Asia Mae.

As they shuttled into the undersea mine, they entered an area that had stalactites and stalagmites outlining crumbling walls. There was rubble in the water everywhere. What should have been above water was now submerged.

But then they noticed a pocket of air at the back of the docks. Parts of the sensory shield seemed to still be in place over this area, protecting it from the sea, but inside, debris, smoke and blasted rocks were strewn everywhere.

"I can't believe it," said Sumer. "The residual fires and satellite debris must have hit this like they hit our vacation sea homes!"

"Oh, no!" said Asia Mae, covering her mouth with her hand. She pointed at the remnants of a ship smouldering inside the air pocket. "Wait, that's not Luca's Pathfinder, is it?"

"That doesn't look like wreckage from a Pathfinder," said Sumer. "It's possible it was a ship from somewhere else on the planet."

"Oh, no, Sumer! There're bodies on the ground!" said Asia Mae. Her heart pounded against her chest.

"Luca might have escaped," said Sumer.

"Or he might have been killed!" said Asia Mae, tears forming in her eyes. *Get a grip,* she told herself. A stab of longing pierced her heart. She knew she might never see Luca or any of her friends again. Their world had changed and nothing would ever be the way it was before.

"Calm down, Asia Mae," said Sumer. "I'm more worried that this whole place might collapse at any moment!"

Part Two: The Wilds

Chapter Forty-Four

So they were in the Wilds. The Garbage Pit. That savage, mysterious place where no civilised person wanted to venture. Where no one could survive. Or so they had been told. That place where barbarians lived like animals and killed Outcasts. Luca and his group were definitely Outcasts now. By their own design, yes, but Outcasts nonetheless.

Luca had flown the Switchblade jet as far as the fuel would allow. As they had passed over mounds of sand that shimmered golden in the sun, they had seen packs of camel-like creatures strolling lazily through the terrain. Other than that, they hadn't seen any life anywhere for the past couple of hours.

The first thing that happened when they climbed out of the jet was that their lungs tightened in jerks and spasms. Luca and the others inhaled deeply and started choking. They all stood there gasping, the air scorching their throats, eyes watering.

"What... what's wrong?" croaked Ceiba.

"It's the air," said Luca, covering his nose. "It's contaminated out here in the Wilds. We're being exposed to poisons we're not used to."

"No, this is what real air is like," added Tanner. "In Acacia Burj, the air was always controlled."

"But we were out on the open docks a lot," said Luca. "Some of us, anyway." He looked sheepishly at Tanner, remembering he had been a stowaway on the *Sibylline.*

"The docks had partially filtered air, as well," said Elton.

They looked in all directions of the salt plain and what they saw was both hostile and beautiful. Desolate. And it was hot as hell.

"Let's wrap some of our clothing around our heads and mouths to keep the sun from scorching us," said Tanner.

"I brought a couple of sarongs," said Elton. "Did you guys bring any?"

The boys shook their heads, bewildered. Tanner ripped one of the sarongs in half and tied it around his head so that it covered his mouth. The others followed suit and they all looked like they were wearing turbans. Luca had to admit that it helped keep the sun off their heads and the heat from his throat.

"Luca, I thought you were going to hide the jet," said Ceiba after he finished fastening the material around his head.

"To be honest, we were almost out of fuel and I didn't want to crash-land," said Luca. "We'll just have to leave it out here and start walking west to look for Beyul Atoll. If we find fuel there, we can always come back and get it."

"It should be all right here," said Tanner, even though he didn't really believe it. "I doubt if any of the stragglers from Acacia Burj or the savages would know what to do with an old Switchblade."

"If everybody has everything, let's get started," said Luca. "We don't know how long we'll have to travel by foot."

"Elton and I have the Neutralisers," said Tanner.

"Hopefully, we won't need them," said Luca.

Luca didn't really know what direction to head in. But he knew the general direction of the west because of the position of the sun. So, they trudged on. The sun popped out from the clouds and beat down on their backs, stinging them like arrows of fire. They were all struggling to breathe the air and sweat gathered in beads on their foreheads, dripping down onto their chins. They dragged their feet across the white ground, stopping regularly to take sips of water from their flasks. No one talked. It was too much effort. There were dark, jagged rocks in the distance, skeletal bushes that looked eerie and dusty plains with scrub tumbling across the ground.

Luca's feet felt as heavy as concrete. He could barely move them. Ceiba, Tanner and Elton dragged behind him. He could hear them struggling to breathe just as he was.

The light breeze picked up and within minutes a strong wind was whirling around them, whipping the granules of salt beneath their feet into a frenzy. The sudden onslaught of particles hit them from out of nowhere, blasting into the sides of their faces. It was like a sandstorm. The boys all crouched down in defence, pulling their clothes and head wear more tightly about themselves. But the salt granules worked their way beneath the fabric, collecting around their eyes and pushing up into their nostrils. They didn't dare open their mouths to talk but moved together into a huddle to try and protect themselves from the onslaught.

Luca opened one of his eyes just a little to look around. In the distance, he could make out what looked like a settlement of wooden buildings that shimmered in the sunlight. *Was it only a mirage?* He had read about mirages, so he knew this could be a figment of his imagination. If only they could get there. He felt too light-headed to continue, but was determined to lead the group to safety, so Luca lugged one foot in front of the other, hoping the others would follow him. *Take one step. And another. Slowly.* Heaving his chest, struggling to breathe, he was determined to get to those buildings. But his lungs rejected the Wilds and his feet were too heavy to move on. There were worse ways to die.

Chapter Forty-Five

Asia Mae couldn't stop crying. They had found a dry area to land, and now she was squatting down to look at the body of a young man who from the back had resembled Luca: same brown hair and long body. When she had turned him over to look at him, she saw that it was not Luca, but another less fortunate soul who had not escaped the attack on Mariana. That's when she broke down, shaking and sobbing uncontrollably.

"C'mon," said Sumer, as gently as possible. She pulled her friend up from the dead body and put her arm around her and squeezed. "I am sure Luca escaped. There's no sign of the Path-finder he was on and these bodies look like a mix of people from the Wilds."

Asia Mae nodded. "I know Luca is probably okay. I just can't stand all this death and destruction."

"Come now," said Sumer. "Didn't you tell me that you had trained in martial arts and was some kind of kick-ass chick in the virtual games?"

"But those weren't real," said Asia Mae. "Sure, I was brave when it was all gaming and athletics, but this is not a game. This is real and I don't know where my friends or my parents are. Or even where my place in the world is any more."

"Asia Mae," said Sumer, "it's gonna be that way for all of us now. But you and I have each other. C'mon, let's see if we can find out anything."

Asia Mae dried her eyes. She and Sumer both walked over to a pile of rubble and began digging through it. Most of the area was flooded and debris from a destroyed ship floated in the water. Water dripped down the walls on either side of them and lights from the Mariana base flickered in the corners of the dry area where they stood. The entire place gave Asia Mae a forlorn, desolate feeling. As if she and Sumer were the last two people alive on Earth.

All of a sudden, Asia Mae heard something behind her. Sumer looked up and shouted: "Look out!"

Asia Mae turned around and saw a huge bald-headed alien coming at her. A white blood-like substance streamed down its arms and neck. The alien hissed at her! Before she could even think, Asia Mae raised her hands in a boxing stance and clenched her fists, then lifted her knee straight up and kicked forward. The alien was too slow, as Asia Mae flung around and kicked it in the gut. When it bent over, she struck again with her foot. The alien swung at her, but Asia Mae dived out of the way, jabbing her elbow into its side. She darted between its legs, grabbing at its foot and twisting it off balance. The alien tripped and fell onto the ground. With that, she kicked it off the ledge into the water, and it sank into the murky depths.

Sumer stood there with her mouth open.

"The girl's got skills!" exclaimed Sumer.

"That felt good," said Asia Mae, wiping the sweat off her forehead. "I hope there aren't any more of them. Did you see those weird white lines?"

"Yes," said Sumer. "Not a good look!"

"And it hissed at me!"

"C'mon, let's get out of here."

Sumer turned around, and then stopped. "Did you hear that, Asia Mae?"

"Hear what?"

"Listen."

From the ruins, they heard someone yelling: "Help! Help me!"

"Someone's alive!" screamed Asia Mae. "Let's go! That voice is human!"

They ran over to a pile of wreckage from the twisted steel, shards of glass and weird silicone-type slabs – and started pulling away pieces.

"We're here! We're going to get you out!" screamed Sumer. "Just keep talking to us!"

"Help!" The voice was faint, but clear.

Sweat rolled off their bodies as they worked for more than an hour to whittle away at the debris. Finally, they saw a hand sticking out. Sumer took the hand and squeezed it. "You're safe. We're here to get you out."

As they pulled away the last piece of glass, the young man was free. Looking up at them with cuts etched into his face, Scar said: "Help me out of here!"

Asia Mae jumped back. It was one of those savages from the Wilds. He was the scariest person she had ever seen. Teeth that were dirty and irregular, like someone had sawed them off with a knife. Clothes that were nothing but holes and tattered remnants of what Retros wore, and some kind of metal tied to his chest with leather strings like a makeshift shield. "Sumer," said Asia Mae quietly. "We can't take him with us. He's a barbarian. A savage!"

"He's a *pirate*," said Sumer. "I've heard about the pirates. He'll help us. We're going to have to go out into the Wilds now, and he can help us get to Beyul Atoll."

"What's that?" said Asia Mae.

"A place my boyfriend told me about," she said.

"Help me, please!" Scar yelled again.

They helped the pirate out of the rubble. His shoulder was bleeding and there was a nasty gash on his leg.

"Can you stand?" asked Sumer. She held onto his arm as the ground shook. It felt like the tremor of an earthquake.

"I think so," he said. "Thanks for getting me outta there. I thought I was a goner."

"Do you know if there are any more survivors?" asked Asia Mae, standing back a little, afraid to touch him.

"Yep, there's another one with me," said Scar. "He should be close by. Don't know if he got killed or not. We can try and find him."

"Another savage?" asked Asia Mae cautiously. Sumer shot her a look.

"I reckon he's *part* savage and *part* outcast," said Scar, giving Asia Mae a look like he was sizing her up. "Not quite as mean as the rest of us... yet."

"She didn't mean anything by that," said Sumer. "She's just scared, looking for her friend, that's all."

"Reckon everyone from the city's afraid of us," said Scar, blood trailing down his leg and shoulder. "But not my buddy Phaeton. No sireee."

"*Phaeton?*" said Sumer. Her heart stopped.

"Et's what I said," said Scar, hobbling over to a boulder to sit down.

"Phaeton, my buddy. A pirate just like me."

"Phaeton, a pirate?" asked Asia Mae, her doe eyes big and wide.

"Yep."

"Where is he?" screamed Sumer, looking wildly at the debris. "What is he doing here?"

"He's somewhere in this mess." Scar leaned back on the boulder, his eyes closed. "He was fightin' with us."

"Fighting *with* you?" asked Sumer. "With the aliens?"

"Yep, et's what I said," said Scar. "Fightin' against the fancy military ship from your big Acacia Burj."

"Luca's ship!" screamed Asia Mae. "You and Phaeton were fighting *against* Luca?"

"Ya heard right." Scar looked Asia Mae up and down again with a sneer on his face. He looked dangerous.

Asia Mae looked at Sumer. "Would Phaeton do that?"

"I don't know," she said, shaking her head. "It doesn't make sense. He was in jail! There has to be more to this story and we have to find him."

Sumer and Asia Mae started clearing the piles again.

"*Phaeton!* Are you there? Can you hear me?" screamed Sumer. "Please, be safe. Hang on! We're going to get you out!"

"Hey, can I get some water?" Scar yelled from where he was perched on the boulder.

"In a minute," said Sumer. "I have to see if Phaeton is alive."

After what seemed like hours of rifling through stacks of debris, they found a body covered in dirt and blood. Sumer turned him over. "No way! It's him!"

Phaeton lay motionless under a big slab of glass. He had bruises and cuts all over his body. His hair was free from his ponytail and hanging in strings across his face. Sumer gathered him in her arms and cried softly.

"Oh, Phaeton, please don't leave me. I've just found you. Please don't go."

Asia Mae stepped back, her hands filthy, her body exhausted, looking first at Sumer holding Phaeton in her arms and then at the scraggly Scar on the boulder. It had to be his fault that Phaeton was dead and she was furious. But just as Sumer whimpered in his ear as she held Phaeton close to her body, he opened his eyes.

"Sumer?"

"Phaeton! You're alive!"

"I... I... think so," he whispered. "Help me up."

Asia Mae ran to Sumer and they both helped Phaeton up from the pile of rocks that had probably saved his life.

"Are you okay?" asked Sumer, tears streaming down her face.

"What are you doing here, Sumer? How did you find me?"

"I'll tell you everything, but first, how are you?"

"I'm sore, I'm aching and my head is splitting, but seeing you is the best medicine a man could have."

Phaeton hugged Sumer and kissed her. They looked delighted to have found each other. Phaeton pulled back, grimaced slightly, and pointed at Asia Mae.

"Who is this?"

"Some kind of queen, the way she acts," yelled Scar from his boulder.

"This is Asia Mae," said Sumer. "I met her in Acacia in the hospital. She's my friend. Asia Mae, this is Phaeton, my boyfriend."

"So nice to finally meet you, Phaeton," said Asia Mae.

"Asia Mae?" said Phaeton. "No way."

"What do you mean?" said Asia Mae.

"Are you Luca Mariner's friend?" asked Phaeton.

"You know Luca?"

"We were on the *Sibylline* together," said Phaeton. "Along with Tanner and some others. All he did was talk about you."

"Is he all right?" asked Asia Mae, blushing. "The last time I talked to him, he was here at Mariana."

"I think so," said Phaeton. "I think he escaped on the Sibylline."

"Well, you all can stand there and love one another up all you want, but I'd like to get out of here," said Scar. "I'm bleedin' and we need to get to one of the outposts on land."

"But you're with the aliens," said Phaeton. "Right? You and your group of pirates."

"Well, it looks like the A'Rmillari and my pirate buds have seen better days and I know when it's time to get out. We fought and didn't succeed. So, I just say let's cut our losses and get back home and you fancy girls can go back to your home in Acacia Burj and leave me and Phaeton alone."

"The A'Rmillari?" asked Asia Mae.

"He fought with the aliens, the A'Rmillari. I'll explain later," said Phaeton. He looked at Sumer and continued, "What happened in Acacia?"

"You don't know?" said Sumer to Phaeton. She hadn't let go of him since they found him.

"What do you mean?" Phaeton asked.

"Acacia Burj has been destroyed," said Asia Mae. It didn't even sound real when she said it out loud.

"It was hit by a major solar flare which brought down the satellite network... literally. We got out just in time on my parent's shuttle. Phaeton, we have nowhere to go now but to this place called the Beyul Atoll in the Wilds that you told me about," added Sumer.

"Well, I'll be!" said Scar. "I told you that the city folks were gonna get what was coming to them, Phaeton!"

Asia Mae glared angrily at Scar but before she could say anything, she was interrupted by the ground shaking beneath their feet, more violently this time.

"Come on!" yelled Sumer. "We've gotta get out of here!"

Chapter Forty-Six

Something was kicking Luca in the ribs. His eyelids fluttered.

"Whoa! Pretty boy just woke up!" said a male voice with a slurring accent.

Luca slowly opened his eyes and saw a strange-looking man in front of him. *A savage!* The sight shocked him. His heart jumped into his throat. The savage looked to be a little older than Tanner's age, but his skin was brown and leathery, and he wore some kind of britches made out of hides, no shirt, and a necklace of what looked like animal teeth. He wore boots that looked like discarded Acacia military boots. He stood by a large, camel-like creature that was pure white and he chewed a wad of something brown in his mouth. The juice dribbled on his chin and flies buzzed around his head. He spat the juice onto the ground next to Luca, just next to his face.

As Luca struggled to sit up, he saw a group of four savages – all chewing on the brown stuff and dressed similarly to the one kicking him – and all of them pressing their boots into his friends' chests to rouse them. He saw that they had roped the Switchblade jet that Luca had abandoned in the Wilds, and were dragging it behind the camel train.

"Giddup!" the savages screamed at them. "You're comin' with us!"

"Who... *who are you?*" asked Luca, his throat still on fire.

"Guess you city folks might call us opportunists," said the one who had kicked Luca. "Some call us cowboys out here."

"*Savages* is what we call you," said Elton, defiantly. His dark eyes narrowed into slits.

"His name is Penan – he's in charge here – and you ain't seen any real savages yet," smirked one of the others. They all laughed like fools.

"Look, let us go," said Tanner. "We don't have any food or jewels or anything of value. And I see you've already taken our jet, so you've got everything we had."

"Nah. You're comin' with us," Penan slurred again. "It's a hand to mouth existence out here in the Wilds. We've gotta get our hands on everything we can to survive."

Two camels stood near Luca, and the boys' meagre provisions were strewn all over the ground. Water bottles had been taken and put in the leather slings the pirates wore on their backs.

"If you don't let us go, our families will come searching for us and you'll wish you had." Elton's stance was defiant, challenging.

"I ain't 'fraid of no city folks," said Penan. "Our ancestors used to live in those places, y'know, back before the climate wars. We been seein' those air machines in the sky for two days. We already seen city folks like you dyin' all over these lands. My thinkin' is that somethin' happened in your city and you had to get out real fast."

"I have friends out here," said Luca. "If we can just get to the Beyul Atoll, I'm sure they'll arrange payment for you. Maybe you could help us get there."

The pirates laughed hysterically again.

"We've heard talk about Beyul Atoll," said Penan. "But we ain't takin' you there." He bellowed a low, guttural laugh and, again, spat the brown juice onto the ground. It smelled nasty, raw, and of the earth.

"So where are you taking us?" asked Ceiba.

"We're goin' to the Jungle," said Penan, puffing up his chest like the Jungle was the best place on Earth.

"The Jungle?" asked Luca. "What's in the Jungle?" As far as Luca knew from his studies, jungles used to be in the southern hemisphere of the planet – a long way from the Wilds.

"You'll see," said Penan. He then turned to two of his companions and said: "String 'em up, girls! These boys are ripe ages. Should get us a hefty price."

"Yep, the King is gonna love these," said one of the other pirates. She had strange tattoo markings curving all over her neck, arms and face. "Oh, and by the way, my name's Shuar. Got it?"

"Got it, Shuar," said Luca.

"And that's *Captain* Penan to you boys. Over there is Moai and that one is Hoya."

Hoya kicked Ceiba. "What's with this one with the white curls? He's almost too pretty to be a boy."

Hoya was a skinny woman with a long pointy nose and whiskers on her upper lip. Ceiba would have loved to kick her back, but he knew the force of it might give away the fact he was a Bion, so he stayed still and hung his head.

"Leave him alone," said Luca.

"My name's Ceibastian," Ceiba said.

"Well, Ce-bas-stun," said Hoya. "I think the lizard might want you all to himself. We don't get too many white-hair boys as pretty as you out here." She licked her lips exaggeratedly.

Penan and the others laughed again. Hoya grabbed Ceiba by the arm and ran her filthy fingers through his hair.

"Get off! Leave me alone," said Ceiba, pulling away from Hoya. His whole body shook.

Luca shot him a look that meant *calm down*. No one could possibly ever know that Ceiba was a Bion. There were no outer markings that pointed to his internal wiring. But Luca knew there was definitely a danger that the pirates would kill Ceiba if they learned he was full of useful circuitry.

"Ooooh, pretty boy has a bit a fight in 'im," said Hoya, laughing.

"Look, pick on someone your own size," said Elton, as he struggled to stand tall. He was only twenty-one, but maybe he thought he could fight Hoya if he had to. Maybe he thought Ceiba was far too thin to take on any of these savages, and it would be up to them to protect him.

Hoya growled.

"Just calm down everybody," said Penan. "We ain't gonna fight nobody. The fightin' comes later."

In many ways, these pirates were freakier-looking than the A'Rmillari. At least with the aliens, they presented what you'd expect – an *oddity* – but these pirates presented a type of *human* that none of them had ever seen before.

Luca really wished Phaeton had survived and was with them. How he had ever survived in the Wilds as an Outcast, Luca couldn't imagine. But it gave him a new-found respect for his friend.

The pirate women took leather straps and tied the boys' hands behind them. Then, they laced a harness across their chests and through their arms, chaining all of them together in a line. If one fell, they would all fall.

"We should take the stuff they brought," said Hoya.

"Might be some valuables in there we overlooked," added Moai, a huge savage with bulging muscles and tattoos on his arms.

"Go 'head," said Penan. "Pick 'em up."

Unfortunately, the pirates had also found the Neutralisers and now two of the pirates carried them as well. With the jet tied onto two of the camels, they were ready to go. Luca, Ceiba, Tanner, and Elton didn't stand a chance against them. They all knew that.

"Please... can we have some water?" Luca said, barely able to talk.

"Give 'em some water," said Penan, nodding to his men. "We don't want 'em dyin' before gettin' 'em to the lizard."

Shuar and Moai took their water bottles and gave Luca and his friends a tiny sip of water. Luca could swear he heard the water sizzle on his dry throat – like ice on fiery coals.

The pirates dragged them like cattle going to slaughter across the dusty plains. Penan and Shuar rode underneath the two camels dragging the Switchblade. In front of them, Moai and Hoya rode beneath their camels, pulling the boys along behind them.

Luca and his friends saw a couple of drones fly overhead. He realised that the savages rode upside-down beneath these over-sized creatures so as to not be seen from above. They also saw craters where small meteors had pummelled the earth and they recoiled when they almost stepped on skeletons lying to the side where vultures had picked the bones clean. The wilderness was harsh and unforgiving.

As the savages on dragged the Switchblade jet behind them, they relentlessly taunted their new captives. Luca had no idea what they would want with a jet that had no fuel; perhaps they thought they could trade the parts for something more valuable. Or perhaps they had fuel.

At one point, a clump of stony grey clouds, ragged with edges of red thundered from above. A hot gust of wind and sand blew across their faces and a jagged blue spear of light pierced the ground in front of them. Luca and his friends had never seen anything like this.

"Did you see that?" shouted Moai who was at the rear.

"Yep," said Penan, chewing on the brown weed. "We gotta get to the Jungle before the blood rain comes."

Blood rain? Luca shot Tanner a look and Tanner just shook his head. None of them had any idea what blood rain was.

As if answering Luca's thoughts, Hoya said: "It rains blood out here in dese parts and if the blood rain comes and hits us, it means we die."

Shuar kicked his camel in the ribs. "We ain't gonna die today. We're gonna feed like kings!"

They trudged on for hours and the old Switchblade lost piece after piece as they made their way out of the salt plains. Surely when they got to the Jungle, they would find a way to escape these pirates – they would find someone who would help them. Luca hoped that maybe they could even repair the jet and find some fuel somewhere so they could fly out of there. Luca figured that the Jungle would be filled with luscious trees and plants and plenty of water. Isn't that what was supposed to be in a jungle?

No one talked. It was too hard to breathe. Minutes disappeared into hours. Sweat plastered their hair to their scalps and rolled down their skin, making their bodies sticky. Whenever the boys felt they couldn't walk any further, they would be dragged with their faces in the dirt until they were helped up by the others.

Chapter Forty-Seven

Phaeton gazed at the destruction around them. He still felt shaky and his head was sore. He wasn't sure what to do.

"We have to go to Beyul Atoll," said Sumer, as if reading his mind. "There's nowhere else to go."

"But what about your parents? Your brother?" asked Phaeton. "And their undersea vacation home?"

"Phaeton, my parents were kidnapped on the Moon by the A'Rmillari," said Sumer. "I'm quite sure they're dead and Elton is still in the military prison, I think."

"Your parents were *kidnapped*?" asked Phaeton, incredulously.

"Yes, it was all over the news in Acacia Burj how the aliens had taken them. We never did hear who the aliens were or why they did what they did, because the news of the solar storm came next," said Sumer.

"They stopped reporting anything about Sumer's parents and the Moon." Asia Mae lowered her eyes. "And, we just witnessed their undersea home being destroyed by the solar blast."

"Yeah, there's nothing left of that luxury undersea compound," added Sumer.

"I'm so sorry, Sumer," said Phaeton. "I know you had problems with your parents, but they loved you."

She nodded. Tears pooled in her eyes. "Let's not talk about it now. C'mon, we need to get out of here. This place smells like death and the flood waters are rising. If we don't get out of here now, we might not be able to."

Phaeton nodded. Hell had just descended on Earth and in the sea. Of course, he had had his suspicions of the aliens and their plots, and had been working as a spy from Beyul Atoll, taking messages back and forth to like-minded people in Acacia, but now it seemed like the aliens had gone to the next step of overtaking the city, maybe the whole planet. Everything was beginning to add up. He still had questions and knew they could find answers deep in the sea, but right now, he didn't have a choice but to try to take them to Beyul Atoll.

As far as Phaeton knew, Luca had the only plans in existence of the secret undersea Sub-Biosphere 2 facility the military had been working on. So, he had to find him. Besides, the Beyul Atoll was where he had told Luca and Tanner to go if they found themselves out in the Wilds someday. And with Acacia Burj destroyed, that's where they'd be if they were still alive and they could get there.

For a moment, Phaeton wondered if the Overlord was controlling him. Had he been imprinted on their ship? He didn't feel any different, so it was possible the procedure hadn't been completed. He hoped so, anyway.

"Let's look around for some Neutralisers – any kind of weapon that's still usable."

"Let's take care of your wounds first," said Sumer, seeing blood drip down the side of his face. "We have supplies on the Zipper. Then, we'll take the shuttle back to the shore and head out to the Wilds. It runs on the land just as well as undersea."

"I'll look for some weapons," said Asia Mae.

"Get as many as we can fit in the shuttle," said Phaeton.

"What about the pirate?" asked Asia Mae, pointing to Scar lying on the boulder.

"Looks like he's passed out from the trauma," said Sumer.

"Let's just leave him here," whispered Asia Mae. "He stinks and I don't like him. He scares me."

"No, we need him," said Phaeton.

"But why?" asked Asia Mae, her hands on her hips. "He said he was fighting with the aliens. He's our enemy. Why do we need him?"

"He'll be able to get us around the Jungle without getting killed," said Phaeton. "And that's the fastest way I know to get to the Beyul Atoll – by going past the Jungle."

Asia Mae and Sumer looked at one another with questioning eyes, but said nothing.

Asia Mae picked up as many Neutralisers as she could carry to the shuttle. Sumer and Phaeton carried Scar to the Zipper and put him in the back on one of the seats. While Asia Mae held her nose, Sumer gently washed Scar's wounds, applied bandages and antiseptics from a kit she had found on the Zipper to patch him up.

Phaeton had taken care of his own wounds, which consisted of cuts and bruises. Nothing was broken; he was just sore and stiff. When he unzipped his military bodysuit, he saw a large black and purple bruise on his chest. He quickly zipped his suit back up so Sumer wouldn't see it. It would scare her and she had been through enough already.

Finally, Sumer powered up the Zipper and they sailed out of the Mariana Mining Base with plans to get to the shores of some outpost south of Acacia Burj where there were still docks standing on the sea. Phaeton knew of a couple that had survived from ancient cities long ago, and he believed that it might be better for all of them to not approach the shores of Acacia Burj ever again. But they needed to dock and get on land so they could make their way to Beyul Atoll. It was their best hope for survival.

Chapter Forty-Eight

Hours had passed. They could smell it before they saw it; the stench of rot on the breeze. Finally, the Jungle spread out before them like a sprawling metropolis of scrap metal and steaming waste.

Luca hadn't been able to figure out why they called it a Jungle, because there were only sparse metal columns amidst the decrepit, rotten, ramshackle buildings. Then, it hit him. It was the mix of people and creatures that made it a 'Jungle': bizarre beings that he had never seen before.

They waded through litter and scrap as they made their way into the settlement. The pirates seemed used to it, but the boys had to hold their hands over their noses to block out the terrible smell. The settlement seemed to have been built on a rubbish pit. It was literally made from garbage. *This must be why they also call the Wilds the Garbage Pit*, Luca thought to himself.

Soaring tree-like pillars made from waste material stretched upwards, supporting a canopy of rubbish that seemed to cover the entire settlement. Sunlight speared down through fragments of broken glass and plastic, and through the few gaps in the roof.

From above, Luca imagined, the Jungle would simply seem to be a scrap yard or rubbish dump. It was cleverly concealed and at least there was some relief from the hot sunshine.

They were walking through what looked like a dilapidated market. Human men, women and children rattled carts and wagons across the dirt road in front of them. They wore tatters of clothes – some, especially the children, only had pieces of rags tied around their bodies and picked at the piles of litter, looking for scraps of food. Savages which looked like the boys' captors stood on piles of rubbish, holding aloft their wares and yelling out the prices to anyone who would listen. It all looked like recycled junk and rotten food to Luca. Several birds with mutant, shrivelled wings and pigs with artificial limbs were picking through the litter. Others stalked around cages packed full of huge, weird-looking mutated creatures which fought each other as they were tormented with metal lances.

Further into the market, the odour of salt and seaweed marked the presence of sea pirates, guffawing amongst themselves. Their tattered clothes blew in the light breeze like the sails of a ship. Some bartered around transparent tanks full of water, inside which all manner of creatures swam. Sharks, glowing eels and colour-changing jellyfish-like creatures. Everything around them was noisy, decrepit and lawless.

Luca had heard Penan and his gang talking one night when they stopped to sleep. Evidently, the lizard king liked the hot weather in the Jungle because it was comfortable on his skin. And they had been a part of the Jungle for a long, long time. Living hand to mouth to survive.

"Keep movin' on, stinkin' Blubbers," yelled Penan. "Nothin' to see here!"

At one point, they passed a particularly neat pile of rubbish. It wasn't food waste this time, or plastic. Luca was shocked to spot an eye bouncing on a wire. He gulped and jumped backwards while Penan laughed loudly. The bodies and body parts of male and female AIs were piled on top of each other, twisted like mannequins with arms and legs missing. He looked quickly at Ceiba, knowing that this would hurt him. Ceiba didn't flinch though.

It was difficult to tell if these were only AI parts or if they were from Bions too. Some Bions could have wandered out into the

Wilds with the other people fleeing Acacia Burj. And now, they were probably being sold in parts to the highest bidder. Luca shuddered, he didn't want to think about it. It was so barbaric.

At one end of a wooden building lingered two tall reptilian creatures. They stood on two feet like humans, and had arms and legs, but featured grey-green lizard skin with wide serpent eyes and two slits for a nose. They wore chest harnesses and long tails slithered behind them.

"Bloody hell," whispered Elton under his breath. "Who knew there were mutant lizards like that?"

Tanner shot Elton a glance, then looked over at Luca. Luca was watching Ceiba, worried about how he was holding up. Ceiba looked as though he was melting, his blonde curls in ringlets around his face, his fair skin red and sunburned.

"Boys, we're here," Penan announced. "Now, I don't hafta tell ya to be on yer best behaviour if you want to survive."

Shuar pulled them into a well-built sheet metal building. It was a small room with wooden floors and sparsely furnished with a couple of chairs and a metal table made out of an old classic car. At one end of the room were wide wooden doors with copper fixtures. Two lizard-like soldiers carrying monstrous Neutralisers were standing in front of the doors, guarding it. They had shiny silvery skin with raised green bumps across their skin.

"Let us in," said Penan. "We've got merchandise for King Lemuria."

The soldier opened the door for Penan and his prisoners. Shuar walked alongside Penan and led Luca and the others, grinning toothlessly from ear to ear. Moai and Hoya trailed behind them, proudly carrying their newly procured Neutralisers.

Lying on his side behind a stagnant pool of water sat the being they called King Lah-mu Lemuria. He was a huge reptile, being even bigger that the two lizards Luca had seen outside. But he was different. He had positioned himself under a spotlight of sun and the scales on his body shimmered yellow and green. His arms looked muscled and strong and his head was larger than the other lizards'. Lah-mu Lemuria's yellow-green eyes bulged bigger and wider, too. He had the same two slits for a nose and a thin wide opening for a mouth from which a wet forked tongue flickered. A row of spiky scales ran down his spine, adorned with gold jewellery and gemstones. Luca could tell right away that he was the leader of the Jungle.

Penan and the rest of the pirates bowed before the lizard. He waved his hand at them, indicating they could stand up.

"Well, well, Captain Penan," said the lizard. "What have we here? Very good indeed. You have kept your reputation." He spoke perfect English, but in a thin, shrill, fine-as-wire voice.

"Prime meat," said Penan, smiling, showing off his rotted teeth. "I think you'll really like the one here with the white curls. A special prize. You might want him all for yourself. I want my usual price fer these boys, plus their teeth after it's done."

"That can be arranged," said Lah-mu Lemuria, taking a sip of something from his copper cup. His long scaly fingers were claws that curled inward with razor-sharp fingernails. For the millionth time on this journey, Luca thought he was going to be sick.

"All you need to do is fatten 'em up a bit and they'll make good fighters," said Penan. "With a little meat on their bones, they should put up quite a few good fights before–"

Fighters?

"Yes, yes," said Lah-mu Lemuria, interrupting Penan before he could continue. "But you will leave the weapons with me. Understood?"

"Yes, King Lemuria," said Penan.

"My soldiers need them," said the lizard king. "But I will reward you well for these fine specimens."

"And the white-haired boy?" said Penan.

"Needs meat on his bones before I'll consider having him for myself."

Ceiba turned ghostly white.

Luca felt sure that the Lah-mu Lemuria wanted Ceiba for a servant or something since his blonde curls and blue eyes were different from those of most of the beings around the Jungle.

The door behind them opened and two tall, slender female beings walked into the room, wearing leather thongs and bras-sieres. They were humans – but *extraordinary* humans. The women looked as though they had been carved out of smooth black onyx. Even their lips and fingernails were smooth black. Their hair was a silky burnished copper that was pinned up in coils on their heads like the mounds of ice cream Luca had enjoyed at the *Game Stop Café*. Diamond and emerald studs adorned one side of their faces in an intricate pattern, curving up around their eye. Amongst the filth, these two beings looked elegant.

"Do they speak?" asked Lah-mu Lemuria, motioning to Luca and the group.

"Oh yeah, King Lemuria, they're high-bred," said Penan. "They even had weapons with them. And we brought back one of those fling-flanged winged flying machines. I'd say they're with the military, which makes it better for us. They should know how to fight. They're 'bout dead though. You'll need to give 'em drink and food."

Lah-mu Lemuria looked at Luca and the boys.

"First thing to remember here in the Jungle is that I am the law. It doesn't matter who you are or where you came from. Forget everything you have been taught. You do nothing here unless I tell you to do it. Is that understood?"

Luca, Ceiba, Tanner and Elton nodded.

Penan punched Luca in the gut with his fist.

"Answer King Lemuria when spoken to!"

Luca and the others shouted as loud as their parched voices could scream, "Yes, King."

"Good," said Lizard. "What are your names?"

"I'm Luca, this is Tanner, Elton and Ceibastian," said Luca, motioning with his head towards his friends.

"I see," said the lizard. "Can you boys fight?"

"Yes, Master," they all shouted.

Penan punched Luca in the gut again. "That's so you remember."

"That's enough, Penan!" Lah-mu Lemuria said. He made a strange snorting sound, wrinkled up his snout and shook his head, shooting something from his left nostril towards Penan. "We have to get them strong if they're going to make me any money," he said, grinning as he watched Penan wipe the slimy snot from the side of his face. The four boys looked at each other in disgust.

King Lemuria turned to the women. "Randa, Sosa, clean them up, feed them, and take them to the cages. First fight is tomorrow."

One of the women said: "Yes, King Lemuria." She took the

chain from Shuar and looked pointedly at her. "We do not need you from this point on."

Shuar bowed. "Yes, ma'am." The other pirates followed suit.

Lah-mu Lemuria took another sip of something from his copper mug and watched as the boys walked past him. He was clearly sizing them up.

Randa and Sosa led the boys into the chamber behind the king. Once inside, they gave the boys water to drink, and then started undoing the leather chains that bound them.

"Sosa, let's take them to the showers, then we'll feed them and show them to their cages."

Cages? Luca longed for the sea. The stars. Anywhere but here.

Sosa nodded and said, "Follow me."

They went down a flight of rickety wooden stairs that took them to the underground. Blasts of cool air hit them, a soothing balm on their wounds and burnt skin.

"Leave your clothes here. The showers are in that room next door," said Randa. "Do not take too long. Our water is limited."

Luca and the others nodded. As soon as the women left, everyone started undressing, eager to feel water on their parched skin. He looked quickly around the room. There were wooden benches along the walls, which were built of stone. The floor was hardened earth. It was obvious they were in an underground cave. They all undressed quickly and headed to the showers.

The showers were rudimentary, but they worked. An iron pipe ran to the shower from somewhere in the underground cave. A leather string was attached to a pulley and when they pulled it, water trickled over their scorched bodies. Small slabs of home-made soap sat on a shelf that had been carved out of the stone wall. The water was cathartic. It smelled of rocks, minerals, and grass, but was revitalising after the ordeal they'd been through. At times, the water would gush profusely, and then it would taper off. Whenever it gushed, they drank as they intermittently scrubbed their hair and bodies with the soap that seemed to be made of a fatty substance.

"Is everyone all right?" asked Tanner. "Anyone in pain?"

"Every bone in my body is aching. I've got blisters on my feet and my face feels sunburned," said Luca. "But I'm all right, I think."

"I'm okay, just exhausted and sore," said Ceiba. "What's going to happen to us?" He lifted his head upward to the water trickling down the rusted pipe.

"We're going to have to fight, I believe," said Luca.

"Fight?" Ceiba's blue eyes darted around the room. "Fight who?"

"My guess it could be each other… maybe other prisoners, or a wolvhyena," Tanner continued. "Did you see those gnarly things on our way in?"

"Yeah," said Luca. "They looked mean."

"Or a vulture beast," said Ceiba. "I've heard about those vulture-type things out here. They might even be worse."

"Or one of those soldiers," interjected Elton. "I wouldn't mind killing one or two of them myself."

"Guys, I think we should try to get out of here as fast as we can," said Luca, his voice low. "Let's keep our eyes on the lookout for exit doors, their locking system, everything we can. They didn't sound like they were going to keep us around for long. We have to get out of here."

"This place is heavily guarded," said Tanner. "If we could find a way to get our weapons, we might stand a chance. But, if we don't have our Neutralisers, there's no way."

"The lizard king has those weapons now," said Elton. "There's probably no way to get them."

"From what Phaeton told me," said Luca, "Beyul Atoll should not be too far from here. I'm quite sure it's a more civilised place. Phaeton wouldn't have told me about it if it weren't safe. Although he never mentioned the Jungle or all the mutants."

"He probably didn't want to scare you," said Elton. "They've been living out here for a long time. That's one reason Acacia Burj authorities never told us much about the Wilds – only enough to frighten us."

Just then the water stopped.

"Guess the shower's over," said Tanner.

Randa and Sosa appeared with surprisingly soft towels. Neither woman said a thing as they stood and waited for Luca and his friends to dry off. Luca noticed that the women smelled like spice. Once they were done, Randa handed them a stack of hides of various colours.

"What are these?" asked Ceiba.

"They are to wear around your bottoms," said Sosa. She gestured towards her hips. Luca could have sworn she winked at him.

"I think these are loincloths," said Tanner. "If you recall ancient history–"

"Here," Randa said. "Don't be long. Then come across the hall where we have food prepared."

"And if you have any trouble tying these things around your hips, let us know and we'll help," said Sosa.

"I think we can manage," said Luca. He could feel his face burning hot and knew he was blushing.

After some analysis of how to wear the loincloths, the boys tied the strips of leather hides around them. They couldn't help but giggle a little.

"Well, well," said Elton. "Looks like Ceiba wins the prize for the prettiest legs."

"Cut it out," said Ceiba, poking him lightly in the arm. "This is embarrassing enough as it is."

They all laughed out loud then. They all agreed that they looked ridiculous, as if they were wearing miniskirts from the Retros' wardrobes. "At least we'll be cooler," Luca said.

Luca felt ridiculous and he knew the others did, as well. The parts of their bodies that had not been exposed to the sun were pasty white. Other areas were sunburned bright red. But the young men were strong – or at least they would be after some food.

They crossed the hallway into another room that looked like a feeding room. In the middle was a long stone table and on it were various platters of roast meat.

"What is this?" asked Elton.

"We have prepared boiled vulture beasts, raptorenas, rattle-snake, wild grasses, pigeon eggs, and fruit." Randa seemed very proud of the food. There was also bread and cheeses and a big pitcher of some kind of liquid.

Ceiba was ghostly white and looked like he was going to pass out from the smells alone. But Tanner's and Elton's mouths watered. The smells were rich and pungent and made their stomachs clench. Luca wasn't so sure he could eat the meat, but the bread, cheeses and fruit looked tasty.

Randa and Sosa stood by, insisting that they sit down and eat. The women poured a thick liquid into rusted metal cups.

When Luca took a sip, it had the consistency of a milkshake, but tasted like a mixture of water and honey and some kind of flower essence. It made him kind of woozy when he drank it though, so he only sipped it lightly. There were no instruments to eat with, so they had to use their fingers. Ceiba barely picked at the food, but Luca devoured the cheese and fruit. Tanner and Elton experimented with the meats, but their faces turned green after a few bites. The food was simply too rich for their perfectly balanced and manufactured plant diets.

After a few minutes, Randa raised her ebony hand.

"Stop! That is enough. You will get sick if you eat more. We will take you to the cages now."

One by one, Luca, Ceiba, Tanner and Elton followed the women down a long, narrow dirt hallway beneath the Jungle. Randa illuminated the wall torches on either side of the hall, lighting their way. They came to an area that widened. This was when the horror really began. The smell hit them first. Faeces, filth and rot filtered in their nostrils. Luca and Ceiba both gagged.

Metal cages lined the hallway as far as the eye could see. Hay covered the floors and on top of the hay were the prisoners. Human men, women and children. They were all filthy and bloodied with straggly hair. Some were wearing remnants of bodysuits from Acacia Burj and others were wearing hides tied around their bodies. Luca wondered if the ones with the hides were the fighters. Now and then, there were mutant prisoners – even a couple of reptile types. But mostly, they were humans, and mostly, they looked like escapees from Acacia Burj.

Some of the prisoners looked up at them and a couple of the children cried, "Help us! Please get us out!"

Randa put her fingers to her lips, shushing them, and the children slunk back into their cages. Finally, they came to the empty cages. No larger than a couple of metres square, they were not designed for comfort. However, in these cages, there was a small bed and a bowl of water. The boys each had their own cage, but they were next to each other so at least they could call to each other. At this point, Luca was trying to find *anything* to be positive about. Randa and Sosa locked the cage doors.

"Here you go, boys. Home. Good luck to you," said Randa.

"Thank you," said Luca.

Randa turned and looked at him sadly. "I do not think you will be thanking me after tomorrow."

Then she turned and walked with Sosa down the hallway. Luca sat down on the floor and put his head in his hands. He was sure they would die here.

Chapter Forty-Nine

Asia Mae smiled at him. Her long black hair gleamed in the moonlight and the wind brushed it gently across her face. Being with her was enough. Her spirit was so light, so beautiful; he never wanted to leave her side again. She put her arm through his.

"Asia Mae, where have you been all this time?" Luca asked her. "I've been looking for you."

She kissed him on the cheek. "I've always been here. I'm always by your side. I'll never leave you, Luca."

Luca leaned in to kiss her; really kiss her.

A loud bell rang out, waking everyone in the cages. Luca sat up and rubbed his eyes. *Damn!* It had just been a dream. And now, *this* was the dream, or rather, the nightmare. A nightmare that was real and never-ending.

All night long, Luca had heard people yelling and crying. Evidently, no one patrolled the cages at night, so people yelled freely. It was almost impossible to fall asleep, but his body was so exhausted, he soon passed out and escaped to his world of dreams.

A bowl of slop was shoved into Luca's cage by a short, squat lizard.

"What are they feeding us, guys?" yelled Ceiba.

"I think it's some kind of porridge – a grain or something," said Tanner. He was in the cage right across from Luca. Elton and Ceiba were next door, across from one another.

"Yeah, remember, they want to fatten us up," said Elton in the cage next door. "That will take a while."

"Did everyone get some sleep?" asked Luca.

"Except for the nightmares," said Ceiba.

Looking at their faces, Luca didn't believe that a single one of them thought they were safe, but the conversation made things feel a little less sombre in a world that was so opposite to everything they had ever known.

"Do you have any family left, Elton?" asked Ceiba.

"I doubt it. My parents are probably dead on the Moon. And my sister, Sumer, probably died during the storm. I think she would have come for me at the prison if she had been alive." His shoulders slumped forward, resigned to being alone in the world.

"Well, maybe your sister Sumer is alive somewhere," said Ceiba.

"I doubt it but at least she's not in this godforsaken place," said Elton. "I couldn't stand seeing her in here."

"None of us know who is alive or dead," said Luca. "Let's not even think that way."

Tanner nodded. "Luca's right. We've got to stay positive or we'll never stand a chance of surviving."

Luca took his fingers and dipped them into the slop. It was thick and sticky. He brought his fingers to his lips and tasted it: grainy like a mixture of wheat and water – it wasn't bad. He ate it all. He wanted to build up his strength for whatever came next. Everyone was quiet as they finished their slop.

It wasn't long before two lizards came for them. They looked fierce with scaled skin and dark, watchful eyes. They unlocked the cages and tied the boys' hands with leather straps, motioning for them to follow. Not a word was spoken. They walked the opposite way to where they had entered, down a long, narrow stretch of hallway where the cages were empty. There had to be hundreds of cages in this underground cave. They came to a stairway that led upwards to the outside. When they stepped through the door, Luca couldn't believe his eyes. The heat filtering through the metal garbage roof pricked at his skin. Long slender shafts of light filtered through the stale arena air onto the sandy ground stained in blood. The boys stood there in the loincloths on a platform in an amphitheatre. Luca felt naked. A roar surrounded them from all sides.

In front of them was a large electro-caged arena. It was filled with row upon row, tier upon tier, where pirates, savages and mutants of all kinds sat cheering into the distance. The citizens of the Jungle were all shouting, raising their fists. It made Luca and his friends sick with fear.

Reclining on cushions on a stage to the side, surrounded by mutant lizard soldiers, was King Lah-mu Lemuria. He hissed into an old-fashioned tannoy system: "Welcome to the Gauntlet."

Everyone cheered. Luca and his group were to be the entertainment for the day.

"What's going to happen?" asked Ceiba. Sweat trickled down his cheeks.

"Yeah, what happened to fattening us up?" said Elton. "We've only had one meal!"

A sidekick standing next to Lah-mu Lemuria took the microphone. "Great citizens of the Jungle: as you know, Running the Gauntlet is not for the fainthearted. Not many survive." Everyone in the arena laughed. "But, if they manage to succeed, they will live to fight another day."

Lah-mu Lemuria interjected, his claws snatched at the microphone: "There are great rewards for any champion who can get past our fighters and face the great Pithekos duel without getting torn to shreds. As long as you win, you will stay alive."

With great ceremony, strange music rang out around the arena. In to the arena came huge robots, metal creatures scratching up against each other, glinting in the bright sunlight. There were ear-piercing screeches as the robots positioned themselves. Luca quickly realised that each robot had a team of supporters in the crowd, and an individual savage controlling it.

The first robot to be announced moved over the ground like a spider; deftly moving around on its slender metal legs which were studded with short, sharp daggers. Luca followed the cheers to locate this robot's team, huddled on the far side of the arena. It was a group of savages not dissimilar to the ones that had led them out of the salt flats. Their dirty, braided hair swung around them as they pumped their fists in the air. At the front of the group, one of the savages was wearing a headset and gloves that looked as though it might control the robot remotely. As Luca watched with narrowed eyes, the savage controlling the spider-like robot spun around, making the robot spin too. As the team cheered, the controller raised his hands aloft which in turn raised the metal spider's two front legs high into the sky, its weapons spinning with circular saws. Luca and his friends shuddered as they started to realise what the Gauntlet truly involved.

"Oh, no," whispered Ceiba. His whole body shook. Luca shot Ceiba a look, worried that his friend would pass out on the ground before he even got to the robots. They were not designed to fight this way and knew nothing about the Laws of the Jungle. They didn't have a single weapon.

The robots continued to emerge, each team making a show of their fighter by getting it to display its deadly weapons. The crowd was getting increasingly excited. Presumably at the thought of bloodshed.

One robot moved around excitedly like an excitable dog, snapping jaws lined with needle-like teeth. Another just looked to be a tracked sphere until it started shooting balls of fire from the pits in its surface. Each metal creature was painted with a colour, matching it to its team of controllers on the edge of the arena.

"So what else is in the Gauntlet?" Luca quietly asked the guard beside him.

"You don't know about the Pithekos?" the lizard asked.

The boys shook their heads and the lizard chuckled.

"The great Pithekos are mutant ape-like beasts. They were quite gentle before we wired them up. But don't worry too much. Have you taken a good look at these robots? You won't even make it past them!"

"We'll see," said Luca, tightening his jaw.

"And don't even think about trying to escape," the lizard added. "You'll be torn to shreds as soon as you try to make a getaway, if not by the robots then by crowd. They like a good fight."

Do not forget who you are, Luca... we are Ancient Entanglers," said Serenissima in a faraway voice that sounded like heavenly music in Luca's mind in the midst of this great stadium of hell. *"Our thoughts are connected."* A cool breeze blew in Luca's face. *"I am here to help you."*

In the middle of the roar of the arena and the sweltering sun, Luca remembered several dreams. He wasn't sure what they meant, but they gave him an idea. He had often played a virtual game at the Arcade that involved fighting robots. He recalled that during all of the games, one skill he had strengthened was his focus. He remembered how it had served him well in all his gaming battles and even when he fought the aliens at Mariana, and on the *Sibylline* on the Moon. Maybe he could utilise this focus again to help win this battle.

Luca stepped forward. "King Lemuria," he shouted, as loud as he dared. He waved his arms and seemed to silence the crowd. "May I speak?"

Lah-mu Lemuria looked at Luca, shocked that anyone dare address him in the arena. The robots stopped their macabre dance as the teams paused to listen. Amused, he said: "Go ahead."

"I would like to make a bet for my friends' lives," said Luca.

Everyone shouted. Ceiba, Tanner and Elton all looked at him like he was crazy.

"You want to barter your life for theirs?" asked the lizard.

"Sir... er... King Lemuria," said Luca, "if I can race through the gauntlet and not be harmed by the robots, and make it safely to the Pithekos, I will then fight the Pithekos alone, and you will allow my friends to go back to the cages without fighting."

"I don't understand the benefit of this," said Lah-mu Lemuria.

"They're still exhausted from our journey," said Luca. "They won't be at all entertaining for your audience because the robots will be bored with them. Keep my friends a few days longer and get them fatter, stronger. It will be better sport for your crowds. But I'm strong enough to give it a go. Let me be the entertainment for today. If the Gauntlet kills me, then do what you will. But let me be the only one that fights today."

"No!" shouted Penan from the stands, waving money in his hands. "I want to see some blood!"

"Quiet!" ordered Lah-mu Lemuria. "This is a most unusual offer, but it is not invalid. I will accept the young man's bet. He will run through the Gauntlet and if he is not killed by the robots, he will be allowed to fight the reigning champion of the Pithekos for the title. We will put meat on the bones of his friends for another day. As he said, it will be better sport."

"Luca, this is insane," Tanner said behind him.

"You can't do this," agreed Elton. "We don't need a martyr."

Tears ran down Ceiba's cheeks. He couldn't speak.

Luca looked back at them.

"It's okay. If anything happens, tell my family I love them, and Ceiba, tell Asia Mae I love her and I will see her in the next life." He choked on his last words.

Tanner couldn't stand it. "Let me take your place!" he yelled. He attempted to throw himself in front of Luca before they took him away but as fast as lightning, a guard flicked out his tail and caught Tanner across the chest. He staggered back, blood dripping from his body.

"Tanner!" yelled Luca. "Don't!"

"Do not be foolish," admonished Lah-mu Lemuria. "The young boy has made a fine deal with me. Do not try that again or I will feed you to the beasts myself."

Tanner flinched and tears stung his eyes. The three boys stood there together, helpless, with their hands tied behind them, blood trailing down Tanner's chest. Luca knew they were convinced he couldn't survive the onslaught of the ferocious, starving beasts in the cages in front of them.

A bell sounded and Luca watched as what had to be two Pithekos – about twenty metres tall – rose out of the underground entrance at the end of the arena and stomped forward. The whole ground wavered as if an earthquake were about to rip apart the land. One of the giant ape beasts was covered with brown patchy hair. Slobber ran down its face. The other had black hair and snorted loudly. Around their necks were bulky collars which served as cabin-like control rooms for the fighters to manually control the apes. The apes cried out and the crowd reacted.

All Luca had to do was get through the robots to the Pithekos. He'd then climb inside the giant ape and fight for survival. He assumed the opposing Pithekos was already being controlled from inside control collar. He could do this. He just had to focus. *Focus. Focus.*

Two lizard guards escorted Luca down to the arena floor, followed by a group of savages riding on the backs of an array of mutant creatures. Some of these savages carried weapons that looked like Neutralisers and others had whips and chains. They were all clad in armour that looked as though it had been cobbled together from scrap metal and leather. One of the strange, giant dog-like creatures snapped its jaws noisily at Luca's back and he felt its hot breath on his neck as it sniffed at him. The guards untied the leather strips that had bound Luca's hands behind him, and he rubbed at his sore wrists, his hands shaking.

"Remember," said one guard, jerking his head towards the entourage of savages and mutant animals. "If you try to escape, this lot will tear you to shreds before we can shoot you. You have to fight. Or die."

Luca nodded.

A gong rang out. The robots stood motionless facing of him. As the slow ringing started, the arena fell silent for just a moment and then exploded again into a cacophony of excited, bloodthirsty screaming and shouting. The robots buzzed and whirred into action, taking only seconds to locate their prey.

Luca assessed the situation. The Pithekos seemed far off. He had no weapon; nothing. He was frozen to the spot, trying to get his bearings. One of the savages cracked his whip sharply against Luca's back. "Get a move on, boy!" he yelled, laughing. Luca cringed in pain. A few of the robots broke forward from the pack, lunging towards him. The spider-like robot flashed its circular saws above its body and another thrashed out with dagger-like arms. They seemed so alive.

Luca watched as the spider robot jumped forward until it was facing him. It didn't seem to have any eyes or a face. *It was just a piece of metal,* he told himself. Without warning, the robot flicked out a leg as if to test itself, catching Luca on the shin.

As Luca looked down at the trickle of deep red blood running down his leg, he knew the fight was on. The robot tried to move closer, kicking out its blades at him and raising its spinning saws over its body. Luca rolled right to avoid the vicious kicks, he tried to form a plan. *This robot was the first of many, but what if he could use it against the others?* He jumped as high as he could, holding his arms into his body to avoid the blades and raising his knees. He had timed it well and came crunching down on the joint of one of the robots legs, temporarily tipping it off balance. Without pausing, Luca threw himself onto the surface of the robot's body, sprawling beneath the spinning saws. Over the terrible whirring sound, he thought he could hear the noise of the crowd drop as they held their breath. *They must think this is over already.*

"Kill him! Kill him!" Amidst the roar of sadistic chants, Luca studied the two deadly arms poised above him. He summoned all his strength and kicked out at one of them, aiming at the side of the joint. It bent, snapped and the saw spun into two or three approaching robots, bursting them into flames. He took a deep breath and slid out from underneath it, kneeling on the robot and grabbing the top of the other arm for balance. The robot jumped around, trying to throw him off but he clung to another section of arm beneath the spinning blade, pushing it towards the other oncoming robots. Sparks flew everywhere, metal shards and hydraulic oil peppered the arena. *What next?*

"I am with you," said Serenissima. She touched his arm. He could feel her energy – *a tingling spark* – and from somewhere ancient that bore no explanation, an incredible strength filled him.

Luca laser-focused on the other side of the arena – past the danger. He envisioned himself there, safely past the robots. A sparkling light surrounded him. He wasn't sure if anyone else could see it, but he could. It was as if points of jewelled, buzzing light flowed from his body.

Just as it looked like one of the robot's snapping jaws would crunch down on his limbs, he saw his chance. Spotting a gap in the chaos, he jumped from the top of the robot and slipped through an opening. One of the robots lashed out at him but he managed to dodge it and began to run towards the Pithekos.

Luca, Ceiba and Elton cheered. The crowds went wild. Some were actually cheering *for* Luca. Others were screaming at the robot teams to kill him.

The robots spun around, confused, looking for their vanished victim. But Luca was already at the other end of the arena, running as fast as his legs would carry him towards the Pithekos. Fearless. The robots scattered after Luca, and just as the fastest few were about to close in on him, Luca jumped again, and this time, landed on the bridge of the Pithekos's back. How in the world had he managed to jump so high? Luca didn't have time to reason out the answer. The robots clashed and clawed at each other on the ground beneath him. More sparks flew as the fans and supports took their rage out on individual robot controllers.

Luca stood on the shoulder of the Pithekos, and gazed across the gigantic stadium. A bell rang out, signalling the end of the robot fight. He punched the air; adrenaline beating through his body.

"The young Luca has earned the right to fight the Pithekos," said Lah-mu Lemuria. "Take the robots away."

The crowd roared, eager for the next, bigger fight. *It would be a fight to the death.*

Chapter Fifty

Phaeton squeezed Sumer's hand as they glided through the sea. It was hard not to notice that there was a difference in the sea after the solar storm had hit. It wasn't a calm and hopeful bright blue anymore. It swirled with turbulence and was a bitter grey. As they neared the shore, they navigated through parts of buildings that were sticking out of the water, as if struggling to stand upright and alive. There were towers from the destroyed satellites floating sideways and piles of concrete and glass where sky-buildings had crumbled. Phaeton knew there had been a smaller mega city south of Acacia Burj, but no one he knew had ever travelled there. And now, it looked as though that smaller city was completely drowned.

Phaeton instructed Sumer to go to a boat dock further south. From the historical maps Sumer had found in an archive panel inside the Zipper, she and Phaeton had located an abandoned ancient village called Evergreen a safe distance north of Acacia Burj. Even this area was considered the Wilds – The Garbage Pit – and had been off limits to the Civils of Acacia Burj. Sumer agreed that it would be safer docking here than risking going back to her home. There was no way of knowing what was going on in Acacia Burj right now.

Asia Mae sat behind Phaeton and Sumer. Scar lay on the makeshift pod-bed behind her. His snoring grated on Asia Mae's nerves. Now and then he would raise his head and yell: "Where in tarnation am I? What's going on?"

Phaeton would reassure him, and with that, Scar would slump back down on the bed and start snoring again.

As they approached the shore of Evergreen, Sumer guided the Zipper through long since abandoned vehicles anchored to the sea floor and hovering in mid water. The Zipper swayed gently while the bow sliced through the long rolling swells. There wasn't much to see. The old pier looked to be rotting and a few wrecked sea craft had been washed ashore. Sumer pulled up onto the pristine beach and powered down.

"Let's get out and see what we can find," said Phaeton. "I need to stretch my legs. Asia Mae, why don't you stay here with Scar?"

"No way," she said, flipping her hair out of her face. "I'm coming with you."

Leaving Scar alone in the shuttle, the three unlocked the hatch and climbed out. Clouds of eerie fog and a swirling mist shrouded the village and it was as quiet as an enclosed medical pod. From somewhere, came the raucous cawing of a bird. Asia Mae shuddered. Phaeton put his arm protectively around Sumer.

"It feels good to stand up again," said Phaeton. He held one hand over his chest and he breathed in deeply, wincing as if in pain.

"How are you?" asked Sumer, nuzzling her head in his shoulder. "You've been quietly moaning ever since we left Mariana."

"It's nothing," said Phaeton. "Probably a couple of broken ribs. I'll survive."

"Promise me you'll tell me if you need something," said Sumer.

"Promise," he said, kissing her on the cheek. They lingered in one another's arms.

"Let's not hang around long," said Asia Mae, averting her eyes. "There could be savages here." She was delighted that Sumer and Phaeton had found one another, but the truth was, seeing the couple together irritated her and she didn't know why. Then, all of a sudden, it dawned on her. She was jealous! Seeing them together made her homesick for her friends. For intimacy. For love.

"Sure," said Sumer. "Let's just have a quick look, and then we'll be on our way."

Asia Mae managed a weak smile, then walked ahead to breathe in the fresh air and give Phaeton and Sumer some privacy. The village was small, but ripe with the melancholy of a lost time. Most of the wooden and brick buildings had caved in on crumbling concrete roads long ago. Wild plants and weeds wound through old windows and rotted doorways. Asia Mae knew it was stupid to wander very far, but she had never seen such tall green trees with fur all over their limbs. She kept walking through the old town, embarrassed about being jealous of Phaeton and Sumer.

At the edge of the town, she stepped gingerly around a dried-out riverbed, covered by a layer of slick rocks and wet, mushy leaves. A few lilac flowers sat in clumps around the rocks. Everything smelled like wet earth. Pungent. Piercing. She stopped and gazed up at the tall fir trees that reached into the moody grey skies. She heard a rustle behind her and assumed Sumer and Phaeton had finally followed her.

"Did you guys decide to explore a little, too?" asked Asia Mae. She flipped her dark hair back from her shoulders and turned around. No one was there. "Sumer? Phaeton?"

There was a crack and rustle of leaves in a thicket of trees. Something large was moving through the woods. Asia Mae froze. *A savage? Another refuge from Acacia?* She silently cursed herself for not bringing a Neutraliser with her.

She couldn't move. She could feel the looming shape approaching her and could smell something... *an animal.* She turned ever so slightly. There stood a mutant bald bear, its matted fur grungy with dirt as if it had rolled around in mud. Even on all four legs, the beast was much taller than Asia Mae. Its dark eyes peered at her, sizing her up. Asia Mae's first instinct was to glance at her sensor-pad to get a reading on the animal and to ask for options. She silently laughed. Sensor-pads didn't work anymore.

Fear coursed through every cell in Asia Mae's body. The bear began to growl as it tensed up in a crouch, baring its teeth. It was so close she could smell its breath, which stank of rotted fish. She was his prey.

She was going to have to run. She couldn't take on a bear, but it was coming closer, swinging forward step by step. She tried to run, but her feet wouldn't move. The bear parted its lips in a sneer that showed its yellowing teeth and it lunged at her.

Just then, something sailed through the air and hit the bear straight between the eyes. The bear groaned and, with a heavy thud, fell on its side. Asia Mea was transfixed by the excessive ripples of blubber as the beast hit the deck.

Behind her stood Sumer. She had thrown a large rock at the bear and has seemingly knocked it out. *Good lord,* thought Asia Mae.

"Got him!" yelled Sumer.

"Wow, thank you," said Asia Mae. "I didn't know there were bears out here."

"I think there's probably a lot of things we don't know about out here in the Wilds," said Sumer, winking.

Just then, Phaeton came running through the trees.

"Oh, Phaeton!" Asia Mae ran to them and put her arms around both of them. "Your girlfriend is something else! I thought I was going to die!"

"Yep, good thing I showed up," said Sumer.

"I say let's get outta here," said Phaeton.

Asia Mae nodded and the three of them ran back towards where the shuttle was docked. Her heart was still thudding and her legs trembling.

"What are we going to do now?" asked Asia Mae. "That bear will come round soon and start looking for us. He's not going to be happy!"

Pushing through the fir trees, the three of them came to a standstill at the same time, their mouths dropping open in shock. The shuttle was gone. Tracks in the sand indicated the direction of travel into the distance.

"He's taken it!" exclaimed Asia Mae. "I can't believe it. Just as I was starting to trust him."

"We should never have left him with it," said Phaeton. "I bet he wasn't as injured as he said he was."

"If my dad was here, he would kill me," said Sumer sadly.

They were stranded on this beach, with nothing around them apart from perhaps more mutant bears. The group talked about what they should do before falling into silence for several minutes as they each reflected on the seriousness of their situation. Eventually, Phaeton said: "I know. Look, we passed some old abandoned boats anchored just off shore. If we can bring one to the surface, I know how to run those things."

"Really?" asked Asia Mae.

"I've driven one or two," said Phaeton. "If they have properly stored fuel cells, then they should work. Some do and some don't."

To the roar of an angry bald bear just beyond the beach, the three of them ran down into the water and jumped into the sea. The nearest and newest looking one was about twenty meters out and five meters down. The three of them dived down and freed the boat from its tether and it broke the surface.

They clambered aboard, realising the bear had tracked them onto the beach. Sumer started frantically cleaning the green slime from the outside, clearing mud from the sealed cockpit window with her T-shirt. It smelled of musty seaweed and dirt. Phaeton lifted the access hatch and climbed in. After several minutes, and with the viewing windows now clear, he happily announced: "A Cruiser! Climb in everybody. Let's start this baby up!"

As if by some miracle, the engine of the boat whispered into life. Grabbing the wheel, Phaeton reversed the boat away from the beach and accelerated away from Evergreen to the open sea. They glanced back only a couple of times, bouncing and bumping over the waves. They were now living in a daring, strange, and archaic world.

Chapter Fifty-One

"Well done, well done," said Lah-mu Lemuria. "Now, it is time to fight our reigning champion. If you beat him, you will be our new champion. As long as you win, you'll stay alive. Please, Champion of the Pithekos, come out and face your opponent."

As Luca stood on the shoulder of his Pithekos, a human opened the cockpit door in the collar-cabin around the neck of the opposing Pithekos and came out to face him. His hair was long and stringy, and he wore a loincloth across the bottom half of his body. He was tall and muscular, and bore a scar across his cheek under one eye. Luca experienced the shock of recognition. The guy standing before him was Thitis, one of the boys who had run after him and his friends that night on the docks.

"Thitis?" asked Luca, shocked.

"Well, well, look what we have here!" said Thitis, sneering at him. "Ready to play with the big boys?"

"Look, let's play this smart," said Luca. *Could he possibly talk any sense into this guy?*

"There's only one way to play and that's to win," said Thitis, puffing up his bronzed chest.

"How long have you been here?" asked Luca.

"Long enough to be a champion that cannot be beaten. You don't stand a chance against me."

"It looks like our two opponents might know one another," announced Lah-mu Lemuria, who had extraordinarily good hearing.

The crowd roared again.

"The Pithekos respond to human control," said Lah-mu Lemuria over the megaphone. He seemed to take great pride in describing the events. "Ladies, gentlemen, and others, we will see if our new opponent, Luca, can take down our reigning champion, Thitis. Let's get started."

The crowd roared, and from Luca's perch, he could see more betting taking place. Ceiba, Tanner and Elton seemed small and far away on the platform. But they were alive and Luca was grateful. If he died, at least he could be at peace, knowing they would survive for a few days and hopefully even find a way to escape.

"Let's get the show started," said Thitis, sneering at him. His eyebrows drawn together, he looked just as mean as he had done back on the beach. *Some people just don't learn*, thought Luca.

He and Thitis climbed into the giant collars around the necks of their respective Pithekos. For a moment, Luca felt like he was back at the Arcade, getting ready for a virtual game. But the reality of the slash on his leg and the churning in his gut told him otherwise. He put on the headset that was hanging from the old-fashioned control board and sat down. He placed his hands carefully around the control sticks and placed his feet in the stirrups.

Luca lightly moved the controls and felt his Pithekos respond accordingly. It felt similar to the old-fashioned Arcade games he had played, but this was too realistic. Then he heard the horn sound. He could do this.

The two Pithekos stood as formidable opponents. It took a long moment for Luca to get his bearings. Before he really had time to act, his giant ape lunged forward and ducked down into a wrestling position. It would be over before it even began if he didn't get it together.

Sweat rolled down Luca's face and he glanced at the crowds in the arena. The momentary distraction cost him as Thitis swung his right arm into Luca's Pithekos. Thitis was coming at him at full force and had the advantage; he must have fought with his Pithekos several times. The two giant animals wrestled and their slamming footsteps shook the floor.

"Luca, focus," said Serenissima. *"Focus. The way is in you. Don't forget who you are. You must believe in yourself. We are Ancient Entanglers and I am always with you."*

Luca struggled. As the giant apes grappled each other into new positions, their two collars were suddenly side by side. Luca looked at Thitus in horror.

"Free the Pithekos," said Serenissima. *"They never wanted to fight like this."*

Free it? What did that mean? And then he remembered what the guard had said. These mutant apes had been wired to fight.

With a new purpose, Luca moved his Pithekos to grab at the wrist of its opponent, twisting it so forcefully that Thitus' Pithekos had to move and bend to try to release the grip. Twisting the Pithekos's arm up behind its back, Luca got a clear view of the wiring panel set into the back of its head.

With his spare hand, Luca reached out and tore at the control panel. He was scared of hurting the creature but he knew he didn't have much time. The panel came away and crashed to the floor far below. The fighting stopped. Wires sparked in the Pithekos's thick hair but it stayed standing, staring into space.

The move had taken his opponent by surprise and Luca could see that Thitus had paused momentarily, looking at him through the window of the collar cabin with a confused look upon his face. Then he began hammering at the controls. But nothing worked. The connection was broken.

A thrill coursed through Luca's veins. He had won! He didn't know what that meant for Thitis, but it had to be good for Luca and his friends.

His massive ape just stood motionless.

Suddenly, a noise shook Luca, vibrating through the control panel. It was Thitus' Pithekos roaring. Luca watched dumbstruck as the Pithekos grappled at the control collar around its neck. Thitus looked terrified as the Pithekos finally managed to tear it off and sent it hurtling into the crowd, right at Lah-mu Lemuria. Luca tore his eyes away. He didn't want to see this.

Everywhere else, the crowds were scattering in terror. Thitus' Pithekos was on the rampage, stomping around the arena and reaching out to grab whatever it could get its hands on. Savages, pirates, lizards and other mutants were running out of the arena and out into the Wilds. Running for their lives.

Luca realised this was the only opportunity they would have to escape. He moved his Pithekos towards where he had left Ceiba, Tanner and Elton, and spotted them sheltering behind a wagon. He held out the hand of his Pithekos on the floor beside them and they hesitantly climbed into its palm. Bringing them up to the control cabin, Luca flung open the door and pulled them inside.

"Luca!" Ceiba flung his arms around his friend. But there was no time for celebration.

"We need to get out of here!" said Luca.

"Is there any way we can release the other prisoners?" asked Elton, resting his hand on Luca's shoulder.

"You're right, Elton," agreed Luca. "Let's see what we can do."

The boys grabbed on to whatever they could to hold themselves steady as their Pithekos awkwardly knelt at the entrance to the building they had been held captive in. It ripped off the door that led downwards into the prisoners' chambers, discarding it to one side. The crazed roars of Thitus' Pithekos still raged behind them, somewhere in the Jungle. Reaching inside with its arm, Luca clenched and unclenched his Pithekos's fist, trying to get a grip on the central cage locking system.

Finally, he felt the bar catch in the Pithekos's fingers and yanked on them. All cage doors flung open in unison and hundreds of prisoners ran free. Tanner directed them away from the mayhem of the arena towards the savages' collection of old automobiles and other exotic looking vehicles parked directly below the arena floor. They would be free!

"Good idea! I think they can look after themselves from here," said Tanner. "Let's just get the hell out of here!"

"Wait," cried Ceiba, pointing outside. "What's that?"

The window of the collar cabin was being pelted by red liquid. The Pithekos wiped it away with one hand but it kept coming back.

"It must be the blood rain they're all so scared of," said Elton.

"Let's go," said Luca. He turned the Pithekos to face the far end of the arena, after which the Jungle fell away and the Wilds opened up before them. He manoeuvred the cumbersome legs of the giant Pithekos through the giant arena doors and out into the emptiness of the Wilds. The blood rain pounded down even harder. The sky lit up when a funnel as high as the sky itself whirled to the side and struck the earth with a sound so loud, it shrieked in their ears.

Luca could see vehicles driving in all directions out into the Wilds – out into freedom. The blood rain didn't seem to bother them. Perhaps only the citizens of the Jungle were superstitious about the red rain.

"By the way, good work, Champion!" said Elton, slapping Luca on the back.

"I hope I didn't permanently damage it," said Luca, thinking of the other Pithekos as he attended the controls. "It wasn't his fault they engineered him to fight. Do you think Thitis is still alive back there?"

"Hey, don't feel sorry for him," said Elton. "That dude got what he deserved."

Luca shrugged. It felt like a small victory. But they had freed all the other prisoners, and he and his friends were alive and free of the Jungle, as well.

Once their excitement calmed down, they travelled for what seemed like hours in the Pithekos's collar. They had long ago been passed by the refugees who had fled the Jungle. The blood rain stopped and finally, the moon started shining through dark, but somewhat calmer, skies.

The boys had taken turns to sleep and navigate to the Beyul Atoll. They didn't really know where they were going – not in the dark. But when the morning came, Luca remembered Phaeton telling him about a ridge of rocky mountains that had white on top of them.

Phaeton had explained during one of their conversations about the Wilds. "Once you see those mountains with the snow, just keep going towards them. Beyul Atoll is in the sea beyond them."

Luca yawned. His muscles were still sore, but for the first time in a long time, he had new hope.

"There, head towards those mountains!" said Luca, excitedly pointing to vast mountains covered with snow.

"They look like they're about a day's travel from here," said

Tanner. "I think we should walk from here and let this Pithekos go?"

As if it had heard them, the Pithekos began to slow down and then stumbled to a stop.

"I think it's exhausted," said Tanner. "Without its help we would never have escaped the Jungle, we owe it our lives."

Luca nodded. He couldn't praise the great Pithekos enough. It slumped down to the ground. They gathered the Neutralisers and their few belongings and shimmied down its hairy arms to the ground. Luca looked sadly at the great beast. Ceiba climbed up around the beast's shoulders and hauled away the control board, groaning with effort as he hauled it to the floor. He carefully pulled out the remaining wires.

"You're free now. Thank you!" Luca said, touching its huge wet nose and looking deep into the creature's eyes. The ape grunted hard and smiled. He felt great empathy for his new friend, the giant ape that had taken them to safety. But they had little time for emotion.

They were still in dry, barren lands under an angry, stormy sky, and the mountains seemed far away. At least they had a clear direction now. Behind them the second Pithekos quietly appeared through the landscape and gestured sensitively to its fighting partner. With a final look towards Luca and his friends their new friend disappeared.

"How in the world did Phaeton travel so easily back and forth from Acacia Burj to out here?" asked Tanner. "It feels like we're so far away from anywhere."

"Thanks to my sister," said Elton. "She provided him with everything he needed to be comfortable out here. He had an old style Bullet super-bike and even a Zipper shuttle at times, when they were available, and when Sumer could sneak them out of the military hangar. It only took him a couple of days to travel back and forth. Of course, I never really got the full story about Beyul Atoll."

"Beyul Atoll has to be better than the Jungle," said Ceiba. "I'll be happy if I never have to see another lizard again."

"You and me both! Beyul Atoll is an Outcasts settlement, and we've seen how Outcasts are treated by the Savages who have always lived out here in the Wilds," said Elton.

"I don't know why anyone would want to go the Jungle," said Ceiba.

"Some people don't know any better," said Luca. "They think that what they have there is the best that life has to offer, it isn't their fault really."

"Beyul Atoll surely has a better way of life," said Luca. "From what Phaeton said, they're a secret community that's just trying to stay off the radar. Now we know why."

As they slogged wearily across the plains, they came across steep drops that led to ravines below, and pools filled with the previous night's blood rain where insects buzzed. Bloated, dead ones floated on the surface. Now and then, they spotted glow-ring snakes slithering under rocks and luminous scorpions scooting under shrubs – all things they had seen before, but never in real life. They noticed strange green plants with arms that seemed to move as they walked passed.

"Don't get too close to those," warned Elton. "Everything is fighting for survival out here."

"And we always thought gaming was wild and dangerous," said Ceiba in a quiet, hoarse voice.

"We were naïve back then," said Luca. "We thought the virtuals were the most exciting worlds to live in. Now look at us."

They walked and said very little, schlepping one foot in front of the other until they were so bone-tired and dehydrated, they could walk no more. Tumbleweed floated by their feet like wisps of cotton and clung to their blistered feet. By now, dawn was drifting rose-coloured up over the distant mountains and if Luca had not been so exhausted, he would have thought there had never been a more stunning morning. Some stars were still blinking like diamonds behind the red and charcoal aster clouds, canopying the world like a giant kaleidoscope of prisms. The Moon was somewhere up there. He just hadn't found it yet.

Grampa Sol's wife, Celeste, Luca's grandmother, had been a star reader. Luca had never known her; she had died before he was born. But, according to Grampa Sol, she had come from a long line of star readers. Luca wondered what she would see in the stars if she were here tonight. He wondered if she was an Ancient Entangler as well.

As hot as the Wilds could get during the day, it was still dangerously cold at this time of the morning. The chill sharpened in their bones like a hacksaw gnawing through them, the wounds from the lizards' tails still stung on their sunburned backs, and their feet were peppered with fat, oozing blisters. Luca and his friends stopped. They could walk no more.

They quietly ate the food Luca had smuggled out of Jungle City, drank the last of the water, and collapsed against a boulder. Animals they weren't familiar with howled in the distance. The wind picked up and moaned an eerie call to them. Huddled against the boulder, they barely listened.

They were freezing cold with ice in their bones in this wild place, but were too spent to care.

Chapter Fifty-Two

"You are almost there," Serenissima whispered. *"Wake up, Luca. Wake up."* Luca opened his eyes. *Was he still dreaming?* And then he saw it, but for a moment, thought it was a mirage. In the distance, a fleet of vehicles was moving across the sand. It wasn't clear from here what kind of vehicles they were, but he counted perhaps fifty of them, shimmering in the sun. Around him, Tanner, Ceiba and Elton were waking up, as well.

Tanner stood up. "Over here! Over here!" he yelled, waving his arms wildly.

They all struggled to stand up. "Help! Help!"

They thought the vehicles were going to pass straight by, but Ceiba angled a Neutraliser so it would reflect the sunlight to attract attention, and eventually a large tracked vehicle slowed, then gradually turned from the fleet and headed their way.

"Guys, not so fast," Luca said. "What if Penan or some of the other savages stole these and came after us?"

"No, it's our guys, look they're wearing uniforms," said Elton. "I think I recognise one of them standing out on that control tower. That looks like an old friend of my father's in the military, Colonel Dixon."

In moments, a very large military personnel carrier pulled up in front of them, scattering sand into their faces as it lowered its access ramp. A couple of Acacia military men were on board with Colonel Dixon.

"How are you boys doing?" asked one of the men.

"We're mostly all right," said Elton. "Just dehydrated and hungry. Are we pleased to see you?"

"Elton Madden, my God, is that you?" asked Dixon.

"Yes, Colonel, it's me," Elton said. "Boy, am I glad to see you!"

"We're escorting military personnel and survivors from Acacia to Beyul Atoll," said Dixon. "We've got a camp set up. Jump aboard and we'll take you there."

"These are my friends," said Elton. "They saved my life."

Dixon nodded. "Good to meet you, boys."

"We heard about an Acacia Burj military trainee leading a mass escape from the Jungle. Was that you?"

He shook his head. "Luca got us out," said Tanner, motioning to his friend, who wore the military trainee suit like Tanner did, although the clothes were now torn and dirty.

"We all worked together to get everyone out," said Luca. "There were a lot of prisoners there."

"Glad to see you made it out alive," said Dixon. "And yes, we've been picking up most of them along the way to join our fleet. It's a miracle you all got out of that hellhole, we've been trying to find their base for years."

"Colonel, sir," said Ceiba.

"Yes?"

"Are there any aliens in Beyul Atoll?"

"Not any that you would know," said Dixon. "The ones there look human like us and they fight *with* us, not against us."

"Sir, have you heard anything about a security guard supervisor at the docks named Red Ammos?" Ceiba asked.

"Red Ammos? His name sounds familiar," said Dixon. "I'll look into it if you'd like, son."

"Thanks, I'd appreciate it," said Ceiba. "He's my dad."

"Do you know anything about my mother, Skye Mariner, and my sister, Gaia?" Luca asked. "They both work for the ISRO."

Colonel Dixon seemed to think for a moment, and then asked: "You're Del Mariner's son?"

"Yes, sir," said Luca. For once, Luca felt proud instead of

ashamed.

"Well, I'll be," said Dixon. "Small world, I guess. I know the ISRO building was damaged. They may have escaped, I can't be sure. There have been numerous convoys leaving the city. When we get back to Beyul Atoll, I'll see what I can find out but it isn't going to be easy."

"Thanks," said Luca. He wondered if Colonel Dixon shared in the beliefs that his father had been a coward years ago. Luca now knew it had never been true and, someday, he'd prove it. Luca also finally acknowledged to himself that their lives were forever changed.

With that, Colonel Dixon's men helped Luca and his friends aboard, and gave them water and hot food. Elton spent some time explaining to Colonel Dixon what had happened to them in the Jungle. Colonel Dixon briefed them on the latest news and said that following the carnage caused by the solar flare, many Acacia Burj military vehicles such as this one had been patrolling the Wilds, rescuing people.

"It's still dangerous in Acacia," said Dixon. "But we're working on plans to take back what's left of our city from the mercenaries. Someday."

"Have you heard anything about my parents or my sister?" asked Elton.

"Not yet," said Dixon. "Sorry, son. All we know is that the A'Rmillari are in control of the Moon and Mars. We do know that two spaceships were seen leaving the Moon in pursuit of the *Sibylline*, but they were apparently destroyed in the ocean at our Mariana Mining Base. However, there were reports of more alien warships in the air right before the solar flare attack, so we're not sure what happened since the satellites went down."

Luca and Tanner didn't mention that they had been on the *Sibylline*. They were too tired to explain.

"So, Elton, I'm sorry, but I just don't know about your parents right now," said Colonel Dixon.

Luca placed his hand on Elton's arm. "We've all lost someone in this fight. We're your family now." Elton nodded, hanging his head and closing his eyes.

The four of them were now a brotherhood. In this new world, you had to adapt and become a family with those who were with you. It was the only way.

"What about Sub-Biosphere 2?" asked Luca, boldly. He recalled the plans he had confiscated from Mariana, however he hadn't had the opportunity to study them. Although he shrugged, the surprise on Dixon's face was noticeable. It was obvious to Luca that not everyone was aware of *all* the undersea facilities. If Colonel Dixon knew about Sub-Biosphere 2, he wasn't going to talk.

"Everything is in flux right now," said Dixon, shifting uncomfortably in his seat. "*Everything.*"

The landscape shifted as they neared the foot of the mountains and the sea appeared between the peaks. Moving downhill, it wasn't long before the fleet reached the water. They left the yellow-leafed trees and dying grass behind them and moved from the beach onto the water, turquoise and clear around them.

The fleet's engines powered down for a moment so that the tide could sweep them gently into shore. Each engine grew to a soft hum again and the vehicles moved up the beach. Ahead were fields full of all types of plants and crops. The men and women working the gardens stopped to watch the convey pass. Even the children started running alongside the vehicles laughing and waving.

"It looks good," Tanner said. "Primitive, but good. But aren't they afraid of being attacked here by aliens or pirates?"

"Sure, but it's something they live with," said Dixon. "Most of them prefer to live in more hidden, protected areas like Beyul Atoll, but some people prefer the freedom of the open spaces.

The road became dappled with sunlight through the trees. The welcome party had faded away and a vast mountain rose before them. Paths twisted up the mountainsides amongst trees and rocky cliffs. The fleet rounded one pathway and stopped in front of a covered opening which led into the side of the mountain. Dixon and his men got out and moved the boulders that blocked the entrance. Then, they got back inside the vehicle and drove through the opening. They got back out and closed the opening. Next, they moved towards an inner cave system that traversed the entire mountainside for a half mile or so to a wooden sign that read:

Beyul Atoll, Home of the New Free

"Amazing!" said Ceiba. "This is a real underground city inside a mountain cave in the middle of the sea! Who would have ever thought this existed?"

"Well, who would have ever thought that the Jungle existed?" said Elton. "Think about it."

"All the varied settlements have been eye-opening out here in the Wilds," said one of Dixon's military men. "And sure, there are some savages and pirates, and a mix of mutants in that dump called the Jungle, but there are also some highly intelligent people who grew up out here after the mega cities were constructed, and they have been very inventive."

At that moment, there was a rumble and they could feel the ground move.

"Don't worry," said Dixon, smiling. "You'll find there's plenty of seismic activity out here in the Wilds. It's usually just small quakes. You'll get used to it!"

They entered a large area within the mountainous cave that comprised the city's heart. As far as the eye could see there were pumice stone brick buildings joined with narrow walkways and souk style market places. To one side of them, there was even an opening to the outer sky where the sun and clouds were shining through onto trees and shrubbery inside the cave. It was an underground biosphere!

Dixon navigated slowly as he explained that Beyul Atoll had rigged solar panels above in parts of the open caverns to let in light and even grow crops in select areas of the cave system. When aircraft was spotted from a radar housed within an observation tower – no matter if the aircraft were friend or foe – they sounded the alarms. The military had been known to patrol the Wilds from time to time to conduct exercises.

When the alarms sounded, Beyul Atoll citizens closed the panels so there would be no reflection to the outer world, and to keep out any aircraft flying overhead that might threaten their city.

Luca and his friends just stared. The air was cool and musty and felt soothing on their parched skin. To think that they had thought there were no civilised people in The Garbage Pit – the Wilds. And now, to learn there were all kinds of settlements out here.

"Just on the other side of this mountain is another ocean," said Dixon. "And it hasn't been harmed by any solar flares or storms.

It's quite beautiful. At night, there is a stream of blue light that the citizens shine from the mountaintop to the ocean – a beacon of hope and refuge to any weary travellers."

"But, wouldn't it also attract enemies?" asked Luca.

"It's risky," said Dixon. "But the people here in Beyul Atoll see it more as a beacon of hope, and so far, it has worked as there's been no trouble. It only shines in the deep of night."

"Most people have homes within this network of caves," said Dixon. "They stay very cool and moderate all year long even when there are storms and snow. And there are streams in the caves that supply fresh water. "What about fresh air circulation?" asked Tanner. "Is there plenty in the caves?"

"There are holes that stream in air throughout the system of caves," said Dixon. "There are numerous open-air regions, too, just like the artificial one in the Mega Cities. We suspect that all these caves and holes could have been formed from bubbles of air that got caught in the cooling lava from a volcano."

The people were an eclectic mix of outcast Acacia Burj citizens, some wearing clothes similar to what the Retros wore – old torn, denim jeans, boots and t-shirts. Some had rags tied around them, reminiscent of what people in the Jungle wore. Some men wore beards on their faces and wide-brimmed straw hats and some of the women were dressed in long, floaty skirts.

"Are there AIs out here?" Ceiba dared to ask.

Colonel Dixon looked at him curiously before answering. "I think there are a few, I'm not sure. There aren't any Personas that I know of – now that our communications have gone, there couldn't be. There will be a few Beyul Atoll Bions, from what some of my men have said, but again, I'm not sure. We're just in the early stages of exploring all that Beyul Atoll has in the way of citizens and capabilities."

Luca thought that all the citizens of Beyul Atoll looked different. Not exactly bad or good, or exactly haggard either, but... *free.* That was it. They seemed unconcerned with their looks or behaviour. Their hair was wild and unkempt, and some of their clothes had stains on them. And some were torn and shredded. Not at all like the perfectly pristine, clean-dressed Civils of Acacia Burj.

He looked down at himself and almost laughed. He hadn't given a second thought to how he looked since that night so long ago at the docks. He looked at the others. Everyone looked the same now; ragged and messy. Luca realised that it didn't matter. Wearing his torn, dirty old bodysuit he was no longer just another privileged Civil living in a Mega City, that life was gone. He was now part of a new beginning, and this time, everyone was starting as equals.

Chapter Fifty-Three

From the distance he heard someone calling his name. Luca looked around and was hit with a shot of overwhelming emotion.

"Gaia?" There she stood, smiling. The sister he thought might be dead. The sister who was perfect and a known genius, who always made him feel inferior to her mad skills. The sister who never had a hair out of place now stood before him in a torn, stained bodysuit, strands of hair hanging haphazardly in her eyes.

"I've found you!" They hugged so hard and she kissed him on the cheek. She used to be very frugal with affection. A hug or kiss from her was rare. "It's so good to see you, Luca. You've had Mum and me half-scared out of our wits."

"Is Mum here?" He rubbed his eyes.

"Not right here, but she's safe, Luca. We're all safe. How are you feeling, little brother?"

"I thought we'd lost you in Acacia. What about Mum?" said Luca

A dark look crossed her face, and then she quickly recovered. "It became too dangerous but the military sent a vehicle to rescue Mum, me and some others. I've been helping the medical personnel since I got here. Can you believe all this exists out here in the Wilds?"

"I know," Luca said. "Crazy, huh?"

"Luca, I heard about what you did at that crazy Jungle town."

"You heard?"

"Everyone's talking about it," she said. "How you freed all the prisoners. I kept hearing about this brave, heroic person who challenged this strange mutant lizard king and freed the prisoners out of cages. I had no idea it was you until Tanner told me."

"You've seen Tanner?"

"Just now," she said. Tears filled her eyes as she smiled. "I thought I'd never see him again. It's just been so awful. He's badly injured but Nurse Lorelai is taking good care of him! She's just an old lady but she's so sweet - her Persona was working in Acacia's hospital but obviously there's no more of those after the solar flare. She knows what she's doing - she's invaluable - we're lucky to have her here."

Gaia took Luca's hand. "We're so *fortunate*, you know? Mum's alive, Tanner's alive and you're alive. Our family is whole again. So many people have lost their loved ones."

"I know," said Luca. "Elton has lost his whole family – his sister and his parents. I don't know what happened to Asia Mae. Have you heard anything?"

Gaia looked down at her hands and hesitated for a moment. Then she said, "No, sweetheart, sorry. I haven't. Mum heard that her parents were on an underwater dig when the solar storms hit – we hope they're still okay – but we don't know anything about Asia Mae."

"I talked to her briefly on my comms just before the storms hit, but we lost all connection," said Luca. "Have you heard if there was destruction in any of the other mega cities?"

Gaia shook her head. "Since the satellites were knocked out, our communications with the other mega cities were stopped all over the planet. I really don't know. I'm sorry."

"I hope Asia Mae's okay," Luca said. "I hope so..." His voice trailed off.

"I feel certain she's looking after herself," Gaia said, squeezing his hand. "I should probably go for a bit, sweetie. I have patients to tend to, but I'll come back to take you and your friends to dinner in a place they call the *Saloon*. It's boisterous, but fun.

They even have a couple of musicians over there sometimes who play an old-time piano and guitars."

"Might be fun travelling back in time."

"You have no idea," said Gaia. "It has been a culture shock, for sure. But I've been enjoying it. Right, I've got to go, sorry."

As Gaia got up to leave, Luca squeezed her hand tighter and said, "Wait, Gaia. I need to talk to you about Dad... and our family..."

She sat back down on the stool and nodded. "Sure. Ask me anything."

"First, I'm assuming there's electricity in this place?"

"Yes, they have geothermal out here. And solar power. It's much more advanced than we would have ever guessed. The electricity is limited, but sure, why?"

"I have an opti-file I need to open," he said.

Luca wondered how much he should tell Gaia and how much she already knew. He looked cautiously around the room. Sunlight from the open solar panels was filtering a stream of dusty golden haze through a cracked window. A reminder that he was in a new world. Luckily, no one was paying any attention to him and Gaia.

He lowered his voice to a whisper. "I'll briefly fill you in."

He then explained about finding the Pathfinder Museum at the docks and discovering an opti-file with a message from their father, and how he had never been able to access the entire message. He also briefly told her about finding the secret files at Mariana and the top-secret underwater research station, the Sub-Biosphere 2.

Gaia wasn't surprised. "Mum told me about the very things you're speaking of."

"So you know about the secret undersea facility?"

"Yes... a little bit." Gaia leaned closer to him. "I'll take you to a place where we can access the opti-file.

Luca followed Gaia out the door. "Where are we going?"

"There's an office set up down the hallway."

Gaia opened the door to a room that was lined with computers and equipment. Luca's eyes grew wide.

"We brought these from Acacia Burj," she explained. "As much as we could. But, Beyul Atoll already had a few."

"This looks great," said Luca. He looked around on the screen for the opti-access zone and then held his hand against it. They waited for a few moments before it recognised his DNA. Then, before him and Gaia, the Key projected their father's image and a slight hum rang through the room.

"Oh, Dad!" exclaimed Gaia, overcome with emotion.

Their father stood before them, dressed in his military body-suit. An emblem that was given to all Pathfinder Champion racers shone on his shoulder. Tears filled Gaia's eyes. "Oh, Dad, how I wish you were really here!"

She reached out to hug him, but it was only air that she grasped in her fingers.

"Gaia, I see that you have joined Luca in this quest. I'm so thankful that you have both found me, for this opportunity, this Key, is vital to our survival on Planet Earth... It is vital to our family and humanity as a whole. Even though I am not with you physically, I can sense your feelings. I am always with you. We are Ancient Entanglers, who utilise Quantum Entanglement, and as such, our bonds are forever."

Gaia looked at Luca with big eyes. A choked sob burst through her lips as tears streamed down her cheeks. She tried to contain herself. The message had changed – evolved – since Luca first heard it.

"Luca, you have activated the Key, son. Once activated, an ancient memory and awareness has been awakened in you. Only a member of the Mariner family could awaken the Key. You will find that you have some special skills you didn't have before, and these skills will grow as you develop. You may already be aware of them. My knowledge is your knowledge. Our entire Mariner family is linked because of our infinite quantum particles, no matter how far away we are from one another in time or space. This lifetime or the next or the next. But you are in danger now the Overlords know the Key has been found and activated – everyone is in danger across the Universe. The Dark Alliance have been waiting for this moment since I hid the Key in my Pathfinder and sent it to the surface all those years ago. I needed to go undercover to establish more about the Dark Alliance"

As Luca watched his father speak to them, he felt this great longing to be with him. It had been so long since he had been together. Luca's father began to sparkle like stars in a cloud-free sky. From everywhere on his body, points of white-blue light glowed like juggling atoms. A multidimensional helix curved out

in a golden spiral, coiling around Luca's father. Blue bioluminescent lights curled in an arc throughout the room, juxtaposed
with Luca's and Gaia's bodies. Luca looked down and saw that
he, too, had white-blue lights bouncing at multiple points on his
body. A graph of blue spheres whirled through his and Gaia's
bodies at intercellular points. *Quantum superposition,* Luca heard
in his mind. *Intrinsically and absolutely linked.* Luca wasn't sure
what it all meant, but he had learned to trust his father and the
mission. Luca's father continued:

*"Humans, under advisement from the Galactic Council, built the
Sub-Biosphere 2 facility many years ago. Primarily it is a self-sustain-
able underwater research facility that contains the genetic and scientific material needed to regenerate biodiversity on the surface of the
Earth in the event of a catastrophic man-made or natural disaster. Sec-
ondly, but more importantly it is the gatekeeper to an interstellar trading port called Murias. Luca, you must find this Sub-Biosphere 2 facility. Your Key will allow you access."*

Luca looked in disbelief at the ring on his finger.

*"From what I have found out, each of these secretive thirteen Over-
lords are tasked to dominate different sectors of the Universe, to destroy
intergalactic trading facilities and to steal and sell whatever planetary
resources are available. I have learnt that it is only a matter of time
before they try to take Earth. Our water is too precious for them to just
blast our planet into pieces. It would cause a great imbalance in the solar
system. They need to take control of Murias to be able to free the water
from Earth's atmosphere. Earth is in great danger. Go there son, and
you will learn more. This is very important. You must help save humanity from extinction, and to save our family's knowledge of the Ancient
Entanglers because we are the bridge between worlds."*

Delmar C. Mariner's image and the swirling lights began to
fade.

*"Never forget that I love you and will see you and your mother
again. Each time you access this message, I will have more information for you. Remember, we Mariners are Ancient Entanglers... and–"*

There was static as if something was interfering with the message, and his father dissolved and the computer room returned
to normal with its wooden floors and boarded walls.

For what seemed like an eternity, Gaia was speechless. Finally,
she wiped her eyes clear and said, "Oh, Luca! I can't believe we

got to see our father! Mum told me about the Sub-Biosphere 2 facility, but nothing about being an Ancient Entangler. What does that even mean, Luca?"

"I'm just learning myself," said Luca. "Now I know it's more important than ever that I continue my journey. As you heard Dad say, I have to go back to the blue hole."

"Absolutely," she said. "You have to go, Luca."

"Do you want to come with me?" he asked.

Gaia shook her head. "I'm needed here. Mum is already there at the Sub-Biosphere 2, waiting for you."

"She's undersea?"

"Yes, and she has a lot to tell you."

"How did she get there?"

"The Vice President sent her with a couple of his associates. They've been friends a long time. The Sub-Biosphere 2 can open the portal too"

"I'm happy she's there," said Luca. "But, how am I going to get back to the blue hole?"

"That's easy enough," said Gaia. "Grampa Sol's prototype Pathfinder is hidden here at Beyul Atoll."

"What?"

"Yes!" said Gaia, nodding enthusiastically. "Evidently, Grampa lived here for a while after he left Acacia Burj. The people here have stored it for him ever since. He disappeared from Beyul Atoll one day and they don't know what happened to him. But his Pathfinder is still here and in working condition, apparently."

"That's fantastic news, Gaia. Really great."

"Right now, let's go get Ceiba and get over to the *Saloon* for dinner. I'm sure you're starving and Tanner and Elton are waiting for you."

¤¤¤

"We have just picked up the Mariner's signal again from Earth," said Pihaa. "It's faint, but it's there."

Chapter Fifty-Four

Gaia, Luca and Ceiba headed towards the *Saloon*. From the opening above, Luca could see clouds rumbling together, but they didn't look too menacing. What Luca noticed most was the crisp smell of swollen creeks nearby in the cave system. He could hear the babbling of water over the rocks. He knew that outside, in the distance, loomed those craggy mountains with snow on top, and on the other side of the mountain, there was the open sea.

The *Saloon* was one of the manmade buildings inside Beyul Atoll and served as a community hall. Even before they arrived there, the clamour of conversation and laughter greeted them like old friends out on the roadway. It sounded more like a party than an evening dinner. Ceiba's stomach growled first, then Luca's. Gaia looked at them and they all laughed. Lured by the savoury aromas, they walked quickly inside. The *Saloon* was packed with people, but once they entered, the conversation stopped. All they could hear was the sound of chairs scratching against the floor around tables, boot heels scuffing, and spoons clattering.

Luca shifted his eyes around the huge room, alighting first on Tanner and Elton who came towards them with big smiles. Before he could look further, someone grabbed him from behind and put their hands over his eyes. He whirled around and there stood Asia Mae.

"I don't believe it!" Luca could hardly speak. His eyes were wide, his mouth open. Never had he been so surprised. "What are you doing here?"

She laughed. He had forgotten how her laugh sounded like music. He enveloped her, wrapping his arms around her tightly, fearful this might be another dream and he'd wake up soon.

"Surprise!" shouted Gaia along with others in the *Saloon*. She stood nearby with her arms around Tanner, delighted she had pulled off such a big secret reunion.

"Luca," Asia Mae said, "I've missed you so much. You've had me worried sick!"

"Me? I've been worried sick about *you!*"

He pulled back and looked at her. She was thinner, but somehow looked stronger. Her eyes were the same wide, deep brown almond eyes he had remembered, and her long hair, black and lying over her shoulders, was still shiny and thick. And she wore Retro clothes – blue jeans, a red plaid flannel shirt over a t-shirt and boots. Luca liked the look on her.

Asia Mae then turned and grabbed Ceiba next and hugged him. "C'm'ere you cutie, you! I'm so happy to see you! I've missed you so much, Ceibastian!"

"Asia Mae," said Ceiba, pulling back from her, and running his hands through his blonde curls. "We've been worried about you. I didn't know what happened to you after seeing you in the hospital and–"

"Shhh," said Asia Mae, putting her fingers to his lips. "We don't have to talk about that right now!"

Luca still couldn't believe Asia Mae was standing there in front of him. He expected to wake up any moment and realise it was all a dream.

"Luca, this is Sumer," said Asia Mae, grabbing the arm of her friend and pulling her over. "I think you already know her boyfriend, Phaeton, and her brother, Elton."

"*What?*"

They all laughed.

"Phaeton! You're alive!" Luca was stunned. He had no words.

"Long story," said Phaeton. He put his hand on Luca's shoulder and gripped it. Then, he pulled him close and hugged him.

"Let's just say I got up front and personal with those A'Rmillari weirdoes down in the mine, but Sumer and Asia Mae found me and rescued me."

"You went to Mariana?" Luca looked at Asia Mae and Sumer. "You rescued Phaeton?"

"We had nowhere else to go," said Sumer. "We went to the military hospital to find you and Phaeton and Ceiba, but the guards wouldn't let us in. So, we took one of my father's Zipper shuttles and went to my parents' undersea home near Acacia Burj, but the solar flare wiped it out." She stopped to catch her breath, but before anyone else could speak, she continued. "We then escaped to the Mariana Mine where you were when Asia Mae last talked to you. When we got there, we found the place mostly underwater and in ruins and with Phaeton buried in the rubble. We were shocked to find him there, and to find him alive."

"That's a miracle! Did anyone else survive?" asked Luca.

"Just an old sea-dog called Scar, as far as we know," said Sumer. "And I wished he hadn't. If it hadn't been for Scar, we would still have my dad's Zipper!"

"The pirates were working with the A'Rmillari at the mines," said Luca. "I saw them."

"Yeah, the A'Rmillari imprinted the pirates' minds to make them their soldiers, but when the A'Rmillari were all destroyed at Mariana, the imprints were disconnected, as far as I can tell," said Phaeton. He opened his mouth to carry on talking but then abruptly closed it again. Luca wondered if there was something he wasn't telling them.

"But wait... how does everyone know each other?" asked Luca. He still couldn't wrap his head around all of his friends being there together in one place.

"I met Sumer at the hospital right after the incident at the docks," explained Asia Mae. "When I went to check on Ceiba."

"Nice to meet you, Sumer," Luca said.

"We're twins," Elton interjected. "Can't you tell by looking?"

"Well, I know who got the *looks* in the family," Luca said, managing a small smile. He was still stunned by the surprise of Asia Mae being there. And by Phaeton being alive. It was all just too good to be true.

Elton grinned. "I know. I can't believe I got all the looks either!"

They all laughed and Sumer punched him in the arm. With

her arm linked in Phaeton's, she turned towards Asia Mae. "And so, this is the man I've been hearing about all this time?" Her dark eyes twinkled. She really did look a lot like Elton, Luca realised.

"Luca, meet Sumer. Sumer meet Luca!" said Asia Mae.

Luca's face was on fire. He was sure he was blushing.

"Well, this guy has saved our butts time and time again," said Phaeton. "And showed some real impressive piloting skills, I have to say."

"Yeah, he was our hero," said Tanner. "He kicks ass in a Pathfinder."

Gaia smiled at her little brother with a look of pride. Just then Ceiba's parents walked over with huge smiles on their faces.

"Ceiba?"

"Pops? Mum?"

Red Ammos and Elsa swooped Ceiba up in their arms.

"I've been so worried about you," Ceiba said. "How did you get here?"

"We'll fill you in later," said Elsa. "You all right, son?"

"Yeah, Mum, I'm great," said Ceiba, sniffling. He quickly wiped the tears from his eyes.

"This is amazing!" said Luca. "This night just keeps getting better and better!" Luca hugged Elsa and shook Red's hand. Luca couldn't help but notice that Ceiba's eyes once again glistened a sky blue.

"Oh my, I'm so glad you all escaped," said Elsa. "It nearly gave me a heart attack just hearing about it!"

"Mr. Ammos, I want to thank you for helping us escape Acacia Burj," Luca said. "You saved our lives."

"I'm just so grateful you boys made it here," he said. "I was worried when I heard about the Jungle." He patted Ceiba on the back. "We have so much to be grateful for."

"We've all heard the stories," said Asia Mae, looking at Luca, "about your escape and how you freed all the prisoners – most of which are now here in Beyul Atoll."

"It was nothing," said Luca. "We all worked together as a team. I didn't do anything by myself. I have so much to tell you but I don't know where to start!"

"Me too," she responded. "But for a little while, for tonight, let's pretend all is right with the world. There is no A'Rmillari race trying to take over Planet Earth, and there is no Jungle and no one has been harmed. Let's just enjoy our evening."

"Sounds like a great plan to me," said Luca, putting his arm around her waist.

"Just another night at the *Arcade*," said Ceiba, grinning from ear to ear.

"Yeah, just another night at the *Arcade*," Luca said, taking Asia Mae's hand. "Anyone else starving?"

They all shouted in agreement and headed for a table which was loaded with food.

Out of nowhere, a loud siren rang out and the opening above them started to close. Asia Mae and Luca both looked up in surprise. Luca and Asia Mae looked blankly at Gaia.

"What's going on?" asked Luca.

"Luca, Corporal Dixon has the Pathfinder prepared for you, ready to go when you're ready."

"That's great," he said. "I'll plan to head out tomorrow. But what's going on with the siren?"

"Mmm, Luca," said Gaia, "I hate to spoil your evening, but Corporal Dixon says they have spotted an alien ship on their radar. It appears that it's headed this way."

"Then I need to get out of here now," said Luca. "I need to take the Key to the portal and give it to the authorities there to keep the place safe from alien attack. If the aliens get their hands on the Key, then they could destroy it or use it for their own purposes. And I can't let them attack Beyul Atoll. It's the only home we have left."

Fear was creeping into their hearts and interrupting what had been a beautiful reunion. Gaia and Luca told Ceiba and the others what they had learned. Ceiba agreed that Luca had to leave tonight. Then, both Ceiba and Asia Mae announced that they were going to go with Luca.

"I don't know, Ceiba," said his mother, hesitantly. "We've only just found you again."

Ceiba looked at his mother carefully. She had the same blonde curls he had and the same blue eyes. But her eyes were creased and lined from worry. He knew she would give her life for him if she could.

"Hon, if Ceiba feels it's important to go with Luca, then we have to let him go," said Red. "After all, he's not a boy any more. He has proven that over and over again."

"I know," said Elsa, with tears in her eyes. She lowered her voice and looked around to make sure no strangers were listening. "I just hate for any of them to go back out in danger. Ceiba, sweetheart, are you sure your... um... wiring is in optimal working condition?"

"I've never felt better," said Ceiba. He generally hated it when his Mum called him *sweetheart*, but right now, he didn't care what she called him. "Pops re-calibrated everything when I was in the hospital. I'm fine, really. And, Mum, Pops, you know I have to go. Luca has been my friend since we were children and I won't abandon him now."

"But it's dangerous," said Luca. "I think you should stay here, Ceiba. You too, Asia Mae."

"No," Ceiba said firmly, folding his arms in front of him. "I'm coming with you. You might need me."

"I am too," said Asia Mae. "You can't talk us out of this. You need us, Luca."

"Think of it like one of our games at the Arcade," said Ceiba. "It's just another game for us. And we always have each other's backs in those games."

"But this is *real*," said Luca. "And we could die."

"It's okay," said Asia Mae. "I have faith in us and in you, Luca."

Luca had to admit that he was grateful they were coming, although he didn't like putting them in harm's way. After talking with their other friends, Phaeton and Sumer decided to stay behind. They felt that they could help with any problems that might arise in Beyul Atoll. "Besides," Phaeton said, "you don't really need me, Luca. You've got Asia Mae and Ceiba."

"And Sumer, from what I've seen so far, you'll enjoy working with the herbs and plants here," said Asia Mae. "This might as well be called Retro City."

"I think I should come," said Elton. "Maybe I can find out more about my parents... if they're still alive, that is."

"Elton, you're needed here," said Luca. "You've got your sister back! And look, we'll find out everything we can about your parents."

"Thanks, guys," said Elton.

"Asia Mae, promise me you'll be back," Sumer said. "You're

my sister, and you, Phaeton and Elton might be the only family I have now."

"I promise you, I'll be back," said Asia Mae, giving her a big hug.

"Love you, Asia Mae," said Sumer, tears forming in her big brown eyes.

"Love you, too, Sumer," Asia Mae said.

"And Luca," said Elton, "brother, you have to come back."

"I will, guys, I promise!" said Luca, smiling. But inside, he was choking. He knew there was a real possibility they would die in the blue hole. He wasn't even sure how he had survived it the first time. He knew he might never see his mum, Gaia or Tanner or any of them again. But this was something he had to do. Luca hugged all of them, not wanting to say good-bye, but knowing he had to. Many of his friends had tears in their eyes. But if Luca didn't stop the aliens, then they would no longer have a home at Beyul Atoll, or anywhere else for that matter.

Gaia and Tanner then led Asia Mae, Ceiba and Luca to the area where the old Pathfinder was stored. Faded lettering on the outside of the hull named it as the Norma Jeane. Similar to the one that Luca had discovered in the old Pathfinder Museum, tiny in comparison to the *Sibylline* of course but it still looked enormous from where they were standing.

"Luca, be careful," said Gaia one more time.

"Don't worry, we'll be back, I promise," Luca said. He hugged his big sister and Tanner. "Take care of my sister, Tan, you'll be needed here." he said.

"You got it, buddy," said Tanner.

The sirens were screaming throughout the underground cave system, warning everyone that great danger was imminent.

Chapter Fifty-Five

As the Pathfinder slipped away into the night, the sirens stopped and Beyul Atoll was in lock down. Phaeton took Sumer by the hand and led her to their bedroom inside the housing that had been sanctioned for the newly arrived Acacia Burj refugees. The air was cool and comfortable. Once they got inside their small room, Phaeton turned on the solar lamp, casting the room in a warm, rosy glow. He and Sumer hadn't been together in their own private bedroom for a long time.

"I feel guilty about not going with them," said Phaeton.

"They'll be absolutely fine," said Sumer. She took Phaeton's hair out of his ponytail so it flowed freely around his face. "I'm too selfish to let you out of my sight again. I've been dying to have you all to myself." Sumer threw her arms around him and kissed him.

The trip in the old boat to Beyul Atoll had been long and cramped to say the least. Luckily, the cruiser was still in good shape and had managed to extend its hull-wings effectively enough to propel the boat out of the water and into hydrofoil mode. The girls had dried off and relaxed on the sun deck during the day but they were on high alert not to be captured by pirates.

Phaeton had learned how to fish and find wild herbs when he was cast out of Acacia Burj, but Sumer and Asia Mae had been shocked at the discoveries. The government and military at Acacia Burj had lied to them all their lives. The Garbage Pit was actually a gold-mine for natural resources and wildlife. If you knew where to look. And then, when they had come to the dry, barren area where the Jungle was, Phaeton had been the one to get them safely across the desert to Beyul Atoll.

And now, he was finally alone with Sumer. He kissed her hard, passionately. It felt so good to be with her, to hear her laugh, to kiss her, to be close to her again. With her short hair tousled all over her head and her wide eyes wild like a panther's, he was *home*. No matter where that home was.

They quickly slipped between the covers of their small bed. Phaeton turned down the light and snuggled close to Sumer. Her skin smelled of the fresh air in the Wilds.

"Can you believe we're here?" said Sumer.

"I know. Life has changed so completely for all of us." Phaeton wasn't really in the mood to analyse their situation. He started kissing her neck. They could hear muted sounds of laughter and people talking in the cave network. But mostly, they could hear each other's heartbeats. Loud and strong. Rhythmic and true.

Something took hold of Phaeton's mind and startled him so much, he stopped kissing. He was standing on an alien ship and there stood Pihaa in front of him.

"What's wrong?" asked Sumer as Phaeton jumped as if a charge of electricity had snapped him.

"I... I... don't know," he said. His mind was split. He could see and feel Sumer wrapped in his arms, but he also could see and hear Pihaa. *Didn't she die at Mariana?* Then, he remembered she was a 3D copy and was probably just another imprint. *Dammit!* He had been implanted.

Pihaa spoke to him as if she were standing right in front of him: "Where's your friend Luca? Think about where the boy went. We need the route to his destination."

Phaeton could see the interior of a spaceship, similar to the one he had been on at Mariana. Pihaa stood there with a few A'Rmillari soldiers.

Phaeton battled with his thoughts. He tried desperately to block out the secret opening where Luca and his friends had left

Beyul Atoll. He tried to erase the A'Rmillari from his mind. He turned his attention back to Sumer. She said: "Don't you dare go anywhere in that head of yours, do you hear me, Phaeton?"

"Sumer, I'm yours," he said. "Completely. You can use and abuse me all you want. My body is yours." He tried to laugh light-heartedly.

She laughed. "You better believe it, Mister."

He answered her by kissing her mouth, determined to turn off all communication with the A'Rmillari. The last thing he heard from the aliens was Pihaa: "Mr Wilding, you are a member of the A'Rmillari – you pledged allegiance to us – and you are under Supreme Order from Overlord Xsar Tiandi to provide us with these details and you will do so without fail. Do you understand, Earthling? To disobey is to die."

At that point, a bolt of pure electricity was unleashed into Phaeton's brain and he writhed around the room in pain.

Chapter Fifty-Six

Luca, Ceiba and Asia Mae climbed aboard the old Pathfinder. The sirens were still blasting throughout Beyul Atoll and the friends knew they had no time to waste.

The *Norma Jeane* was much smaller than the newer Pathfinders and only had two levels. It was designed for undersea travel, the first of its class, but was very capable on land with its huge monster wheels. As they scrambled into the cockpit Luca held his hand against the screen.

"Verification authenticated. Mariner DNA identified."

An optigraphic data scan of the ship's interior sprang into view on the panoramic screen. There were sleeping quarters and a supply room off the bridge, as well as engine rooms and an empty room that didn't seem to serve any purpose. There was also a small storage and kitchen area on the lower level. Built into the *Norma Jeane* were orb blasters, albeit a much a more basic version of the weapons used on the *Sibylline*. Luca also had a Neutraliser with him that Tanner had given him before they left. Luca slid it under the controls. He hoped he didn't have to resort to weapons and even though he had successfully piloted the *Sibylline* and fought the alien ships, he had been helped by Dr

Tycho's Persona. This time, he was on his own and he wasn't so sure he'd make it. Sure, he had sailed the *Sibylline* out of Mariana by himself, but he had ultimately wrecked it when he was swept into the blue hole. He was nervous. Right now though, before anything else, they had to lure the aliens away from Beyul Atoll.

Ceiba and Asia Mae sat behind him as Luca took his seat before the control screens. As he voice-activated the controls, light-infused maps and data switched on in the panels and invisible straps automatically locked around Luca and his friends. A stream of sweat trailed down Luca's forehead. Asia Mae touched his shoulder. He looked back and met her eyes. It gave it strength.

She smiled at him. "I have faith in you."

"Is this thing actually going to get us to the bottom of the ocean?" asked Ceiba.

Luca just smiled, then shifted in his seat and placed his hands on the panel. A slight buzz – a pulse – inside him activated as if he were connected to the panel in the same way as he had done on the *Sibylline*. Luca powered up the engines and they drove the *Norma Jeane* on a makeshift road to the secret opening in the side of the cave. From there, they rolled out towards the sea. A few stars were sprinkled overhead and the Moon was half-hidden behind thundering yellow storm clouds. It was already late into the night.

Luca drove the Pathfinder towards the sea and away from the Beyul Atoll as fast as he could along the narrow coastal paths. On his screens, Luca spotted a spaceship emerge out from the clouds directly behind Beyul Atoll. He swiped at the control screen to get a view of what was happening and was horrified by what he saw. Dozens of A'Rmillari were materialising out of thin air at the entrance to Beyul Atoll; armed and dangerous.

"Look," he said, pointing at the screen. "They're attacking Beyul anyway!"

"Oh no," cried Asia Mae. "I hoped they'd just follow us and leave everyone else alone!"

But as they watched, the alien spaceship moved from its location above the mountain but didn't stop. It was following them after all. Luca charged the *Norma Jeane* straight into the sea and towards the co-ordinates for the blue hole. He dived the ship as fast as he could. They sank deeper and deeper into the darkness.

They were on their way back into immense danger.

"Do you think the solar flare could have destroyed the Sub-Biosphere 2 compound?" asked Asia Mae. She looked out into the dark waters as they zoomed through the water.

"Surely it will have an alternate power grid," Luca said.

"Tanner said that all of you almost died the first time," said Ceiba.

"Well, sort of," said Luca. "I don't remember much, to tell you the truth. We all lost consciousness and next thing I knew, I was in the hospital."

All seemed to be going smoothly until Luca heard a buzzing noise.

"Do you guys hear that?" he asked Asia Mae and Ceiba.

"Hear what?" asked Asia Mae. Eyes wide, she looked around the command centre. Suddenly, a multidimensional helix arced out around them. Blue lights juxtaposed on their bodies. Manifesting before the three friends were real life aliens with flashing bands of colour and patterns pulsating across their skin. That meant they had to be A'Rmillari.

"What the..?" Luca mumbled.

"Who are you?" Luca asked. His throat was dry and his heart nearly shot out of his chest. How in the world was he going to deal with this?

"You may call me Xsar Tiandi," he said, bowing slightly. "I come from the Markarian Galaxy."

Asia Mae jumped. This was the one she had heard when they were at the Arcade. She shot a glance at Ceiba and he nodded. He knew what she was thinking.

"And this is Pihaa." The female had wild, yellow catlike eyes. She smiled, baring bright, even white teeth.

"What, what do you want?" asked Luca. He swallowed hard. "And why have you sent soldiers into Beyul Atoll?

Luca seemed transfixed by the dancing textures across their bodies. swirls of colour and particle of lights pinged around the two entities and whirled around the room. How could this be happening?

"For now, we want to make a trade," said Xsar Tiandi. The Overlord swept his hand through the air and another room opened up for them to view. There appeared the opti-images of President Halley Madden and his wife, Rosalie. They were seated in a room on the alien's spaceship and seemed scared, but unharmed.

"You have the president and the First Lady?" asked Luca. *My God! What in the world would they want to trade?*

"Yes, they are unharmed, as you can see," said Xsar Tiandi, motioning to his hostages.

"What do you want from us?" Luca asked. He looked back at Asia Mae and Ceiba. Their faces were as white as ghosts. They all knew what the A'Rmillari wanted, but didn't want to admit it.

"You know I want the Key," snarled Xsar Tiandi. He folded his long fingers in front of him. "Not everyone can get through the portal, which is why we need your Key. A simple trade. We will send you the president and the First Lady. You will give the Key to me. Neither you nor they will be harmed. But be warned, if you do not give us the Key, then we will have no choice but to dispose of you and your president and the First Lady."

"Luca, you can't!" gasped Asia Mae.

Xsar Tiandi shot her a sharp glance.

"She's right," said Ceiba. "This is a trap."

"If you listen to your friends, you will all die," said Pihaa placing her finger on her lips.

"You can manifest them physically onto our ship?" asked Luca.

"Yes," said Xsar Tiandi. "Once you voice-activate the panel. It should be matched to your DNA."

Luca didn't know what to do. On the one hand, he could free the president and the First Lady. He had promised Sumer and Elton that he would do all he could to find out about their parents. But on the other hand, if he gave the Key to this A'Rmillari alien, then he and his friends would surely die and all of Earth would be in mortal danger. Of course, if he didn't give them the Key, then everyone would die, as well. He had to buy some time. *Time to think. To plan.*

"It would be best if you gave them to us before we get to the blue hole," said Luca. "It's dangerous going through the blue hole and there's no guarantee that any of us will survive it."

"Maybe you won't, but we will," said Xsar Tiandi. "The blue hole isn't a problem for us. It's the portal at the bottom of the blue hole that has kept us from entering all these years. And only your Key will allow us through. So, we will not give you the president and the First Lady until we get through the portal."

Luca could see that he had no choice.

"No," said Luca. "Once we enter the blue hole, I will activate the panel that allows you transfer your captives onto our ship. Once they are safely on board, then I will give you the Key."

"It is good to know that you have more sense than your grandfather and father," said Xsar Tiandi.

"Now, please, get off my ship," said Luca.

"We will see you soon," said Pihaa, laughing. "I might just have to come on board myself to meet you in the flesh."

The aliens disappeared and Luca sat there staring at the control screen before him. This was an impossible position to be in.

"Luca, what were you thinking? We can't give them the Key!" said Asia Mae. "You know he wants to enslave the Earth and steal our resources."

"There has to be another way," said Ceiba. "They're going to kill us, whether we give them the Key or not."

"It's possible," said Luca. Like a dark storm cloud, the task ahead rolled over him.

"What are we going to do?" asked Asia Mae.

"We have a few more minutes before we reach the blue hole, according to the data onscreen," said Luca. "Just enough time to plan a strategy!"

Through the rest of their journey, the A'Rmillari war ship stayed close behind them, making them nervous. So much depended on Luca and his friends.

Chapter Fifty-Seven

For a long while, the *Norma Jeane* had been moving over the ridges of an underwater canyon. The waters were relatively shallow. All too soon, as the morning sun shone down through the water, a plateau spread out beneath them. And there it was. The blue hole. Vast and perfectly round, the sinkhole was a dark blue vortex, disappearing into the sea floor. Luca saw it first on his display panel.

"Look! We're almost there."

Asia Mae and Ceiba were engrossed by the sight as the *Norma Jeane* drew closer.

"So this is the way to the portal?" gulped Ceiba. He ran his fingers through his curls. *We're going to die,* he thought.

"Yes," said Luca. "I've been here before."

His palms were beginning to sweat. This definitely seemed more dangerous than he had anticipated.

"Hold on, everyone!" Luca glided the *Norma Jeane* down through the cold, lifeless ocean. The distance between the Pathfinder and the A'Rmillari ship closed rapidly. Luca had to admit to himself that his heart was beating unusually hard. If he failed, they would all die. It was not an easy thought, and now he desperately wished he had come alone.

Just like the last time, the Pathfinder suddenly dived automatically towards the blue hole.

"Whoa!" said Ceiba. He gripped the handles of his seat. "This is weird."

"Yeah," said Asia Mae. "Just like a virtual game. C'mon, Luca, you've got this."

Luca realised that he was more afraid this time because Asia Mae and Ceiba were with him. He didn't want anyone harmed. He heard nothing but the hammering of his heart. And maybe Asia Mae's and Ceiba's hearts. Yes, he was sure he could hear their hearts, as well. *Where was the voice of Serenissima?*

"Put on your oxygen masks," said Luca. "The oxygen level is about to be depleted. We have extra ones we can give to our new passengers when they arrive."

Both Asia Mae and Ceiba reached for their masks. As they spiralled down into the eerie darkness, the pressure inside the Pathfinder rose to critical levels just like it had the first time.

"Maybe we should turn back," said Ceiba, taking his oxygen mask off for a second.

"No, not now," said Luca. "We have to move forward."

Luca felt light-headed. He looked over at Asia Mae and saw her struggling to breathe, too.

"Oxygen is at critical level of 30%. Target location is 7,000 metres" appeared on the screen.

Luca guided the ship further down into the blue hole; into the abyss. And waiting there would be Serenissima?

"Do you see her?" Luca asked his friends.

He started to hear a soft, angelic voice, *"Luca, you cannot go through the portal until you stop the A'Rmillari from following you. You have to face them now,"* said Serenissima.

"But, Serenissima, the A'Rmillari are right behind us," said Luca. "They want the Key and I don't know if I can fight them."

"Do not give them the Key," said Serenissima. *"You have the ability to fight the A'Rmillari if you trust yourself."*

"I heard her," said Ceiba. "I heard the sea creature speak!"

"So did I!" said Asia Mae, excitedly. "Luca, we can hear her, too!"

"She helped me the first time," said Luca. "Maybe she'll help us now."

All of a sudden, the ship started to screech and groan. Luca was sure that the hull was giving way under the extreme pressure and would eventually buckle against the force of the water, drowning them. He had to get the Pathfinder through the blue hole and to the portal. But before he did this, he had to face the A'Rmillari.

As Serenissima had instructed, Luca directed the ship's power source to pause their trajectory. The *Norma Jeane* stopped and hovered in the vortex, as if in suspended animation. The A'Rmillari ship paused, as well. A few more engine thrusts and they would breach the portal to the Sub-Biosphere 2. And then it would be too late. The A'Rmillari could take control.

As Luca, Asia Mae and Ceiba watched, the A'Rmillari ship seemed to blur and wobble. Its edges vibrated and shook. The friends looked at each other, speechless, watching as the ship morphed into a huge figure. As the shape shimmered and moved, it sharpened into focus. The figure clung onto the side of the blue hole with one hand, sinking its nebulous fingers into crevices in the rock.

"It's him, Xsar Tiandi," whispered Asia Mae. Luca nodded, speechless.

In a bellowing voice that enveloped them, the figure said: "We exchange here, now."

As the figure of Xsar Tiandi spoke, it reached out and wrapped a hand around the Pathfinder. The ship shuddered as the strange shape took hold. Luca nodded. "Proceed to open docking area for the entry of the president and the First Lady," he announced.

"Opening confirmed," the command centre replied.

Pihaa escorted President Madden and Rosalie and boarded the *Norma Jeane*. The captives' arms were bound behind them. Pihaa carried a sleek orb weapon in her arms, poised, ready to shoot at any time.

"Are you all right, President Madden?" asked Luca, temporarily ignoring Xsar Tiandi.

"Yes," he said. From what Luca could see, the president and his wife were fine. The president was a tall, statuesque man with salt and pepper hair, cut short. The First Lady was shorter, with big doe eyes, and short hair like Sumer's. They were harried and dishevelled looking with a few bruises, but they had no serious visible wounds.

"And what about you, Mrs. Madden?" asked Luca.

"Stop!" interrupted Pihaa, pointing her weapon at Luca. "Can't you see that they're all right? We did not harm them. Now, give me that Key."

Luca was surprised at how good her English was, in spite of her strange accent.

"Don't give it to them," said President Madden. Luca saw the same defiant look in his dark eyes that Elton had. "I'd rather she killed us."

Pihaa whacked him around the side of the head with her weapon, cutting a small gash into his temple. He staggered back-wards.

"You said you wouldn't hurt anyone!" cried Luca.

"That's if everyone behaves," said Pihaa.

"Look, we're doing what you wanted," said Luca. "There's no need for this."

"I am tired of conversation," said Pihaa. "Give me the Key so I can get off this puny ship."

Asia Mae and Ceiba stayed sitting as if glued to their chairs. But they were ready. They all had their roles to play in the next few seconds. Luca started sweating. His mouth went dry. His heart palpitated. Could they do this? Without drawing any attention to the control screens, Luca discreetly laid his finger over an activating panel and closed the entry to the docking area, sealing and locking the door. Part one of his plan.

"What have you done?" Pihaa shouted as she shot a crazed look at Luca. Before she realised what had happened, Luca grabbed his Neutraliser from under the control screen.

"Drop your weapon!"

Just as Pihaa aimed her weapon at Luca, Asia Mae – as quick as lightning – jumped up, turned sideways and roundhouse-kicked it out of her hands, then jabbed her hard in the gut with her fist. As Pihaa bent over, clutching her stomach, Ceiba grabbed the orb blaster as it fell to the floor. Luca quickly shot the stun phase of his Neutraliser and knocked out Pihaa. She slumped to the floor like a rag-doll.

"Did you kill her?" asked Ceiba.

"No, I just stunned her," said Luca. "We might be able to use her as a bargaining tool later."

"What?" cried the voice of Xsar Tiandi. They all felt the ship shake violently in his grip.

Asia Mae quickly untied President Madden and his wife, Rosalie. "You need to sneak out of here," she whispered. "Take the escape shuttle to the surface, hurry."

"I can't thank you enough," said President Madden as they scurried away, hand in hand.

The ship shook again and there was an awful creaking sound. Luca slipped back into his seat in the command centre. He was shaking and his throat was constricted with fear, but he tried to look calm and collected. On the screens surrounding them was a display of the external environment, sonar data, GPS, depth and speed. Charts, symbols and numbers glowed on the instrumentation panel. Warning lights flickered off and on. He had no idea what to do. *Help us, Serenissima*, he called out in his mind.

Luca scanned the command centre and found the appropriate panels that activated the weaponry systems. He ordered the firing of the orbs as well as the kinetic impactors. But when he fired, the figure of Xsar Tiandi warped and bent to avoid the weapons. He roared and the *Norma Jeane* rocked again, its seams screeching and moaning.

"Oh, no!" said Ceiba. "He's not letting go, Luca. He's crushing us! And we're taking on water fast!"

Chapter Fifty-Eight

As if answering his call, Serenissima appeared before them in the command centre. Wearing a long turquoise silk dress that billowed out onto the floor, her long green hair flowed down her back to her waist. Her aquamarine eyes glistened like iridescent jewels. Blue bioluminescent light radiated out from her body. Serenissima touched the sides of Luca's head and diamond-studded light shot out of her fingertips. He smelled fresh seaweed, the perfume of the ocean. The others watched with their mouths open, their eyes fixated on Luca and Serenissima.

The data scans read that the *Norma Jeane* had a breach at the bottom of the ship. The Pathfinder was being crushed in Xsar Tiandi's grip. Luca was failing in his efforts to save his friends, let alone Earth.

But Serenissima's voice and the music of flutes reached out to him. *"They cannot defeat you if you believe in yourself,"* she said. *"You have my power, my strength. You have the power of all the sea nymphs before me and all the Ancient Entanglers of the Mariners. Use Quantum Entanglement. Do not let them win, Luca."*

"How?" asked Luca in his mind.

"Look on the control screens," said Serenissima. *"Grampa Sol*

equipped this ship with Quantum Entanglement. You can face up to Xsar Tiandi and fight him in the sea right here, right now."

"What?"

"Trust in yourself, Luca. Trust the Ancient Entanglement in all of us. Believe in your ability and focus your mind."

Luca saw the letters *QE* written on a panel to the side. That had to mean Quantum Entanglement. Remembering Serenissima's words, he let go of his preconceived thoughts and ideas about reality. Defying all logical thinking, Luca stared at the *QE* icon and imagined himself standing in the sea outside the Pathfinder, like Xsar Tiandi was.

"Grampa Sol must have created a chamber here in this Pathfinder that is like a gaming room," Luca frantically explained to the others. "It showed up as an empty room on the scans earlier, but that has to be it," he continued, gesturing at a plan of the *Norma Jeane* on the control screen. "I remember that Grampa was instrumental in designing some of the first games in the Arcade. I don't think anyone knew about the virtual room on this ship."

Asia Mae and Ceiba nodded, looking confused.

"You guys need to keep an eye on the control screens while I'm gone," said Luca. "You should be able to see everything that's happening. I'll be back soon." He smiled at Asia Mae, trying to look more courageous than he felt inside and ran out of the control room and through the knee high water down the corridor.

When Luca entered the Gaming Zone, a soft violet hue emanated throughout the chamber. As Luca looked around, trying to figure out how to turn on the game, he found himself being lifted from the floor, elevated in zero gravity into the centre of the room. He held his breath, feeling scared and exhilarated at the same time. His vision blurred, he felt dizzy and his eyes watered.

Luca blinked and looked around him. He was in the inky blue sea. As his vision cleared, he realised that he seemed to be built of clear blue quantum particles that rotated and churned into spinning bursts of light. A helix coursed through his arms and legs, circulating up through his heart. He felt himself sinking and grabbed out wildly at the side of the blue hole, kicking his legs until he managed to grab a hold in the rock. He looked at himself again, at the giant arms and legs which were covered with pinpoints of light trailing down the veins and arteries. Whatever

Quantum Entanglement was, it was allowing him to do this. A science he didn't really understand at all.

From here, Luca could see the bubbles escaping from the hull of the Pathfinder, where the water must be streaming in. They didn't have much time before they all drowned. The figure of Xsar Tiandi still gripped the *Norma Jeane*, but because he was holding onto the rock, he had no spare hands. He seemed to shrug, then release the ship, letting it drop through the water, as he saw Luca opposite him.

The figure drew his now free hand to his chest, forming a fist and then releasing a massive orb of fire. At first Luca was worried it was heading for the *Norma Jeane*, but then he realised it was shooting through the water towards him.

He let go of the rock and let himself image the orb exploding before it reached him. It did. It exploded and fizzled out before it reached his shoulder. Luca grabbed onto the wall again and tried to clamber up, keeping one eye on Xsar Tiandi. With little warning, a second orb hit him, blazing into his arm.

But then, as if from heaven itself, a group of sea nymphs encircled him. They brought with them a vortex which whipped around Luca, quickly healing his pain. Luca instantly knew that Serenissima and her friends were nearby and would help when needed.

Bursting into action, Luca knew he had to get closer. He let go of the wall and pushed forward. He swerved to miss another of Xsar Tiandi's orbs, before lifting his right arm and shooting an orb back. This caught his opponent by surprise. Quickly recovering, Xsar Tiandi came at him, firing orbs from both hands. Luca leaned forward and met fire with fire. Rays of light shot out from Xsar Tiandi's centre like a fuse had been lit and he threw Luca back hard again the wall. It knocked the wind out of him.

"Remember who you are," whispered Serenissima urgently in Luca's ear.

While Xsar Tiandi was raging, Luca focussed his mind and clasped his hands together. He felt a familiar energy building up in his hands. He couldn't wait any longer in case the A'Rmillari was about to launch a counter attack. He hoped it was enough. He pulled his hands apart, feeling the tug of electricity. Suspended between them was a colossal red ball of pure energy.

"In three... two... one..." Luca whispered to himself. With all his strength, he leant forward and thrust the orb deep into the chest of Xsar Tiandi. A great explosion of fire shot blinding rays outwards in all directions. It sounded as though a bomb had exploded. In seconds, the alien figure disappeared from the sea in a trail of particles.

There was nothing, just darkness. And then Luca opened his eyes and gasped, blinking at the violet light surrounding him. He smiled to himself as he felt his body being lowered to the floor. He couldn't wait to get back to his friends. But the Norma Jeane was still sinking fast.

As he landed with a splash, Luca hurried back into the command centre, now chest deep in ice cold water to a chorus of cheers. Asia Mae and Ceiba swam to meet him, squeezing him so tightly he couldn't breathe.

"You won!" exclaimed Ceiba.

"That the end of it, right?" said Asia Mae.

"I hope so," said Luca.

"Pihaa has gone," said Ceiba. "She's dead."

"How can that be?" asked Luca.

"If what Phaeton said was correct about her being a printed copy, then when we took out their power source, I think we killed her," said Asia Mae.

"But if she's a copy, then they can print more. Now," said Luca. "We've got to get through the portal to Sub-Biosphere 2 before the ship implodes, we don't have much time."

¤¤¤

The roar – savage and menacing – shook through the sea and the galaxy, sending ripples into the universe. The fury and anger from Xsar Tiandi coiled upwards from the sea into space. He did not accept defeat lightly.

"Prepare for Overlord Xsar Tiandi's arrival," said Pentu, one of the Dark Alliance observers aboard the A'Rmillari mother ship, which was stationed directly behind the sun.

"Did he retrieve the Key from the Mariner boy?" asked Kadoo, another of the Dark Alliance's observers.

"No," said Pentu. "And his war ship was destroyed. Xsar Tiandi – all of us – underestimated the Mariner boy."

"Do we still have a tracking signal from the Key?"

"No, it has stopped," said Pentu. "They must have entered the portal."

"The Dark Alliance is going to tear the universe apart," said Kadoo.

"We will have to report this back to them right away to devise an alternate plan. And Xsar Tiandi will have to take part in the Warrior Death League to maintain his position as an Overlord. He has failed and must prove himself worthy again."

"He will win and he will lead another attack," said Kadoo. "If he is defeated, our home planet and all that we've worked for will be destroyed."

As their ship orbited the Sun, they looked out into space and at Planet Earth, which shone brightly below *Ramessu*. Never had anyone wanted control of a planet as much as their alliance. Never had anyone had so much to lose as they. Yet, they knew that with persistence, they would one day take this galaxy as their own.

Chapter Fifty-Nine

Water still raged through the bottom of the *Norma Jeane.* It might only be minutes before it completely filled, so Luca had to act fast. He searched the control screens underwater and found a digital opening, then took off his father's Key from his finger and inserted it. A buzzing sound whirred throughout the command centre.

"Authentication for entry into Sub-Biosphere 2 confirmed," appeared on the screen.

Automatically, the main propulsion extended the ventilation mast. The low-pressure blower pushed the water out of the tanks through the grates at the bottom. The Pathfinder was pulled by an invisible, magnetic force through the bottom of the Blue Hole and into the portal. The water had nearly completely filled the *Norma Jeane.* Luca held his breath in his lungs and braced himself has he dived down again to look at the control screens.

Despite wearing their oxygen masks, they couldn't breathe, the air had all but run out. The only air available was a small pocket at the very top of the control room and it was disappearing fast. They were surely going to drown here and now. *Where are you, Serenissima?*

Luca and his friends discarded their masks and inhaled their last breath before the air pocket disappeared. They noticed a glow emerging from the darkness. From inside the *Norma Jeane*, they began to hear a loud humming sound that gradually built in intensity, vibrating throughout their bodies. There was a magnetic pulse in this portal that linked to other galaxies; a humming that oscillated with time itself. Green and blue luminescence pulsated in a sharing halo twice the size of the ship. Shooting out from this halo was a fusion of blinding white light that spun in concentric circles – so blindingly bright it rivalled the sun. Everyone shielded their eyes underwater. A cloud of electrically charged particles enveloped around them, pulling the *Norma Jeane* into the vortex, and to the bottom of the blue hole. The sound and light encompassed them, carrying them effortlessly onwards. And there, right there before them, was Sub-Biosphere 2, beaming like a beckon in the distance.

Water rushed in bubbles outside the *Norma Jeane*. A strange calmness engulfed them all and, suddenly, their ship was surrounded by scores of bioluminescent sea nymphs. Their long blue hair billowed out around them. Long, flowing translucent materials covered their arms and legs... creatures of the sea. All around them, there was music that sounded like a million harps and flutes. Luca could hear their voices.

"Serenissima sent us. We are sea nymphs, here to help you. We long ago found refuge here in the blue hole, and formed a symbiotic relationship with it over thousands of years. Now, we are free to travel the universe, helping beings in the universal ocean. We are part of you, Luca."

At that moment, the sea nymphs seemed to swim through the control screens and the friends felt ghostly hands reaching out to touch their hands. Their skin tingled at the touch.

They were all transfixed as they struggled to hold their breath underwater inside the badly battered Pathfinder. As they exited the portal Ceiba pointed wildly towards the giant, glittering structure. Sub-Biosphere 2 seemed to be bursting with life.

The structure was formed of giant, bubble-like pods joined by spokes to a huge central hub. The pod nearest them seemed to be filled with lush gardens. Brightly coloured birds that none of them had ever seen before flew between the trees and rain was falling lightly onto the glossy leaves. In other pods, Luca could make out dark forests, shimmering lakes, snowy landscapes and scorching desert. These were things Luca and his friends had studied in iT school, but had never seen for themselves. There were no such places in Acacia Burj; no such places left on Earth. Or so they had thought as the control screens began to flicker.

Guided by the sea nymphs, the *Norma Jeane* was automatically pulled through a sensory shield in the central biome of the Sub-Biosphere 2. The place was truly intergalactic. There were spaceships and alien creatures of all different shapes, colours and sizes freely moving around. Tall luminescent beings with blue-green skin floated past nonchalantly. Their backs were covered in bioluminescent spines that pulsated with blue sparks. Several of these creatures escorted the Pathfinder into a docking bay.

Suddenly, the *Norma Jeane* stopped dead on the deck and one of the beings motioned for them to exit, urgently waving its fin-like arms. Luca desperately tried to open the hatch, they all did. Everything on the Pathfinder seemed to have given up. Luca looked around underwater at his companions, perhaps for the last time. They joined hands. Suddenly the whirring of the ships power stopped and they were plunged into total darkness.

The doors wouldn't open and the last of the air was gone. Everyone was holding their breath, feeling the pressure pushing and straining at their lungs.

Chapter Sixty

"I'm sure they'll make it," said Sol quietly, rubbing his hand against Skye's back. She nodded without speaking, biting on her thumbnail and staring at the floor.

"Oh, Sol, if I don't see him again..." said Skye Mariner, with tears in her eyes.

"I know, I know."

The two of them stood watching in horror as a team worked on trying to open the *Norma Jeane* hatch door. It seemed well past the length of time that anyone could possibly hold their breath and hope was fading fast.

When Skye had first arrived, she had learned that Sol had gone to Beyul Atoll after leaving Acacia Burj all those years earlier. He had then accidently travelled here, to Sub-Biosphere 2. After a tearful reunion, Sol had told her he was quite sure Del was still alive, but that he had gone into hiding for safety. He just wasn't sure where. And Skye didn't want to hope for too much.

When she heard that Luca would be travelling through the blue hole again, she had been afraid. She knew that it was dangerous. After all, he was an inexperienced pilot. Granted, he had the ancient entanglement connections he needed to be a champion racer like his father, and granted, he had handled some extreme situations recently, but still, he was only sixteen. It wouldn't be so dangerous for him once he managed the melding of his consciousness with that of the other Ancient Entanglers, but that could take years. Fortunately, Skye was able to monitor a lot of Luca's journey through her own entanglement with her family, but she had to be careful. This was one of the great secrets she was trying to protect. Right now, she had no idea if he was alive or dead.

They were still hugging each other when the hatch finally flung opened and a soaking wet Luca, Asia Mae and Ceiba burst onto the deck in a cascade of water. Looking up with a cry, Skye ran straight over to him. Bursting into tears, she threw her arms around him.

"Luca! Luca! Oh, my goodness! Talk to me!"

With a cough and a splutter the three friends started to move.

"Mum, is that you? I can't believe you're here!"

"You're all alive! The sea nymphs reached you in time, thank goodness." Skye said, as the others started to sit up. "Asia Mae, I'm so glad to see you. And Ceibastian, I'm so happy you're here!"

Skye grabbed all of them and hugged them close.

"Do you know about Beyul Atoll? What's happened? Are the people safe?"

"Yes, I had a transmission from Gaia a few moments ago to say that they've managed to hold off the aliens that landed there. And they've also picked up the President and First Lady from the sea. They're all safe. They've sent light signals up to the moon base and have established communication."

Skye released Luca, Asia Mae and Ceiba from her tight hold and they stood back and looked at each other, smiling.

"That's amazing," said Ceiba. "Now I can really relax!"

"Phew," said Luca. "They were just copies, like Pihaa, so they probably died when we destroyed their ship."

Just then, from around a corner, Sol C. Mariner stepped out of the shadows. Luca looked at him and, for a moment, was speechless. And then, he ran to him as if he was a little boy again. Sol opened his arms and wrapped his grandson in them. "Luca, I am so proud of you."

"Grampa Sol, you're alive!" Luca said hoarsely, pulling back and looking at his grandfather. It was the same Grampa Sol he remembered. His face had a few more lines, but his eyes still flickered an ocean green-blue, he still looked sturdy and strong, and his hair still had a lot of black intermingled in the grey.

"Where have you been? You never came back after all those years."

"Luca, I'm so sorry but I've been needed in Beyul Atoll. I've been looking for your father all over the planet, to tell you the truth, and finally, I came here," Sol said. "Then, I started trying to work with you from *here.*" He tapped his heart, smiling. "We'll talk about this later. I know you have a lot of questions."

After their excitement subsided over seeing one another, Asia Mae said: "If it's possible, Mrs. Mariner, could you find out about my parents? They were on a dig on the sea floor – I just don't know where."

Skye nodded. "Of course, sweetheart, we'll do our best to find them."

"Not many people are admitted into Sub-Biosphere 2 unless they've been selected by the Galactic Council or our Government," Grampa Sol explained. "This means that each of you are extremely brave. From now on, you will be able to do extraordinary things, like breathing underwater! You will be invited to join the Intergalactic community, I'm sure of it."

"Even me?" asked Ceiba.

"Yes, even *you*," said Skye. "You have shown remarkable courage and skills." she said, shaking his sodden hair and smiling.

Ceiba blushed. He had never thought of himself as courageous. Little by little, he was forgetting that he was mostly a Bion.

"Why would they want me?" asked Asia Mae.

"Your knowledge of music and the arts is something that we need as a way to create a cultural paradigm in life on this planet and others. Music is a universal language and one that my ancestors used to make contact with other planets."

"Mum, you've never talked about your ancestors," said Luca. Sol stood quietly by and when Skye looked at him, he nodded for her to continue.

"That's because my parents came from another galaxy," Skye said. "I didn't want to tell you or Gaia about it until you were older."

"*What?*" Luca was stunned.

"They're humans like we are," said Skye. "In fact, our race

came to Earth long, long ago – way before recorded time – and we were instrumental in what we have developed here.

So, his mum was part-alien? But apparently, most or all humans were. Weren't they?

Luca and his friends were all trying very hard to absorb the information. None of them realised that after stepping into Sub-Biosphere 2, their very cells were being refined and re-tuned to match a new vibrational level of existence. Of life. One that encompassed a magic as old as time itself.

Skye further explained that Sub-Biosphere 2 was a safe haven for protecting biodiversity and humanity in the event of a catastrophic natural or man-made disaster on the planet's surface. It remained the best hope for the long term survival of all life on Earth. Stored within Sub-Biosphere 2 was the genetic and scientific material needed to reinvigorate life on the surface and potentially abate the harsh environmental conditions that forced people to live in vast mega cities in the first place.

"We have people working in Beyul Atoll," said Skye. "And, we did have people in Acacia Burj – I was one of them – but after the recent solar flare attack, we have mostly relocated our scientists to this place, and to other outposts on the planet."

A little while later, Sol took Luca to a quiet balcony off the main biome, away from the others. From their position on the edge of Sub-Biosphere 2, Luca could see out through the glass onto the activity below. Researchers were busy moving shuttles between various pods and Luca could see humans and all kinds of aliens moving around everywhere in the structure. A group of tall, limb-less and elegant creatures were gathered on another nearby balcony, like a shoal of jellyfish. Soft fluorescent lights ran in trails down the length of their bodies. His mother stood amongst them, moving her hands around in strange ways. It was clear she was communicating with them somhow, perhaps even in their own language. But it was what lay beyond all of this that took Luca's breath away.

"Look, Luca. What do you see?" Grampa Sol was pointing out into the darkness beyond the lights of Sub-Biosphere 2.

"I have no idea," whispered Luca, amazed.

Above them on the distant ceilings of this cavernous sub-sea world were perfect replicas of the constellations, copied from Earth's starry night skies and illuminated by bioluminescence.

They were totally immersed in a 360 degree starscape. They marked gateways to other galaxies, Sol explained. It was an intergalactic portal from which you can travel anywhere in the Universe.

Straight ahead of them hung a vast sphere, the epicentre of this stunning world, spinning like a planet on its axis. It glowed iridescent and pulsated through the darkness; its surface seeming to ripple with waves. As Luca's eyes started to focus, he could make out spaceships travelling to and from its enormous central sphere.

"We call it Murias," said Grampa Sol. "It's more ancient than you could imagine. It's the nucleus of everything. It connects us to every other galaxy, in every other special planet that holds water-based life. Sub-Biosphere 2 was not only built to protect life on Earth, but also to research this greater secret. These portals are the most precious thing in the Universe. From here, we can travel anywhere. From Murias, we point at the star we want to travel to," explained Sol, pointing upwards, to one of the distant constellations, "and we go, in a flash of light, boom!"

Luca looked warily at his grandfather. "And has all this got something to do with me?"

Grampa Sol chuckled. "You're learning quickly! More and more will be revealed to you as time permits. We mustn't let this place fall into the wrong hands. Earth is still in danger."

"I know. I have Dad's message and his Key," said Luca. "He explained a lot about the Dark Alliance."

"He recorded that for you before he ventured to sea on his last race," said Sol. "The message will change as you mature because of our entanglement. I have been hoping that, eventually, his message will reveal where he is – if he's here on Earth and if he's still alive. Serenissima hasn't been able to locate him precisely. It could be that he's being held captive with monitoring sensory systems that hinder his abilities to communicate. We're not sure. I believe he thinks it's too dangerous for us to know where he is."

"I will help you find him Grampa," said Luca. "I miss him."

"Me, too, Luca, me too," said Sol.

"Grampa, just who is Serenissima exactly? I've been hearing her a lot in my head and we've seen her, too."

"She's a high priestess, nymph from the sea. Some might call her an angel. But, she's much more than that."

"Will I get to see her again?"

"Oh yes," said Grampa Sol, smiling. "Now that you've connected, you'll see her whenever she has something to teach you or whenever you need her. You might see her tomorrow when Skye and I take you and your friends to Murias."

"We're going to Murias?" said Luca hesitantly.

"There will be a Galactic Council meeting with local dignitaries from all over the galaxy. They want to meet you, to explain how they think you could help us in our fight to save the Universe. Do you think you are ready?"

"I'm ready for anything now," said Luca with a look of determination.

He would worry about the Overlords tomorrow.

www.ingramcontent.com/pod-product-compliance
Lightning Source LLC
Chambersburg PA
CBHW031657170626
46808CB00005B/1492

* 9 7 8 1 9 0 9 4 7 7 2 2 3 *